THE **PALE**

A. D. Wittman

ISBN: 1451580088
ISBN-13: 9781451580082

W*here am I going to be attacked from? Which direction?*
A voice around the corner hissed the words, "Hol Chaan"...
He's here.
I backed away from the snake-like voices, pulled my dagger out of its sheath and moved silently onto the side walkway.

"Hello there," a smirky, masculine voice said behind me.

Well, shit, I thought, *I'm surrounded.*

✧ ✧ ✧

"A.D. Wittman's fresh, funny and biting dialogue will take you on a wild ride that will leave you fascinated. This new author has crafted a fast-paced story that will have you looking over your shoulder for things that go bump in the night... *The Pale* delivers!"

– Alicia Wiggins, author of *A Place Like Home.*

THE PALE

A. D. Wittman

Dedication

The Pale Series is dedicated to a master inventor and an imaginative writer. Grandpa Rudman and Poppop Wittman, you are always over my shoulder guiding me in my work. I miss you both everyday.

Acknowledgements

If it wasn't for Erica Hoagland, my brilliant and patient editor, this book would have sucked! Thank you so much for helping me put meat on the bones of my skeleton work and correcting all of my bad grammar habits (which I'm sure there are tons in this section since I didn't let you edit it! Ha!). I look forward to working with you on the rest of the series – if you can put up with me!

Thank you, Alicia Wiggins (my friend and mentor) who read my messes several times and threw me, kicking and screaming, into the right direction. Your wisdom and good dinner picks have helped me get my act together enough to publish this. I can't wait to read your next book!

Andrew Wittman! Thank you so much for letting me use one of your photos for the cover work to The Pale. I'll be waiting for a signed copy of the picture you get into Sports Illustrated or National Geographic (or when your band is on the cover of Rolling Stone.)

A big thank you goes to Brian Wittman for designing a book cover that I think may actually be scarier than my book! It's awesome! Thank you so much for doing it!

Chuck Wittman also had a hand in the book cover as well as reading through both the early and last versions of the book. You're a true poet! Thanks for all the great ideas.

To Ruth C. (the other half to our 2-person book club), Reyna W. (who puts up with me daily) and Emily (the coolest librarian chick I know!) – thank you all so much for reading the early versions of this book. Your suggestions and enthusiasm have been a gift (you will be so surprised at how this one turned out!!)

Tish R., thank you for the use of your awesome description of Devon's car. I hope you don't mind, but I'll be coming back to you for more!

Thanks to Tracey T. for helping me with the PD stuff. Let me apologize in advance since I changed a few things to make it suit the book.

Thank you to Nicola Sage who came up with a wicked cool name for one of the characters. I can't tell you enough how great it is that you joined The Pale Series Facebook page! I hope you've got some more names for me! LOL!

Katie B., Joe & Joy R., Hope N., Audra S. & Ellen G. (Holy crap! I just got published, can you believe that?!?) You all have helped keep my sanity over more years than I would ever like to admit (because, no matter what, I will always be young). You've had no easy task, but I love you for it! (You guys rock!)

Romeo – Miss you, little guy.

To Souleymane Marzouk – Wherever you are – you are pure inspiration. When I'm down, I think of what you've accomplished and I get back to work!

Thanks to my coworkers (past & present) and neighbors who have been so supportive of this adventure.

To my family – especially Cindi, Mike, Chuck, Mary, Jen, Doug, Bodhi, Grandma, Nana, Linda and Nan – thanks for all your support, love, craziness, and drive to, well, wherever we're going! (And if you see yourself in any of these scenes, it's purely coincidental – I swear, Ma!)

Aaron – You're the best! Thanks for letting me bounce chaotic ideas off of you and being honest about when they suck (and when they're good!) Thanks for swooping in and helping me through writer's block and my railroading! After I met you, the ocean became bluer, the scenery more dramatic. You didn't fulfill my life, you enhanced it and I love you for that and am, as always, crazy, but happy.

I would like to thank Stephen King, whose hard-ass words in *On Writing* helped get *The Pale* through some tough times during the editing process when I had to read all of the red my editor kept giving my work. Also, the first book that I ever really fell in love with was *The Phantom Tollbooth*. Thank you, Norton Juster, for writing a book that was so fun and interesting that it actually gave me a different perspective on life and on art.

My biggest 'thank you' goes to all the people who've joined The Pale Series on Facebook. What a wild ride! (And you've been there since the beginning – especially you, Alison C-H. (the very first person to sign up), Abby B. (the first to "friend" me), and Nicx L. (who was the first person to say they are my #1 fan)! I hope you like *The Pale* enough to stick around for the next books! Your insights, comments, discussions and everything else have really helped this book fly and keep me laughing. Thank you! Thank you! Thank you! (Did I mention, 'thank you?') I'll see you all on the site!!!

If you would like to follow *The Pale Series* on-line, check out the following:

On Facebook: The Pale Series
T's Blog: http://thepaleseries.wordpress.com
Follow on Twitter: http://twitter.com/ThePaleSeries

Or send an email to me, A.D. Wittman, at thepaleseries@gmail.com

One final note…. GO BOILERS!

Table of Contents

Prologue

The Troublemaker

Heavy fog rolled in from the bay and enveloped the woman as she stood on the roof of the blue warehouse at the back end of the wharf. The town that unfolded in front of her was lit sporadically with street and bar lights muted by the white-grey moisture. The April evening was colder than most, but it was no matter to her. Whether heat or chill in the air, they were both the same feel against her porcelain skin.

She scanned the humans milling about on the sidewalks of Commercial Street, searching for her prey. He would be any easy target. *Any human would be at this point,* she mused silently. She laughed to herself as the inept humans kept coming up short to objects in front of them. Although they couldn't see more than a few feet of their own paths, the woman's eyes cut through the fog as if it wasn't there. Regardless of the shrouding weather, no human would see her there, not this far away from the main streets of the town. *Weak, clumsy things.*

The wind blew her waist-length, silky, crow-black curls around her pale face, making them skirt around her blood red lips and crystal blue eyes. The moisture encased a few strands, catching them on her cheeks. She wiped them away in a generic motion, practicing; she needed to be as human-like in her gestures as possible if she was to keep her prey from knowing her intentions.

She watched and she waited.

Shifting her position, a slight lean to the left instead of the right, was the only sign that she had seen who she was waiting for. A group of five young men came around the corner from Union Street to Commercial. As one of the bigger ones tripped over the curb, she let a tiny girlish giggle escape her lips, *Practicing.*

One guy's teasing of the off-balance kid floated across the dense night like sounds reaching across a lake, "Ya just get those feet yesterday, Sam?"

"Ah, shut the hell up, Gabe," another said as he helped the fallen back up.

The murky wetness would have been as heavy in her lungs as it was in theirs, if she had needed to breathe. *Thankfully, there is no reason for that constant boring human response.*

The boys, *for that was what they really were,* stopped for a moment and huddled together. One with glasses, the smallest in the group, divvied the rest of the teenagers what looked like credit cards. She narrowed her eyes, zooming her focus in the distance.

No, not credit cards, she thought, *driver's licenses.*

Her sharpened sight kept on the boys as they crossed the street and headed toward Chuck's Pros, a bar overlooking the wharf. She traced her tongue against her lips, tasting the air. She found her mark for the night facing her, recognizing him instantly from the birthmark on his face. Pensively, she considered the scene unfolding.

That's right, she caught on the slight but important discrepancy on one of the new licenses. *He wouldn't be old enough to get into the bar after hours. Tasty, young thing. I'm going to enjoy this game tonight.*

At the thought, her eyes transformed to black as if something from her pupils crawled out to overtake all of the color in them. A thin, dangerously beautiful leer crossed her lips before she reigned herself in and the blue hue returned to her eyes.

Careful. Do not give in to the cravings, she reasoned with herself, *You'll feed soon enough.*

She licked her lips again, capturing the plethora of scents in the night before jumping down the three stories onto the cement. She landed with only a slight whip of her thick coat as it whisked around her like wings of a dark bird of prey. It didn't phase her that many people were out at this time. Community college boys mixed in with lobstermen, both groups hoping to pick up sweet young things for the night. Old beer and fish mingled with the overpowering perfumes of the girls out for a good time. None of these things mattered – only her kill for the evening. Melting in with the shadows, passing people quickly like a rush of wind blowing, she barely moved the fog out of place. The woman crossed the street and slid past the bouncer, through the open door at Chuck's Pros without anyone noticing.

KEEN

Chapter 1

It All Started When...

✧ ✧ ✧

How Much Trouble Can I Get Into?

I handed the waitress my newly minted ID along with the other guys. Jeffrey's uncle had produced them for us as a late graduation gift. The only thing different from our actual driver's licenses was the year we were born, giving us roughly 2 to 5 years more than what our normal age was without confusing us with other details. *Some of us are not very good liars,* I thought. And we would never be able to get away with fake names since the locals knew enough to recognize us from our childhood. But we might be able to fudge our ages in their minds. *Especially if they've had one too many and then try to do the math.*

I didn't think she was going to go for it. Although the bouncer really didn't take more than a glance at us or the IDs, this waitress, Veleda, the name tag read, looked smarter than the big oaf. *And she was.*

Shit.

She gave the five of us a look. Not just a look, but THE look of knowing. *Shit, shit, shit.*

I held my breath as she moved the cards to her chest in a move to confiscate them. Not looking at the others, I just kept a big smile plastered on my face, and only imagined the fear and defeat of having the cards removed from us within just a few moments of having received them. *I knew we should've gone out of town for the first go of these.*

She swished her brown hair from side to side, the blond streaks darting around making her hair seem to dance with light, and winked at us through small, square, black-rimmed glasses as she handed the IDs back. A collective sigh of relief flew through the table. *Guess I wasn't the only one holding my breath.*

She left with our order and not our cards. The guys all started a round of congratulatory laughing while slapping each other on the backs. *A year out of high school and they are still as immature as ever. They can't really believe we got away with it, can they?* I rolled my eyes.

"You-a ready for the game tomorrah, Keen?" A thick New England accent broke my thoughts.

I turned to Jeffrey, "Against West Eng? It'll be a piece of cake," Our lacrosse team had already played a few games this season and we were doing pretty well. Although it was my first year with the team, I had made first string attackman for the University of New England. I was actually on scholarship for ice hockey, but since the hockey season ended back in March, I had decided to pick up lacrosse to keep in shape. It was either that or golf, and for me, that's more of a game of relaxation, whereas I loved contact sports. *Bruises and broken bones? Bring it on!*

Western New England was our upcoming game and they were having a wicked weak season so far.

Poor Jeffrey, he couldn't play a sport to save his life. I've known him since kindergarten. He got the brains of the group, but he certainly didn't get any muscle. *Or height.* I'm actually surprised the bouncer let him in. With his glasses on and clothing picks, he looked more like a 14-year old pimply half-pint than the 18 year-old he was.

The waitress plunked our drinks down along with a large wooden bowl of complimentary popcorn. Looking at the rest of my friends, sharing brews for the first time in an actual bar, I was still amazed that we got in. *I didn't think we had a prayer.* Chuck's Pros, or just Pros as the locals call it, never lets people under 21 in after 9 PM. Most bars in the area don't. Families and tourists have the run of joints during the day, but nighttime is for the locals. *The 21 and older locals* – which, thanks to Jeffrey's law-bending and slightly crazy uncle, we are able to be part of now. *Besides, who wants to be a college student who can't get into a bar? I mean, seriously, what else is there to do in this town, but drink stout and eat oysters?*

But it's good to get out with the guys and not be stuck up in a dorm room waiting for the Resident Assistant to bust us. Especially if he used to be the first string attackman before I came along.

"You gotch-your lucky charm on you," Gabe asked in a lilt, trying his best at using an Irish accent – a very poor excuse for an Irish accent at that. Gabe looked his age at 19. As the star quarterback in high school, he could get into anywhere just flirting with any woman or man. Things didn't change for him when he hit college either. When he wanted something, he wasn't picky about how he got it.

I pulled out the slim gold chain that was around my neck and tucked under my shirt. A small, gold medallion hung from it, something I've had since my Jewish parents adopted me. It was a short Hebrew word, chayyim, meaning 'life.' I wore it most everyday, but on my first few games that I played hockey in high school, I took it off as a precaution. However, I lost those games. One game, I forgot to take off the necklace and I scored a hat trick, three goals during regulation play. Ever since then, any game I've had the necklace on, we've won. I guess, after awhile, I became superstitious about it and I always made sure I had it on me – especially on game days.

"You keep that bad boy on, Keen, and we'll win. No worries," Noah said, as if he already knew what the outcome of the game was going to be. He had a dark and dangerous demeanor. People usually didn't bother him; and those that did usually ended up in the hospital. Since the ripe old age of thirteen, he has known his way around every dark alley of the Old Port, the original area of the downtown, none of which I'd ever want to be in alone – with or without him.

Then there's Sam. Sam and I could pass for brothers. Both of us had blond hair and blue eyes and stood at 5 feet, 10 inches. But with hockey and lacrosse, I most definitely had a six pack whereas Sam just carried around a keg. But, he was the comedian of the group so he always kept us laughing.

This is so cool! I thought after our second round of beers. Well, Noah was on his third or fourth round – I hadn't kept track. Studying had kept us so busy that we'd only had time to hang out on Thursdays – all colleges' official unofficial start to the weekends. As I was laughing at a joke Sam had made, bringing my mug of Guinness up to take another swig, the hairs on the back of my neck suddenly stood up. A bad rush of feeling came from my stomach to my head.

A warning.

Glancing around Pros, scanning across the bar's yellowed walls and dark blue wainscoting, people were in their own conversations while they sat at the old wooden pub-style tables. The benches could handle up to eight friends on backless seats on either side, so some of the tables were wicked rowdy. The walls had strategically placed, five-foot-wide mirrors with brewery logos across them. Shipyard, Bass and Guinness were the beers most everyone paid tribute to in this town so there were a bunch of shiny, neon and mirrored alters all around the bar.

The rest of the tables were either tall with bar stools or normal four person ones. Most of them were filled with several people standing around the lucky ones who had scored the stools. There were several tables on the back wall that were four person booths – comfortable and out of the way. The middle of the place was held up with wide, red-brick walls with three open-ways through them and I was able to scrutinize those walking around opposite to where we were sitting. My friends and I were at one of the pub-style benches near the windows and away from the bar.

Quite the random mix of people out tonight, I thought. Older groups of people sat next to those barely of age, *and some of us who aren't old enough to get into the bar.* Most of the patrons, in typical East Coast fashion, were wearing flannel shirts of various colors and jeans with hiking boots. But there were some women who were walking around in low cut shirts, designer jeans or skirts, and spiky, high-heeled shoes.

The bad feeling only got stronger as I stared at the door area. Maybe it was because of the music that was playing in the background, Pink Floyd's *Hey You.* The guitar melody always made my skin crawl with its haunting tone and it was making me want to jump out of my seat and run to the nearest hole I could find, burying myself for a really long time – *Or at least until I get hungry.*

Something bad was about to happen and I could feel it. Anticipation made my forehead sweat and my mouth go dry. Luckily, the guys were so into their own beers and conversation about the upcoming lacrosse game that they didn't notice that I was sitting there worrying like a little old grandma.

I've always had this knack of knowing when something wrong was about to occur. My friends called it my "Spidey Senses". *Yeah, well, Peter Parker can have them back for all I care. We need to get out, but how to explain to the guys without looking like a total tool?*

My hand automatically went up to the necklace that was hanging around my neck, fiddling around with it like I always did when I was nervous. The metal felt hot in my hands as I thumbed it. *Is a cop around? Maybe we're about to get busted for underage drinking* – the 'No Tolerance' laws were really strong in this town. *Maybe I should tell them, tip our waitress and then get us the hell out of here.*

Thinking of beer, my eyes drew to the bar. They danced past the green framed kitchen window where a cook was dinging the order-up bell in triumph with a goofy grin on his face. At first, I didn't see anything unusual with the people at the bar.

But then, I saw her.

Skin tight pants.

An even tighter red corset laced with black ties.

And they were tied only slightly enough to cover her breasts. A black leather jacket flowed around her like a bat ready to swoop her up and fly off.

My gaze finally wandered up to her face. *Absolutely the most beautiful woman I have ever seen.* Angelina Jolie couldn't hold a candle to this woman and every man in this universe, gay or straight, could tell you that's saying a lot.

Her hair…the most perfect, glossy mess of black curls hanging down her back.

And her eyes…

Pale ice reflecting the harbor…

Dropping my hand away from my neck and taking a sip of my beer, I spat it out in surprise and knocked over the glass at the same time. *No fricken way! She's staring right at me!*

My bad feeling!

It ended when I saw her.

No, that's not right.

It started when I saw her. *Well something started when I saw her,* I thought as a jolt of sudden longing oozed into my body. My mind went completely blank and it took me a minute to realize that Sam's hand was waving in front of my face as he called my name. My eyes focused on him and then on the others. I stammered, "Oh shit, Jeff! Sorry 'bout that!" My projectile beer had hit him in the face and his shirt. Helping him, Gabe tossed a bunch of napkins from the holder in the center of the table. The waitress, Veleda, came over and handed him a bar towel.

"You boys aren't going to cause anymore trouble are you," she asked in a I-will-throw-you-out-myself tone.

I flushed, "No, sorry. We've got it."

She raised an eyebrow at us, distrusting us, but she took the wet towels from Gabe and Jeff, wiped off the rest of the table around them and walked away.

Sam turned to me, "Dude, y'are totally zoned. What the hell?"

"Yeah, you better not be this out of it against West Eng," Noah slurred his words so it sounded more like Wes-ss-sing, "I've got big bucks riding on it."

Fantastic, that's all I need. A debt to Noah if he loses. That's how it always works out. Somehow, I always owe him if he makes a bet on me. *Well, on the rare times I've lost.*

"No worries," Jeff said, still patting his shirt dry with napkins, "as long as he wears that lucky charm of his you'll get your money Noah. Right, Keen?"

I smiled at Jeff and turned to Noah, accusing, "Don't tell me you made a bet with Jeff's uncle again."

"Ok, I won't tell you," Noah smirked and sipped down the rest of his beer. "Shoulda ordered a pitcha," he mumbled.

Well, at least I know that if I lose, Noah won't get his arm broken this time. That's a little pressure off. I shoved the necklace back out of view.

"Anyway, Light Weight," Gabe laughed, "What the hell is your problem tonight? Can't take the drink, buddy?"

"It's not the beer guys," I said, defensively, "There's a woman at the bar and she's checking me out." My voice cracked like a prepubescent. In my head I understood how absurd that sounded, *This woman can NOT be looking at me.* But raising my head back to her, it was true…She was staring right into me – like she could see every fault I had, every slight dishonor I had made over the years, such as all the times I swiped my dad's Maxim magazines and got busted. *Yes, more than once.* I felt guilty just being in the same room with her. *It's unnerving.*

"Come over here and buy me a drink," A sultry, sexy voice whispered.

I blinked. Her lips hadn't moved, yet I swear I had just heard her. *Must be wishful thinking.*

"Don't make a girl ask again," The voice was so clear, it was if she was sitting next to me, sighing in my ear. I shook my head side to side, glancing around to see who really spoke. But no women were around me and with all the music and burly crowd around, *I must be losing my mind.* Then I saw her bat her eyes in that kind of come-hither look you only see in movies. I was not the guy that always gets the hot girls. *That is Gabe.*

Jeffrey said, "The hot one in the leather?"

"Yeah, that would be the one," I said, "She's staring at me."

"Right Keen," Gabe said, "In your wet-dreams, buddy."

"No, seriously, look."

They all turned, but the woman had swerved around her bar stool away from our direction and was flirting with some local in a flannel shirt. The guys looked back at me as if I was crazy, but she moved her gaze right back in my direction at the same time.

"She's doing it again, I swear," *Maybe I am going crazy after all.*

They looked again. "She is definitely not looking at you, Keen. What would a woman that fine want with a college boy, anyway?" Sam asked.

"Yeah, anyway, if she's looking for a real man, she'd be staring at me," Gabe said. He finished the rest of his beer, slamming it down onto the table and belching as if to make his point, "I think I might just go get her number for my wall."

Ah, Gabe's infamous wall, where all his conquests' numbers and forgotten names were hanging on a board in his dorm room closet. We laughed as he went up, mine being a little more nervous than the others for him, since I still couldn't shake that really weird bad feeling. For that moment, it had backed down to just a dull hum in the depths of my mind. We watched Gabe go up in his classic I'm-so-cool look that usually made girls drool. He could puff out his chest and women would swoon. *He's an idiot if he thinks he can pull that off with her! But he is usually one lucky bastard.*

After a conversation that lasted less than fifteen seconds, Gabe was back at the table, face drained of all color from shock of the rejection. He was dumbfounded, "Apparently you're right, Keen. She asked me to send you over."

"No way!" Jeffrey cheered.

"Don't keep the lady waiting," Noah teased.

I couldn't move, "Are you guys out of your mind? What about Maddie? She would kill me." I reminded them of the girlfriend I've had since our sophomore year in high school. Unbeknownst to the guys, I was going to ask her to marry me once she graduated. She was still back in high school, in her senior year and I was counting down for the big day in two months.

Gabe mocked glancing around the room, "Well, I don't see her here. Besides, what's one drink to talk to the hottest woman ever? I'm shut. Boys?" They all nodded but couldn't keep from smiling and joking about my new found interest. A couple of them made the sign that they were locking their lips and throwing away the key although, in classic Gabe form, he added a few more vulgar signs prior to that.

"Last chance, buddy," the sultry voice in my head warned in a breathy way. I looked up again as the lady at the bar glared at me in an incredibly sensuous manner – her chin down, her lips slightly pouting, elbows resting against the bar, her eyes securely fastened on me. *Some guys have all the luck.*

I should've listened to the warning, let her move on to the next guy, but my body reacted to her voice in my head and shut off my mind from further disruptions. My legs were suddenly shaky as I stood up and put my beer down on the table, almost knocking it over.

"Go get her, tigah" Noah said as he shoved me toward my mark.

I walked over to the woman. The guys gave me plenty encouragement every time I looked back over my shoulder at them. I was so nervous, my heart felt like the rumble of a herd of Clydesdales running by at full speed. I could feel the air slightly chill my skin as I started to sweat. I had this vision that I was a walking waterfall of perspiration and wondered how in the world I was going to talk to the woman at the bar while I dripped all over her. *I should just turn around now and give this up.*

I chided myself for being a coward since I wasn't really sweating, but I couldn't slow my heart. The room in Pros seemed suddenly longer, like I was never going to get closer to the bar. Tables passed in a slow, drawn-out fashion, as if they were stretching along with my every stride. The beer mirrors became twenty feet in my mind instead of the five they were. The music slowed as if to let me hear every syllable in every word, every note that each instrument played. *A vertical vertigo – whatever the hell that means.* But, after forever, I made it through the crowd to land myself awkwardly next to her.

"I thought you would never get over here, Handsome," The voice was deep and sexy. *Better than hearing it in my head.* Her accent was mottled and definitely not from around this town, nor was that style of dress either. *Well, not at these kinds of bars that were near the wharf, maybe the ones uptown, but not where drunken sailors and fishermen hang out.* The girls here wore plaid flannels with low-cut, tight shirts under them and tight jeans. *Wharf rats.*

She tossed her glorious hair back, flirtatiously. Seductively.

"How did you do that?" I blurted, grabbing the back of the bar stool next to her to help my stance appear a little more manly, even though it was more to help my balance.

"Do what?" Her voice was silky innocence.

"I heard your voice in my…" I trailed off, feeling a little more than stupid at saying that out loud. This woman was going to think I was crazy. But then she put a hand on mine, smiled sheepishly and batted her eyes again. My mind flashed white like a surge of electricity had hit it – the touch of her was flame and ice, and my body couldn't handle both feelings at the same time. *Man up, Keen! She's just a woman. A totally hot woman, granted. But a woman none-the-less. Don't be such an ass.*

"I'm Alexandra," she purred.

Sweet God, she just purred. "Keen."

"Why don't you sit down and buy me a drink?"

I had no restraint. I did exactly what she said, totally enthralled by her beauty and forgetting about everyone else in the bar, even forgetting a little of myself under her divine spell.

She moved slightly toward me when our drinks were put in front of us, giving me an inviting peek at her breasts. I tried really hard not to look down, *As if it isn't hard enough being a guy and trying to show some self-control!* I could smell her perfume – sweet and musky, the smell of lavender and newly wetted earth.

✿ ✿ ✿

Exit Reality, Stage Left

Alexandra took my hand as she led me out of Pros. I felt heat surrounding the cold that came off her – hot like the feel of blood as skin touches skin, but cold like smooth river stones that have been sitting in the winter air for months. *I can't believe I'm walking out of here with HER! What am I thinking? What am I doing? The guys are no help at all. Typical.*

The fog wrapped around us like a blanket as we strolled down Union Wharf and headed toward the water. It never mattered what time of year it was, if a fog like this moved in, there were two things a person could count on: the first being that the temperature was going to drop several degrees and the second was that the fog would last for days if not a week or more. Most people would find this kind of weather spooky or even evil. I mean, Stephen King wrote an entire book on it – *Well, mist, anyway.* But fog like this made me feel like I was the only person on earth – that this weather was for my benefit only. I always welcomed it… *Until now. This one is creeping me out!*

Something was about to jump out at me. *I can feel it.*

Stop being a big baby, Keen, my mind reprimanded.

The ugly feeling muffled itself for the moment, like a child crying into a pillow, it seemed only as a slight drum in the back of my head. *Maybe there is really nothing to worry about. Or maybe it's because you have a girlfriend, Dumbass. What are you doing? If Maddie catches you walking down the street…*I couldn't finish the 'what if.'

Alexandra's perfume wafted around me as if she knew what I was thinking and was trying to entice me into the here and now. A chill ran through me like metal forks against metal plates, but I chocked it up to the wind going down my shirt, not that I was possibly balancing on the line of the cheating zone. *Well,* I countered myself, *only thinking about that cheating zone.*

Like that makes it any better.

We turned down between two buildings and out of view of any stragglers walking the street this late at night. Lobster traps were stacked all along the sidewalk edge, slinking up near to the lifeless boats moored in the water. I tried to shake off the bad feeling – *Or is it guilt?* – but Maddie's beautiful heart-shaped face kept coming into my mind. I thought of the hurt this would cause her. *I hate when she cries.*

Alexandra's pale-skinned profile shoved Maddie's face out of my sight as she pushed me up against the red building forcing me to face the water. The movement was quick and scary as all hell. *I've never seen a person move that fast,* I thought as I shook off the suspicion that I was somehow prey to her.

"Wow, you're strong," *I honestly cannot believe the class 'A' dork comments that keep burping from my mouth.* I'm not sure if it's nerves or not, but I needed to shut the hell up. *Or maybe if I keep talking, she'll think I'm a total idiot and give up on flaunting her hotness at me,* and I can go home with nothing having happened and nothing needing to be said. *Coward.*

She smiled a sly smile at me, licked her lips playfully and began kissing me on my ears and neck. She moved her knee in-between my legs, rubbing it gently against me. *Oh crap. Now there's no way I can tell her I don't like this.* My eyes rolled back into my head with the need of it, *God, that feels good.* My mind reeled, self-control trying, unsuccessfully, to take my body back over from the inside out. *Ok, this needs to stop!*

"Alexandra, whoa, wait a sec. Hold on. I'm sorry. I can't do this. I have a girlfriend," I gently put my hands on her shoulders to push her back, *Or hold her at bay,* but it was like trying to move a stone statue. She didn't budge.

"I don't think we need to worry about her right now," she pushed through my hold and divinely purred in my ear, licking the lobe and nibbling on it gently as she began kissing me again. She wrapped her hands around my neck and into my hair roughly, as if she was telling my body that she owned me.

After smelling the sweet, muskiness of her and trying hard to remember who Maddie was and what I was doing, I gave in. I had no resolve. I was her captive and I couldn't find my senses to fight her off.

I want this.

I want her.

It was like knowing I was hungry and just needing to eat right at that moment or choose to die within reach of sustenance. No other time would do, *It has to be now.* This incredibly, absolutely sexy being was kissing me and I wanted to kiss her back.

I'm not going to lie – part of it was because I would have bragging rights with the guys. But the other part of me wanted to make sure that I had no reservations about asking Maddie to be my wife. If I could get through this, I knew Maddie would be the only girl for me. *Right?* But if I can't…

What a stupid argument. That is not justification for this, Moron, I chided.

Eventually I gave in and kissed Alexandra back as she slid me down the wall, sitting me on the ground and leaning me up against the building. My hand reached up to feel the black curls dangling around her face. Her hair was softer than I thought it would be, softer than chinchilla fur. *No, that wasn't right.* I had never felt anything like this before.

She broke her lips from mine and stood above me in her tight black leather pants and red corset. All I wanted to do was reach out and touch her again. Tossing her hair and catching one curl in her painted fingers, she twirled it slowly.

Oh my God, she is driving me crazy! My eyes couldn't leave her mouth. Perfume swirled in my direction and my mind started to blur. I began to wonder what my own name was let alone who in the world this Maddie person was and why I was so damned worried about her. The drum in the back of my head began beating louder, "Listen to the warning," it cried. But it quickly became clouded and dull, muted by the strange woman's scent. I was caught in her pale eyes, her luscious lips and high cheek bones. *And that body – so many things I want to touch.*

Alexandra's hands slid down around my chest and the next thing I knew, she grabbed my shirt and ripped it. Buttons flew everywhere. She kissed me again on the lips and gave me a teasing look as she slowly moved her hands down to my belt and zipper. It was so hot; my excitement swelled further. *I need her. Now.*

Her mouth was back on my bare chest and I caught her eyes as she looked seductively up at me. I gasped, taken aback. There was something different about her eyes. They were no longer pale. They looked odd. Wrong. Suddenly hateful. *No, not hateful…*

Evil.

They were completely black, no white showing. *Demon's eyes.*

The drum in my head beat louder, but I was stunned into submission by her. I couldn't even move my arms or hands to touch her. *React! Damn it, push her off!* But it was like I was waking too quickly from a dream, my arms and legs still asleep in unconsciousness.

I tried to move my arms again, but they lay limply at my sides as I sat there in amazement and fear. *I'm in a nightmare. This isn't real!!*

"What the hell are you?" was all I could manage to breathe out, my voice barely audible to even me. The sound of it raised panic, so I asked her again in a louder more strained voice, still trying to maintain some control. She bared a smile, showing sharp incisors and hissed at the same time. Then she dove for me. I was horrified. My voice froze up so my mind took over the screaming, *Get Up! Get UP!! GET THE HELL UP, KEEN! MOVE!! MOVE! MOVE!!*

But it was too late. Searing pain ripped through my neck as she tore through me. I felt my necklace break against her teeth. A screech came from me in surprise, in fear, in pain, unlocking my voice but it turned into a guttural sound as my throat and mouth began to pool with blood. I could taste the metal of it, but tried not to swallow. Tried not to choke. I could smell it in the air as it began to flow from me – hot wetness dripped down my neck and out from between my lips.

The beautiful monster dug deeper into my neck, and I felt the swoosh, swoosh, swoosh of blood leaving my body. It was painful. It was sultry and seductive. It was simultaneously excruciating and exquisite.

Why didn't I listen to myself before? She's killing me, if anything, I at least recognized that.

My ears turned off from the outside world, like I was iced up, solid. The only sounds I heard was my heartbeat drumming against my head. Darkness was falling around me, *Or is my face buried in the luxurious curls gracing my killer's head? They'll be the death of me.* I laughed to myself before grimly thinking, *I'm dying. This is it. Maddie, I am so sorry. I am so stupid!*

But then, out of nowhere, a different sound began to form in my brain. Slowly, like removing cotton from my ears, I heard voices over the commotion of her ripping through my flesh.

"What the hell are you doing?" and "What is this?" The deep voices yelled.

The feeling of her lips left and I almost cursed the release of death taken away from me as she turned to answer her new distraction, "Back off boys. It's this one's time."

Her voice was purring again and my body shifted towards her as if under a spell. I wanted more of the pain. *If I have more than at least I know I'm alive.* But this… this was agony. Blackness in my brain, clouding and closing in on me. *I just want to hold on to the pain. Please,* my mind begged although I'm not sure if I actually tried to speak the words out loud, *Please let me have the pain.*

The desire of it was great and I edged closer to her, finding the smallest bit of strength to inch towards my doom – it was calling me to grasp on to her and never let go.

"We don't feed raw in city limits. Time to go, lady," a deep voice said in a calm anger of disgust.

"Well then, catch me if you can," She said gleefully, "or save him. Your choice. Either way, he's mine."

Well, this is new, I thought dully as I felt my body being lifted and then flung over the boats and across the water. My necklace, *My chayyim necklace,* slipped from around my head as my own life slipped from me. My brain went giddy, *Is this what it feels like to have an out of body experience? Maybe I died. The stars seemed so close. Am I above the fog? Oh good, the pain is leaving.* My eyes dimmed. Tunneling. But suddenly it was cold and the pain was back again. *So this is what death feels like.*

Halfway between being out-of-body and in reality, I understood finally that I was being wrapped in the cold, cold April waters of the bay. This was it for me. Searing pain heaved through every muscle and every joint when I tried to move. It rippled me like putting a finger in an electrical socket over and over again. My neck was ripped all to hell and my arms and legs still felt that dream-like paralysis. And now my worst fear was about to occur, and I wasn't going to be able to do a damn thing about it. *I am going to drown.*

Some guys have all the luck.

☆ ☆ ☆

This is the Last Time I'm the First Person to Pass Out

"Get out of the way, Bree!" My arms swept above me to dislodge the damn cat from the skylight. When the weather began to get warm, the cat would go outside during the day to terrorize the rabbits and birds, only to return at night to tackle the house like a rock climber. To top it all off, she would sleep in between my open window and the screen. She always blocked out the sun with her big, gray-and-brown-striped body. But I wanted to see the sun, *No, I need to see the sun,* and she was a terrible pain to wake up.

I missed the screen, it was usually a pretty far reach anyway, and I would have to shift my body to a sitting position to just barely hit her with my fingertips. That usually surprised her enough to move. But as I kept edging my body up, I didn't feel her fur through the tiny holes of the screen. In fact, I couldn't feel anything but air. *Uch. Just open your eyes.* After the long night and freaky dreams I'd had, I knew I wasn't ready for that. *What an awful sleep.*

My eyes were groggy and heavy. My dreams had never been that life-like before. *Must've been the alcohol. Is it possible that Guinness can even go bad?* But a final decision on the matter forced my eyes to open to the murkiness of shadowed light. *Stupid cat.*

Propping myself up, I put my hands slightly behind my back. But I didn't grab the soft edge of the mattress like I normally did when pushing myself through sleep and into wakefulness. My hands squished back behind me, sinking a little bit, throwing me slightly off balance and I slipped back down onto my back making a soft 'splat' sound. My eyes popped open in surprise and my body lurched back up into a sitting position. *Oh, crap. This is not my room. So where the hell am I?*

What I thought had been my bed of soft comfortable blankets had actually been a pile of mucky sludge and grass. The shadows through my eyes weren't from the body of my cat in the skylight, but of the thick fog still leaching around, blocking the sun in dark-stained intervals before bright patches leaked through randomly. Blinking a couple of times to clear the haze, my left eye suddenly closed in a sharp heat of pain. My right eye went in and out of focus as my left began tearing up. Then my right eye clamped down in a sympathetic gesture of pain.

"Ow, ow, ow, ow, ow!" I grumbled trying to force my left eye back open through sheer will, "Damn contacts!" It didn't work. Both eyes remained down as if the lids were sewn shut and my eyebrows folded over them to help hold them in place.

The pain was razor sharp, cutting my eye out. This had happened to me before; I had slept in my contacts one night last year and they had dried out. My right eye had been fine, but my left cornea had been scratched and I ended up spending three days keeping my eyes closed in my darkened bedroom. Another two weeks of wearing my glasses, and being called "Four-eyes" by my friends, completely healed it.

"Shit, shit, shit." It hurt worse, "Ok Keen, just relax." I hoped speaking out loud would help loosen my tightened face up enough to calm the hurt even a little. Then, I worked on reopening my right eye. Light broke through and I felt myself relax more when I was able to see clearly from it. *One down,* I thought, *One more to go.*

Bringing my hands up to my left eye, I went to touch the lids, trying to peal it open. Underneath, my eye was dampened by thick, gel-like tears, *I better not've gotten an eye infection from this. I'm going to be so pissed.*

My eyes tensed back shut, and I deepened my breathing. A stench of salt and fish hit me. *Just fricken great! I'm blind. My eye is probably going to fall out of my head and I'm sitting in mud near the ocean. Could this get any worse?*

Do I really want to know the answer to that? The voice in my head was the mocking version of myself, sounding a little bit like my dad when he says to be careful about asking questions you don't want the answer to. *No, not really,* I mused, trying to again calm myself and handle one task at a time. *Just open your right eye first than work on your left.*

Once again, I struggled to open the right eye, but once it was open, I concentrated on just my immediate surroundings and not the pain in my left eye. I needed to remain calm in order to open it and get the contact out before it did any further damage.

Marshy grass ran past me and I realized I was in one of the estuaries where the over flow of the ocean comes up during high tide. Lucky for me, it looked like it was low tide *For now. Ok, so we,* As in me, myself and I, *are safe for now. Let's work on getting that eye open.*

Ah, good, a team effort, I laughed, helping me to relax. Wiping away the viscous wetness under my eye with my right hand, I reached over with my left middle finger and pulled up the lid.

"Oh shit, that hurts! Mother-fu," I cut myself off as my right thumb and pointer quickly snatched out the contact from my eye. Both eyes clamped down again as I winced in pain.

I can't believe I scratched it again. This blows. My thoughts flicked back to those three days in the dark and the following weeks. I went through a lot of audible books and hours of music as I sat there in my room, blinds completely shut, a thick blanket tacked over the sky light, and the cat lying on the bed with me.

Ech, I don't want to wear my glasses, my thoughts whined. No one, not even Maddie, had ever seen me in my glasses before last year and I got endlessly ripped on for it. Yes, I know, I'm practically legally blind, but that didn't mean that I needed to show it. To top it all off, my glasses weren't even the right prescription.

This blows, I thought again. Taking in one more deep breath, I opened up both eyes. Clearing away the rest of the haziness and gunk from the infection, I looked at the contact, bringing it up as close as I could to my face so I could focus on it. *Near-sightedness sucks.* There was nothing on it. The thing was completely clear. Whatever debris had been scratching my eye must've been actually on my eye.

Wait a minute. Why doesn't my eye hurt anymore?

Looking up quickly, past the contact, I realized not only did my left eye not hurt anymore, but I could see just fine. *No, that's not right. That can't be possible.*

Winking my right eye down, I stared through my left. Everything was clear – grassy marsh to my left, tiny granules of dirt in the muck. I could even see insects in the grass at a short distance away, beginning to encroach on the area I was in to come over and check me out.

I shut my left eye and opened my right. *Holy shit!* Same thing!

Reaching up, I grabbed for the contact that should've been in my right eye and I poked my eyeball instead with the pads of my fingers. But that didn't hurt either. Opening both eyes, I could see something in the far distance that brushed into my view, a slight curve to a horizontal shape. It skimmed in and out of focus. The fog wasn't helping or hurting the view, but it took me a bit to realize I was looking at a foot bridge about one hundred yards away. It overhung the wide mouth of the estuary, connecting its two sides.

"Holy shit! What the hell? I can see? Without my contacts? What the hell?" I rambled, "No fricken way!"

Excitement began to rip through me. *This is so awesome!* I gave myself a moment to be excited before reality knocked to be let back in, *Nope, this must still be a dream.*

Well, damn it. Disappointment sank my shoulders into a slump.

But it didn't feel like a dream. In fact, I felt completely awake. A little disoriented, but awake none the less. *Well,* I thought, *either way, I'm going to need to figure out where I am.*

Pausing for a moment, closing my eyes and listening around me, I hoped this would distinguish exactly where I was. *I'll have to figure out the why/how I got here part later. Car horns and truck tires?* The sounds faded in and out, sharply one moment and then muted by the thick fog. *That almost sounds like the highway. Where the hell am I?*

Not wanting or ready, really, to move, I went back to looking at the bridge. I shifted, listening to the cars, music blaring out their windows, water lapping at the beach and the lighthouse fog horns crying their mournful tone of warning in the far, far distance. My eardrums suddenly began to hum as the sounds of cars were drowned out. The ground around me began to rumble, I felt like I was in an earthquake. The vibrations felt like they were bouncing me around, but I hadn't moved. Out of nowhere, a huge plane flew up over the bridge – very low and very loud, landing gear out.

Holy shit! The jetport? Jesus, how did I get all the way out here?

Then it hit me. As if the plane broke the hull of my memory.

Alexandra.

My hands jolted immediately to my neck when I thought of her name. My body slammed into attention, feeling feverishly around for the holes that creature had made in me. I searched for damaged skin, muscles pulled away from my neck.

Pain.

Anything.

But nothing.

No hole.

No damage.

My skin was intact, although I felt a small bump of puckered skin, like a healed over scar. A scar I hadn't had before.

Or just a couple of new zits, I reasoned with myself, the best of my own personal Gollum coming out in me. *I must've been dreaming this entire time. And I must've been really wasted.* Alexandra had to be a vision in my highly drunken state. *You know, go to bed at 2 with a 10 and wake up at 10 with a 2. I bet she never existed.* My panic subsided as I began to come to the conclusion that Gabe must've had something to do with this.

Punked. I will so get them back. My own personal April Fool's day prank. I must've passed out first and they had to've driven me all the way out here. Who the hell did they know that could get them onto the runway access road?

Oh right. Noah knows someone, I'm sure of it.

"Assholes," I yelled at the top of my lungs, knowing they couldn't hear me, but feeling better all the same.

Or maybe they're hiding around here. But looking around and listening for laughter didn't turn up anything. *IF they left me out here, they really left me out here by myself to find my own way home.*

Assholes, I concluded.

But then, I looked down at my shirt, and fear took hold instantly. It was ripped open – buttons were missing and there were splattered and dried stains that could only pass for blood. I could smell the hint of metal to it and the memory of the taste came back into my mouth. Seawater and mud stained the rest of what was left of my shirt.

I needed to take stock of what had happened to me, so I began looking down at my ripped jeans. One of my sneakers was missing. "Ahhh!" A strained yell came out of my dry, cracked throat as I jumped up ridiculously fast in surprise. At my feet was a huge seal, mauled open from the neck down. It was disgusting. Claw marks stretched from mid-back to its hind flippers. Guts, blubber and blood all drained into the incoming tide. I turned my head to retch, but all that came was a dry heave from the clear lack of food in my stomach.

What the hell?

I walked over to the seal, and tried not to beat myself up for being such a wussy. It wasn't working. The animal was long dead, but I couldn't help think the damn thing might just pop up at anytime, and bite the crap out of me. I'd already had that happen once last night; I didn't want a repeat.

My brain thrummed with pulses like a heartbeat. I put my hand to my chest and tried to slow down my breathing. My hands jumped away. *What??* I put my hands on my chest again. The pounding of my heart was in my head, but I couldn't feel anything in my chest. I put my hands on my wrist. *No pulse.* I moved to slide my pointer and middle finger onto my neck just below my jaw bone.

Nothing?!?

But the pounding in my brain would not slow down as I bent over to look closer at the seal's head. *Get a grip, Panofsky. You're being ridiculous. The seal is dead, and you are not the Tin Man stuck in Oz without a heart.*

I turned my attention back to the seal. It's eyes were glazed over. One ear had been ripped off, and the mouth was frozen in a silent, pained bark. The smell of the blood and decomposing flesh wafted up into my nostrils and my stomach turned. But not in the need-to-retch way as before.

My stomach growled in what felt like hunger.

Ok, time to go. I don't want to run into whatever the hell attacked that thing anyway. I turned around.

Arrg! What the...

I dropped to the ground, grabbing my head. Not in pain, but in shock. When I turned to move into the opposite direction of the seal, away from the water, I ran smack into a tree, which broke at the point my head banged it. The problem was that this tree was four inches in diameter and, as I looked back at the seal, I realized that in less than a second, I had spanned fifty feet away from it to reach the tree line.

What the hell? I thought for what seemed like the millionth time, *This can't be happening!*

Chapter 2

The Boogey Man

✫ ✫ ✫

There is Something Very Wrong Here

Isat next to the broken tree for what seemed like hours trying to calm myself and think rationally. A losing battle.

OK, let's start at the beginning. Two hands, two arms, two legs. Feet still intact, though missing a shoe. I looked down again at my pants and did a quick shift and smiled. *Yup, that's still there. Good sign. You never can be too careful when it comes to the family jewels.*

Breathing in and out, though, didn't feel natural like it should. It didn't even feel like my lungs were expanding or contracting at all – which reminded me of my heart that I couldn't feel either. I slid my hands up again to my neck. And again, there was nothing. Focusing on my internal functions, I tried to feel the blood pulsing through my veins, for my heart beating. But there wasn't even that odd pounding in my head that I had heard earlier. No thump, thump, thump in my ears.

I wrapped my thumb and index finger of my right hand around my left wrist and squeezed. Hard. There wasn't a pulse there either, *And the hits just keep on coming.* The color of my hand never changed to the reddish-purple it should when it's starved of oxygen and blood. I let go and pressed a finger back into the hand. The skin where my finger touched did not turn white. Actually, it was all white. The entire hand, my arm, everything was pale like I had never been in the sun before. *This is quite the hangover reaction. Usually I just puke it out of my system. Maybe I have alcohol poisoning.*

Or maybe that crazy lady stole your heart and lungs like that stupid urban legend where someone wakes up in a tub after having their kidney stolen. I shrugged that thought away. However, something else came to mind.

I wonder...

I looked down at my still working watch. It was about eleven o'clock in the morning. *When the second hand hits twelve, I'll hold my breath and see how long I can do that for.*

Tick, tock, tick, tock, and GO!

Around the second hand went.

And then again.

And again.

And again.

Ok, ten minutes of this and my lungs aren't burning nor is my brain screaming for oxygen? This is not good. The only sensation I had during that little exercise was that I became bored and mildly annoyed from not being able to smell anything around me. *Well, apparently, breathing is now over rated.*

"Hmm, does that mean I'm dead?" my voice shook, "Because that would really suck and I don't want to be dead." I checked out the area around me, then up at the foggy sky, and yelled at the top of my lungs, "Seriously, if this is heaven, it's really fricken dirty. And why are there planes?"

Of course, there was no answer. Only the sounds of the highway and the passing planes were there to keep me company. *For now, I will excuse this as NOT dead, but as a really bad hangover, or a really, really messed up dream.*

As I breathed in the air again, the wind began to swirl the fog around and the scent of the dead seal came over to me. Again, my stomach growled. Hunger pains took over and I could feel my blood-sugar drop. I became immensely dizzy and suddenly very agitated. A searing pain went through my eyes, nose and mouth. My mind sent waves of panic like I just *had* to eat and I *had* to eat right then. I'd been at this breaking point before. I needed food fast or I was going to pass out.

Too late, I thought as my eyes began tunneling and darkness passed through me.

✵ ✵ ✵

Where the Heck did I Go?

When I awoke again, it was dark. Boogey Man dark. The fog was still heavy in some areas, but I could tell it was beginning to lift. The tide had come up and was showing signs that its visit for the evening was over. I checked the time on my watch, needing to hit the glow button. *It's 2:30 am. Yeah for water proof watches.*

With only a few nearby street lights reflected off the water, I couldn't see too much, but from what I could tell, I wasn't in the same estuary anymore. I was sitting at the bottom of a beach carved from rough stones. The beach turned quickly into a tree lined hill, but it didn't look unmanageable to climb. Since it was so early, there weren't any planes flying over. Nor was it late enough for the lobster boats to be out yet.

My clothes were clinging to me in that uncomfortable wet, ripped and bloody mess kind of way, but at least I was no longer hungry. *Take the positives when I can!* My stomach felt full, and my mind felt clear. I had no idea how I had gotten there and was beginning to think that I didn't want to know.

Making sure I was fully awake, I went down to the ocean and splashed the cool, crisp water onto my face. Dark saltiness dripped through my fingers and I watched it make its way back down into the water, creating tiny ripples. Moonlight peaked through the clouds at that moment and I jumped in shock of the horror the water reflected back at me. *That's not me, right? It can't be me! No way in hell is that me!* Sharp rocks cut into my palms as I tried to keep myself from falling backward onto my ass. I turned to make sure no one was standing behind me, someone with the face that created the reflection. But no one was there. It was just me.

Just great, I moaned in my head and took stock of my hands. Although the cuts looked ragged like they had been made with a serrated knife, it didn't hurt. A clear liquid, which didn't resemble blood, dribbled out of my left palm as I removed the shard of rock that was embedded there. I threw the rock and watched it skip a couple of times on the water before sinking into the depths.

Turning my attention back to my injured hand, I flipped it over and back and then looked at my right hand. The cuts were gone. Only a trace of the clear liquid that had flowed from them was left. "Ok, this is just crazy!" *Or maybe I'm going crazy. I am talking to myself, which is the first sign.*

I removed the rest of the debris and dipped my hands back into the water to wash them, all the while trying not to catch my reflection. *I am not ready to see that again.* I tried to enjoy the coolness of the water and the briskness of the mist as it curled around me. The moon peaked through and, after a couple of calming breaths, I looked again.

My face was barely recognizable, *A dead man's face.* The water reflected the moonlight upon my skin, showing a paleness to it like new-fallen snow. My face seemed drawn. *Thin.* Tired and hollowed out at the cheeks. As an athlete, I was thin and toned, but this was different. I appeared plain skeletal. Anorexic. *Disgusting.*

I had never considered myself all that great looking. When Gabe was around, heads turned towards him. But, I could hold my own in a regular crowd. *Now, I'm not so sure.*

Dried clear 'blood' was caked on my forehead – some still dripped from my lips and under my nose. Moving my hands up and down my face, mapping the hollows in my cheeks, I tried to get used to the creepiness I had become. *I don't think I can. This is just not me. Maybe I really am dead. Maybe I've become the Boogey Man.*

The thing I was seeing in the ghost of the moon's reflection didn't seem real. I smiled and humorless lips smiled back at me.

"Holy crap!" My hands automatically went to my mouth, "What the hell are those?"

My fingers flew up and traced my lips and teeth, "Ow! Shit!"

I pulled my hands back to survey the damage. Spiked holes were quickly healing where my teeth had poked through.

I brought my face down as close to the water as I possibly could, my nose almost touching it, allowing enough light for me to see. I smoothed my lips over my teeth, gently this time. Baring my teeth at my reflection, a hissing sound came out of me. High pitched and snakelike. *Ok, that is all sorts of wrong!*

My non-existent heart raced in fear, beating in my head like an echo of what it should've sounded like. *What have I become?*

I pulled on my teeth, touching the bottoms of them, feeling them scrape against the pads of my fingertips. *This cannot be possible.* They were so long.

So sharp.

So revolting.

And dangerous.

I pursed my lips together and accidentally bit the inside of my mouth. I could feel the blood. It was warm and gooey. But it didn't taste like blood – it was bitter, rank and gamey. I spit out what I could, but the taste still lingered. The fluid that had landed on the rocks was the same clear-like goop that had come from my fingers. *I don't have any blood at all?* Pushing that to the back of my mind, my thoughts went back to my teeth. *How am I going to eat with these things? How am I ever going to kiss Maddie again without hurting her?*

"You can't. Either way, you can't," I answered myself out loud before thinking, *Yes, I'm losing it.*

This is insane, I must be going insane. There is no way my teeth could've grown this quickly overnight. No fricken way.

I'm going to ignore this. I choose to ignore them. They are not here.

I smiled at that stupid thought but stopped immediately when my reflection showed the little puffed out spots above my lip from my new, sharp teeth. Those things I was trying to deny were actually there, digging into the insides of my cheeks. *Gross.* Childishly, I hit my reflection in frustration. *What the hell is going on with me?*

I wanted to scream. Actually, I think I wanted to cry. I *knew* I wanted to wake up from this night terror.

The moon retreated, thankfully, taking away the grotesque image of me in the water. *Maybe I should disappear with it and drown myself.*

With no immediate answers coming to me about my predicament this entire day, I decided to quickly clean the rest of the blood and mud off my face and hands and walk up the hill to figure out where I was.

☆ ☆ ☆

Finding My Way Back

The hill wasn't as steep as I thought it would be and I moved easily up it to a clearing at the top – a field, not particularly manicured, but definitely not ignored. I continued to the middle and realized there were lines painted on it. *Ah, a soccer field.*

Turning left, walking past the grayed benches, I moved beyond the dilapidated recreational building onto the main drive. The access road opened up to a real one. *Osgood Street. Libbytown. Good. Not too far from the docks.* Taking Osgood, I crossed over Hobart to get to the old railroad tracks and followed them to the right. They would lead me into town.

While I ran down the tracks, I took everything in. Thinking, smelling, seeing, planning – all, it seemed, for the first time in my life. *Well, this life. The one after Alexandra – my own version of AA – if I don't wake up from this.* Something had clearly changed in me, but I couldn't figure out what. *How in the hell could I have changed so quickly over a night? It's just not possible. This is just not humanly possible.*

I thought back to the night before with Gabe, Sam, Jeffrey and Noah. I wondered if they thought I had gone home with her. I wondered if they had made it home themselves, or if Alexandra had gotten to them too. *When the sun comes up, I'll go check on them and make sure they're all right.*

I began to think of Alexandra again. I just couldn't believe that I was so completely immersed in her will that I hadn't listened to myself when the warnings hit. That was so unlike me. I usually listened. But she was so beautiful. Maddie is very pretty, but this woman was some kind of super model. *Stupid male hormones.* And ego.

And what the hell keeps blurring by me? Stopping dead in the tracks, I realized that I had been running so fast that the scenery had become just lines of color surrounding me. Unable to explain my pace, I continued to run and in no time I was back on Commercial Street where the old industrial buildings and the mouth of the estuary intersected. According to my watch, the few miles down the tracks had taken me less than five minutes.

That can't be right. It takes me longer by car. My head hurt just thinking about it. *For now, just queue the Twilight Zone theme music.*

I flexed my muscles and stretched my legs, feeling the movement. Even though I could sense every muscle, there was no soreness, no pain, no hurting. *This has to be the most bizarre dream ever.*

I didn't feel any stronger. I didn't feel any different at all, actually. I picked up a rock and threw it. Instead of it hitting off the metal building like it normally would do, the speed of it caused the rock to go directly through the building, leaving a hole in the wall, metal denting inward. I could hear it crash through other metal and glass before the small 'tink' sound of it dropping to the ground. It sounded like it went completely through the entire building.

Man, I hope these buildings are still vacant. Let's not do that again.

Either way, I decided to take off in case someone was coming by. I let my thoughts skip around in my mind again, finally resting on the fact that I needed clean clothes and I couldn't continue into the downtown looking the way I did. *Why not just show up at the precinct and admit to a murder? No officer, I'm not sure whose, but I think it may have been mine.*

Making an effort to appear normal, I became painfully aware of my pace. *This feels ridiculously slow,* I thought, feeling oddly annoyed. Passing underneath the Bay Bridge, I stopped at the old international marine terminal where boats used to leave for Canada and other trips. I remembered the fight this bridge had caused within the town. Since the new bridge had not been tall enough to dock cruise-liners without drawing it, town-folk wondered why it had been built at all. Now the big ships port at the old Iron Works docks, where they used to build and service Navy vessels. *Well, at least that worked in my favor tonight. No one is out now.*

Ferries would not be running at this hour, and the water taxi... Well, I didn't think it would be prudent to scare anyone. So I looked for a dinghy I could borrow. A narrow two-person one was resting near a lobster boat off of Holyoke Wharf. It was pretty banged up and didn't look like it could hold a seagull resting on it, let alone me, even with my nearly hollowed out frame. But it was all I could find, so it was going to have to do.

I hopped on more silently than I expected, untied the little boat from its mooring and began to paddle away from the docks. The boat had a small motor, but I didn't want to risk calling attention to myself with all the noise until I was well away from the port. It was easy to stay hidden since the thicker fog still rolled in from the ocean. It muted any noise from the small wakes hitting the bow.

Curiosity got the better of me and I checked to see if my arms were as quick as my legs had been or if they seemed to be suddenly stronger than they were before. I waited until I was past the 'no wake' zone to test my theory. I was an experienced boatman, or so I liked to think. I used to race kayaks and two-man canoes in high school, and did fairly well.

I let my arms and hands run free, paddling into the water. At first, it was awkward and I found myself very comically boating in circles instead of a straight line. I wondered if before 'the incident' of Alexandra, my left arm had been stronger than my right, and if that had been magnified with these new changes. I stopped and couldn't help but laugh. *If only Maddie could see me now!*

That thought sobered me up, real quick. *Maddie can't see me like this. I don't even know what 'this' is let alone explain it or how I got 'this' way.* I imagined how the conversation would go:

Maddie: Wow Keen, what happened to you? You used to look so hot and tan. Well, tan by Northeast standards.

Me: Oh funny, you should ask… I went to Pros with the guys and this really hot chick picked me up. Yeah, we fooled around a little, and when I woke up, I just looked like this.

Maddie: Huh. At least she was hot.

Then I would get to enjoy watching her backside as she walked away for the last time.

I sighed and got back to paddling, adjusting my long strokes to keep me straight. The wind in my hair, the salt splashing up, the light sounds of the water. *This is the best part of being on the ocean.* I tried to enjoy myself, my mind taking me back to a time when I raced, but I would see Maddie's face waiting on the bridges over the finish line and it would bring me back to the present.

The lighthouses and forts seemed to pass quickly by as I paddled the boat. The fog and darkness of the early morning blocked most of the view of them, but I'd taken that route many times on the ferries, I knew where each of them was. The fog was very useful, though, in blocking me from the sight of the late-night protectors of the barges that were anchored in the area. I could see the water splashing against the tankers, strong enough to break a two-person boat if caught up in them – four hundred and seventy-five feet of iron and steel melting into the water. Their cargo bays held oil, chemicals, wine. Who knew? I shuddered at the thought of what could happen if one of the hulls were ever damaged in the small bay.

I continued more confidently, honing in on controlling the sounds of my movements as they quickened. I still splashed around a bit, but it wasn't nearly as bad as before, and I only went in circles when I wanted to. *Much improvement.* Sweeping past Hog Island Ledge, which held the long abandoned Fort Dune, and House Island, a secluded island with one large house, I thought about how I used to joke with Maddie that we would call it home someday.

Well, I can kiss that fantasy goodbye.

Aiming directly at Gordon's Wharf, I changed my mind at the last minute and decided to cut left, out of range of any lights coming from my intended landing. I continued edging just off-shore of Sweet Haven Island to the slight beach where kayak tours were launched. That seemed to be a pretty good place to land as the local and foreign stoners, I mean summer help, would not be at the bunk house that early in the season. Only the owner would probably be running tours for a while yet, and he lived in the center of the island. But in a few more weeks, the landing zone would smell of mildewy plastic and "special" cigarettes, hand rolled for a more flavorful kick.

Ech! I only tried the stuff once during a trip Gabe took us on to visit our 'next door neighbors' in Canada. But toking up and drinking beer along with it did not give me the laughing, munchy frenzy feeling my friends were enjoying, so I dropped the who-ha thing. *Being giggly is not my thing anyway.*

I scraped my borrowed boat up the beach and hid it in the thorny bushes of the island roses that were not yet in bloom. The fog had been thick on and off the bay, but on the island it was thinning, ghostly spirits swirling around. This was probably the first time I was even vaguely skittish about it, still thinking that Alexandra was going to jump out and finish the job, as it were.

I used my new-found speed ability to run silently up the dirt and gravel road until I passed Miss C's, the only grocery store on the island. This talent was beginning to amuse me – I always liked going fast, but it was nicer knowing that I was going fast on my own volition. I went up the back way to my parents' house and waited at the edge that marked the property, looking at the place that I had called home for most of my years. Of all the places we had lived, this was my favorite. It was a two-story blue-gray captain's house. Although it was smaller than most houses on the island, it was still comfortable for a family of three.

"I can do this," I whispered sounding much louder than expected in the silent night. I stood straight, fixing my shoulders back with the confidence I tried to force myself to have and then rolled my eyes at how stupid that must've looked. I turned toward the house. I brought in a deep lungful of the cold crisp night air and noted how the salt in the wind was less distinctive here in the middle part of the island.

Well, I thought, *I can't put this off any longer.*

I headed to the porch.

✵ ✵ ✵

Home, Sweet Home

The fog was clearing and I could see the gray-blue shaker shingles of the two-story house. As I slowly walked up the patio steps, I remembered sneaking in late once last summer, having spent most of the night with Maddie on the mainland. I was so late that there were no ferries and I had to take the water taxi back. It had cost me a whole week's worth of tips from blue-hairs down at Mike's Lobstah Bake but it was worth it. I couldn't believe my parents hadn't caught me then, and I gave a silent prayer that they wouldn't catch me now.

I started picking up more changes in my senses – objects around me felt different than before. The flavors of the wood wafted up to me as I shifted up step by step. The scent was so familiar, yet now so distinctly changed through the unusual heightened senses I'd gained. The different layers of grains in the woods seemed to cause different vibrations in my ears. Before, I could only hear the sound of creaking wood when I walked up the steps; now it was a buzzy, humming sound that was occasionally muffled by moss or louder scratching noise due to the slight rotting of the wood. I could even tell that my left leg hit the ground a bit heavier than my right, but I was still silent in the night. I smirked; *Ninjas have nothing on me.*

I got to the top of the steps and played with my new senses to take in everything on the patio. The linseed oil on the patio furniture was rustic and peaty. The iron on the fire pit smelled red-yellowy of leaves and carbon from the wood mixed with dankness of melted snow. The house was almost a hundred years old and had the odor of molds and mosses, rain-weathered wood, sun-baked glass and paint. And dryer sheets.

Ma must've run the wash. What I wouldn't give to be in clean clothes right now!

I reached the sliding back door and hesitated. I could see on the other side that my parents had not locked it or put the bar down. There wasn't a real need for security on the island as nothing ever happened, but I had always been a worrier and preferred to keep the house locked up. *Then again,* I thought, *they could just be leaving it unlocked for my return.*

Two full-time police personnel drove around the island or waited by the docks in shifts. Summer Sundays were always the most active due to reggae at the main patio-bar down by the dock. Between the good music, decent food and assortment of drinks, it could get pretty rowdy when the mainlanders and tourists showed up. But for the most part, the island was crime free. The closest thing to theft here was when people accidentally left items too close to the curb where they were then picked up as "other man's treasures." One note on the grocery's bulletin board was all it took to retrieve the "stolen" item along with apologies from whose misunderstanding it was. It was one of the more amusing aspects of island life.

I sighed and decided it was now or never. The door opened with no sound and I slipped through, shutting it quickly behind me in one small fluid motion.

The hunger pains came back immediately.

☆ ☆ ☆

The First Attack

My eyes began to narrow into the depths of a freakish tunnel vision. My stomach reared up in a hunger pain so intense that I thought my insides were turning outward, exploding from anger. The back of my mind throbbed a warning signal that coming home may not have been a great idea after all.

I was starving and all sorts of food smells bombarded me. My instincts tore through me and I was unable to deny them. I had never felt so overwhelmingly hungry in my entire life. I bee-lined it to the kitchen and opened the fridge. It reeked of foulness and rotting – spoiled milk, sulfur smelling eggs, meat that had become a science experiment. My parents had always cleaned out the fridge so I had to find out what smelled so badly.

I grabbed items, sniffing them and then pushing them aside to sniff the others, trying to figure out what the God-awful smell was, and looking for anything green, black or feathery white with mold. I checked the expiration dates on everything.

Nothing.

The food was not old. Nothing was near its expiration date. But yet, the smell was so bad it almost sent me into dry heaves. I thrust the door shut and it immediately dislodged the nasty smells – not killing them completely, but lessening the stench. Unfortunately, they were replaced with an overwhelmingly powerful scent that caused my hunger to show again and I doubled over in pain.

My legs automatically switched directions and I started running through the house. I had no control. I jumped over sofas and chairs like they were a slight speed bump. I trashed through one of the side tables, not seeing it before I hit. A rain of papers and envelopes fell around me, but I hardly noticed. My body had a clear goal and my eager hunger allowed me to ignore everything else.

My mind couldn't govern the actions of my body until it was too late; I tore through the glass and wood frames of the partially opened French doors. They knocked off their hinges as my shoulders barely grazed them. The tantalizing smell of food burst through as the doors opened all the way. I couldn't wait any more. I needed to satiate my stomach. I could hear it growling, or maybe that noise was coming from my throat. I was in such a frenzy of need that I couldn't tell.

Not being able to contain myself any longer, I dove for what my blood was calling for.

I went in for the attack.

I heard a scream.

I saw a sharp movement as a body flung itself at me and began hitting me in the chest, feeling no more than just a pat. But the atmosphere held the anger and fear behind it as my nostrils filled with the scent, exciting me into more of a frenzy. I bent down, my instincts intent on the feeding.

But I was jolted suddenly. I heard my name being called.

"Keen! Keen! Please," the voice was insistent. I faintly recognized it, but couldn't place it.

It was enough, however, to cause my brain and my instinct to war. Not knowing what to do, I pushed the form down and away from me. It knocked into a dresser and slumped to the floor.

That's when I realized I was in my parent's bedroom. I looked at the form and understood that it was my mother that had screamed at me. It was my mother who I had just knocked into the dresser. It was my mother that I almost attacked, *but why?*

I tried to rationalize what had happened. But the hunger... the pain... the flavors tickling my tongue and drawing through my nose and lungs were intense. I couldn't concentrate.

"Oh my God", I barely whispered in shock, *what have I done?*

I had attacked my mother.

✵ ✵ ✵

I'm on the Milk Carton

Running over to my mother's crumpled form. I stopped inhaling when I realized that she was the cause of my stomach pains. Memories began to inundate my mind when I touched her arm: My mom teaching me how to sail, my father showing me how to kayak for the first time. Thoughts of some of the Jewish holidays we celebrated over the years also came to me: Chanukah, also called the Festival of Lights, and Purim, a holiday where children dress up in costumes and read from the Book of Esther. Both holidays commemorated escape from persecution. A comedian once summed up Jewish holidays as, "They tried to kill us, we won, lets eat."

Shouldn't've thought the word 'eat'! My stomach reeled and my fangs felt as if they were going to fly out of my mouth just to bite. *Find some control here, Panofsky! Pull yourself together! Now, damn you!* Looking up and away from my mother, I saw a picture on her dresser. It was of her, my father and me at one of the "Adoption Day" parties that the community held annually. I think I was five- years-old in that photograph. My nerves began to calm more, my teeth pressed less against my lips and the hunger began to flee.

Turning to my mother, I felt for her pulse, but I could hear it like it was the same warning drum that had been beating in my head. Her pulse was steady. She was knocked out. *Good,* I thought, *Now what to do?*

I looked over at the bed to see that it was empty. *Oh,* I was relieved, *That's right, dad would still be in Boston this part of the week.* He was a computer software consultant and traveled down in Boston every week. Picking up my mother, I laid her on the bed, covering her with the bed quilts. It didn't look like she would be bruised from her landing. Guilt flooded through me. *What kind of horrible creature had I become?* I needed to make it look like I had never been in my parents' room or messed up the house. *Everything needs to be put back in its place – like a monster didn't just go ballistic and try to attack her. Make her think this was a bad dream, matching my own bad dream except that mom will wake up from it and I won't.*

I moved away from my mother and looked at the doors to her room. They were only slightly off their hinges, with no other noticeable damage to them *I can fix this if I hurry.* Risking a breath, because I was starting to feel uncomfortable and disoriented without having the sense of smell to ground me, I quickly sucked in air through my mouth. *That monster, Alexandra, has clearly turned me into something evil and I am going to fight it.*

Memories of my family seemed to help before so I began focusing on those and not the fact that, after I got a few things from my room, I would probably never see them again. I took another deep breath.

Home. This time, I smell home – The lingering lilac perfume mingling with Old Spice cologne. I allowed myself to smile at that and filled my head with more memories to keep the hunger at bay. Focusing past the still lingering smell of rotting food, I mentally dulled their overpowering aromas and tried to imagine what I should have smelled when I was normal.

Mom had clearly made one of my favorite dishes this evening – tuna fish cheese melt with...

I sniffed...

… tomato, hold the onion.

I had been able to replicate the three bread layer-y goodness oozing grilled cheese, tuna and garden grown tomatoes. I just couldn't master the amount of love and butter that went into such an unhealthy but delicious concoction. *Odd that there's no onion, though.* Especially since I could smell the waiting onion bulbs hanging in the mud room between knotted lengths of nylon, *Thank you, Alton Brown for that bit of advice on how to keep onions longer.* My parents always ate their tuna and grilled cheese sandwiches with raw onions and tomato, while I opted for the less stanky version of hold-the-onion-tomato-only-please. I did have a girlfriend to kiss occasionally, and nothing is worse than Panofsky onion breath.

I breathed deeply again, relaxing, thinking of home, mom, and dad. I let the air dance around in my lungs, getting me used to normalcy, and ignored the twitches of hunger pain in my body. I wished my mouth would salivate over my mother's dinner. I missed wanting to eat with my parents instead of wanting to actually eat my parents. *What a frigged up thought that is!*

The flavors of the leather couch and an old, dusty radio in the living room, I noticed, were the strongest. My upright piano and djembe drums were only slightly less muted. I could smell my own scent radiating from them. *Damn, I smell good. Thank the Lord for that small favor!* I picked up the scent of my clothing and my room upstairs, but they were more mellow, not nearly as strong as my parents' scents around the house. I'd only been gone a few hours, having left here before going to the bar with the guys. *Weird.*

I ran downstairs into the basement where my dad's workbench was and grabbed one of his many screwdrivers. I went back up and over to the French doors to fix their hinges. The entire effort took me less than ninety seconds.

I paused again. A smell of something else was in the house. Something I had not smelled in a long time and never this strong. It took me a moment to remember what it was, but it triggered...

Sadness?

Yes. That's exactly what it was. Sadness and heartbreak. Like when my grandfather died of cancer two years ago. It was so strong back then that I thought dad was never going to recover from the anger and shock of his father passing away. Even though death is inevitable, I knew then that I never wanted to feel that again. *Ever.*

But there it was, lingering and mixing into the pleasant, homey smells of my childhood. It obscured the life of the house and its ambiance within – the home that never had so much tragedy or pain that it couldn't recover. *But why was it here now? What happened since last night?*

I shrugged and got back to work. I walked over to the sitting room where I had knocked over the side table and bent down to pick up all the letters and mail that had scattered. There were magazines, junk mail and a school bill. *Yippee.* Flipping through everything, a small piece of scrap paper fell out of one of the envelopes. I bent to pick it up and realized I didn't recognize the handwriting at all. In fact, I didn't even recognize who it was written to. The scrawl read:

Em –

My half is gone. Do you still have yours?

– J

Who in the world is Em? And Who's J? My parents names are Miriam and Kalman. I put the letter back in the envelope and something else caught my eye. The newspaper.

The Press Herald headline was nothing special, and most of the articles running were about the Sea Dogs and the Boston Red Sox starting up spring training. *No big surprise there.* But the article that stopped me dead was about a missing college student... me.

"Local College Student Still Missing After Two Weeks.
After a night on the town with friends, Keen Panofsky, a University of New England student and star athlete is still missing."

Two weeks? I was dumbstruck, *No way. How could I be missing for two weeks? Two days at most. But two weeks?!?* I checked the date on the paper. If it was in fact that morning's paper then all this craziness did start two weeks ago. *How could I have missed two weeks of my life? How is that even possible?*

My knees started to buckle in shock, so I sat down on the chair in front of me. I continued reading, catching only the snippets of detail that my brain would allow me to read.

"Friends say 19-year old Keen had not been drinking. 'Keen told us he needed to catch the next ferry back to Sweet Haven,' Gabe Butler said."

"He said he wanted to get a good night's sleep in order to play against West Eng," Jeffrey Lafayette said in reference to the UNE Lacrosse game versus the Western New England team where the Nor'easters, without their 1ˢᵗ string attackman, lost 6 to 13."

Damn it, we lost!
And another section read:

"A shoe was found on Union Wharf Street matching the description of what Panofsky was wearing that night. Although divers have been in the bay, signs of Panofsky have not been found.

'Foul play has not been ruled out,' advised Captain Lowry Jameson of the Police Department.

Panofsky has been described as 5'10", medium build, blond hair, blue eyes. He is on scholarship as a center for the ice hockey team at University of New England and recently joined the Lacrosse team. He's in the B.S program in Environmental Sciences.

If anyone knows his where-a-bouts, please contact the Police Department at..."

I guess that's as good a use for my senior photo as any. I should check the milk carton; hopefully they haven't put me on there yet! I set the paper down and headed up to my room. *I just need to get my stuff and get my ass out of here before my mother wakes up again.*

When the house was built, the upstairs was split into three closet-sized bedrooms. However, after we moved in, my parents had combined two of the rooms into a bigger one, and used the third one to create a tiny, but full bathroom. My parents had also built a master bedroom off the living room. They already had a full bathroom, in true East Coast fashion, off the kitchen.

I went into my bedroom, but didn't need to turn the light on. Not only did I know the room like the back of my hand, but the moonlight and fog through the skylight helped me see. My room was pretty much how I left it – messy. Clothes and books were everywhere; the bed was not made, typical of any college student.

I laid down on the bed and stared at the skylight, my legs hanging over the side of the bed, and wished this had never happened. I'm not a "Why me?" kind of person, so I didn't go there. But I did go to "What next?" Sighing, I got back up, reminding myself that I should only stay as long as I needed to. *Dawdling isn't a good idea right now.*

My backpack was lying at the foot of the bed, so I grabbed it and emptied out the school books and notepads. I threw some clothes from my drawer into it and grabbed some camping gear from the closet. Looking down at myself, I noticed it was time for a change. I switched out of my ragged and bloodied clothing and put them in a plastic bag. *I'll throw them out away from the house later.*

God! I can't even imagine what Mom had thought when she saw me in them. Man, I hope she doesn't have nightmares from it.

The final gear I threw in my bag was my if-I-was-stranded-on-an-island-what-would-I-take items: my laptop, iPod and energy sources. Without music, nothing would be sane in my life and I needed that now more than ever. Also, too many private thoughts, *Not to mention a hidden folder of porno,* were on my laptop and I didn't want to leave that behind for prying eyes. *Hopefully, nobody had searched through the computer yet. Well, it doesn't look like anyone has touched it, so maybe everything is safe.*

Not much believing in banks and not owning a credit card, I had a stack of cash in my sock drawer that I took and threw that into my bag too. *There, done.*

Except for one thing: Even though I really didn't want to show signs that I had been home, I needed to let my parents know that I was at least, well, alive, if not necessarily ok. But as I was definitely not ready to face them, especially with the persistent and nagging hunger I was trying to ignore, *I'm going to try to figure out what's going on and learn some control before I get in the same room as them or any person or animal, for that matter,* my best option was to just leave a note for my parents. *Maybe, they won't find it for a few days, but I can't worry too much about that.* Tearing a page from my notepad, I wrote:

> "Mom, Dad, I'm all right. Something's happened that I can't quite explain. I'm not in trouble, but I need to figure it all out. Please don't look for me. I will come back as soon as possible. I love you. Keen. P.S. Please tell Maddie that I love her and I'm sorry. Please tell her to move on from me."

I dropped the letter on my bed, grabbed my bag and walked out of my room, for what I was hoping was not the last time. *I'm not sure how it can be otherwise though,* I thought as I felt the weight of all the changes suddenly hit me. My shoulders slouched in distress. Checking on my mom one more time, I held my breath as I approached the room. The rise and fall of her blankets and her stronger heartbeat told me she was sleeping now, instead of just being knocked unconscious. She looked peaceful.

It broke my heart to have to leave like that, *But what choice do I have?* I could feel big goopy drops falling from my eyes and I swiped at them. The liquid was thick against the back of my hand. *No longer tears, but that evil inhuman fluid.* Saddened further, my heart fell through my chest and into the barrel of my stomach as I turned around and left.

❖ ❖ ❖

Ah, Lunch

I walked silently down the porch. Engulfed in the fog away from the house as I approached the edge of my parent's property, I heard a motion to my right, stirring the mist. Three blurs skittered past me, one almost knocking into me. *Oh. Deer.*

I'd forgotten about them. The family of deer had always slept through the nights on our property. Our family fed them regularly, which is more than I can say about any of us mowing the lawn. We also had left salt blocks by the start of the wood line on the left side of the property clearing.

The scent of them blew past me like a shallow after thought. My eyes began to narrow and my stomach felt the same urgent hunger pain as it had in the estuary and in the house. The smell was sweet, woodsy – mixed with grass and newly bloomed island flowers. It melted in my mouth, and like Pavlov's dog, I began salivating. The surprise of it made me breathe in deeply, which only made my senses more alive. Heightened and frightened by the lack of control I was beginning to feel again, my body moved instinctually, shifting to the direction of the deer. This time, I let the impulse take me. I was done fighting it. I was tired. I was hungry. It was time to figure this thing out and see where it was going to take me.

I lunged.

My arms wrapped around the doe. Fear swept in her eyes as I brought her down to the ground. She bayed and struggled against me, but I was stronger. My mouth bore down in sharp precision. I was no longer horrified by the sudden confusion of it. Eating sent a surge of ecstasy to my mind. The hot blood pulsing through my mouth filled my soul. The heartbeat of the deer was transferred briefly into my body. And I sucked more on her, wanting that feeling of being alive to be in me again.

I fed.

And it was good.

Chapter 3

Scene of the Crime and My New Friends

✩ ✩ ✩

Don't Go Swimming After a Large Meal

I watched the slightly weakened doe hobble away from me. She was trying to get her legs under her in a way that reminded me of Bambi when he first stepped onto the ice. At the same time, though, she was shaking her long, beautiful neck as if it prickled with flies landing on her. The marks I made in her flesh were already healing. Staring at the dripping holes that were getting smaller and smaller with each passing second, the desire to pounce again was hard to resist.

But hadn't I just done the most disgustingly, horrible thing ever? I had attacked an animal and stole some of her life blood away from her.

So why am I not as repulsed as I should be? My brain and instincts warred again. My brain wondered in anger at the disgusting creature I had become, what ever the hell I had become. *Did that evil woman make me into a demon? Am I evil? I don't feel evil.*

When the hunger went back to the deep recesses of its cage, I didn't feel any different. Before Alexandra's attack on me, I had never noticed that my heart beat, my lungs breathed. *Why should I worry that I can't feel them now? That when I breathe, it feels more out of habit than necessity? I mean, I don't have the urge to bring about the apocalypse and that's what evil does, right? Right?*

But what have I become? I don't think I'm human.

The deer would be fine, and that gave me some relief. I hadn't killed her. I don't know how I would've reacted if I had. *But this isn't exactly like I was ordering a steak at Oceanside Steakhouse. This was an attack on an innocent creature with my bare hands and my teeth!*

But I didn't kill her.

At least, I hoped she would be ok. I hadn't taken that much from her. Just enough to feel human again. *NO! That's not the right word. Feel alive? Maybe?*

Thank God the cat wasn't around! Would I've gone after her too? She must be out hunting... Maybe I should've joined her. A hysterical kind of laughter ruptured from me as I pictured the two of us stalking rabbits side by side. It was the nervous giddy kind that's hard to stop and it took me a couple of minutes to salvage what was left of my mental capacity.

I wiped the blood from my mouth with the back of my hand and bent over to brush my hand on the grass, hopefully, ridding me of the brutal evidence that I was not right in the head, or body, for that matter. Looking at my blood stained knuckles caused me to lick them instinctively. My eyes turned to that black tunneling haze and I went to bite my own hand. Fighting the yearning, I jerked my mouth away and held my breath.

What is wrong with me?

I need music. That's what's wrong with me. It had apparently been weeks since I'd heard any. Something needed to be done to calm my nerves, put my head back on right. In my fury to get my dinner, I had dropped my backpack a few feet away from me. It took less than a second to stand, jumping to my feet faster than I had the thought to do so. The movement was so quick that it threw me off balance. I hadn't expected my body to react quicker than my mind was giving orders to move so I overcorrected – swaying like a man who had drunk about ten more drinks than he should have.

Taking one step got me to my bag, almost like I had willed it to come to me. But in reality, I had just moved that fast and it was now in my hands. *Almost the second I thought to reach for it.* I found my iPod in another instant, threw the ear-buds on and hit play.

I doubled over in pain from the sound hitting my ears but to my surprise, the volume level was barely a fourth of the way up. I turned it down as low as it could go and tried to get used to even that loudness.

Well, that's just flippin' perfect! Even my iPod is against me. Gnarls Barkley's "Boogie Monster" played in my ears. *Ah well, it fits my mood perfectly.* I ran back to the dinghy, pulling it from its hiding place and made my way back to the mainland as the song continued to play.

It's time to find a new home. A new life, I thought. When I arrived on the other shore, I returned the boat to its rightful resting place and put everything back exactly where I found it, just like a good boy-scout. No one would be the wiser. The song was on its last, most fitting, stanza and I thought about the meaning, *Like I need to be reminded that I will forever be that monster staring in the mirror.*

The fog had been steadily decreasing since I had stepped on the island and come back. The black early morning sky peaked through every once in a while with an eclectic mix of larger-than-life stars, upper-atmosphere clouds, the occasional roaming satellite and the moon. It was like the heavens were creating a peep show – *Just put your money in the slot and look 'til your heart's content or your sixty seconds is up.*

My feet took me to Union Wharf, to the scene of my... *What? Crime? Murder? Rebirth?* I needed to see if there was anything left to remember from that night two weeks ago. It was unfathomable to me. *Two weeks. Just gone.*

And you'll never be able to get them back, Keen.

The streets were still empty, the lobstermen not yet needed at their traps. But now I was exiled in my town. I kept to the shadows. The area had been cordoned off by police tape, although, after two weeks, it was starting to come down like a lazily strewn streamer at a party that had already ended. *The tape isn't going to last much longer.*

Turning the corner and seeing the place where the vixen had taken me gave me more of a shock than I had expected it to. My eyes clouded up with viscous tears and I had a hard time swallowing back the sorrow. It was like trying to swim against the current as it pounded itself against cliff rocks. The emotions consumed me as I dropped to my knees in sadness, heartbreak and a little awe. The memory of the incident wasn't what brought me to my knees, however. What broke my strength in two was the impromptu shrine that was there against the wall where I had lain, mutilated by a demon before being thrown into the water. I may have even taken my last human breath in that spot. *I don't know.*

A framed and enlarged senior picture, the same one that had been used in the newspaper clipping, was leaning on the wall and several stuffed animal black bears and Stormin' Norman dolls, the mascots for my high school and college, surrounded it. Pictures were dangled around the site and glued to handwritten signs and notes. *I'm stunned. Overwhelmed. I never thought so many people would miss me.*

Getting my courage back, I got up and ducked under the police tape to get a closer look. The wind had blown out several candles that had, at some time, been burning in front of the ode to me. I could still smell their ashy wicks and flavored waxy scents. Someone had been here merely hours before. *This is so weird.*

The poster boards read:

'We miss you Keen!'

'Come home soon!'

'We're praying for you!'

'We love you, Keen. Please come back!'

There were smaller notes, but I was so moved by everything I felt I couldn't possibly read any more. It would have incapacitated me with grief. *And I need to get through this. On my own.* Turning my attention to the photographs was probably not a good idea either, but I did. There was a picture of me and the guys all dressed in drag for a Halloween party. Gabe made the best looking woman out of all of us. *I'm sure no matter what he wore, someone would fall for him.*

Another picture was of a group of us hiking up to Naughton Peak on Mount Larson. There were photographs of me on the hockey rink, in uniform for the basic team shot as well as some while I was playing. There were even pictures of boating trips I had gone on in middle school. *Wow, did I look like a baby then!*

One picture, however, caught my eye and I had to fight back the tearing feeling again. It was of Maddie and me after my senior prom. She still had her hair up and makeup done, but she was in a casual jean mini skirt and a tank top. I was in jeans and a T-shirt. I had my arm around her neck and I was kissing her on the top of the head while she looked on at the camera laughing. *I've never seen this one before. Did Maddie put it here?*

After glancing around at the other photos one more time, I picked up the one of Maddie and me and put it in my bag. Everything else I left alone. It was time to concentrate on the real reason why I was here: to see if there was anything that could lead me in the direction of Alexandra. Staring at the building, and the surrounding area, I could smell the scent of chemicals that they had used to clean away the blood. *My blood.*

My sharp eyes examined every square foot of the scene. I had bled profusely from her attack and it amazed me that all visual traces were gone. *Something must be here. Some evidence that she might have left.* The newspaper article said that the police had found my shoe. Of course it wasn't there, presumable taken into custody as evidence or maybe given to my parents, *'Here's what's left of your son. Sorry Ma'am.'*

Nothing was left, though. No sign of Alexandra. No sign of me. *And soon, once time moves on, the items people left here will be gone too.* Stolen? Lost to the bay? *No. Forgotten.*

Feeling a gust of wind, movement caused me to glance over at the police tape. It had finally abandoned its duty, falling to the ground as if it were a sign agreeing with me. I went back to looking at the memorial when something just beyond the group of pictures fixated my attention. In what remained of the candle light, a tiny hint of gold glinted from in-between the metal of the build-ing and where the ground met. I went over to it, fascinated by the dull light. My mind tried to process all the things it could possibly be as I delicately pulled at the object. It was a test of my patience to retrieve it from its confinement without breaking it, but, eventually, I was able to get it out intact.

My Chayyim! I couldn't believe it. The gold metal was bent and it looked like there was a fang mark from Alexandra, but it was in one piece. "Holy shit," I muttered as I bent the medallion in my palm so that it was flat again – I could do nothing about the tooth mark.

Turning my back from the altar, I sat down on the edge of the wharf, dan-gling my feet inches above the tide water and staring at my lucky charm. I stayed that way for a few minutes, deep in thought of all that I had lost and at a loss as to what to do next in my life. *If you can call this a life.*

The water lapped against the wall, lulling me into a trance-like state. Physically, I wasn't tired, but emotionally, this new reality was getting to me. I thought of all my options, *Who can I call? Where can I go?* But kept coming up blank when thoughts of someone would invoke my stomach to hunger. Friends and family were definitely off limits until I could figure out what was wrong with my system. *In fact, for now, I think it best just to leave all the human population alone.*

"Good idea," I responded aloud.

"What's a good idea?" A gruff, base of a voice, two octaves too low for any normal person to hear, questioned from behind me.

I startled to a jump, turning so quickly that my iPod ear-buds went flying off my head and I almost fell into the water. In the same quick motion, I recovered, shoving my iPod and my Chayyim into my front pocket and faced something I had never seen before in my life.

A monster. It was five, no, six feet taller than me and I had to crane my neck up to look at its face. It was humanoid in shape like a Pats defensive lineman that had been dumped into a nuclear reactor. He, I assumed 'it' was a 'he,' was dripping in water, but looked like he was made of water all at the same time. The drops would fall and then rejoin him, making the areas darker with the dirt and grit it had picked up off the cement. Those darkened spots would go to the center of his massive body, and then would turn clear again before going back through the process. *His heart?*

He laughed and rumbled, "You're quick. That's good. More fun to play with before I kill you."

This creature from the black lagoon that had just threatened me was no more than 10 feet away. *So close.* "What?" I said stupidly. *No one actually tells you they're going to kill you. Not in the really real world, right?* I heard a deep, guttural growl and almost backed away in fear until I realized it was from me. If I hadn't been so freaked out about the thing in front of me, I would've thought that pretty menacing of myself.

It stepped toward me and I felt the real danger of him. I could smell it coming off of him like a whirlwind of destruction. *Keep him talking.* "Why would you want to kill me? I haven't done anything to you," *I am really not good under pressure,* I thought.

"Fun. Bored. Pick a reason. You're here and more entertaining than most humans," it paused and sniffed at the air. "Ah, but you're not human, are you? No matter. That just means it'll be even more exciting." The place where his eyes should have been looked gleeful, almost childlike. And that scared me more than anything.

I had to think. *How do I get out of this one?*

He started toward me again. Grabbing at my shirt, he threw me before my brain could engage. I was in the air and then slammed up against the wall a few feet above the place where I had been bitten. Some of the posters and pictures dropped from their spot on the shrine as the vibrations of my hit got to them. *This is like de ja vu. Does everyone just want to kill me right here?* I began laughing at the thought.

Not understanding that my sudden outburst was not directed at him, my laughter goaded the creature like a cattle prod. He slammed his fists into my stomach, knocking air out of me and drenching me but not doing much else. Actually, I barely felt anything. Except anger. That guttural growl escaped my lips once more. It was louder now and more threatening. My eyes began tunneling, like when my hunger hit. But this time was different. This hunger wasn't for blood. It was for water.

He picked me up in his left arm and pummeled me with his right fist. My head swung side to side with every hit. I noticed again how the water dripped from him and then would reconnect with his body. It reminded me of something and I tried to figure out what as he threw me around like a hacky-sack.

Oopl-ick!

That's it! Cornstarch and water. A simple and stupid toy my mom used to make up for me when I was getting in her hair while she worked in the kitchen. She'd combine cornstarch, water and sometimes food coloring. If you slammed something into it, the thing would be rock solid. But if you gently touched it, you could put your hand straight through it. *Let's see if this theory will work.*

The creature grabbed my shoulders with both hands and lifted me up, "I am getting bored with you. I think it's time to end this silly game. Don't you?"

"Yes," I snarled. Lifting my hands up, I grabbed him at where his elbows should be. He looked at me and a second later grasped what I was about to do. His reactions were too slow.

I squeezed.

His grip on me broke immediately as his arms fell off. Together, his appendages and my ass landed in great splashes against the ground. My head banged into the cement, somewhat cushioned by the water. It felt like I had landed hard into a water bed.

He howled in what sounded like pain. I only had a few seconds to do something else as he was willing his droplets back to his body, dark and mucky, turning his bluish-gray to brown.

I went to put my hands through where I thought his heart might be, but he head-butted me. The surprise caught me off guard and I fell back to the ground. By the time I got up, his arms were back together and he was reaching for me again. I backed up against the building; the wall was dented and broken where he slammed me into it. He cocked his entire arm back and grabbed me with the other one to keep me still. Not wanting this to be it for me, as I wasn't sure if my changed body could handle more punishment, I finally let my instincts take over.

My eyes tunneled into tiny pin pricks. I could only see what was directly in front of me. My other senses took over. I was no longer Keen as I had understood him. I was a creature backed into a corner, looking to kill my attacker before he killed me. As my arms and legs flayed out in utter disorder, trying to beat him off however I could, I began to become aware of other voices.

"Kaellan! Let him go," the first voice said in an almost jovial and amused tone.

"Drop him Kaellan, or else," the second voice was deeper and more powerful than the first.

The creature, Kaellan, with his hands still on me, turned to the voices, "Or else what, little creatures?"

"Or else we'll boil you like we did the last time," the jovial one said.

Kaellan's grasp weakened only slightly.

"You remember that, right?" the larger voice spoke.

"Yeah, exactly how many days did it take you to put yourself back together?" the jovial guy said, with a hint of laughter in his voice.

The larger-voiced guy questioned, "Two weeks?"

"No," the jovial voice turned cruel, "the way I hear it, it was a month."

"A month?" this time, the man with the larger voice laughed, "Now Kaellan, do you really want to go through that again?"

Kaellan's hands completely dropped off of me. But I was entirely too far gone. I couldn't reign myself in. Kaellan headed toward the water and I bolted after him. I was ready to grab him and sink my hands into him, the only way I knew how to beat the living crap out of him. My anger was over-powering and I couldn't control myself.

Two sets of hands pulled me back and away from him. I roared and screamed. I couldn't see who or what had a hold of me and, frankly, I was tired of being grabbed. I again tried to punch, hit and kick anything in reach. But the other two were able to keep me just at arms length – keeping me under control. They were both extremely strong individually, so I had no chance with both of them holding on.

"Looks like we have a lively one, D," the jovial one said.

"Take care of him," the other replied.

"My pleasure," the jovial one spoke to me directly, "We've got to stop meeting you this way."

I felt a sharp prick in my neck and I was out cold.

※ ※ ※

Groggy, and out again

Music.

I heard music and it was blurring in and out; I couldn't quite make out the words or the sweet sound. *What is it?* It sounded so familiar.

Why can't I open my eyes? I tried shifting.

I can't move either. My muscles were incredibly relaxed.

Is it because of the music?

No, that didn't seem right.

Drugged? The thought ripped through my head instantly, clearing it. I realized I was hearing the beautiful crooning of Billy Holiday. *Okay? That's wicked odd.*

"He's coming around," the deep voice from the dock said, "Stick him again. We don't have him secured yet and I don't want him coming up swinging."

The phrase 'don't have him secured yet' should've bothered me. But how can anyone feel bothered when Billy Holiday's velvety voice is singing in the background? Even my 'ass is in trouble' warning sign wasn't going off. *Is it because I'm drugged? Is the 'stick' thing another drug?* I tried to open my eyes again. But they didn't even move to slits.

The jovial voice was exasperated, "What the hell? I gave him enough to take down three of him and an elephant."

"He's a newbie, and he looks like he was in pretty good shape before he was turned."

Turned? What's he talking about? Oh yeah, me, the demon. I wanted to roll my eyes at the thought, but again, nothing would move.

The deep voice continued, "Just stick him already, would you?"

"Hey D, I know we saw this guy a couple of weeks ago, but doesn't he look like that college student that.."

I blacked out again before I could hear the rest.

✧ ✧ ✧

Tied Down... Again

The sounds came to me quicker this time around. The music that had just ended was 'Don't Fade on Me' by Tom Petty. *Wildflowers. Good album. Are they really called albums anymore since I can just download individual songs? Well, did we ever even say 'good CD'? Nope, I think I've always only heard album. Huh. Weird.*

OK, apparently whatever happy juice they shot into me is making me loopy.

The next track was even more fitting to my dazed and confused state: 'Blue Foundation.' *Whose ever play-list this is, I like their style.*

Oh wait.

This is my playlist. I'd like to blame the previous dumbass-ness on whatever drugs I was given. I kept my eyes closed and I listened to my music, allowing it to relax my mind, fill me up with patience and calmness. Letting it push out my fear. *I'll take stock of my predicament in a minute.*

I took a deep breath in while keeping my eyes shut in feigned, groggy sleepiness – filling my chest with the plethora of new smells, but mostly checking to see if any of my captors were in the room.

They weren't. *Good.*

Listening for a good ten minutes, I got to hear a throw back to Guns N' Roses, a song from the soundtrack 'The Village' and a more recent song by Cold Play. *Ah, Cold Play. They throw an excellent concert. I wonder when they're coming back into town?*

It smells like a funky dorm room in here. Like Gabe's and Sam's place at the college where they are roommates. I hope that crazy vixen didn't get to them too. Reviewing the smells, I came up with cardboard, earthy cloth, wood mixed with strong cologne and sweaty socks. The next breath was smaller, less offensive. I concentrated on distant scents. I could smell metal that flowed around me. It wasn't coppery or rusty and it didn't have a brassy flavor either. *Steel? No... Silver? No... Hmm I'll move on for now and see what I can get from it when I open my eyes.*

Now is as good of a time as ever. I was in a strange room – a metal ceiling, dull white-painted walls, a shut door and no windows. There was a light, *Maybe a desk lamp?*, coming from behind me, but I couldn't crane my neck around to see. The room itself had computer desks, a couple of chairs and medium-sized, cardboard boxes everywhere. A sudden, quick terror filled me. I tried moving my arms to get off of whatever surface I was laying on, but I couldn't. I glanced down the line of my body. My arms and legs were strapped down to a table or bed of some sort. Metal with only a thin layer of leather protecting my skin was what was holding me in place. There were straps across my chest too.

Taking several calming breathes to ease myself back from the point of really freaking out, I tried to separate myself from the situation and *How far deep into shit am I right now?* Luckily, nothing seemed to be needled to me or coming out of me. I was a little concerned about that possibility. But with the mess the room was in, it looked like the straps might have been for my safety, if not everyone else's.

My tranquility only lasted a few seconds as I shifted and the straps tightened slightly. Panic set in further. Worming around, I tried to reposition myself up and down, side to side, even diagonally on the table. It was like a straight jacket. The more I moved, the tighter the holds grew. It became hard for me to bring air into my chest, not that it was necessary anymore. I was becoming increasingly crazed. *Admit it… Scared.*

Within just two short weeks, I've been attacked, murdered, then beaten up, and now strapped down. What the hell else is going to happen? Can I be killed twice? Is that why they have me strapped down? They, whoever 'they' are, know I'm some sort of evil freak and I need to be killed – again?

Lashing against the straps, hoping against hope that something would budge or give a little, they tightened even further. The leather began to cut into my skin and I could feel the wetness of clear goop seeping through. Defeated, I stopped struggling and concentrated on the music in the air around me, willing myself to relax. The straps began to release their hold just enough to be comfortable and allow my skin to begin healing – the skin stretching itself over the wounds.

Ok, time to meet the jerks behind this set up. Either being brave or stupid, not sure which, I called out. "Hey! Hello! I'm awake now. Can you get this crap off me?"

The door at the end of the room opened in a flash of wood covering metal and I was instantly surrounded by two men who were larger than life.

One guy was toned like me, or like I had been, but taller by a few inches. He was very tan. California beach volleyball player tan. He had brown hair with blond spikes in them. *Do guys really get highlights?* He was wearing a blue polo shirt with a large team logo on it, plaid shorts and white Converse high tops. The other guy had extraordinarily dark brown skin, like I was looking midnight in the eyes. He was my height and extra beefy. He was wearing a T-shirt from one of the more upscale clothing stores, jean shorts and work boots. With a green four-leaf clover tattoo on his neck and a scowl on his face, he had a very commanding presence.

"Ah, Sleeping Beauty wakes," the tall one jumped up in a crouch over the bed I was on and leaned in close to my face as he spoke, "How are we feeling this glorious evening?"

I didn't move, "If you're coming on to me, I'd rather be on a first name basis."

"Well, then," he moved in closer, "My name's Tom. And you are?" He was too close for my comfort and I couldn't tell if he wanted to kiss me, eat me, or was just screwing with me.

The black guy said in an authoritative and very menacing voice, "Tom, stop messing around and back off."

Tom jumped back down, crossing his arms and laughed, "What's your name, kid?"

"Keen."

"This here is Devon, the guy with the wonderful personality," He hit Devon on the shoulder. Devon didn't budge.

"Where the hell am I and why am I tied down?"

"For your protection," Tom paused dramatically, "and for ours," he smiled.

"I don't understand."

"Well, let me ask you again. How are you feeling?"

"I didn't realize I had been strapped down by psychologists with a flare for fashion," I nodded towards their preppy threads.

"This is no joke," Devon advised, "If you want us to let you up, you will need to tell us how you are feeling."

"Annoyed, angry, pissed-off. Do those work for you?"

"Yes. But more importantly, are you hungry?" Devon asked.

Ah, that. At the mention of the word 'hungry' my stomach twitched and my eyes narrowed.

"That's what I thought," Devon said, "We'll need to feed you before we can let you up."

"What the hell does that mean? What do you mean, 'feed me'?"

The agitation clearly showed in my voice because Tom said gently, "Just calm down and we'll explain everything."

"No you calm down! I want to know what the hell is going on. Why did I react to the word 'hungry'? What the hell are all these weird things going on with me?" *OK, that was irrational.*

Then the tantrum started. I began screaming things out like a five-year-old, a waterfall of craziness as it occurred to me. "I almost killed my mother after having been missing for apparently two weeks. Which, by the way, I have no recollection of what happened in those two weeks, let alone that I was missing for that time. I attacked a deer and I hate venison. I got beat up by some weird-ass water thing, and then I wake up to find that I'm being tied down until I eat. I don't even know what that means or what the hell is going on!"

"Keen, you need to calm your ass down for a minute," Tom was firm, but patient, "We're going to help you, but you need to chill out first."

Then I smelled it. I realized that I couldn't smell anything unusual coming from these guys as I had when I was in my parents' house. But then I smelled that sweet, metallic, drenching-your-hunger scent that had almost catapulted me into direct instincts before. The strange feeling that kept taking me over and over again the past few hours – it was nearby and I wanted it. *I need it.* I craved it like nothing else. My hunger was unbearable and I began to pull and twist underneath the straps, trying to break them. I needed to get at that smell and eat until my pain was satiated. My eyes dulled into deep murkiness as if someone had turned the light down to the lowest setting possible. I felt as if the darkness was going to entomb me into insanity. The silhouetted shapes of the burly men came toward me. The straps tore into me again as I struggled against their attack.

"Oh crap!" Tom said, all patience and goodwill leaving his voice.

"Hold him down by the arms, Tom. I'll grab his legs." They swarmed onto me, locking me down in their vice grips against the table. I turned my head, the only part of me that could move, toward the scent, as they did too.

"T! Get the hell out of here! It's not safe for you right now. Go to Veleda's. I'll call you in a bit," Tom yelled out in the direction of the door.

"What ya got in there, Tommy? Another Newbie?" A girl's voice responded through the closed door.

"Yes. Now get going. And hit the fans, would you?"

A swooshing sound started and slowly increased in speed. The air in the room started to circulate. The smell relented and my hunger began to ease. "Why am I so hungry?" I whined, "Can you help me? How can I make this go away? This can NOT be normal!"

My eyes began to adjust and un-strain, my body relaxed more. Tom let go of me and walked out of sight behind me. I heard the opening of the rubber-sealed refrigerator door and some clanging of metal and glass before he came back into view. "Here, drink this," he said while tilting my head up.

"What is it?" *Do I want to trust this random guy to not kill me? Do I have a choice?*

"Just drink. This will help." He shoved the bottle down my throat, clicking against my teeth. A sweet, cooling drink quenched the fire in my throat and stomach. Its odd combination of fizz and yeast reminded me of drinking a brew with the gang, but this was no ordinary beer. It tasted like a gamier version of the deer I'd had earlier.

I immediately felt better. I was able to lock my animalism completely behind the doors it kept crashing through. I felt alive and energized. *Human again.* "Man, that's good stuff. What was that?"

"You're drinking boar's blood."

I turned my head and spat out the liquid that remained in my mouth. Dragging my tongue against my teeth to get as much off as possible, I spat again. Thick, red splatters hit the floor and Tom's shoes and I said, exasperated, "What the?!? What are you trying to do? Poison me? You are kidding, right?"

"Hey, you're the one that said you already attacked a deer," Tom smiled.

"That was different! I didn't know what I was doing. I've been out of my mind lately, there's no way I'd ever do that again."

Tom's face turned into a big grin as he started laughing.

"What?" I barked at him.

"First of all," he said through a grin, "you owe me new shoes. And second, these drinks were made for people of our nature. Bloody Captain's is a reputable brewery. No other company even comes as close to the freshness of the meal without having to do it ourselves."

I am so confused. Bloody Captain's? Never heard of it. Sounds like something out of a lame horror movie. "What do you mean 'people of our nature?'" I asked him, tensely, and then muttered to myself, "maybe I was right, she did turn me into a demon."

Tom snickered, but didn't answer.

Fine, if he isn't going to answer my questions, maybe Devon would be more reasonable, "I think you can let go of my legs there, Devon."

He stared at me for a moment, his dark eyes debating, but then warily let go.

"So, seriously you guys going to let me up, or what?"

"In a little bit. Maybe," Tom said.

I looked more closely around the room. The disheveled appearance of it, with boxes and their contents strewn about, implied a transitory state like someone was just moving into a college dorm room *Or a workshop that had exploded.* There was a lot of high tech equipment that hadn't been put together yet. "You do this kind of thing often or do you always have straps lying around for a good time?"

"Occasionally, we run across a kid in your, uh, predicament, and we try to help them out," Tom answered.

I didn't miss the emphasis he put on 'try,' "What happens if the 'try' fails?"

"If they're good, they move on. But if we fail, they are put down," Devon advised cold and calculated.

I asked, trying not to sound shaky, but I'm pretty sure I gulped, "So what happens next?"

"Well that depends on you," Devon advised

"I'm listening..."

"What can you tell us about the woman who turned you into a vampire?"

A full raucous laugh escaped me, "Now you guys are screwing with me. A vampire? Whatever. Are you out of your minds? That's a good one. But a vampire? Please! I was only kidding about the demon comment." I stopped laughing when I realized they hadn't joined me, "Ok. Joke's over, let me go." Struggling against the binds again, I tried to get up. *How quickly I forget!* As the restraints tightened against my body, I whacked my head down against the table, grunting in frustration.

"Keen, I hate to break this to you, but this isn't our first meeting. We saw you with the black-haired woman. Think about it. Did her eyes go dark when she attacked you?"

I only half nodded, and curtly at that.

"She was a vampire," Devon started.

Tom broke in, "We tried to stop her attack on you, but we realized it was too late."

I kind of remembered – that night's sounds flooding back, "You were the voices I heard?"

Devon nodded, "We patrol the greater city area looking for trouble before it finds any. Then we handle it. We were, unfortunately, too late for you." He paused, "For that, I am truly sorry."

They both looked sad and failed.

"She did a number on you. When she tossed you into the bay, we thought you were already dead," Tom remarked.

"Tom still jumped in after you. He couldn't sense where you'd gone and the water was wicked deep where you'd been thrown."

"But here you are, two weeks later, fighting a water spirit," Tom finished the story.

"Got the best of him too, briefly," I smiled weakly.

"Yeah, nice job on that one," Tom broke in again, "That was a slick move. I'll have to remember it for the next time he and I cross paths."

"So," Devon continued, "Who was that vampire, and what have you been doing since we last saw you?"

I filled them in on everything that I could remember about Alexandra, when I woke up next, and visiting my house. It was a fairly short discussion owing to the point that all but two days of the past two weeks were missing from my memory. When I talked about my parents' home, Tom got a look of shock across his face. When I asked him why, he said that we would get to that. I hurried the rest of my story along so I could get more information from them.

"That everything?" Devon asked when I finally got up to the part about the water spirit.

"Yes." *Like there needs to be more?*

"What enhancements have you seen in your body's reactions to things?" He continued his questioning in a direction I thought was a little too personal.

"Enhancements?" Even though I knew my situation was precarious, my mouth spoke before my brain caught up to the fact that I should probably not annoy these guys.

Devon crossed his arms and puffed up a bit, which made him look like a pissed-off bouncer, "Don't play coy, kid. You know what I mean."

OK, fine, no reason to hold back. They seem to know more about me than I know at this point. "Well, let's see. I'm definitely faster than I was before. And stronger. I was able to take a few hits from that, what did you call him again?"

"Kaellan? He's a water spirit," Tom answered.

"So, not as breakable. My sense of smell is continually on overload, and my eyes do some crazy shit when I'm hungry. And speaking of which, why am I having these weird hunger pains? And why do my eyes dim to the point of me passing out when I feel this way? And how do you know for sure that I'm a vampire? Who was the person you told to leave? Am I always going to look like this?"

"Any other questions?" Tom asked, amused.

"Yeah, when are you going to let me up? These ropes are beginning to chafe," I did my best to smile in order to make them believe I was in my right mind. Instead, my face grimaced, *Even I don't believe I'm mentally stable yet.*

"Done?" Devon said, with a tone that made me realize he didn't want to hear anymore questions from me.

"Yes, I think so."

Devon began, "First of all, let me start off by saying that Tom here and I are vampires too."

"Really?" I felt a little awed and repulsed. Maybe that was why I couldn't smell them. *Maybe I can't smell vampires the same way as humans. I mean, I could smell Alexandra. Or was it just her perfume? Or is everything completely different because I'm a so-called 'vampire' now?*

"Tom was bitten about 2 years ago," Devon said.

"Two years, five months and three days. But who's counting," Tom broke in.

I turned to Devon, "How long ago were you bitten?"

"Unlike Tom, who can be very anal about certain things, I lost track. But it wasn't that long ago, only ten years. I was bitten when I was 23. Tom was bitten at age 17."

"So you're 33 and Tom is 19 now?"

"Well, technically yes, but we will never age from the time we were bitten," Devon said.

"You mean I am going to be 19 forever?" *That's awesome!*

"Try being 17 forever. I'll always get carded when I try to go into bars," Tom said in a huff.

"Well, technically, you're still not old enough. But I do have a friend that can get you a fake ID if you need it," *Maybe bribing will get me out of here quicker.*

Devon continued, "The point is, we know what you are, we know what you are potentially capable of, and we can help you get through this if you want."

"Do I have a choice?"

Their eyes pierced into me.

"Apparently not," I whispered to myself.

"No, Keen, apparently not. You will take our help, or we will have to take you out behind the shed, and.." Devon said.

"Ol' Yeller style?" I finished his innuendo.

Tom smirked as he started to unlock the straps by way of reaching under the bed-table I was on.

"Look, we are going to try to help you through this as much as possible. It's hard to be a newbie in this form."

"Yeah. How the hell you managed to not kill your mother tonight is beyond any understanding. I've never seen that before with newbies," Devon said.

"How did you do it?" Tom asked.

I shrugged as I shifted my legs to one side of the table and sat up to face my captors better, "Maybe it's because I don't know what I'm supposed to do or how I'm supposed to act. And I have pretty much grossed myself out when I stopped to think of everything. All I know is that one minute, I was lying on the ground with my neck torn open and the next I was doubling over in pain from a hunger that I don't even know how to begin to satisfy."

"Well, whatever your restraint is, you will need to find it again and soon," Devon's tone was ominous.

Chapter 4

New Things

✧ ✧ ✧

My Days Locked Up

"Hey Newbie, you awake in there?" It was Tom, knocking at my door at 9 a.m. having left me alone for a few hours. Of course I was awake. I hadn't been even remotely tired though my human-self would've crashed dead hours earlier. *I'll have to ask Tom if I'll ever get tired again.* After they had given me a couple more blood beers, they had left and I started moving the furniture and boxes around to give myself some semblance of a room. They had picked up my bag from the wharf when they had taken me and I had found it on a chair next to the table I had woken up on. They had already set up my laptop and iPod gear on one of the small desks, although how they figured out the password to my computer so quickly was a mystery to me.

I had been listening to music through my ear buds instead of playing it through my computer when Tom had peeked in. Slipping my iPod off and putting it into my pocket, I turned in the desk chair away from my computer to look at Tom as he opened the door all the way, "It's time to get used to the new you, Newbie."

My right eyebrow rose in its automatic questioning response, "Whaddya mean?" Since they had released me from the table and left me to my thoughts, I had been Googling the term 'vampire,' trying to find out as much as possible. They had a wireless connection to the internet that I was able to hook into with my laptop and download information. Although, most of it seemed completely dated and full of superstition, I wanted to know what was real and what wasn't.

"Well, you may feel like the ultimate fighting machine and able to leap tall buildings in a single bound, but we need to make you street legal," Tom had a couple of blood brews and handed one to me. No one else was in the apartment, but the small whiff of meandering human scent still hit my stomach when Tom opened the door, and my eyes started to go into their narrow pitch.

Turning my focus to the bottle and trying to practice some restraint, I read the label – 'Beaver's Milk… For when no other rodent will do.' *That doesn't sound pleasant.* But I twisted the top off and took a sip anyway. I drank the bottle quickly. It was gamey and fishy, like the taste of frog's legs, but it staved off the complete attack mode I had gone into the moment before.

After I finished it, I asked, "What are you going to do to me?"

"Well, actually, today we thought we'd go easy on you. We'll kick your butt into shape tomorrow with training. So today we get to play 'Twenty Questions.'"

"Where's Devon at?" I asked.

"This was never his favorite part of getting Newbies prepped for the outside, so he's taking patrol for today," Tom replied.

"Patrol?"

He laughed, flashing a sly smile, "Careful, Newbie, or else you'll run out of questions."

"If you want, I can ask my questions as two– and three-parters," I responded with my own devious smile.

Putting his hands up in surrender, Tom said, "Ok, Ok, ask as many questions as you want. Like I said, today is just a relaxing day for you. We'll be testing you soon enough as it is, so go ahead and hit me with what's on your mind."

I decided to start off with some softball questions, like the one I had thought of earlier, "Am I ever going to be tired? Need sleep, or anything?" Daily naps used to be part of my regime. I actually scheduled classes around the afternoon just so I could take them! *I wonder if they're even necessary now.*

"This is actually pretty cool," Tom began, "The old rumor that vampires could only come out during the night started because we sleep in the afternoon only. We're never outside between 1pm and 4pm."

Weird. "Why? Do we fry?"

He laughed again, "No! It's not that we can't, it's just that it's really the slowest time of day. Your body enhanced after you turned, but one of the things the human body needs is to rest in the afternoon. Didn't you ever feel sluggish after you ate lunch as a human?"

"Well, yeah, of course."

"That part was enhanced. It's the hottest time of day, you usually have fed right before, blah, blah, blah. I mean, it's just like how some European countries take siestas, the afternoon lunch-nap time. When I first turned and Devon had me locked up in this place, it was the weirdest thing. As you can see, no windows in here, but my internal clock just knew when it was time. Which is funny, because I totally took naps in the afternoon when I was a human, so it worked out just fine for me," Tom explained.

"I guess that makes sense, but then why don't I need any sleep at night?"

"Again, along with the enhancement, we are able to condense the time of sleep needed to regenerate our energy. Well, that and drinking blood, of course. Besides, all the freaks come out after midnight, so why shouldn't we?"

"Freaks? You mean besides that crazy water guy and us?"

"Oh yeah!" Tom's eyes got wide with excitement, "There are tons of non-humans out there. Like right before we ran into you, we had to deal with some Kabouters from the Netherlands. They had just landed and we were giving them the lay of the land, so to speak."

"Ka-bou-ters, what the heck are those?" I tried to replicate the word I had never heard of before.

"Close enough," he said about my attempt at pronouncing the creatures, "They're like these gnome beings. Actually, they look exactly like those stupid, tacky statues people put in their gardens, though why anyone would want to attract a Kabouter is beyond me."

"Why, are they bad?"

"Not exactly," he hesitated, trying to think of an explanation, "They just can do a lot of damage to gardens. They dig them up to plant mushrooms… very inappropriate mushrooms that they sell on the black market."

"Drug dealing gnomes?" I laughed, "You're kidding, right?" *I can just picture these little two-feet tall things with big pointed hats standing on a street corner and flashing one side of their jackets, saying, 'Hey kid, ya wanna try something really fun?' Yeah, right!*

Tom continued, "Not all of them are bad. Some are just here to get legitimate landscaping jobs in the States, but we have a list from the Netherlands of Kabouters that need to be extradited back to their home. It wasn't pretty. They have significantly sharper nails and teeth than one would expect. We were covered head to toe in miniature bites and scratches for a couple of minutes. It was so annoying."

My overactive imagination took control again as I pictured Devon and Tom swamped by these little guys and I had to stifle a laugh. He didn't look too happy about the memory. So I changed the subject, "You said that Devon was on patrol right now. What do you guys do exactly?"

He gave a quick headshake to jump him out of that last lingering memory of the Kabouters and he answered, "We work for the police department as part of the 'Immigrations' team. Meaning we meet non-humans as they come in from their respective countries and introduce them to the laws and regulations here."

Taking a sip of his beer, he continued, "We basically tell them not to harm the humans and definitely to not eat the humans within town limits. Let the other cities handle their jurisdiction, but whatever happens here is our responsibility."

"Has anyone ever gotten past you?"

"Sure," he nodded, "We don't know how many cross through the bay that we don't catch. Only Devon and I are on this unit – although my sister helps us more often than I'd like her to. We usually only go down to the docks if we're warned in advance that there are immigrants being transported in. But most aren't here to hurt anyone. Some are on vacation or visiting family or looking for work. We don't really control the number of 'whatevers' that come through this way. We don't have that kind of manpower."

Tom finished his drink and took both of the bottles to the bag that was meant for recycling. "I mean, don't get me wrong. Sometimes creatures get by us and can completely wreak havoc."

"For example?" *This could be good.*

"You met our 'for example'"

"Huh?"

"Your swimming buddy, Kaellan."

Oh yeah. Him. My skin crawled at the thought of that jerk.

"Kaellan had come across by latching himself to the bottom of a cargo ship. We completely missed him until we caught him destroying a wharf full of lobster traps just for the fun of it. Since we couldn't catch him, we tried a heat gun that Devon had created for other purposes. But it worked for what we needed. We shot at him from a distance and he boiled into steam. That kept him busy for awhile. But he turns up every once in a while when he's bored."

Clearly! I got that 'bored' feeling from him.

"So anyway," he continued matter-of-factly, "That's pretty much what we do on that front. This place is a hub of activity for demons, water spirits and other things that go bump in the night. But it isn't really up on the nation's list of high 'terrorist' related activity, so we don't get much backup."

"Ok, so what else do you do on the squad?"

"Just normal patrol."

"A regular Batman and Robin, eh?" I laughed but then I was in the air so fast, I didn't even realize it until I landed flat on my back on the floor. *Man is he fast!* Shoving quickly up from the floor, I righted myself and sat down on my bed as the desk chair I had been in before was now splintered into very sharp pieces, "So I guess I shouldn't ask which one of you looks better in tights?"

"Not if you want to live longer than tonight, Newbie," he grinned jovially.

"Well, will you at least get me new desk chair? I was starting to like that one."

"Maybe… If you're good," he bent down to pick up the shards of ruin he had created. Before I could even react to his cleaning, he completed the job. *Batman and Robin nothing! This guy has to be faster than Superman!*

Tom dumped what was left of the chair into the trash bin, "What else ya got for me?"

Still having more questions, I wanted to jump ahead to the important one in my mind before I forgot or pissed off Tom anymore and he destroyed the rest of the furniture in the room, "What do you know about Alexandra?"

"Unfortunately nothing more than the information you gave us about her tracking and attacking you. It was weird, though. She came in a few weeks before you were attacked. We kept tabs on her for only a couple of days. She seemed pretty harmless at the time."

Yeah, harmless. As harmless as a starved shark in seal-infested waters.

"She really gave us no idea of her plans to attack anyone. And when we saw you," he breathed in deeply and released the air slowly through tight lips, not whistling, but as almost a sigh. He began again, "When we saw you, the marks she put in you… Well, you shouldn't've survived it. I've never seen anyone so mutilated live."

I'm sure I winced at that. *Keen, the boy wonder.* Putting on a brave face, I asked, "Why do you think I survived?"

He again took one of those long breaths in and out. I was beginning to think that was the only way he could think, "I have absolutely no idea. My theory is that the water was so cold that it slowed the poison down enough for your body to absorb it and change you instead of kill you."

No argument against that theory. Not like I have any of my own!

His eyes turned wide again, like he had figured something out, "Didn't you wake up next to a seal?"

"So?"

"So? Sooooo, you did say that it looked pretty wasted like something had mauled it, right?"

I shrugged, a little in disgust. *Ech, I know where he's going with this one.*

"You probably latched onto it, drinking his blood. I bet that's how you survived your own mauling."

I felt as if I paled more than I was.

"Dude, you ok?" Tom asked, a little worried.

"I never put two and two together. Until now." *Blech!* That made me the starving shark in seal-infested waters. *Just like Alexandra.*

"Don't worry too much about it. Your body did what it needed to do to survive. I don't think your brain was conscious enough to know what was going on. Turning is not the best thing in the world. For those who remember it, they say it hurts like hell. But everyone's different in how they handle the poison."

"How did you handle it?"

"I, thankfully, was completely out of it."

"What happened to you?" I asked, curiously.

Now it was his turn to have the pale face, but his skin color never changed.

"As I said before, each vampire's turn is slightly different. I only remember the circumstances leading up to mine," his face darkened in memory.

"Forget I asked. I didn't mean to open that can of worms."

"No, no. I don't mind. I've just never told it before."

"Devon and T don't know?"

Tom sighed, "Actually, they do. They were both there."

✳ ✳ ✳

Tom's Story

"I guess I should start back at what led up to my being turned," Tom hesitated before he went on, his eyes tilting down as if to remember, "T was thirteen and I was fifteen when our parents were lost at sea during a race from Marblehead to Halifax Ocean. I'm sure you've heard of it. They were part of a crew that races yachts over a forty-eight hour period?"

I nodded, *What else can I do? Saying sorry for a loss so many years ago seems very irrelevant.* At my silence, he continued in a withdrawn voice, as if he was a story-teller trying to be energetic about it – like this wasn't the story that happened to him but to someone else instead. *Maybe that's his way of dealing with the bad in the past.*

"A rogue wave caught them and several boats. Everyone was pulled out, except my parents. Their bodies were never found. We don't have any family that we know of and my parents didn't have that much money to begin with. No one claimed us so we were sent to separate foster homes. Luckily, though, we were always able to keep in touch with each other. Whatever the hell we were going through didn't matter as long as we wrote or one of us sneaked a call."

"How long were you there for?" I asked.

"We were bounced around a lot. The last place that T was at treated her and the other kids like their own personal servants. They forced all of the children to work behind the scenes in their restaurant."

I was appalled, "Didn't child services hear about it or do something about it?"

"Child laws don't apply to parents or guardians who give permission for their kids to work."

"Oh that is total crap!"

Tom spread his hands out in a 'that's-how-it-goes' gesture. He became silent for a second. Regrouping, he continued, "Anyway, at fifteen, my sister decided that she'd had enough of the bullshit and ran away."

"Strong-headed, is she?"

His laughter was fond and endearing, "Like the devil. But she's a good kid."

Getting up unnaturally quickly, but slowing to a human speed when he paced around the room, Tom said, "Like most run-a-ways, she fell into a bad crowd. She was caught breaking into a club to steal some liquor."

"Police catch her?"

"Unfortunately, no," he stopped walking and looked at me, "That would've been much better. Instead, the owners caught her and two other street kids. What the kids hadn't known was that the club they were screwing with was owned by vampires. Very bad vampires who wanted to keep to the old ways of feeding on humans within town limits."

"But your sister isn't a vampire, is she? I smelled a human that day when you brought me in and had assumed it was her," *I'm confused.*

"You're right, that was her and she is still human. The kids were captured and were hooked up to tappers."

"Tappers?" *That sounded unpleasant.*

"It's a machine that drains humans or, really, any animal. It 'taps' into the blood stream and keeps the vampires from accidentally killing the 'tapped' which can and mostly does happen when they feed on humans for real. So they could always get their fix of human blood without losing their suppliers immediately. It looks almost like an intravenous hookup that's flowing backward." He went back to his pacing for a couple of minutes before giving up and sitting back down.

Helping him get on with it, I asked, "So what happened next?"

"At first, the vamps kept the kids drugged. But as they got weaker, they decided to not waste the good stuff, i.e. the good drugs, on them when they could sell it and make a profit. That was their mistake. T is a very good actress when she wants to be and hid that she was getting stronger. I don't know if she swiped one of their cell phones while they weren't looking or what, but she called me and was able to give me a rough description of the club."

Tom continued with his story, "I found it. Almost by accident, but I found it. Some older foster kids I knew had told me about this crazy club that I should sneak into sometime. That it was, 'freakishly Goth and totally awesome,'" he made air quotes around the last part. "I don't know, but I think my parents must've been looking out for us that day."

"How so?" I interjected. *Lay off, dumbass. He's going to tell you. Stop acting like an overactive five-year old.*

"I went into that club, guns blaring. Well, 'guns' as in I was running my mouth, yelling for my sister and had no idea what I was getting into. But I found out as soon as I got there. Someone grabbed me from behind and took me to a back alley where two females attacked me."

"Two females? Was one of them Alexandra?" Excitement hit my voice as if maybe all of us were connected.

"No, Newbie. Don't give yourself a stroke. Remember, we didn't meet Alexandra until a few weeks before she attacked you."

Damn. My adrenaline deflated. *I really need to pay attention to details.* "Oh yeah, sorry… Got a little crazy there."

"Yeah ya did. Now shut up and let me finish," that large smile of his crossed his face again briefly before he continued, "Anyway, as I found out later, just as these vamps were killing me, Devon and his squad had come into the club to bust the owners on human trafficking. Devon had been working on breaking this ring up for months since they were selling human blood to other vamps. It just happened to be the day they raided. Had they come a day later, I wouldn't be here to tell you this."

"So Devon found you in the alley?"

"Actually, T found me first. She's a little Wile E. Coyote. When she heard me, she broke out of wherever she was and found me. The vamps had already taken flight when they heard the cops enter the place, but they thought they had done their job to me. Devon found T huddled over me. Apparently, she lashed out at him quite a bit. Of course he didn't get hurt, but it took a lot for him to get her to calm down and let him see me."

"Did he think you were dead?"

"If he had been human, I think he would've just called in the coroner. Devon brought us both back here," he looked around the area, "I stayed in this very room while I healed and turned. I never felt a thing of the change. I think Devon must've given me that stuff we gave you that first night to keep you asleep. I remember the taste, though, of all those blood beers he kept feeding me. Odd that I remember those. And T…"

His face fell into another darkened stance, his eyes pierced into nothing in particular, but full of emotion, as if he was holding back tears. "She never stopped holding my hand," he mumbled so softly that I could barely hear him.

Tom got up again and went over to a box of miscellaneous electrical cords and mish-mashed crap, "Anyway, we've been here ever since. Working together with Devon. I owe him my life and hers."

Letting out my own sigh, I thought about how my parents had adopted me so young. My birth parents were rarely in my thoughts. All I knew was that they had died, so I was never bothered to wonder about them. *As far as I am concerned, I am part of the Panofsky family. Well… Was,* I amended my thoughts.

After a brief moment, he turned back to me with that good-humored glint in his eyes, the seriousness completely gone, "Well that was depressing! You have any questions of a happier nature?"

"Guess I won't ask you about Devon's story. Not after that one!"

"Probably a good call. But I will tell you that he was bitten back in Ireland while on vacation from Scotland. He had been visiting friends. But I'll let him tell you the rest. Not my story to tell."

※ ※ ※

And the Questions Continue Along

Another question came to mind, "Alright, since story time is over, how about this one. What the hell is going on with me? Why do I look like the Night of the Living Dead, and you look like... well, you?"

"Why? Jealous?" Tom flexed his muscles and did several ridiculous body building poses.

Yes, "No."

He didn't believe me either, "Yeah, right. How can you not be jealous of this." He then did a standing backward flip and landed on one hand to do a push up and vault himself back up right.

Show-off. "Tool," I said.

Totally jealous.

"Ok, so really, Tom, when do I get to do all the circus freak tricks?"

"Well, Newbie, your body is going to be weak for a while. Remember, your blood has been completely drained. Nothing is pumping in that body of yours. No heart, no lungs, no internal organs. The only thing that works is your brain and your..." he looked down and back up quickly, "other brain."

Oh! Well that's embarrassing and... good.

"Your body has to rely on the strength of others to keep you going, but at the same time, it steals that strength and holds onto it longer. Things are going to get a whole lot better soon. Already, you've seen your speed go haywire, your ears are better and will continue to improve. You're an enhanced predator."

"So what else changes?"

"First of all, your strength. Your physical body is going to remain the same as it was before you turned, so don't worry about the walking dead thing, your looks will improve as best as it can for you."

"I think you just insulted me."

"I think you're right," he smirked and hit my arm, not hurting it.

"Ok, so strength. What do you mean by that?"

"It's going to be immeasurable. You're never going to tire. You will be able to lift objects only machines can lift."

"That's cool."

"Oddly enough, it comes in handy a lot more than one would think. So you'll have to practice being human," he pulled a few baseballs out of a box marked 'Toys for Tots' that was laying on one of the steel tables and began to juggle, "No one likes a show off."

"This is true," I said remembering his little acrobatic act he had just put on for me a few minutes before and now watching this. Just for my own amusement, I caught two of the balls out of the air to throw him off. He let the others drop as if he was bored of it already.

Tom pulled out a small, red rubber ball and threw some six-pointed jacks on the floor. It looked like there were about thirty. "Speed and strength are really the most standard changes. But everything is relative to the individual vamp."

He stooped down low to the ground, bounced the ball down and picked up ten jacks along with the ball before it could bounce again. "Each one of us was different in human form and it's the same in this one. Some vampires can hear up to five miles away. You may eventually only hear up to two or three. That's true with vision and scent as well. It's really dependent on the person. Now you try."

He handed me the ball. I hadn't played the game in, I don't know, *Never?*

Frowning, my face giving away my ignorance to the game, he continued with, "Let's see how many you get. The most jacks I have seen any human pick up was fifteen. See if you can do better."

"OK," I said, reasonably unsure of myself. I glanced at the distance each jack was from each other and mentally calculated a plan. *This is never going to work.*

Throwing the ball down, I swooped my hand down dragging it on the floor and grabbing as many jacks as I could. I closed my fist around the ball before it could hit the floor again.

"Show and tell," He laughed. I think he already knew how many were in my hands.

The metal of thirteen jacks shined dimly in my palm. *Man, I suck at this game!*

Tom threw back his head in a throaty laugh, "Geez, we have a lot of work to do with you!"

"Hey, give me a break. This is the first time I've ever played this. And besides, I picked up more than your lousy ten." *There, that should shut him up.*

To my surprise, he continued to laugh and stole the ball from me. It bounced again. His hand was a blur of tan skin. My eyes couldn't adjust to the movement, it made me a little queasy to watch.

Twenty-nine jacks left the floor before the ball could bounce a second time. Trying not to be impressed, I smiled as mean as I could, "You missed one."

He shrugged, not at all offended by my comment, "Yeah. One day I'll be able to do it. I'm going to blame it on my hand size. Too small."

Smiling for real I said, "Sure kid, you keep holding on that dream."

It was good to laugh. And we did for several minutes, joking with each other. *Maybe, this might turn out right after all.*

We both settled down pretty much at the same time. Tom turned to the clock on the desk and I followed his motions. "Ok, ok, getting back to business.

I still have a few minutes before I have to relieve Devon, what else do you want to know?"

My thoughts went darker this time. I couldn't protect myself when I was a human so I needed to know, "Tom. I want to know what kills us."

"Ahh, yes, the ultimate question. What can destroy a vampire? Garlic? Sunlight? Various religious symbols?" He mocked my question playfully.

"Well, does any of that?" I was definitely unsure of all the superstitions. *How many of them are real?*

Tom reached into the neckline of his shirt and pulled out a small cross on a gold chain, "Dipped in holy water when I was baptized. And I'm not dead yet. Want one? I have a couple of other crosses lying around here."

"Nah, thanks. I'm Jewish," I pulled out the little Chayyim from my pocket to show him, "I think my parents would be a little pissed if I converted now." A pang shot through me as I finished that sentence and I blanched inwardly, returning the medallion to its residence. *God, I hope my mother is alright from what I did.*

Not noticing the battle going on in my head, Tom shrugged good-naturedly, "Suit yourself. But if you ever change your mind…"

I recovered and gave him a weak smile, "Yeah, you'll be the first to know."

"So back onto the subject. None of that superstitious shit does anything. Those were all old wives tales. And my guess is they were probably put in place by vampires themselves for protection. I mean, should Superman tell the world that he's allergic to Kryptonite?"

"Bad example, dude. Lois Lane printed that in the first Superman movie. That's how Lex was able to trap him, remember?" *Man, I loved those movies… Except Superman IV. Wasn't a big fan of that mess.*

"Oh yeah, that's right. Anyway. So we're not allergic to garlic, holy water or sun. Silver, however, is the one superstition that is partially correct. It can be deadly to us, and it certainly causes a lot of damage. But we can heal from it."

He paused, thinking, "What else? Hmm, oh yeah, fire is bad. Very, very bad. And certain magic."

"Magic? That's real?"

"You're a vampire and you don't believe that magic is real? Oh silly boy."

"Well? I'm not sure I'm ready to believe in this vampire crap either," And besides, w*hat's one got to do with the other?*

"Yes, Newbie, you are really a vampire and magic is real. It can be very deadly to us. Also, very rarely non-humans can harm us and vampires are capable of killing other vampires. As far as I know, it doesn't happen very often, but that doesn't mean that it can't."

"So in other words, look out for non-humans, magic, silver and fire."

"Yup, that pretty much sums it up."

"Ok, so how long do vampires live for? I mean, are there diseases that we can die from or any other weird things out there that can kill us?"

"Barring a run-in with any of the four things we talked about, a vampire can live a really long time. I don't know how long for sure, though. The only other vamps that I know or have met are the rest of the guys in our department and the few that have come across through immigration. And only one of them has been alive for more than a couple of centuries. The rest are relatively newly bitten vamps, not more than fifty years living as a vampire."

"Huh. Interesting."

"Yeah," he agreed and then changed the subject, "Hey, are you hungry? Do you want another blood brew before I head out?"

Mmm. Food. Damn, my eyes are narrowing again.

"Never mind, I see that you are," he said sympathetically.

"Well, that's your fault. I seem to be hungry whenever someone mentions it, but if no one says anything, I seem fine. Any thoughts on that?"

"I have no idea. That does seem a little strange. But again, to each his own," Tom didn't seem too worried, so I decided not to be either.

He headed for the door, "I'll be right back."

Tom darted out the door. Not smelling anyone outside of the room, I assumed he would know if we needed to worry about humans being in the apartment. But I didn't need to worry about having a reaction if I had smelled a human as he was back holding two more blood beers before the door could casually swing shut. *He has got to be the fastest vampire ever. Seriously!*

This time the blood brew was Caribou, 'For the Wild Game in You.' *These labels are cracking me up.*

After taking a sip of the caribou beer, I had to ask about them, "Do you have time for one more question?"

"Depends. Was that it?"

"No."

"Well, I guess I could do one more, but make it quick, Newbie, or else Devon will kick my ass for being late."

"Ok, this'll be quick. What's with these beers you keep giving me? Where do they come from? How are they made?"

"You said 'one question,' Newbie. That was like three," Tom teased.

"Yeah, sorry. I was never good with math. And I lied, I still have one more after this." I tried to give him my best charming look, but it usually never worked on guys. *Only teachers and Maddie.*

He rolled his eyes, "You're in luck. This shouldn't take too much time to explain."

Cool, it worked.

"Ok, here it goes. Although non-humans try to remain pretty much on the down-low, we are involved in every faction of every business across the world. So businesses have marketing directed totally at the different species of us weirdos. Over the past couple of decades, many breweries recognized the vampire niche and began brewing pure animal blood concoctions. Bloody Captain's Brewery was the first one created that made several different kinds of ale and is located here in the downtown. The blood is from all organic, free-range, hormone-free and locally butchered animals."

"A real feel-good favorite to the bleeding heart, tree-hugging vampire crowd?" I mused.

"Basically. The brews are bottled and sold same day. Butcheries and fisheries catch the blood while processing normal meat for humans. They filter it for any impurities and hand it off to Bloody Captain's Brewery who bottle it in different flavors. They either bottle the pure blood of a specific animal, combine two or more animal blood types, or they mix it with spices and/or other human food flavors. The last type is to help older vampires make the transition back to 'normal' human foods by using the bottled blood as a daily supplement, not unlike vitamins to humans."

This sounds good, "What do you mean by transition back to human foods?"

"Well," Tom explained, "It's possible for vampires to assimilate back to foods they ate before they were turned. It may take a few years and not all vampires can make the transition, but it is possible. Some choose not to, some just never really get the taste for it again. Some vampires just want to leave their humanity completely behind whereas other vampires just can't let go of it."

This sounds really good, actually. Maybe there is real hope for me yet! Becoming optimistic, I asked, "How does that work?"

"Vampires who had their first meal on human blood will almost never go back to eating the food they ate before the change. They just never get a taste for anything but the best."

Did not drink human blood first. Check the mental box under 'success.'

"If a vampire's first meal was an animal, then the transition can occur but will be difficult. They may only stick to the fresh or bottled blood. It's a fifty-fifty shot that they'll want to eat normal food."

Crap. That's my category. Mental checkbox equals 'fail.'

Tom continued, oblivious to any checklists that were occurring in my head, "However, if a vampire is like me and is caught before his or her first meal and given the bottled blood first he or she has the best shot for assimilating back into human society and eating what the humans do. It may still take a year or two to get close to where they were before, but they eventually do."

"Still a fifty-fifty shot for me, though. Right? I may not need to continue living off of these?" I swirled the beer around in front of me.

"Well, not to burst your bubble, but we will always need blood. We cannot survive without the life force of others."

I frowned. *Aw, damn.*

Tom patted me on the shoulder, "Aw, don't be sad Newbie. I'm sure there's a lobster roll and clam chowder in your near future."

"Gee, thanks. But right now, I would just prefer to not find humans so appetizing."

"Don't worry so much, Keen. I'm sure it won't take you anytime to get over that part of it."

"Did it take you very long?"

"Honestly, no. But T was with me during the entire time and I think that helped. I was always smelling a human and Devon was continually shoving those damn beers down my throat."

"So do you think I have a shot?" *Please give me the answer I want to hear.*

Tom quirked, "Do you think you have a shot?"

Not the answer I wanted, "I don't know. I hope so."

Giving me a reassuring smile, he said, "I hope so, too. And I'm sure you'll do fine."

"Ok, last question. How many people fail at this? How many for real?"

"Does it matter?"

I thought about that for a minute, *Wouldn't it just be better if I didn't know my chances?* "No. I guess not."

"Good, that's the spirit!" He hit me hard on the back as if I had just scored a goal and he was the team captain congratulating me.

He looked at the clock again, "Ok, now I really need to go before Devon calls the S.W.A.T team to get me out of here. You should get some rest. We're going to start on your training when we get back tonight."

"Hey, I thought you said I get an entire day of relaxation and questions."

"Yeah, I lied," He laughed as he walked out of the room and locked the door behind him.

Chapter 5

Training

✧ ✧ ✧

This Sucks

Hmm, Tom was right about the napping thing.* I was able to catch about a forty minute cat-nap although I couldn't be sure. The table had become my make-shift bed, straps securely hidden underneath though still readily available, if needed. By the time my head hit the pillow, all the thoughts about my question session with Tom and all the questions I had yet to ask disappeared into LaLa Land. My eyes shuttered down and the next thing I knew, Devon was knocking on the door, waking me.

He didn't seem like he was going to be as friendly as Tom was, so I thought I would try to keep my questions to a minimum with him. Knowing me, that was going to be hard – like trying to get to sleep before playing in the Frozen Four Hockey Championship game.

Pushing aside the bed-table thing gave the room a significant amount of extra space. Devon moved it while I cleared the random boxes of computer gear and home improvement supplies out of the way. *Instead of shopping in the Martha Stewart section, apparently they shop the collection by Bruce Wayne.* After our redecorating, Devon placed two small dumbbell weights in the center of the room.

"You think these five-pounders are going to cut it?" I joked.

He stared the laughter right out of me, "Why don't you try picking them up."

That statement made me a little nervous. *I think I'm about to know what a fool looks like.* Reaching down, I braced myself for either a shock of electricity or some kind of pain. When I felt none, I wrapped my hands around the center of the dumbbells and pulled.

Nothing.

I pulled again. And then again.

They wouldn't budge. *Yup, a fool looks just like me trying to pick up dumbbells.* Standing back up I asked, "What the hell?"

A brief sneer turned up the corner of his lips, "Tough, is it Newbie?"

I shrugged, trying to be nonchalant, "A bit."

He broke out in a less creepy grin, his bright white teeth blinding against his dark, black skin, "Good. If you were able to pick them up at the vampire age you are now, I'd be a little concerned. I'll dial them down for you."

"What's 'dial them down' mean?"

"They're magnetized," he bent over them and turned a dial on each of the outside bell parts, "See?"

I leaned over to get a better look. The range of numbers on them were between 0 and 30 with intervals of 2. In the center of the dial read 'Tesla.'

Even though I didn't want to ask more questions than I really needed to, curiosity got the better of me even, "What's a Tesla?"

"You mean other than the sweetest and most expensive electric car in the states and the last name of the inventor of the radio? It's the unit of measurement for these bad boys."

"What did you have these two up at?"

"Their max. Thirty Tesla. I'm putting them down to five Tesla."

I just couldn't stop myself, "How much is that?"

"Well, let's just say that half a million times stronger than the Earth's magnetic field is somewhere between 25 and 30 Tesla."

"No shit?" That was awe inspiring.

"No shit," he replied in his cool manner. He finished turning the magnets down to four, "Try this level. Let's see what you've got."

I went back to the dumbbells. *The ego crushers. The five pound humiliators.* They moved more easily this time, but it was still a struggle. I didn't feel stress or strain on myself, but they just wouldn't work with my muscles.

As soon as I lifted them up to chest level, Devon laughed, "That's more like it."

"What am I going to be doing with these?"

"Your muscles need to be built up, so you're going to lift them regularly. Once you get used to a weight, we'll up the Teslas on them. These will help us determine how fast you're developing."

"Well, how much can you lift?"

He seemed pretty amused by that question, "More than four Tesla."

Clearly, he's not going to tell me.

I did a couple of reps of twenty before dropping them. My muscles stopped working. Again, they didn't feel tired, they just couldn't move anymore, as if I was trying to lift a car in my human form. *Which never would've happened either.*

Moving the dumbbells with greater ease than I had, Devon put them to the side and tied a rope to the door knob. He held onto the other end and stretched it taught across the room, "Now, what I want you to do is to jump over this rope."

"That sounds easy enough," *In fact, it sounds down right stupid.*

"Easy if you were a human. But this is actually a lesson on control," his eyes glanced at the ten-feet-high ceiling, "We wouldn't want you to hit your head, now would we? I'm not really in the mood to replace that again."

"So just to clarify, you want me to jump four feet up and try not to hit the ten-feet-high ceiling?"

"Yup. It's not as easy as it looks. I want you to barely brush the top of the rope."

"Okay," I answered, but I wasn't really sure of myself at this point. What was left of my competitive, arrogant-side thought, *Hahaha, what a lame exercise. Anyone can do that.* But the new, so far less-egotistical side said, *Dude, you are so going to fall on your face and Devon is going to laugh his ass off at you.*

I banked on the second part to be right, all things considered, so I was cautious as I moved toward the rope, facing him and keeping it to the right of me. There it was, one teeny tiny obstacle, not more than a quarter inch thick of twisted hemp only four feet off the ground. It was just daring me to jump over it and land on the other side, if not gracefully, than at least on two feet. And the kicker was that I couldn't hit my head on the ceiling. *How can that be so hard?* But I hesitated.

"Let's go, Newbie, I don't have all day," Devon wasn't harsh, but he wasn't trying to reassure me either.

I crouched down and sprang up. My hair only dusted the ceiling, which I was thankful for, but I landed on the same side that I jumped up from, "Crap."

"Well," his grin was almost as friendly as Tom's could be, but he was definitely hiding his amusement better, "That's a start. At least you didn't put a hole in my ceiling."

He rattled the rope, "Try it again."

"Wait, any advice?"

"Yeah, don't trip."

"Very funny. But seriously, what do I need to do?"

Taking a second to think about it, he turned a critical eye at me, "Your starting form was good, but you need to shift your weight more to your left leg, to push off in the direction you want to go. Now don't over compensate or else you'll go through the wall."

Pleasant thought.

Crouching down again, I leaned a little more on my left and pushed off. I felt my left toe fling me over the rope. Briefly I thought, *Yeah! I made it and I didn't even come near the ceiling!*

But that was when I came crashing down on the bed, knocking it over and into the wall.

Laughter rose from behind me, "Well, at least you got to the other side."

Devon swung the bed off me easily, even though I could've done it, and extended his hand to help me up. I took it and awkwardly bounced to a stand.

"I want to try again." *This stupid little rope is not going to get the better of me.*

But over the next couple of hours, and even over the next few days, that stupid little rope did get the better of me.

✵ ✵ ✵

Changes

For most of the following four days of that first week that I spent with my new friends, Tom and Devon, we worked out with the Tesla weights, the rope, and other devices that they had selected to torture, I mean, train me.

Monitoring my appearance in the bathroom mirror, I could tell I was changing more and more back into my original, physical-looking self with only a few minor changes. The first thing I noticed was my skin's color and feel. Like any human teenager, I had my share of pimples. I also had freckles and sun spots. *Despite popular belief, it is possible to get a sunburn this far north.*

What was really incredible to me, though, was the complete disappearance of a birthmark I had on my right cheek. It had looked like a dragon crawling its way down from my eye to my chin. When I was in elementary school, kids would point at it and tell me I had dirt on my face. The tan mark had always been a part of me. *And now it's gone.* It made me wonder how Devon's green tattoo could stand out so solidly against his black tone. *Did he get it after he was turned vamp or does ink just never go away?*

At least my color is coming back a bit. No more sallow, hollowed out skin. No longer Night of the Living Dead.

This is true.

And no zits.

I smiled at that thought. I had tried not to be self-conscious of them as a human, but it suited me just fine that they were gone.

My body recovered to look as muscular as I had been before the change. The blood brews really saw to that. My favorite was the Moose Pale Ale. Before my change, I had thought that moose tasted less gamey than deer, for whatever reason. Most people think just the opposite. Anyway, I had retained the same preference between the two flavors of the blood beers.

Either Devon or Tom would bring me a drink every two to three hours. *Like I'm some fricken newborn baby.* The drinks were very helpful in staving off my hunger. Besides the moose drink, I also favored the Black Bear Red and the Ship Wreck Three Bloods Brew. I had no clue which animals the latter was made up from, but I wasn't to a stage of really wanting to know totally what I was drinking either.

Actually, when I stop to think about it, I was really grossed out by the drinking blood thing, but the beers tasted so good and I couldn't bring myself to eat any of the foods I had eaten when I was a human. Every time they opened the door after they had eaten normal food, all I could think of was how rotten it smelled. None of the foods were appetizing anymore. But I didn't want to starve, so I did what any other guilt-ridden vamp would do... sucked it up and tried not to think about it. *Drinking like I'm tossing a few brews back with the boys.*

Checking myself out again, the only real difference I saw in my face were the color of my eyes and the slight puffiness surrounding my lips. My new fangs were the cause of the last issue. The two that I had seen when I first turned were now joined by two more on the bottom. The bottom ones grew in slightly closer together than the top fangs, allowing my mouth to completely close, but pushing my skin out just the same. Like a saber tooth tiger

My eyes were a few shades lighter than they were before, except at times when I became hungry or angry. Then they became black like Alexandra's eyes had right before she attacked me. I had watched my reflection once when Devon had given me a blood beer and I waited a few minutes to drink it. Even though I felt as if my vision was tunneling into pinpoints, what I saw in the mirror was that the pupils actually expanded, filling the complete whites of my eyes. Watching my eyes change into deep pits of blackness was scarier than going up against Kaellan and more surreal – like the out of body experience I felt right before I 'died.' Sometimes, my temperament was like Jekyll and Hyde – one moment I was fine and then I would smell the scent of sweet blood, human or animal, and I would physically go into a frenzy. *Hell, someone could just mention the word 'food' or say they were hungry and that would set me off.*

I think to keep me off thoughts of food, the guys tried to put me on a schedule to work through everything else that was changing for me – physically and mentally – as I became stronger in my vampireness. In the mornings, we worked on testing my hearing capabilities. Devon was a master at listening, *Which I'm sure would come in handy with that special someone someday.* He helped me learn how to literally turn a deaf ear and filter unimportant items out. Between Tom and him, we regularly tested how far I could hear. My record at the end of the four days was two miles. Tom had left my room, then the apartment, walked to the car, and drove away, all the while talking to me until I told him I could no longer hear him.

Tom and Devon both have a five mile range of hearing, but only Devon can drill down to singling out a specific person he's trying to find that far away. Tom can do that up to three miles, but hears sounds from further away.

Those kinds of tests actually helped me learn to focus on just who was talking to me or who I wanted to hear, or rather, eavesdrop on. And, although it wasn't guaranteed, with practice, there was a possibility that I'd hear at about the same distance as the other two.

I assumed that my eyes were getting sharper in this time period as well. It was hard to test because the other two wouldn't trust me enough to let me go out of the room. But it seemed that my eyes were able to focus more on smaller objects like dust particles and slight cracks in the walls. I got to stare at those a lot in the times that the guys left me alone and I didn't feel like surfing the net. And, regrettably, seeing through walls is not a trait that normal vamps pick up. *And here I thought I was becoming Superman.*

On the fifth night, the door opened to my room, *I guess it's become my room,* while I was still checking out things in the bathroom. It was both Devon and Tom. They had given me a heads up the day before that it was going to be the night that they started to get me used to the human population again. *Starring Tom's poor sister as the guinea pig.*

"Hey Newbie, you ready for us?" Tom called.

I came out of the bathroom, wearing my favorite dark blue cargo jeans and throwing on a black shirt to cover my bare chest, "Yup. What's the plan?"

Devon was moving the bed-table back to the center of the room, it had been there since that morning's training. I had just slept in one of the chairs in the room for my afternoon nap instead of schlepping the bed back in place.

"It's about 8 pm, and T is going to be home soon. Sorry Newbie, but we're gonna need to strap you down again before she drops by. The plan is to just watch how you're reacting right now."

Even though the beers were fulfilling, I still lapsed into blood sucking urges every time I smelled a human. What sucked was that the human I kept smelling was T, Tom's sister, who shared the apartment with Devon and Tom. If T was in the apartment, the vamps would have to strap me to the table and leave me alone until I calmed down. This was problematic for everyone because I tended to stay keyed up until the human left either the apartment or hid in her room. Unfortunately, her being in her room and my door being shut didn't keep the smell of her away. *I must be ruining her life. She probably doesn't feel safe in her own bed even with two locked doors between us and I know at least one of those doors is vampire proof. Poor thing.*

Until I learned to control my urges, the guys would not let me out. And, regrettably, after that first day at my parent's house, I hadn't been able to control myself. I think it was because that other than T's lingering scents, I hadn't had any human contact, no possible way to relate back to humans. That, along with my self-preservation instinct to feed, prevented me from keeping my impulses from taking over. *That's my theory at least.*

The pressure was on too. A deadline was looming; Devon and Tom would only wait a few weeks before they would take me out "behind the shed". It wouldn't matter how much they'd come to like me or I them. Their system had been proven and it had rules. Rules that could accurately classify me as uncontrolled.

Rules that will call for my destruction if I fail.

※ ※ ※

Try, Try Again

Tom's sister got near the door again as they had instructed her to do. As soon as her scent hit my nose, my eyes slanted with hunger pains and my body jolted into straight instinct. It didn't matter that they kept telling me she was going to approach the door. My urges always swept through me, making me an animal, willing my body to struggle against the chains that held me down. No matter how much I prepared, I was losing the battle.

This went on for days. The first night, we only tried it a couple of times and had no success. The next night, we tried for a couple of hours. Tom's sister would approach the door, and I would instantly freak out. At the end of two weeks, they tried to have her just surprise me. That was a really bad idea. Once they didn't have me all the way tied down before I smelled her. None of us believed how quick I had become.

WHAM!

I left a dent in the four inch thick metal door, shaped like my shoulder.

Why is this so damn hard? I was so angry with myself.

After Tom's sister left, I could hear Tom and Devon murmuring on the other side of the door about how this should not be taking so long. They had no idea why the nature to attack was so strong. After a few minutes, they came back in. Tom looked sullen. Devon, was, well, Devon.

Controlled.

Devon had his arms folded across his chest, "This isn't working, Keen."

Fear dropped into me.

"Please guys. Just a few more times. I know I can get this. If I can just keep practicing," God, did I hate to beg. *And failing is not an option. I like myself way too much for that.*

They looked at each other, silently discussing options with their body positions and faces. I could tell they had done this many times before. I think it was Tom's eager face that got Devon to agree.

So we kept practicing.

As such, week three started much better off than week two. My strength continued to grow with every blood drink given. Although my body structure was still the same toned frame it was before, my muscles somehow became stronger within the confines of their appearance. Devon told me that vamp bodies are pretty much frozen in time, but that the older we get the more adaptable the physiology of our bodies become. Sometimes these things come quickly, sometimes it takes centuries. Luckily for me, my body was filling out sooner than later. *Must be my competitive side.*

During the times we weren't struggling to keep my attack-the-human instincts under control, we worked out in my small room and continued testing hearing, sight, and speed. I was able to bench press four times my weight. My muscles never felt any fatigue either. That was the coolest part. Imagine never stopping because you're tired, but only because you're bored or have other things to do. Some days I didn't miss my old self at all.

If I could just get past this entire wanting to eat people thing, I decided, *I would join their merry band of fighters – well, if they'd let me.* I didn't want to leave the area. Although, I knew I couldn't see my parents again – at least not face to face – I didn't want to leave them unprotected, now that I knew what kinds of things were skulking around the docks.

I was also on a mission to find Alexandra and take all of what I had lost out on her. Maddie was constantly on my mind and the thought of her kept me going as I tried to reign in my new, ah, cravings.

By the end of the week, I was still having problems when T approached the other side of the door, and I realized I was seriously running out of time – I knew the guys were losing their patience with me. So at the beginning of week four, I asked to try something new.

"Boys, today, I want to use a different tactic."

Devon raised an eyebrow at me.

"Tie me down again, and ask Tom's sister to stay for a few hours on the other side of the door. No, listen. Maybe if I just get used to her scent, I can really beat this thing. It's just that every time she comes near, it's a new shock to my system. Maybe I just need to get used to her."

They had the silent conversation again.

Then Tom spoke, "I'll ask her, Keen."

He left the apartment.

Devon and I sat in silence for a few minutes, him watching me as if he was waiting for me to turn into a bat or simply freak out. He was definitely waiting for something bad to happen; his posture was alert and controlled. Meanwhile,

I found a small, discolored spot on the wall that was no where near him that I suddenly found very interesting – mainly so I wouldn't have to look at him. He was making me very nervous, like he was anticipating that my idea would fail and he would have to kill me. I struggled with the concept of my death, and evaluated possibilities of a break-out. Since I had not been outside of the room and I had no idea where the escape routes might be, I didn't think I could get out of there before either one of them grabbed me. *This has to work, or I will die.* Staring at the spot on the wall, I did something I hadn't done in a very long time. I prayed. *Please God. Please give me the strength to keep my humanity. If there is anyway to do this, please let me find it. Thank you. Amen.*

The sound of an annoying ring tone chirped and Devon reached into his pocket to answer his cell phone, "Yeah?" He paused, "Ok," he closed the phone with a click, "They're on their way back."

I hopped up on the bed, shook the fear from my thoughts, and smiled slyly, "All right, big guy, tie me down, but don't enjoy it so much this time."

Oof! He pushed me against the table and tightened the lengths of straps more so than usual. *Good thing I don't need to breath for real. Not much chance of that happening.*

Devon got the last binding strap down as Tom's sister's scent wafted into the air from the other side of the door. The will to attack came on quickly and this time it was painful – like my mind and body were battling it out and my will would have to wait and see which one would win. Either way, both sides of the battle were torturing me. I flailed against the ropes, causing them to cut deep into my skin. My shirt became wet with my thick, clear blood, allowing the ropes to chafe me further. A growl in my stomach erupted and it bellowed all the way up through my lips before turning into a hissing snarl. I screamed madly with the anguish of wanting the human blood that was waiting for me on the other side of the door. *What the hell, this reaction is so much worse than the ones before.* A weird thought popped into my mind at the same time as my neck began to tingle that something bad was about to happen. *This is it. This is when they decide if I live or die.* My neck prickled more fiercely and I knew that my last thought was dead on.

Devon came over to the side of the table and pushed my shoulders down against it. The familiar 'fwick' sound of a bottle opening sent me into a darkening spiral. *They're going to feed me a blood brew to calm me. I should take it, I need help with this.*

My mind may have thought that, but the word that came out of my mouth was a long "NOOO!"

Tom was in my sight with the blood drink, "Drink it Keen, it'll take the edge off."

"No!" I pursed my lips shut. *If they give me that than I'll never beat the instinct to attack. I'll have failed and they will kill me.*

"Take it, Keen," Devon commanded.

I shook my head side to side violently and thought, *No way in hell. I'm not giving up.*

Tom went to the top of the table to hold my head down, but I shook him off. He looked over at Devon with the question on his face as to what he should do.

Devon's eyes went hard, "Keen, we're at the end of the line here. This is just not going to happen for you. Let us give you the drink."

The tunneling in my eyes began to grow darker in fear. The desire for hunger was still there, but a more immediate instinct breached the surface and outweighed it. *Survival. How can I get out of here. I need to get out of here.*

Calm down. Breath. The only way out is to control yourself.

I can't.

There IS no other option.

If Maddie was here, she'd help me out of this.

My thoughts flung to her face, *My beautiful, sweet, funny, Maddie.* Memories flooded through the physical and mental agony I was going through. The first time we met, it was in band at high school. She was trying out for the drum line and bending over a snare head to tighten it. I ran right into her as I was trying to get my own instrument prepared for try-outs. I wasn't paying attention. She bruised her knee and I knocked my nose hard enough into the drum that I broke it. I asked her out shortly after that. We went on so many dates before I got up the courage to kiss her.

Light began to seep back into my vision as my body began to relax. I continued to focus on thoughts of Maddie – all the awkward school dances we went to together, shuffling back and forth, trying not to step on each others' feet. I thought about the first time I kissed her. We were sitting on her porch swing having just come back from the homecoming dance. We were watching a storm blow out over the ocean. Lightening was flashing far away from us, but close enough for the thunder to make her jump. We laughed and I brought my hand to her cheek. She was so beautiful. I leaned in to touch her soft lips with mine.

Maybe Maddie would accept me one day.

That did it.

That glimmer of hope was exactly what I needed. That is what finally broke my hunger pains.

"He's coming back to us," Tom said.

Devon grunted, but I couldn't tell if it was in agreement or if he was waiting to see what my next move was.

Blinking my eyes, I could suddenly see the room more clearly, the guys were huddled over me, staring. Taking in a deep breath, I smelled the human. *Her name is T,* I reminded myself, and suppressed cringing into instinct again. I went to sit up, forgetting that I was strapped still. My head was fuzzy like I had somehow slipped into unconsciousness and was just waking from a nightmare.

Tom put his hands up, palms facing me, "Whoa there, kid. Relax. Thought we lost you there for a while."

My brow furrowed, "A while? How long have I been out?"

"Well, let's see. You freaked out on us when we tried to give you a drink and then you stopped moving all-together for about an hour," Tom replied.

"What?" *That doesn't make any sense.*

"Yeah, it was weird too," Tom said as he shifted around to lift my head up so he could give me a blood beer, "Your eyes were completely open. To tell you the truth, it was pretty creepy."

He tilted the bottle to my mouth and I drank it with his help since my arms were still strapped down. It tasted so good. The fiery pain in my throat cleared up and my thoughts cleared further.

"Did you try to wake me?" *Why didn't they just kill me when they had the chance?*

"No, we've never seen this before, but you weren't dead. Usually with that kind of stress level, the mind just self-destructs the body and the vampire dies," Devon said matter-of-factly, "and your body showed no signs of degenerating – which is something that would've occurred the minute you died for real."

"I don't understand," I struggled slightly against the straps, *This conversation would be much easier if I could just sit up.*

"Every Newbie we've taken in has gone through a kind of final battle between their vampire instincts and their humanity. Some make it through the mental overload, some die trying, and some we have to kill if they can't keep their fangs off of non-consenting humans."

My eyebrow quirked in question.

Tom answered, "Vampires police each other and the universal law prohibits any vampire from feeding off of humans – unless it's a little love-bite in the privacy of their own home," He gave a quick sly smile before getting serious again, "We're to put down any vampire who kills a human being."

Devon continued, "We've used this room before as a 'rehabilitation' for any new-made vampires we find before other vampires get to them and aren't so nice."

"Yeah, I kinda remember you telling me this when I first got here. Why didn't you kill me when you had the chance? Why don't you just kill me now?" *Not that I really wanted him to, but I had to know.*

"We're not murderers, Keen," Tom sounded defensive, "We're just here doing our job. You haven't hurt anyone. It's been ten minutes now and you still haven't made a move toward the door and I know you can still smell my sister."

This is true. I shrugged in agreement.

"Don't get me wrong, as I've said before, some vampires still do use humans as food and will finish them off, but the laws in this country are against that practice," Tom said.

"Ok," I said. It was quiet for a few moments as I let things sink in. I decided it was time to thank the person behind the door that had helped me through. *She, a stranger, gave me so much of her time just to give me a real chance at surviving my new life. I should get her a gift or flowers or something. Well, if I don't end up killing her,* "Tom, I'd like to meet your sister and thank her."

Tom studied my face, deciding what to do and then nodded. Devon began un-strapping the binds on me as Tom called through the door to T, "You decent, sis?"

"Yup," called the girl's voice back.

"We're going to open the door and unleash the kraken. You ready for us to do that?"

"I was ready to be done with this awhile ago, bro. Let's get on with it."

Tom smiled and moved to flank my right side. Devon went to the door. Both were ready to pounce on me if things went wrong. The door opened. Her smell was even more tempting than when it was muffled by the door, filtering all of its beautiful sweetness. Honeysuckle and cloves, her flowery smell hid the metallic of blood yearning to be drunk.

My eyes went instantly into tunnel vision and I briefly wondered if all of the hassle had been worth it. A quick fear hit me, *was I going to attack her?* I clenched my teeth, gritting down tensely, "I… can… do… this…"

Devon and Tom began crowding me, gearing up to take me down. I looked over at Tom's sister, trying to force myself from the tunnels, and doubled over.

She looked…

I snuck a peak again from my bent over position… *Yup.* She looked.

Bored.

I began laughing. Unfortunately, it was more of the maniacal psycho version than a reassuring human-like one. Devon pushed Tom's sister back out of the doorway and shut it superhuman fast. Tom was all over me. He knocked me off balance and threw me back on the bed. Devon was on the other side of me in no time and they had me pinned in two seconds, with me still laughing.

It took me a few minutes to get my composure. Clear gel liquid was coming from my eyes. In normal terms, I guess they would be tears of laughter. I blinked several times to get the fluid to clear from my pupils and then I realized they had indeed strapped me back down. Panicked, I shifted my eyes back and forth between Tom and Devon, "I'm ok guys. I swear, I wasn't going to attack her," I rambled on, "She just looked so funny standing there, completely bored out of her gourd. Here I am, could'a probably broken her in half, she's so small, and she looked at me like 'are we done yet?'" I mocked the last bit in my best high-pitched girly voice.

I continued, "I couldn't help myself. It was just funny. I swear, that's all."

Devon gave Tom a look like 'It's your call, dude.'

Tom shrugged and began undoing the binds. Devon followed suit.

I sat up, "Hey Tom, no offense, but your sister?"

He glanced at me, waiting.

This is where I should've shut up, but my nerves and adrenaline caused me to brain barf, "She's smoking hot!"

Hmm, I didn't realize how much I liked my nose until it was then broken for the third time in my life. The first time had happened when I took a puck to my face in hockey practice, then again on Maddie's snare drum and now by Tom. *Thankfully the guy hadn't hit me with a slap shot. That would've been more than a broken nose!*

I flew back on the bed with my head up toward the ceiling, and clear liquid gel flowing from my nostrils. I landed on it so hard, the bed shifted several feet from its original position, "Ok. Let me correct myself. Tom your sister, for the brief few seconds I saw her, looks like a very beautiful young lady."

Devon grabbed my hand to help me back up, "Tom, come on. Chill. He's right, T looked really bored," he paused, "And she IS cute." He winked at me.

Tom squirmed and turned a stony look at me, "Let's get one thing straight, dude: that is my sister and she is not here for your entertainment or your meal. She is off limits, or so help me, I will break every little bone in your body before I cut off your head and then burn your body until it is less than ash. That clear enough for you?"

I nodded. *Don't touch Tom's sister. Check!*

Tom reached forward, and I jumped back, cowardly, I know. But he grabbed me quickly by the nose, "Let's fix that, shall we?"

"I'm not sure you're the best person to do.. OW Man! That hurt!"

He slapped me on the shoulder and finally smiled, "Fixed."

"Gee, thanks," I said sarcastically.

Devon bellowed out a laugh and Tom joined in. We heard a knock just then and a muffled voice called through the door, "Hey! What's going on in there? Let me in! Is everything all right?"

Tom looked at me, serious tone again, "We cool?"

"Yeah, we're cool."

"Devon?"

"She'll be fine, Tom. We'll try again."

"Guys?" Tom's sister called, this time more worried.

"Hang back, lil' sis. You ok to try this again?"

"Yeah, ok," the bored voice was back.

Tom looked at me, "Ready?"

I nodded again.

Tom signaled Devon, who opened the door.

This time when I breathed in her scent, my eyes and my hunger were securely in my command. *I am finally broken.*

She stood in the doorway again with the same bored-ass expression on her face, but this time I finally got to really look at her. She had bright, bubble-gum pink hair that hung in chunks to her shoulder. Her pale, porcelain skin showed off her eerie green eyes shining through thick mascara. She was short, maybe 5'3" in her platform thigh-high boots with three inch heels. She had a black miniskirt and black crop knit on. *Very Goth looking. And the exact opposite to her brother.* Tom had olive skin and dark hair and he was very angular whereas she was all curves – soft and round. The only similarity was their peculiar green eyes. *That is so weird. For a human, her eyes seem supernatural in color like Tom's. I wonder if she wears contacts.*

I walked over to her, trying to keep my tongue from rolling out of mouth. *Come on, dude. Think of Maddie. You know, the one that you're hoping to get back with.*

"Hi," I said, trying to remain cool, I reached my hand out, "I'm Keen."

Tom's sister checked me over and debated, then finally reached up to shake my hand, "T."

Sparks didn't fly between us, but something weird happened when she grabbed my hand. A blue light pulsing with gold flecks suddenly encompassed her. I dropped my hand immediately, but it didn't go away. The change in my face didn't go unnoticed by the boys, either. As I stepped back, they stepped to the sides of me.

"What's wrong?" Devon asked as he raised an arm, crossing it in front of me in preparation to hold me back, if needed.

"How are you doing that?" I asked her.

"Doing what?" She looked slightly annoyed.

"Why are you surrounded in blue?"

"Huh?" She shifted herself to glance around her and check out her back side.

"You have a blue light around you. Gold and blue. Does that happen often?" I was curious now, shifting my hands to try to grab the light. Reaching and searching. Then I noticed my hands. They had a gray glow around them like I was wearing clear gloves with gray LCD lights that pulsed. I looked at the rest of me, as T had done to herself, and the gray surrounded me as well. My entire body was enveloped in a strange coloration. *Weird.*

Devon and Tom's faces were weary.

"Do you not see that?" I pointed at them as they were both also surrounded by the gray glow, "The three of us have gray, but she's surrounded with blue. Do you not see that?"

Don't freak out, I thought, even though I had spoken with hysterical worry in my voice. This didn't seem normal by any standards. And I didn't want them to remove me just because of some oddity.

Tom patted himself down as if trying to feel something crawling on him, "I don't see anything. Dev?"

"Hmm," was Devon's only reply.

The light began to dull away from all of them, almost like it was creeping back into their bodies. My own gray was shrinking back as well. It became suddenly silent, and they were all staring at me.

"It's going away," I broke the edge, "What do you think that was? And why was I the only one who could see it?"

"Not sure," Devon said, "but we'll check it out. Let me know if it happens again and try to remember what you were doing at the time."

"Aye, aye, Captain." I shrugged, hoping not to ever see that again. It was too weird and I hate hallucinating.

✵ ✵ ✵

Your New Home.. Here, Take the Tour

Wow, I thought, *Has it really been five weeks since I got here?*

Tom had come in and let me know that it was finally time to, and I quote, "Get off your lazy ass and stop mooching." The next challenge was to be that night: out on the town. *Contact with humans and others.*

Gulp.

I was nervous, to say the least. I hadn't even been out of the room that, for all intents and purposes, had been my home. It didn't matter that they left the door open to let me wander. There was no need to leave. Not with a shower, a fully stocked fridge of Bloody Captain's, and my iPod and computer connected to their wireless network. *Why should I leave this room?* I had not been ready. *I'm not ready now, and they want to take me out around the humans? This doesn't sound like a good idea at all.*

I eyed Tom as he smiled at me. It wasn't reassuring. He smiled at me with eager humor in his eyes, either because he thought I was going to fail or because he thought it was going to be funny when I did so. Or maybe I was just terrified and that was what I was projecting myself to see.

"Let's go, big guy, you can do this," said Tom.

Nope. Still not reassured.

But also not a coward.

I stepped out of my little room and into the biggest apartment I had ever seen. Not to mention it was the messiest place as well. It looked like a bomb had exploded in a high-tech store and threw its contents into LL Bean. Junk was everywhere! I could barely see the old hardwood floors and brick walls that were customary in this town. Computer gadgets and items I could only think were some kind of weaponry were scattered among layers of camping equipment, flannel shirts and other random male crap. There may actually have been furniture under all of it, but I couldn't be sure.

"Did your maid die or something?" I joked.

"Yeah," Tom said, "We think she's buried in here, but we haven't gotten around to looking."

"I thought my room at home was messy," brief nostalgia stumbled me for a second, but I recovered, "Geez, look up 'Bachelor Pad' in Wikipedia and they'll just have a picture of this place, no explanation needed."

I walked over to what resembled an entertainment area with two couches sitting perpendicular to each other and a coffee table in the middle. I picked up a handful of wires and what looked like some sort of gun. "What is all this stuff?"

"Tools of the trade, my boy," Devon said.

"Are the computer game stations also 'tools of the trade?" I said glancing at not one, but two different gaming devices sitting next to a large stereo system and a mini fridge. "How do you find anything in here?" I was unsure if I should be grossed out or in awe.

Devon shrugged, "It's an organized mess."

"Yeah?" I raised an eyebrow, "I call bullshit."

Tom laughed, "Let's give the man a tour… This is crap pile #1, this is crap pile #2," he announced, pointing at various mounds of trash, equipment, and left over food boxes.

"Very funny, Tom. Why don't you give Keen the real tour," Devon was reproachful.

"Ok, fine," Tom then turned to me, "Right this way, Señor."

Starting at the room I had been staying in, we went counter clockwise, "This is Devon's office."

I looked past the doorway to see a room only lit up by one giant window. The furniture was dark and included a desk covered by piles and piles of paper, on the desk, chairs and a small table in one of the corners. Tom pointed at the window, "We occasionally use the fire escape to get to Devon's car quicker since we park it in the alley back there."

"Cool," I said as he led to the next area. It was an open space with what looked like a large dining room table in it, but with small boxes of nails and tools on it, I couldn't be sure. The table actually looked like it was being used to build things.

"This was our formal dining room, but now it's used as a catch-all for miscellaneous stuff."

"Did you ever use it as a dining room?"

"No not really. And here's the kitchen," Tom said.

That room was actually clean. The triangle shaped breakfast bar and the tall counter tops were cleared. Dishes weren't sitting in the sink. Overall, it was the nicest looking place so far.

"Devon is really particular about keeping the kitchen clean, so if you make a mess, make sure you clean it before dad gets home from work," he laughed.

"No worries there," I replied as I smelled human food scents and my nose tried to close itself off, "I think I'll be sticking to my beers for now." I stopped breathing in air as we walked by.

From the kitchen, there was a freestanding wall that was created to separate the entertainment center from a hallway. We took the hallway. As we passed the first closed door, Tom said, "This is Devon's room. The door straight ahead is mine. That one in the corner is T's. And this is your room," Tom swung the door we were standing in front of open with a smile, "Feel free to mess it up however you feel best."

Other than a queen-sized bed and a five-drawer dresser, the room was completely empty, but huge – more than three times the size of my room at home. I walked over to the window and peered out. The sun was just setting, the shadows beginning to lurk around down the street. My view was of Exchange Street. I could hear the cars and the footsteps of the people going by. I could smell them, faintly, through a small crack in the wood of the window, but I had no reaction. It was good.

I turned to Devon and Tom and noticed that T had joined them. I hardly sensed her scent anymore.

"Who pays for all of this?" I asked, not able to hold my curiosity longer.

"I do," Devon replied, nonchalantly, "Plus we get some funds from working with the police department."

Tom smirked.

"How can you do it? I didn't think that the PD paid well," I questioned as I tried to mentally calculate the cost.

"They don't," T said.

"We pick up a lot of 'odd' jobs," Tom laughed, "and Devon is ridiculously loaded."

"Can't wait to hear that story sometime," I hinted.

Devon smiled, deviously.

Chapter 6

Night on the Town

✧ ✧ ✧

Can I Get Any Privacy Here?

It was around eleven o'clock at night and I was in the bathroom singing to an old-school Michael Jackson song that was playing in the background when I felt a pinch on my lower left butt cheek. Well, it was like an annoying mosquito bite feeling more than anything.

"Nice ass," I turned to the open door to see T peeping at me with ornery eyes. Her hair was blond – bouffant would be the correct word for it. She was wearing a floral skirt, skin-tight sweater and cowboy boots.

"Dolly Parton called, she wants her hair back," I said, trying not to blush at her comment as I played with my green-and-white-stripped button-down. *Should I tuck it in or keep it open and out over my polo?* "How many wigs do you have, anyway?"

Thankfully, she hadn't noticed me checking out my fangs in the mirror. I was still trying to get used to them. And I couldn't even begin to think of all the mocking she would've given me if she'd seen that.

"I don't know. I've lost count. Big night on the town, huh?"

"A'yup. Dev is finally going to let me out of here."

"Oooh! Mortal population beware," T had a sweet and teasing smile as she swept her hands up to her throat as if to cover it from a bite.

"Funny," *Like I'm not nervous enough without that little reminder that I could kill anyone within a heartbeat if I didn't remain completely in control.* I annoyingly shoved the shirt into my pants and left a few buttons open to reveal the faded orange polo underneath. *Ah, sweet compromise.*

"Well, good luck. And no bringing chicks back to the pad," T said.

"Why? Jealous?" I flirted.

She smirked and turned to leave, "By the way, big guy. Your fly is down."

I could feel my face burn, even though I knew it couldn't, as I checked myself and zipped up. *Smooth, Keen. Real smooth.*

I could hear her light laughter as she walked away.

✧ ✧ ✧

Leaving the Nest

I came out of my bedroom shortly afterward to see an unexpected sight: T, Devon and Tom were all crowded around a mass of computer screens and electronic gear that was up against a wall I had thought had been a giant closet.

There were sections of the wall that were flipped down, holding the equipment. There were miscellaneous armaments scattered about – maps of the city, blueprints of cargo ships and several amateur radios tuned to police and truck frequencies on the surrounding tables and unoccupied chairs. Piles were tediously balanced on a thread, a gigantic Jenga board. It was like I had entered into a small war room. Had I had my human hearing, I would not have been able to discern the several dozen murmurs and beeps coming across. I cleared my throat to let them know that I was in the room. *And not to shoot me.* "What's all this?"

"Tools of the trade, Newbie," T said.

"It's like a broken record in here," I responded.

"What?" She looked slightly taken aback.

"Devon said the same thing to me earlier. Tom, do you want to enlighten me or are you also going to call me a 'Newbie' and tell me this stuff is just 'tools of the trade'?" I probably sounded more annoyed than the joke I intended my question to be.

He smiled his big, mischievous smile that reminded me of the Cheshire cat from Alice in Wonderland. *More like American McGee's Alice.* I laughed inwardly at picturing the surrealistic video game of the Goth and angst-filled Alice. I rolled my eyes, "That's what I thought."

Devon came over to me and handed me a small plastic insert, "This is how we communicate back to T at nighttime. You'll need to put it in your ear. It acts as both hearing piece and microphone. All you need to do is whisper and we will all hear you. Never leave here without it as it is also a tracking beacon in case someone decides to walk off with you."

"Do you expect that?"

Devon just shrugged.

"It wouldn't be the first time," Tom tried to keep a straight face.

Seeing the tiny thing, I suddenly had this awful mental vision of a metal bug crawling into my ear and taking over all my brain functions so that aliens could move my body around. I actually shivered visibly at the thought. But I placed the little nugget into my ear anyway. It was tinier than any hearing aid I had ever seen. I was just hoping it wouldn't slide all the way down into my canal. Luckily, though, it had some kind of foam texture to it and puffed out to form around the space. It didn't hinder the sound around me at all either. *Cool.*

Tom put a similar hearing piece in his left ear, but Devon hooked on what looked like a Bluetooth phone head-set, you know, the ones that make people look like the Borg from "Star Trek Generations". I pointed to it, questioning.

"Camera," He said.

"Ah."

After a little practice to make sure that all of our hearing pieces worked, Devon told me to pick out a weapon. He moved us over to a table full of handguns and knives, short bows and maces. He explained each weapon to me and said that we would eventually practice, but for now he wanted me armed – just in case.

The morning star looked interesting, but with its long pole and huge spiked metal ball at the top, I thought concealment would be an issue. I wanted to hide something that was easily accessible, preferably in my pants, and there was already a large enough weapon there. *Hehe.*

There were several throwing weapons on the table including Japanese shurikens and their lighter cousins, stars. One weapon caught my eye. For a brief second, I thought the metal glowed deep black, if that were possible. *That had to be a trick of the light.*

I carefully picked it up, respecting the eight inch curved blade that ended in a sharp turned-up point. The top of the blade was thick and slinked to a ragged but smooth cutting edge. The handle was black with a silvery frieze carved into it. Running my fingers up and down the handle, I couldn't figure out what it was of, but I knew the moment I touched the blade, the dagger was for me.

"Where did you get this?" I inquired.

"I got it during one of my travels to Egypt," Devon replied.

"Business or pleasure?" I joked.

Devon tossed me a warning look, "Revenge. He didn't get very far. I took it from him."

"What are the markings?"

"No idea. I cleaned it up as best as possible, but I still can't tell."

Cool. "Do you mind if I use this one?"

Devon looked thoughtful for a brief second, "No. It's yours. The blade is pure silver. It can kill most non-human creatures. And since you are no longer a human, do NOT cut yourself on it."

Oops, that was close. I had been skimming the blade against my nail to check the sharpness like my dad had taught me when we used to sharpen hunting weapons and other cutlery. I just missed nicking myself as Devon gave me the warning. I decided that now was a good time to sheath the knife, just in case. "So one cut and I'm dead?" I asked. M*aybe I shouldn't take this one after all.*

"Depends on the cut," Devon responded.

"Guess I won't be using this to shave," I laughed.

"As if you would ever need to again," Tom said.

"As if you ever needed to before. Ya gotta face like a 15-year-old girl," T said.

"Very funny, T." *Everybody's a comedian.*

The covering had the same markings on it, but I still couldn't figure out what they were. Looking at them was like seeing someone whose name was on the tip of my tongue, but kept slipping from my mind once the words started to form. It seemed, almost, that the markings were even moving around, snaking into different positions, not allowing me to understand what they were.

Funny trick of the light, I thought again.

I shifted the dagger around in my hand and tried to find a good place for it on my person. I finally decided that it would be fine on my left side, attached to my belt, and pulled my plaid shirt out, completely unbuttoning it now. The dagger barely left a bulge and, for pure silver, it was incredibly light.

Watching Devon and Tom find places to hide weapons was pretty hilarious. They had, of course, knives in the usual places around their belts and hidden in straps tied to their ankles, and guns were in various pockets of their light jackets and cargo pants. But there were some weapons that were of their own creations. They looked bulky in hand, but somehow they managed to hide them without showing. It was like they were using a bag of holding, a magical bag that holds items larger than itself from the role-playing game Dungeons and Dragons. I sighed at that image, and thought about my other friends – Gabe, Sam, Noah and Jeffrey. We used to play D&D every Wednesday night from the time we were in high school until.. *Until Alexandra. One day, I'll have to let them know I'm all right.*

I felt completely useless just hiding a dagger. "What the hell kind of trouble do you think we're going to get into tonight?"

"You never can be too prepared," Tom responded.

"Spoken like a true Boy Scout," T joked.

"Yeah, but seriously," *I really want to know,* "Should I have something more than just this?" I pulled the dagger out from its hiding place on my left side.

"Nah, if shit hits the fan, just stay behind us," Devon said, "Besides, until we teach you how to handle any of these special toys, they are off limits. You will hurt yourself or one of us, so just stick with the dagger for now."

"Gee thanks. I feel so much better now," My voice was as sarcastic as possible. Once all of us were armed, we left the building and stepped out onto Fore Street. All of the tourist shops were closed. Only the bar across the street was still open, the bouncer sitting on the stool looking big and toad-like.

I could smell humans everywhere. I sneezed. *Maybe I'm allergic to them,* I laughed to myself. After only a brief lapse of concentration, I managed to control the urges. Devon and Tom continually gave me sideways glances, always at the ready to strike me down. That both worried and relaxed me. *At least if I do give in,* I thought, *maybe that will give the human a fighting chance.*

T danced past me, "Have fun boys... I'm off like a dirty shirt."

"As long as you're not off like a prom dress," I joked reflexively. It was what Gabe used to say to us when we were getting ready to leave.

Tom took a fatherly tone, "Hey, Newbie, that's my baby sister you're talking to. Do you want me to break your nose again?"

"Nah, I'm good," I brought my hands up to my nose protecting it in memory of before, "Only trying to be funny."

"Well, don't quit your day job because you suck at funny," trying to be serious, he grinned anyway.

"Everything set up, then?" Devon asked T.

"Yes, sir!" She saluted and winked at me. She turned to give Tom a kiss goodbye on the cheek and then ran up the street, disappearing into a crowd of people as she turned the corner.

"Where we headed?" I asked.

"Docks," Devon grunted.

Tom allowed, "We're meeting some vamps from New Zealand. Nothing big, just a meet and greet."

I raised an eyebrow.

"Just welcome to America… Don't eat the humans within town limits… That sort of thing," Tom laughed.

We walked down to Exchange Street and crossed over Commercial. Crossing that one road, the air thickened with the deep scent of ocean, fish and salt. Sporadic laughter clung to the walls and echoed on the streets. Things you never had trouble finding in this town were the pubs, clubs and bars.

I glanced at the humans around us, sitting at ease, not even knowing that predators were in their midst. I squashed that thought quickly as it began turning my stomach in hunger and my eyes to black tunnels. I reminded myself that I had eaten before I left and tried to imagine that I'd be full and sluggish if I had another bite.

Four kids my age were either standing next to or sitting on top of the newspaper box stands. Each had a cigarette in hand and laughter lighting up their faces. The two girls were in tank tops and cargo khakis. Sandals strapped their tiny feet, which they swung either nervously or flirtatiously as they sat on the stands. They dressed like sisters.

The two boys were hovering close on either side of the girls. Every once in a while they would take turns leaning in, whispering, making the girls laugh or giggle or blush. I thought of how Maddie and I used to flirt in the beginning of our relationship – sweet, innocent, maybe pushing innocence, trying to figure out how far we could go before making the other uncomfortable.

In the first few months of dating her, and we hadn't even gotten to second base yet, she would play this game with me called "Color." She would rest her hand on my knee and ask, "What color am I thinking of?" I would guess. If I guessed incorrectly, and I always guessed incorrectly according to her, she would slide her hand up my leg ever so slightly and ask me again. She would continue moving up my thigh until one of us would get too nervous to continue. Though I hate to admit this, I always blushed first and would push her hand away just as she was getting to my upper thigh and I could begin feeling my excitement towards her. She would giggle and clap with excitement that she won the game. Then, she'd kiss me. *God, I miss her smile.*

I glanced over at the teens. Just what I thought.

"Devon, the kids are all in blue again."

"Huh. Ok, what else do you see?"

I turned toward them and noticed a guy I hadn't seen before. He was standing about a block away toward the old factory turned self-storage building. His face momentary lit up in the yellow glow of a cigarette. In that brief second, I could tell that the guy had shoulder-length stringy hair. Maybe it was dark blondish? He was wearing a worn, brown leather duster over faded jeans and a black t-shirt. From this distance, he looked like he was as tall, if not taller, than Tom. He reminded me of a cowboy that had lost his hat or a knight that had lost his sword. Either way, I could tell he was tough and didn't want to be messed with.

I nodded in his direction, "The man over there is glowing gray. I assume that he is one of us?" It was more of a comment than a question.

The two vampires turned to face the same direction.

"Ayuh," Tom said.

The vamp nodded at them, and Devon and Tom returned the gesture.

"Who is he?"

"Acair. He works with us on the PD. He lives near here," Tom responded.

In a blink, Acair was gone. The glow around everyone seemed to fade within themselves and I told Devon as much. He shrugged. Nothing seemed to phase that guy. *Well, I won't let it bother me either, then.*

We walked down to one of the small commercial docks. It was more or less a parking lot for lobster boats. A few private sailboats had moorings there. The water was quiet. Still. Dead. The air was heavy with fish, salt and humidity. As my father always said, "Storms coming". Although it always sounded like, 'Stahm's comin',' with his heavy East coast accent.

'Stahm's comin',' indeed!

For then, though, the night was cloudless and moonless. Stars were thick in the sky as they always were up north. They blanketed the sky and were so close I thought maybe, with my new abilities, I would be able to jump up and reach them. "Yeah, right," I muttered to myself, causing the other two vamps to look at me funny. I just shook my head at them to ignore me.

In winter, the stars were even closer. I loved standing at the bow of the last ferry of the night in the dead of winter, the wind brisk and waking as it hit my face. Feeling the excitement like a dog hanging his head out the window, I would just look at the stars, wishing I could grab them to save for Maddie.

"Oh Maddie," I sighed sadly. They looked at me again. I shrugged. I needed to learn to keep my thoughts to myself so I wouldn't freak them out.

Maddie.

She kept creeping into my head when I least expected it. I needed to think of a way to get over that girl and let her and I move on. I mean, really, how could I ever see her again? I wasn't even a human anymore. How could she love that? *Love me?*

I hardly noticed that we had moved to the end of the dock. I was suddenly melancholy over the life and love I had lost. Taken away from me. *Ech, here comes the anger.*

"Keen, seriously dude, you ok?" Tom asked.

"Fine. Just fine," I held the words, speaking slowly.

"It gets better, you know? Trust me. I don't even think of it anymore. I just enjoy it."

"What are ya, a friggin mind reader?"

Tom smiled his engulfing smile, "You're an open book. That's a terrible trait for a vampire, bud."

"Reign it in boys," Devon broke into our conversation, "Time to work."

Devon's eyes drifted out to an oil boat in the middle of the bay, out near Fort Dune. From even that far away, my specially enhanced eyesight kicked in and in the gloom of the light I could see Cyrillic letters naming the vessel, though since I couldn't read Russian, I had no idea what the boat was called.

Shadows of human forms drifted their way down the side to a waiting speed boat. Although there was a ladder at the location where they were coming down from, their movements showed they weren't using it. Even from afar, they didn't look human to me. Not, at least, by the way they were moving. They looked like they were drifting down through the fog at a fairly quick and even pace. Their belongings had floated down before them and a man in the boat was already situating them in it.

"How are they doing that?" I asked.

"They probably have a witch with them. My guess is he's their servant," Tom said.

"Do vamps usually have servants?"

"Only the very old and the very wealthy. The job is extremely hazardous to the witch's health."

"You mean to their life?"

Tom laughed in agreement, "Yup, something like that. Not all vamps are like us and humane. But on the bright side, it pays well!"

As the speed boat approached, the other two vamps tensed, which made me nervous and I felt my own muscles clench in anticipation. I could very clearly feel my fangs against the inside of my lips. My eyes went into a focus mode, not quite the agitation level of the tunneling that occurred when I was hungry, but more alert.

A glow around the human shapes became apparent once they were a few hundred yards away. It was as if they were being backlit by the sun: colored halos clung to them. Three of the beings, two men and a woman, glowed gray. I assumed they were the New Zealand vamps. The man driving the boat had a blue glow with a hint of red sparks surrounding him. The last male gave a yellow-green hue to the air around him. In the lowest voice I could, I told the guys next to me what I was seeing before the glows pulsed out again and the strangers returned to their un-lit selves.

The boat slowed and turned parallel to the docks. The tide was in the middle of its run, so the water had gotten a little rough near land. The boatman looked a little nervous, his eyes darting at his wards through long-banged hair. But he tried to keep his face calm. I admired his will. I didn't know if he knew who his customers were, but he knew there was just something off about them.

I had to agree with his sentiment. Something was dangerous and disturbing. I was a vampire, and even I was nervous. *So much could go wrong here, the least of which I could end up accidentally killing this guy. Or maybe getting killed by these visitors.*

Or maybe I'm feeling this way because this is the first time I've been near other vampires besides Devon and Tom, good guys, and the demon, Alexandra that made me. Odds are still in favor of nice guys, two to one, but still, maybe Dev and Tom were unusual for vampires. Maybe most are like Alexandra.

What a mess I'm in.

I felt quickly for the blade at my side. *Still there. Calm down.*

Tom caught the ropes easily and cautiously, only slightly faster than a human's normal movements. Practiced. He tied the boat up securely at the front and back.

The vampires and witch stepped off the boat, the boatman handing them luggage as they disembarked. The new vampires straightened and both groups looked each other over, distrusting. The tension around us was like watching an adult giraffe being stalked by a ferocious lioness – you knew that the giraffe was going to die, you just didn't know when.

Should I introduce myself? What's the protocol here? My hand wanted to lift to shake theirs, but I fought the desire. *I mean, maybe there's a difference country to country on how to greet, like there is with normal people. As in with Americans, give us three feet of space or we're agitated. Or is there something universal between vampires?*

Man, I wish these guys would've prepared me better for this! For anything, really. I made a mental note to ask a lot more questions when we returned to the apartment.

Finally, after what seemed like eternity, Devon spoke, guardedly, "Please state your name and business here."

The shortest vampire male, who may have stood at 5'5", stepped forward and responded with outstretched hand, "I'm Sherman." He had shoulder length blond hair tied back, with a single small section wrapped with different colors of thread. He was wearing khaki shorts, a white t-shirt and a big toothy grin.

Score! At least now I know I won't be a hoser for doing that in the future.

He shook hands with all of us, using both his hands in the nicest, most cheery and joyful way. I couldn't help but like him. Even Tom and Devon eased up as Sherman turned to his fellows.

"This is Karl," He nodded to the tallest male, another vampire.

Karl was wearing black pants and a black button down shirt with a black blazer over it. His belt flashed a gold buckle in the light. He had a single gold, diamond stud earring in his right ear that stood out against his black hair and bright blue eyes. It looked like he had been in his early 20's when he had been bitten. His hand was cold, and his shake was confident, but not over-bearing or threatening. *But not friendly either,* I thought.

Then Sherman held out a hand to the female vampire who stepped forward, "This is my wife, Zara." She took his hand and they looked at each other in a loving way, almost disappearing into the other's eyes and retreating into their own private world. She stood about as tall as the other vampire, so she was probably 5'11". She had to look down at the tiny Sherman. She had a red sundress on, low cut and sweet. It flaunted her beautiful figure, platinum hair and deep tanned skin. Like Sherman, she appeared to have been bitten in her thirties.

Karl coughed a stiff laugh and said, "Newlyweds. Geez, get a room!"

"Ahem," Sherman shook himself out of his young-looking bride's eyes, "We're on vacation for the next two weeks to the Big Island." He meant Deckard Island, one of the wealthier islands in the area where there were very few year-rounders living.

"And who is your friend," Tom asked.

"Mark. He is our human servant."

Mark nodded, but kept a very neutral face on.

"A witch?" Tom questioned Sherman in a manner which informed Sherman that we already knew what Mark was.

Sherman inclined his head slightly. Mark was dressed in black as well, although not as tailored looking as Karl. He held more of a bodyguard's stance than a butler's demeanor, with his crossed arms and piercing gaze. His head was clean shaven, but his face was encircled by a black goatee that didn't quite look like his natural hair color.

"Ferry's are done for the evening, where are you staying tonight?" Devon drilled them.

"We have reservations up the hill at the Hilton. We'll be heading to Deckard Island in the morning," Sherman responded, pleasantly.

"Ok. Please keep in mind that if you keep to the old ways, there is no hunting in city limits, which also includes the islands. We follow those laws to the letter," Devon emphasized his meaning with a pause, ensuring that the visiting vampires understood the unspoken consequences of breaking said law. "However, there are several breweries in the area that provide all that you need here. You will be able to see which ones they are by the markings on their signs."

Geez, there is really a lot I don't know about, I thought while I listened to Devon.

"Thank you for the information," Sherman said in his up-beat voice and heavy New Zealand accent.

"Enjoy your stay here. If you run into any trouble, please contact us immediately. We are the eyes and ears of this town for non-humans," Devon handed Sherman a business card that just had his name on it. When Sherman lifted it up to look at it, I saw that the back was empty.

I really, really have a lot to learn. How was he going to call him? Yell his name? Yodel a cry for help? Send off smoke signals? Seriously, how is a card with nothing other than a name going to help? There wasn't even a phone number on it!

"Thank you again, Devon," Sherman said as he placed the card in his weathered leather wallet. He then turned his attention to the boat driver who was trying unsuccessfully to hide that he was listening to the exchange, "Thank you sir, you may go now," he slipped the man several bills as a tip. It was at least enough to keep his mouth shut if fear from the weirdness and danger didn't.

The boatman looked very relieved and scurried around to where the ties were to the boat. Tom unwrapped the lines and tossed them back in for the driver. He sped quickly away, not paying attention to the wake zone he was in.

The New Zealand vampires shook hands with us one more time and grabbed their luggage in a completely normal way – by the handles. The witch followed behind with a few more bags. They began their walk up toward town, pointing out buildings and signs like tourists would.

"Ok, so now what?" I asked when the small group had crossed the road into the old port.

"We patrol the area and make sure none but humans are out to play," Tom said.

"So do you ever step in when it's human against human?"

"We try not to interfere, except to call for our human police counterparts. If that is out of the question and they won't get there in time, we help, but only if we can by not showing them what we are. Tom, here, always has way too big of a heart, so we almost always end up doing something. Can't help himself. The freak." Devon's face cracked into a small and rare smile, as if remembering something humorous.

We walked away from the dock. Clouds were beginning to move in. The air began to crackle with displeasure and the distant rumble told me that the storm was fast approaching.

We headed back across Commercial to check out the Old Port. The white cobblestone streets were a sharp contrast to the red brick sidewalks that marked the newer sections of town. Well, if you could call a hundred years old 'new.' But I guess compared to a few centuries old, it was really new.

Remembering some of the questions I had at the dock I asked, "What's the symbol on the bars to let us know that we're welcome there?"

Tom answered, "It's a universal symbol with two small holes in the logo of a business sign linked with a red line that only people like us can see. It's actually kind of a joke in our world."

"How so?"

"It looks like the mark we leave when we bleed a human."

Ew. But my stomach growled in hunger. I moved on to the next line of questioning, "Do all vampires shake hands like humans?"

"No," Tom and Devon said in unison.

Tom continued, "We're going to have to watch them. Vampires never shake hands unless it's with humans. There's something strange about that group. I don't care how lovey-dovey they act."

Devon agreed, "There's definitely something up with them. I got their pics and they've already been uploaded to the system. When T gets back from her errands, I'll ask her to see what she can find out about them."

"Ayuh, something is afoot with them," Tom said.

❊ ❊ ❊

A Task

"Radio to Sarge!" A deep and husky voice shot over our ear-sets, scaring so much of the bejeezuz out of me that I ended up three floors higher on a fire escape landing next to where we were walking, adding another layer of surprise to the initial shock.

Tom looked like he was going to birth a seal pup laughing so hard and in between 'guffaws,' he said, 'You'll.. haha.. get... hehe.. used to.. hahaha… that.. haha… eventually… newbie…whew boy! Did you jump!!" He was holding his sides, shuttering with amusement of me.

Jerk.

Although smiling mildly, Devon had my back, "Leave the kid alone, Tom. You know you spooked worse than that the first time we got a call over the headsets and you landed in the water."

Now it was my turn, and I laughed as I jumped down from the building. *This is so cool.*

"Sarge, are you there?" The voice called from the ear-set.

Devon turned his attention to it, "Go ahead Mo, what's up?" The microphone picked up his voice easily, so Tom and I heard him in stereo.

"Who's Mo?" I asked Tom, speaking with such a hushed, quick voice, that people would not be able to hear.

"He's our radio operator back at the station. He works exclusively with the non-human teams," Tom answered just as quickly.

"Is he human?"

"Yes. Originally from Somalia. Now shut up. I want to hear what he's saying," Tom chided.

Our conversation ended before Mo continued at his slow, accented human pace, "Disturbances located in the water off of Adrian Island. We need your team to check it."

"And you're telling me it's not due to the storm coming, is it?"

"Doesn't appear to be that way."

Devon said something that sounded a lot like 'cac. Damnu air!' but I couldn't be sure. Every once in a while, he was prone to swear in his native Gaelic, and I just assumed that was what he was doing.

"Where off of Adrian Island?" Devon followed up.

"Back side and it's heading toward the island pretty quickly."

Devon swore again, this time in English.

I looked at Tom for some reassurances. He just smiled with thin lips of amusement, not willing to share with me if he knew anything.

Sometimes that guy can be really annoying!

"Affirmative, we're on it," Devon said, "Anything else tonight, Mo?"

"Nah, that's it for now, although the Captain is on the warpath so whatever is out there, be careful this time. You know what happened the last time the sea stirred liked this. Chandler Island is still recovering. Captain does not want a repeat. Got it?" Mo's slightly accented voice was more entertained than disapproving.

"Can't make any promises."

"Yeah, yeah."

"Say 'Hi' to that pretty wife of yours for us," Tom broke in before Mo could leave.

"Will do. Stop by for a visit. You know she loves to try new recipes on you boys."

"Ayuh, we'll be by soon."

"Good. Well, remember to go easy tonight boys."

"Ayuh. No destroying Adrian Island. Got it."

And with that, the clouds opened up and we were hit with a down pour.

☆ ☆ ☆

Gonna Need a Bigger Boat

Twenty minutes later we were idling off the ocean side of Adrian Island on Devon's fishing boat and I was practically drowning in my clothes. It was a twenty-foot, wooden lobster boat with a captain's cabin. I was surprised that boats of that kind were made anymore. Usually, lobster boats that size were fiberglass. When I asked about it, Devon just replied that it was about 30 years old and that he had bought it from a fisherman's widow. He said that it was in pretty poor condition when he first got it, but he had rebuilt it to its current beauty. In his reconstruction of it, he had added an exceptionally fast engine. So our travel out to the island took only half the time as it would have normally.

He called her *Carmilla*, named after the main character of the first book written about a female vampire. *Huh, what do you know, he does have a sense of humor. Occasionally.*

Adrian Island was odd shaped, for lack of a better word. It looked like an 'A' with the right stem of the 'A' broken in half. Located behind Sweet Haven and Cutter Islands, by normal boat it took about half an hour to forty minutes to travel to.

I remember when Maddie and I used to take the mail boat out here and hop off to visit the ice cream shop before hopping back on. As any local will tell you, the mail boat is one of the best ways to visit the islands out here. The boat stops twice on only two islands, so just don't miss getting back on if you step off. It'll either be a long swim back or a cold night's sleep if you do.

The rain was pounding on us. Besides a couple winking street lights from the island, the only light source was from Devon's boat. Either the summer renters hadn't come back yet or the year-rounders didn't care how dark it was this early in the morning.

With my improving eyesight, I could see the outline of where the island grew out of the bay. The flashes of lightening would momentarily light up everything around us like daylight and then drown us in dark and water. The light from the boat highlighted lobster trap buoys in neon green and pink. Red ones were mixed in with pink, yellow and orange – all of them marking the territories of individual lobstermen. Any colors that didn't belong would promptly be cut the first time and recognized with a shotgun blast across the bow the next. People knew not to mess with the livelihoods of lobstermen!

Devon killed the lights. He was standing at the wheel in the cabin looking out the small window toward the island and even with my new and improved eyesight, it was hard to see his dark, black skin against the shadows. A flash of lightening reflected off his four-leaf clover neck tattoo and made him look creepy. I turned toward the direction Tom was staring as we stood shoulder to shoulder on the port side of the boat.

"What are we looking for?" I yelled, not thinking. Maybe it was because of all of the thunder that I had forgotten that the vampires could hear me even if I whispered. Tom flashed a mischievous smile. I wasn't sure if it was at my question or at the way I had asked it. Suddenly, I was knocked off my feet, bumping into the guardrail and landing on my butt as something rammed the underside of us. "What the hell was that?' I asked, panicked, as Tom swiftly grabbed my wrist and yanked me unceremoniously back onto my feet.

"Still have your land legs, Newbie?" He asked laughing.

"Why are you not concerned that some THING just bumped us?!?"

"It was just a love tap," Tom assured.

"Jesus, it felt like a whale hit us!"

"Not quite, but the size is about right," then he mumbled under his breath, "Well, whale shark size that is."

Ok, Maybe I don't really want to know what this thing is. We were knocked around again, but this time, I remained on my feet.

Tom said, "Ah, looks like you're getting better at this."

"You're gonna need a bigger boat," I quoted the line from *Jaws*, not sure I was happy to have a reason too.

Tom rolled his eyes.

Devon called out in his calm, cold, deep voice, "She's coming back around. Tom, ready the tires."

"She? She?!? How do you know it's a she?"

Tom motioned me over to the back of the boat where several truck tires were roped together, "Ok, all of these need to go into the water when Devon gives the word. They are all tied up. Do not get caught up in the lines."

A sound of clicking noises broke the through the tapping of the rain drops and the thunder around us. Tom and Devon heard it too. Devon moved toward us while Tom and I stared port side. In the troughs of the waves the storm was creating, a swell began. It grew nearer and nearer, starting to bulge the water like a mountain pushing through the surface, the crests of the waves temporarily hiding it.

I started to back up to starboard before realizing there was nowhere else to go. There was a monster that was about to come out of the water and eat us. There was no way around it.

"Oh… my… God…" I said as the thing broke through the surface. Two ginormous eyes, larger than the 18-wheeler tires, were staring up at me. The bulbous head reached out. Back behind those scary eyes, a beak, sharp and dangerous, was what was causing the clicking sound I heard.

Why is it staring just at me?

A long tentacle whipped out of the water and tangled around the port railing. I was surprised at how quickly the huge creature could move. But before I could finish my thoughts, another one shot out like a whip and wrapped around me. I struggled against the flexing and squeezing muscle as it drew me up high above the boat and began to drag me closer to its head.

Please don't eat me.

I turned my head back to the boat; it was the only motion I could do. Even with my new found strength I could not free myself from the creature. Tom and Devon just stood there, stone-faced. No panic and not moving. *What the hell?!?*

"Help me! It's going to eat me!" I yelled at them, willing them to move from, what, shock? They didn't move, and I could've sworn Tom had a slight smile on his face.

The monster brought me in close enough to see several hundred tiny, razor-sharp teeth hidden in its beak. I continued to struggle, but shut my eyes and turned away from my impending death. I had a fleeting thought, *Really? This is the way I'm supposed to die? How humiliating.*

I decided I wasn't going to go out a coward. I opened my eyes. It had moved me closer. I struggled again and was able to free one hand. *If only I could reach my knife!*

I twisted and turned, bending my arm around the thick gripping tentacle and, just as I was about to reach the knife from behind my back, I felt this huge, sharp spray of water. The monster had spat on me. I was covered in ocean water and a thick, jelly mucus of leftover fish guts.

And then I heard... *Laughter?*

Quickly, I felt the release of the tentacle and I dropped back into the boat. My legs gave out from underneath me as I tried to recover from confusion, fright and... anger.

Devon and Tom were laughing at me.

The beak clicked again quickly, *was it laughing too?*

Devon leaned over port side. The monster's head had moved closer to the boat. It looked like he was petting it. Devon looked over at me, "Keen, meet Scylla. She always likes to have fun with the new guys," He turned back to her, patting her head like she was a Labrador retriever, "Don't ya, girl?"

The creature sounded like it was making cooing noises through the beak that I had gotten an all-too-intimate view of.

"Scylla? This thing has a name?"

Another tentacle ripped out of the water again and I jumped back out of its way before it landed where I had just stood.

"Careful, Newbie, don't insult the little girl," Tom said, moving forward and stroking the tentacle as he moved it back into the water gently. Another tentacle had creeped its way under the boat, coming up starboard side and beginning to bump against my leg. I jumped back again, really unsure of the creature's intentions.

"Pet her," Tom said, "I think she likes you."

Yeah, maybe as dinner.

I hesitantly bent down and picked up the arm. It felt bumpy and leathery like a football, not at all what I was expecting. The color of the creature, what I could see in the darkness, was dark burnt sienna on top and melted into white on the bottom.

"What is she?" I asked.

Devon had a tentacle wrapped around his chest and arms. It looked like Scylla was, I don't know, *hugging him?*

Devon responded while patting the arm around him, "She's a Kraken. I picked her up on my travels over to America. She's supposed to be up near

Constanze Island. Aren't you, little girl? I visit her about once a week, but since we've been babysitting you I've had to miss. She came down here the last time we were working with a newbie."

"She just about tore down the docks around Chandler Island last time this happened," Tom broke in.

Devon continued, "She's a relative of octopuses and squid. Intelligent little buggers with an IQ probably higher than most professors, but with an attention span of a three-year-old. And the temper of a woman scorned."

He turned his attention once again to Scylla, "Caught you early this time, didn't we girl?"

She clicked her beak.

"Let's take you back home, huh?" Devon made little cooing noises at her.

Cupping my hand to my mouth, I turned my head away for a second, trying not to laugh at the scene. *Aww, shucks, Devon has a soft spot.*

She slapped her tentacles on the water around the boat, spraying us.

"Ok, you're right. I'm sorry it's been too long, but as you can see, we're training a new guy. We couldn't leave him alone," Devon pleaded.

She slapped again, this time knocking the boat around.

Devon slumped his shoulders down, "It won't happen again, little girl, I promise." He smiled over at her, "Besides, we brought you some more toys. Do you want them?"

She clicked her beak and squealed.

Devon nodded at us.

Tom and I went over to the tires, tossing them out. They were tied to the boat with thick, knotted ropes and they bobbed up and down in the storm waves. Tentacles began slowly wrapping around them and gently tugging them below surface.

"Ok girl, let go and give us a head start," Devon petted her.

She dropped down completely below the surface and the tires popped back up.

Devon turned the travel lights back on and turned the boat northeast as the storm finally stopped dumping on us and the lightening moved off to the horizon.

We traveled very quickly, but occasionally the boat would jump back a couple of feet as Scylla would catch up, grab onto the tires and pull. I never did get used to that. And as Devon said, her attention span was that of a kid. A few times, she turned away chasing off after something, so we had to turn around and go get her. But for the most part she stayed with us.

Constanze Island is the home of Martinelli National Park and I knew from scuba diving around in the area that there were some great places for her to stay. Scylla's home was in an underground cave tucked well into one of the northern coves of the island. When we got there, Tom told me to cut off five of the eight tires. I pulled out my knife, admiring it for a second before touching it to the ropes. To everyone's surprise, it snapped the ropes without me having to cut through.

"That ever happen before when you used it, Devon?" I asked.

"Nope. What did you do to it?"

"Nothing," I said, "I just took it out and touched the ropes. That was it."

"Huh, weird."

"Yeah," I agreed, "Weird. Maybe she frayed the ropes and it just needed an extra slice before it gave way."

Devon picked up the end of the rope at our feet. It not only looked like it was cut off by a straight edge, it also looked like it was burned on the end to seal the bottom from fraying. It wasn't a nylon rope, so that should not have been possible.

Devon just shrugged and dropped it, "Let's keep an eye on that thing. There's gotta be something out on the net about those markings."

Scylla dragged the tires underwater, but not before smacking her tentacles against the water to spray us one last time. I could've sworn I heard her chirping a laugh as she headed back home.

"It looks like she's got you wrapped around her, uhm, tentacles," I threw Devon a sheepish grin.

"Yeah, every last eight of them," Tom smirked.

Devon got stone-faced again, "We're heading back in. That took a long enough time."

"Hey Dev, before we go back to the mainland, can we make a stop? It'll be fast, I promise," I asked, kind of timidly as I wasn't sure I wanted the answer to be 'Yes.'

Devon glanced at the horizon. Light was just starting to peak through. "We'll have to do it quickly."

Chapter 7

Strange Things

✧ ✧ ✧

Son from afar

I stared, hidden behind a willow tree, at the middle-aged couple as they moved around the kitchen in the early morning hours. Sadness hung in their eyes as they did the everyday chore of cleaning their breakfast dishes, something I knew they had always done together since they were first married.

The last few weeks since I had disappeared had not been kind to them. Their motions were less noisy... a little less fun... a little less happy. They had aged considerably and their faces had more wrinkles. Their hair was now stained with gray streaks. My heart broke to look at them. *My parents.*

My mother absent-mindedly looked through the window and I shifted deeper into the shadows. She seemed to lock eyes with me and her pain burned into my heart. I couldn't take it, but I didn't want to turn away. *Not yet.*

My father came up behind her. I could hear him even at this distance and through the closed window. "We'll find him, my love," his voice sounded hopeless though.

She turned to look at him and hugged him tightly. I could see small tears dropping from her face. They moved away from view. I felt an arm on my shoulder as thunder rumbled in the distance again, "It'll get easier, Keen."

"Yeah, Devon, I know," I said as a white light momentarily struck around us.

Devon smiled at me in understanding and shook me from my lonely trance, "Come on, we still have work to do."

The rain began to pour on us again as we looked at the house one more time, then walked away.

✧ ✧ ✧

Look at All the Pretty Colors

After we tied off *Carmilla* at a private boat dock, Tom, Devon and I hoofed it up the couple of blocks to the apartment. The town had already begun to bustle with early morning traffic and pedestrians heading into work. Since June mornings could still be a little cool this far north, there were only a few tourists up this early shuttering cameras at what, to me, looked like the most insignificant things. Occasionally, there would be a true photographer in the area, but they mostly preferred the fall since the world around here would then glow in a plethora of colors, making even the dirty streets of the town look romantic.

We got to the apartment, grateful to get out of wet clothes that could hinder us in an actual fight, if there needed to be one. I took a shower, although it was very unnecessary. All the rain had pretty much cleaned off any funk I may have had since the Kraken spat on me and it wasn't like I could ever get cold again, so there was no need to warm up. But out of pure human habit, I took one.

Besides, the smell of tea tree and patchouli always brought me back to my senses, even if for just a moment. I also don't like to smell bad, so although we vampires don't sweat, I still rolled some Old Spice on before I walked out of my room. Maddie always loved it when I wore it.

Damn it. There has got to be something that won't remind me of her!

Annoyed at myself, I shut the door a little hard and splintered the frame slightly.

Whoops. I've got to get that in check. This is exactly why I can't see Maddie again. I could break her as easily as the door.

"Who pissed in your Wheaties, Keen?" T asked from the kitchen as she began turning up Nine Inch Nails on the radio, clearly not really wanting to hear what I had to say. I answered her anyway.

"Nothing. Nothing. Just stuff I need to work out," I walked over to the fridge and pulled out a *Morning Brew*. 'A relaxing cup of blood enhanced with the essence of coffee. You'll never miss the real thing again,' the label read. I poured the contents into a mug and heated it in the microwave.

T was wearing a forest green wig that shaped the hair just around her cheek bone. It was amazing how real it looked. I mean, if people were born with green hair, this was exactly the color it would be. Her eyes were shadowed in dark green and bright pink, reminding me of England's punk rockers of the 80s.

"I have some news for you," she said as she dumped the rest of her breakfast, leftover macaroni and cheese courtesy of the blue box, into a reusable storage container. I really wished that had been appetizing. It was my favorite quick meal. Throw in some leftover chicken, peas and onions and voila! A cheap-ass casserole that lasts a week.

"Wat'cha got for me?" I took a sip from the steaming cup. *This morning brew IS better than plain old coffee. Mmmm.*

"I researched your little human glow stick problem last night at my friend's house. Veleda. She's a Wiccan and I thought she might be able to point me out in the right direction."

"Veleda?" I repeated the familiar sounding name, but I forgot about it when I heard slight movements coming from the other room that told me the guys were heading over to join the discussion. In less than a second, Tom was standing next to T and Devon was leaning against the sink with his arms crossed.

"Go on, lil sis. We're all dying to hear this," Tom sniggered.

"You're such a tool, Tom. That 'dying' joke is really getting old," T smacked her brother on his arm.

She flashed her bright eyes at me, "Turns out, you're seeing people's auras."

"Huh?" I grunted.

T was thoughtful before answering, "For lack of a better explanation, you're seeing people's life force and mood. You said you saw blue when you saw me. Did you see blue with other humans?"

"Yes."

"Were there any other colors?"

"Yes, each human had a start of blue, but there were other colors that wrapped in and out of the blue. I only see gray when I look at Devon, Tom or other vampires. There are no other colors with them, so far. And a witch I saw was like a greenish color."

"My friend said that anyone who is 'among the un-living,'" she made quotes with her hands, "would not have a true aura color. But everyone else should."

"What else did she say?" I was curious. *This is an interesting trick.*

"Well, she didn't know too much about it, but you should probably try to figure out the nuances of it. Her mother could read auras, but she passed away a long time ago, and Veleda doesn't have that ability. Her mom rarely talked about it, and used it only while she was working as a palm reader to figure out who was going to be a paying customer," she walked over to the stool next to me and grabbed a book that was on it, "However, she did give me this."

I took the book from her – it was thin with a colorful, kind of cheesy rainbow on it. The title was 'Knowing Auras – A Collaborative Discussion of Light.' No specific author was listed. Flipping through the book quickly, I didn't see any discussion type sections either. The format had paragraphs and diagrams and was more like a science book than some weird, earthly magic book. "Hmm, thanks, T," I said.

"Keen," T said my name harshly to pull my attention back to her. "This is my best friend's book that she got from her mother."

"Uh-huh," I said, still a little distracted with my thoughts, *Auras. Huh?*

She put her hands on the book, protectively, "I want it back in one piece."

"Yeah, yeah. Ok, T. One piece. I get it," I responded, pulling the book away so I could flip through it again.

"Ok, then," she was still hesitant that I wouldn't damage the book, but she asked me another question, "By chance, did you have this ability before you were bitten?"

I turned my gaze to her, "Nope. But I had pretty good intuition. I used to be able to sense when there was a problem or when I was in some sort of danger and needed to get out of a situation quickly," I bragged.

"Yeah, I see how that worked for you," She said sarcastically as she gestured up and down at my now 'undead' form.

"Hey, it wasn't fool proof."

"Clearly."

I had absolutely no comeback, so I turned to the guys, "Hey, help me out here."

"Sorry, Bro, you're on your own," Devon said, then rethought, "Although, T, can you do another sleuthing job since your such a good Nancy Drew?"

"More like Inspector Clouseau," Tom said, which earned him another loud but fruitless smack on the arm.

"You know that dagger we gave Keen to use the other day?" Devon ignored the bantering between the two siblings.

"Yeah, Dev?" T responded.

"Well, see if you can find anything on it. Where it came from, its uses during its life, etc."

"Keen, let me see that for a minute. I want to get some scans of it," T said.

I pulled up the back of my shirt and took it from its sheath. I handed it over, a little sad.

"Don't worry, puppy eyes. I'll give it right back," she darted out of the room, fast for a human, but still no where near as fast as us. About three minutes later she came back with the dagger and handed it over.

I felt relieved; it was an odd feeling for only having the thing with me a night, but I was growing fond of it – like I didn't feel safe or right without it on.

T took the scans of the dagger with her when she left, "Don't wait up boys."

"We never do… but you better be in before us," Tom said as the door shut behind her.

"What's on the agenda tonight," I asked Devon.

"Oh, the usual. Mayhem, recklessness and other-worldly."

"Cool."

"Ayuh."

✻ ✻ ✻

Meet Mr. Carmichael

The evening was actually quite uneventful, which Devon thought was a little too bad. While we drove around town, he and Tom talked about the lack of non-human, and I sat in the back seat reading up on auras. Apparently, auras are forms of energy that surround a being, regardless of where they are in the food chain. In other words, since I was seeing auras on the living and the undead, I should be able to see them on animals as well. These energies depict the feelings and emotions at that immediate moment. *Interesting.*

One of the graphics grabbed my interest as I was speed reading, *Well, to someone normal, this must be speed reading,* that made me stop and flip back to it. The picture had two human, asexual, silhouetted shapes with the captions of 'Normal Aura' and 'Heightened Aura.' The normal aura human shape had colors of the rainbow that were drawn around it. The heightened aura had the same color design as the other picture, but it included little sharp flicks of light, shaped like the Hebrew letter, lamad, ' .' *This is exactly what I'm seeing.* I skipped to the 'Heightened Aura' paragraph under the pictures:

> "Auras are energies that are vibrations which refract light, cre-
> ating color around the body. Significant uses for aura reading
> in the past few centuries include doctors using aura patterns

to heal sicknesses as well as police using aura reading techniques to assess and diffuse dangerous situations. Anyone can learn how to read these vibrations to some extent (for practice exercises, see Chapter 5: Teaching Yourself to Read Auras.) However, Heightened Aura readers are a phenomenon that have rarely been observed in both the spiritual and scientific senses.

Heightened Aura readers can see not only what emotion or disease is being energized in the body, but they can also see the element the body is made from. In other words, what energy source keeps the body living. For example, human beings and land or water-going animals come from the same energy source, water, so their aura will appear blue in color. Flying beings, such as birds, bats and insects will be surrounded in white as their energy source is air. See appendices A and B for detailed color charts on both Normal and Heightened Aura vibrations.

As of now, there are no scientific reasons for why only a few cases of Heightened Aura reading has been documented over the past several centuries, but there are theories which are discussed in Chapter 8."

I didn't really care about theories, but I did suddenly have an intense and desperate urge in me to find out what it meant to have my aura so I flipped to the back appendices to view the color charts. *Ok, so I can see energy sources. Great! But what does it mean that vampires are gray?*

The answer I was hoping for was not there. I skimmed both color charts again and again and there was no mention of what a gray aura meant. *As far as I can see, every other supernatural creature is listed with a corresponding color. Where is mine? Where is gray? Does this mean that there is nothing natural that is keeping my body going? Does this mean I have to go back to thinking that I really am aberrant? Evil?*

"You know, you're awfully quiet back there, Newbie," Devon said as I jumped at hearing his voice directed at me.

I shut the book, not wanting to see it anymore, and breathed in to gain composure over my thoughts, "Just reading the stuff T gave me."

"Anything good?" Tom asked.

"No," I spoke a little too quickly.

"Oh, come on," he continued, "There's gotta be something that's got you so enthralled."

Ok, just pick out a random fact and don't think about the evil thing, "Well, the way I'm seeing auras is different than normal. I guess I get to see what people are and not just the moods they're in."

"So the colors you're seeing have lined-up according to the book?" Devon asked.

"Ayup," I answered, "The book says that humans are blue, witches are like a yellowish-green color, vamps are gray." *Yup, that'll work. That's a good misdirection. Just lie about the gray part, they'll never know.* "That seems to match so far. Now, I'll just have to study the actual 'mood' colors to keep our butts out of trouble. But there are a ton of colors listed."

Devon said, strategically, "Well, since that should come in handy at some point in time, you better keep studying."

"Good call," I agreed as I opened the book back up.

Tom turned completely in his seat and reached a hand out to the book, "Hey, can I see that?"

"Uhm, w–why," I stuttered tensely, and jerked the book out of his reach, "why do you want to look at it?"

"Just curious," Tom said, surprised of my movements.

"No, I should really get back to this. Devon's right, it might come in handy and there are a lot of colors."

"Ok, ok, don't be so touchy, Bookworm. I'll just check it out later. I just hope your memory is better than your manners when it comes to sharing," Tom laughed in amusement as he turned to face the front of the car again.

I bent my head down over the 200-page book and read it from front to back three times within the hour we were patrolling. With my enhanced reading speed and improved memory, I would have been able to regurgitate the information verbatim, if someone had asked. *This would've been so useful in high school and college. Why couldn't I have had this skill then?*

With no mayhem, nor recklessness nor even other-worldly to be found on our patrol, we headed back to the apartment. This time, we parked the car in the alley, taking the back way up three flights of fire escape stairs and through the back window. Before I headed up the ladder, I took one more admiring look at Devon's '65 GTO hardtop, *Nightwatch blue. Black interior, bucket seats, floor shift. Three hundred and eighty-nine cubic inches of pure power. What a beautiful car.* I just wanted to pop that baby open and see what was under the hood. Knowing Devon, it wasn't street legal, and it would be tightly under wraps. No one got to drive that car but him.

Before I got up to the apartment window, I could tell something was wrong. I could hear wind against jagged edges. The boys were standing just outside. The window was unceremoniously broken.

"Again?" Tom said dryly, "We just fixed that damn thing three months ago."

"Well, I have nothing to lose," I slapped the tall guy's belly as I passed by him to walk through the window. Devon followed closely behind.

An unmistakable click of a gun cocking echoed against the dark walls and made me stop, causing Devon to run into me.

"We need a better security system," I said.

The light on Devon's office table snapped on, illuminating a man in his chair, predictably pointing a gun at us, "Don't you people ever use the door?" he said.

"We could ask you the same thing," I retorted, "but I think, instead, I'll just start with, 'Who the hell are you?' I know, it's a big cliché."

"The question is not 'Who am I?' but, really, 'What do I have to offer?'" the skinny man offered his own cliché as he clicked the safety of the gun and put it down on the dark mahogany wood of the desk.

"We're listening," Devon barked, "Now start talking."

Tom came up to stand near us.

The stranger leaned his salt-and-pepper-haired head back in the chair and crossed his feet upon the desk, "Mr. McCorrigan, Mr. Smith and Mr. Panofsky, besides the work you do with the police department, I heard you were in the, ah," he paused, briefly, "in the locating business."

"Yeah, something like that," Devon replied.

"Don't interrupt, boy," the man nodded toward the gun, "I have very little time and very little patience."

"Well, shooting people you need isn't going to help your time schedule much, friend, now is it?" Tom called his bluff as he knocked the stranger's black leather shoes off the desk, "Now why don't you stop wasting our time and tell us what you want."

Huh, Tom can look a little scary when he wants to.

Regaining his balance as his feet hit the floor hard, the stranger coldly looked at Tom, "I don't like your mouth, young man. You might want to be careful that someone doesn't try to shut it," the man made a move toward Tom, "Just remember who has the gun and the special, pretty silver bullets."

His aura was glowing blue with red-orange sparks, which, from the book I had left in the car, meant that he thought he was a powerful and ego-filled man. That didn't necessarily mean that he was. I challenged by closing the space and said tersely, "Being that you're human and we're not, I'd be careful what you threaten, old man. We can easily take that gun from you."

Devon caught me by the shirt and it ripped a little, "If you two are done with your little pissing contest, I'd like to get this conversation over with so I can eat." He lifted his head up to show bared fangs.

I had never actually seen Devon flash his fangs before. It was so menacing.

We all looked at Devon. My same thought was in everyone's eyes.

"Gentlemen," the man sat down in the chair again, hitching his gray pin-striped, fashionably-tailored suit pants up for comfort, "Do you recognize this man?" He asked as he reached into his inner coat pocket to pull out a photograph.

Devon took the picture and handed it to me without looking at it. I held it up in the light. Tom moved over to see it. The man in the photo was probably in his young twenties, maybe younger, with light brown, reddish hair and pale eyes, not blue, but not quite green either. He was getting into the driver's side of a blue Toyota sedan and looked tall against it. He was a slender but solid guy, whom neither Tom nor I recognized. We both shifted our heads slightly back and forth and Devon answered aloud, "Haven't seen him."

"His name is Adam Carmichael," the man paused that long pause of his, "He's my son."

"You want us to kill your son?" Devon said, not that horrified, all things considered.

Ok, so a bit of shock may have briefly crossed my face as the boys had never told me that was the other job they did. In fact, they never actually mentioned anything other than working for the police department and odd jobs, but it partly explained the affordability of all their toys, weapons and the rest of the awesome apartment. *I guess this is what they meant by 'odd jobs.' And here I thought they just fixed things for people.*

Mr. Carmichael's voice snapped me back into the conversation; I was just going to have to ask about that later. "Actually, no. I have reason to believe that he is being held against his will. I want you to find him and dispose of the people who took him."

"That's not exactly our kind of business," Devon replied as he handed the picture back to the man, "WE don't go after humans."

"Ah, but you see, the thing that took my son was not exactly human. I was there when Adam was taken. We had been walking back from our usual monthly dinner. A black blur flashed in front of me as something hit me hard and I fell. My son was flown away by a winged creature of some sort. It was larger than a human. And it had sharp features like a sculpture. I've seen my share of other-natured creatures, such as yourselves, but never have I seen anything like this before," Mr. Carmichael's eyes widened as if the creature was standing there in front of him.

"A gargoyle," Devon said as my ears perked up, and he then continued mumbling almost to himself, "what the hell is it doing in my town?"

"What do you mean 'gargoyle?'" *This did not sound good.*

Mr. Carmichael broke in before Devon could answer, "I don't care what the hell it was, I just want you to get my son back."

Devon looked at him, "Mr. Carmichael, you must have some pretty big enemies, or your son does, to have one of those take him away."

"Uhm, excuse me, but what is a gargoyle?" I asked again.

"I'm prepared to pay you a large sum for your troubles, gentlemen," Mr. Carmichael said, ignoring my troubled voice. He slid out of the chair, barely a sound of leather shifted, and picked up a briefcase that had been sitting, without notice, next to the desk. He opened the case to show rows of money. "There's $250,000 in here. You'll get the other $250,000 when I get my son back, alive and unharmed."

"Well, I'm not sure about unharmed, but we can aim for alive. Can't promise you anything, though," Tom said.

Devon shot Tom a sharp look to silence the younger vampire. He turned his eyes to the human, "What kind of business are you in exactly, Mr. Carmichael?"

He ignored the question, "So, do I need to take my money elsewhere?"

"No," Devon replied, "We'll do it. How long ago was he kidnapped?"

"Three days ago. My son drives down from the University at Orono once a month to keep an old man company." The man turned to leave, but shifted and turned back around, "Oh, there is one more thing. The gargoyle dropped this as he flew off." He handed Devon what looked to be a coin. One side had on it what looked to be a gate, a 6 pointed star and a backward "C". The other side had a bird with a helmet perched on top.

This looks really familiar. Where had I seen those markings before?

"Who knows about your monthly dinners?" Devon drilled him.

"As far as I know, only him and my driver, Eammon," He pronounced the name 'A-mon.' The old man turned to the direction of the apartment's front door.

Stopping him, I said, "And you're sure this Eammon character doesn't have anything to do with it?"

"I'm certain of it. Eammon wouldn't hurt a fly," he walked toward the steps with the three of us following him, "Gentlemen, I must go."

Tom asked, "How are we supposed to get a hold of you?"

"You're not. I'll get a hold of you in three days' time to find out your progress. I found you before, and from the looks of it," he looked at all the laundry strewn around the studio, "you're not going anywhere soon."

Thankfully, all the computer gear and secret hidey-holes had been hidden away and sealed securely. It didn't look like he had touched anything.

"And exactly how did you find us, Mr. Carmichael," Devon requested.

"A friend of mine owed me a favor. Let's leave it at that," the man unlocked the front door, and exited the correct way.

As soon as the door clicked, Tom began darting around the apartment in such an un-humanly rate that he was a blur. He was calling for T in a strained manner.

Geez, what a jerk I am, I hadn't even thought of her.

Well, there was a gun that was pointed directly at me. With silver bullets and all.

Then I argued in my thoughts, *Yeah, maybe a gun that couldn't do much damage.*

Counter-argue, *Well, who can blame you for still thinking humanly?*

That helped my guilt, but only a little.

Devon stepped into Tom's path and he skidded backward a few feet when Tom's body slammed into him. He grabbed Tom in a bear hug, "Stop, bro! She's not here. Smell."

Tom lifted his nose, sniffed and then stopped struggling. Relief flew through him. He walked over to the fridge and pulled out three Bloody Captain's Black Bear Red Blood Beers, 'A Wild Kind of Bear,' and tossed them to us as Devon and I walked back to the desk to review the money.

Not to sound like a broken record, but, "So what the hell is a gargoyle, anyway?" I asked.

Devon closed the briefcase and sat down on the old, 70s brown-plaid couch after shoving some clothes haphazardly onto the floor. He took a swig of the sweet metallic tasting beer before answering, "Gargoyles are warriors. Evil creatures. They even scare each other. They're protectors, and once they start protecting something, they never stop. Like machines. They will stop at nothing to protect it. It's not actually like them to do something like this, though. Not on its own. Usually their object of protection is an actual object, a building or artifact. But a human? That's unheard of."

Devon paused again for another swig and looked distantly, "It's definitely working for someone. All brawn, but nothing on top, that's for sure."

"Have you ever seen one?" I asked.

"Aye, once. When I was back home," meaning Scotland, where he was born. Living in the states had killed only a little of his accent, "Damn thing near' tore a buddy of mine in half. Never book with a shark whose goombas are gargoyles. If you owe money, it's not pleasant."

"They sound wonderful," I replied, a nice thick amount of sarcasm in my tone.

Devon threw me a look, "I'm being serious, Keen, these things are crazy. Just be thankful it's not an Aswang."

Before I could ask what the hell an Aswang was, T came walking up the stairs. I knew she was coming in well before she did since I had heard her walking from up the street. I had been focusing on the outside of the apartment ever since Mr. Carmichael had left. Her laughter flowed up through the window like a familiar song as she spoke on her cell phone. I heard the slight click as she turned it off, put her key in the lock and then turned the doorknob, her heels clacking the entire time.

She had changed her wig again, bright blue spiked short and choppy. She was dressed in Goth style clothes with wild makeup on. I couldn't help but look her up and down. She had on a red bodice shirt and a tight, red plaid skirt that went to her mid-thigh. Where the skirt ended, ripped, spider-web stockings began and went down all the way to her silver stiletto heels. She looked like she had just stepped out of a Hot Topic store and her outfit showed off some curves I hadn't noticed before. She glowed bright blue briefly, with sparks flicking through it the color of her hair.

Wow. She looks hot!

Whoa, where the hell did that come from?

Trying to remember my manners, I thought, *How does any woman walk in those shoes? They look like a twisted ankle waiting to happen.*

T walked over to the fridge, opened the door and bent over. As she checked out the goods in the fridge, my eyes followed and checked out her goods. That earned me a nice thumping on the shoulder from Tom.

What is wrong with you? Tom said with his protective brother stare.

Finding nothing of interest, T shut the door and plopped down, not so lady-like, on the couch.

"'Hi' to you too, T." I teased, "Why don't you make yourself at home?"

T rolled her eyes, "Don't start."

"I see someone's in a fantastic mood tonight."

She stuck her tongue out at me, baby like, "Just been one of those days." T was an artist in her fifth and final year at the community college. And sometimes it just wasn't a good day to create. "Schmuck professor," her mumble was low and grumbly, but we all heard her clearly enough.

"What's up?" She asked her brother who was still very much staring at me.

"We have an assignment," Devon said, pulling the briefcase out into full view, "A well-paid assignment."

She whistled at the full case, "Very, very pretty. How much?"

Tom filled her in on the details. She sat in silence for a few minutes, playing with the metal bracelets that wrapped halfway up her left arm. They jangled noisily. Letting the recap that Tom told her sink in, she asked, "So what's the catch? There's always a catch?"

"Well," I replied, "Hopefully just the gargoyle."

"Oh that does not sound good."

"I don't know, though," Tom said, "I think T is right, there's something more to it. I mean, come on, this man breaks into the apartment, tells us some story, gives us money, promises us more, then leaves without giving us a forwarding address?"

"Thanks for the recap, Andy Rooney," I said to Tom. *Damn it, he had just stopped staring at me too. Why, oh why, can't I keep my mouth shut?* I smiled at him like nothing was wrong.

Devon, meanwhile, pulled up some old slabs of wood from the floor of an unused closet and hammered them over the broken window.

"Well," Tom turned back to Devon, "There's one thing I don't understand."

"One thing?" T chimed in.

"If he can find us, why can't he find his son?"

"I don't know and I don't care," I said. "For that amount of money, I'll do just about anything – fight a gargoyle, whatever the hell that is. Hell, I'd even kiss you for that amount of money."

"Gee, thanks," Tom held his arm across his forehead and stumbled backward, acting hurt.

"I'll take whatever I can get," I said as I sat down on the couch next to T, putting an arm around her shoulder.

T turned her body toward my arm, one hand on mine, the other extraordinarily high up on my thigh, making me ridiculously nervous and, well, let's just say nervous. She looked deep into my eyes, her face moving close to mine, and in a sugary voice said, "If you think I am part of that 'take whatever I can get' crap, than you are sorely mistaken."

She knocked my hand off her shoulder, making the guys laugh and leaving me figuratively red in the face about my reactions to her. And then I guiltily looked away as I thought of Maddie and my insane attempt at flirting with T. I decided to believe that my craziness was all due to the gun that had been aimed at my face. *Yes, that's gotta be it. Even not being a human that can die easily, a weapon is a weapon.*

"Let's go you guys. We're wasting time," Devon said.

T got off the couch and offered her hand to help me up, "Come on Special K. Dad.. I mean Devon, says it's time for work." We all headed for the door.

Tom put a hand out, "Not you, baby sis."

"Oh come on," she whined.

"You're on radio duty tonight."

"Tommy, I'm always on the radio," only she could get away with calling him that.

"Tough shit, baby sis. We need you here," he hugged her and then kissed her on the forehead.

She pouted, her bottom lip sticking out so far it was almost comical, but nodded her assent.

"We'll be back later, Shorty," I smiled at her as we tromped down the steps and out the door, leaving her to man, that is, woman the radio.

I turned to look at her; she was already settling herself into the leather chair in front of one of the unassuming computer stations around the room. Once her log-on was complete, the wall in front of her opened up to reveal a series of televisions that were recording several angles of the alley with Devon's GTO, scenes from inside and outside the apartment and property, as well as several views of the sewer system and strategically placed cameras around the city. I heard her in my ear-set mumbling curse words when she put hers on and tuned into our frequency.

She really could move fast for a human, I thought as I stepped through the apartment door into more rain and locked her in behind us.

☆ ☆ ☆

The Watch

After much debate, we decided to go back around to the alley where Devon's car was. Tom got in the back with myself riding shotgun and, of course, Devon driving. Since Tom was reading the aura book I had left in the back of the car, I paid more attention to the outside as we passed it by. We drove up Exchange Street, all the shops were closed, and crossed Middle Street. We slowed down to about five miles per hour as I checked out the very small Post Office Plaza area. The trees were in full bloom and hid some of the benches that were on the all-brick park, but my eyes had no trouble focusing through the dark holes between branches and leaves to make sure nothing was amiss. In the rain, even the supernatural don't like to come out, let alone regular people.

Nodding my head to Devon to let him know that he could drive on, I continued searching the streets in front and around us. The old brick buildings were dark with rain. Not many lights were on inside at this late hour, as most of the populace were asleep. The street lamps were dull from another fog that had come into town. It wasn't a deep fog yet – more like a threatening mist.

We drove up to Congress Street and hung a right to head to the cemetery. If there was any trouble to be had, the cemetery was usually the place that had it. After circling it twice, though, we didn't see any living or un-dead thing, so we drove down a side street near some apartment buildings where a small playground was hidden from street view.

"Eh, Dev, slow up," I said as flashes of color were weaving in and out through the jungle gym.

"What do you see," Devon asked as he stopped the car in front of the tennis courts that were to the right of the kid play area.

"Two blue auras, followed by a small greenish-brown one," I paused, thinking of what the book said about the coloring that was new to me. "I think it's something whose energy comes from the ground." The blue auras were sparking with muddy brown lights and the greenish brown had yellow light within it. "It looks like the humans are afraid, but the thing following them doesn't mean any harm to them."

"Wow," Tom said as he checked the book in confirmation, "He can be taught. Did you memorize that entire book already?"

Not amused at his teasing, I gave him a short, "Yes."

"Huh," was all that came from the back seat, but it sounded impressed.

I turned to Devon, "What do you want to do?"

Although there was a lone light in the playground, the shapes had moved to just beyond the reach of the light. Devon could easily see the shapes moving along with his vampire sight, "Let's take a look." Devon opened the car door as he unfastened his seat belt.

"Crap," Tom whined, "Why does it always have to rain? Can I just stay in the car?"

Devon swung around to face Tom and gave him a dirty look before getting out of the car. He stuck his head back in, "Well, you can have an extra minute."

Tom smiled widely before Devon continued, "Call this in to the station. Get Garik down here."

"Fine," Tom huffed and radioed in the request. Then he pushed Devon's seat forward so he could get out as well.

The auras blinked back into the beings and I lost them for just a second as my eyes adjusted. The group of three ran back into the light toward the jungle gym again. I asked "So what's following the humans?"

Neither vamp answered, other than to run towards the group. They moved quicker once they heard a female's scream. The piercing, soprano octave of her screech shocked me and I almost stopped running, but I got to the group about a second after Tom and Devon did. A human girl about fifteen-years-old was on the ground in a fetal position with her eyes tightly shut in fear. Her rain jacket was soaked through and her hair was tumbled around her face, but she didn't appear to be hurt. The human boy, about a year older than the girl, was standing with his back against the ladder of the playground slide with his fists angled down toward a creature that was no taller than four feet. *This poor kid looks like he's about to go into a boxing match that he can't win.*

The creature also had his fists up as if mimicking the boy. He had goat-like horns, a human upper body with dark feathers coming out of his back and two furry legs. The kid was screaming, "Stay away from us! You just stay away!"

Glancing at Devon, a smirk crossed his lips before he called out, "Donagh! Why are you harassing these poor kids?"

The little goat-thing's ears perked up as he slowly turned away from the boy to face us. His features were sad and craggy with deep wrinkles of skin. In a high-pitched, squeaking voice he said, "Devon, I only wanted to talk to them. They were having such fun on the playground! I wanted to play!"

"Come over here," Devon commanded. Donagh slumped his shoulders, but he came over to us.

Blue flashes of light broke through the darkness and reflected off the jungle gym as a police car came into the area. The little boy eased up as he saw a small man in uniform walk towards us. The kid ran over to the girl, "Missy, Missy! Are you all right?" She stirred and the boy helped her up. He wrapped a protective arm around her and stared at us, waiting for something. *Maybe direction?*

The police officer went to stand next to Tom, his aura glowing gray. *A vampire cop? In uniform? I wonder if Devon and Tom also have police uniforms.* The thought made me crack a smile. When I took a good look at the policeman, I realized he looked no older than the boy that had been harassed by Donagh. He was short, about 5'5", and he had an unusually round baby-face. It was as if he hadn't gone through the thinning period most every boy goes through during puberty. *Maybe he just looked young when he was turned.*

"Devon, Tom," the new vampire said and then gave me a once-over. He nodded an acknowledgement that I was with the other two vamps.

"Garik," Devon responded, then was silent.

Tom, speaking to the humans, said, "Want to tell us what happened?"

The kid's voice cracked as he began to ramble through his tale, "We were just sitting on the swings when this thing," he shot an arm toward Donagh, "came up and pushed Missy from behind. She screamed, and when he pushed again, she jumped off the swing. I ran after her and it... he started chasing us!"

Donagh put his head down in shame. If I hadn't know any better, and I didn't, it seemed as if he had been hurt by the boy's comments.

"Donagh," Devon said, "apologize to the kids."

"But, but, but. I just wanted to play with them," Donagh said, kicking the dirt with his goat-hoofed foot like a little boy in trouble.

Devon put a hand on his shoulder, trying to reassure him, "I know Donagh, but you can't sneak up on people like that. They don't like it."

The boy cried out, "It has nothing to do with him sneaking up on us. What the hell is he? That is just NOT natural!" The girl buried her head deeper into the boy's shoulder, hiding her face completely. Tom shot the kid a warning glance to shut him up.

Devon spun Donagh around to face the kids, "Say you're sorry, Donagh."

Donagh puffed out air in a sigh, "Oh, all right. I'm sorry for scaring you. I just wanted to play."

Tom said to the kid, "Now you will accept Donagh's apology and forget that this ever happened."

"What? No way! If there are creatures out there like him, than people should be warned!" The kid argued.

"Oh really," Tom said as he flashed his fangs, the orange playground light glinting off of the four pointed teeth, "I would be more worried about creatures like us rather than creatures like him, young man."

Silent and unmoving until then, Garik put an arm across Tom's chest before stepping closer to the kids. He said in a gentle voice, "Look at me, please."

The kid stepped back in fear, dragging his girlfriend with him, "What are you going to do to us?"

Garik moved like a bullet to close the gap between them and cupped each of the teenagers' chins. He repeated in the same, calm voice, "Look at me, please."

Of course they couldn't do anything but look at him. The vampire was holding their faces directly at him. The humans' eyes widened in fear and then turned to a glossy calm. "You had a wonderful time tonight," Garik said, "but it's past your curfew and it's time to go home now."

The kids nodded very slowly as if they were in a trance.

Garik continued, "Be careful on your way home. Remember, there is no reason to ever come here at night."

The kids nodded more urgently in agreement. Garik let go of them. The girl and boy shook their heads a little bit to get out of the daze that Garik had created, but didn't move.

"Now go! Get out of here," Tom said. He stepped forward as if to antagonize the kids should they decide to stay.

The boy didn't hesitate. He grabbed the girl's hand, pulling her away with him as he said, "Let's go Missy! Come on! Let's get out of here!" They ran to one of the cars in the parking lot and drove away.

"Thanks, Garik," Tom said as he laughed at the nervous teenagers driving away.

"Just doing what the PD pays for," Garik smiled, humbly, but there was a twinkle in his eyes that made me feel like he actually enjoyed doing his job a lot. Garik turned to me, but spoke to Devon, "And is this your new protégé?"

Devon replied with a crooked grin. "Something like that. Keen, Garik. Garik, Keen," he said by way of introductions.

The short, teenage-looking vampire bowed his head slightly, "Pleasure to meet you."

"Uhm, thanks," I said, awkwardly, "you too." I didn't look him in the eye as I wasn't exactly sure what his job at the PD really entailed, but, judging by the reaction of the kids, it wasn't something I wanted tested on me.

Tom smirked at my reaction, "Our friend, Garik, is the resident mind-control freak."

"Eh?" I questioned, and gave my best perplexed look.

"Oh Tom, stop being ridiculous," Garik said, patronizing. Tom shrugged but glanced away. Garik turned to me and said in the same gentle voice he had with the humans, "I can suggest ideas while I'm talking with someone to get them to do things. For example, while I was talking to the humans, I was telling them one thing, but suggesting a new memory so that they wouldn't remember Donagh or us tonight."

"Does that work on anyone," I asked, still trying not to look him in the eye.

"No. Just humans. Unfortunately, I can't manipulate more complex creatures, including other vampires," Garik replied.

Oh good, I finally got the courage to look at him.

Immediately, he was right in front of me and reached up to my face, "Except, it might work on you. Here let me try,"

I shut my eyes tight and tried to push his hand away. He was a lot stronger than me, so my action didn't do any good, but he let go and started laughing. Tom and Devon joined in with him and I even heard high-pitched squawking from Donagh. I ventured a look, not happy with the joke Garik played on me.

"Very funny," I said.

"Ah, newbies," Garik said, "So gullible. But seriously Keen, I can only affect human thoughts and memories. They won't remember anything from the time right before they met Donagh until the time they left here and it'll be like no time passed."

Mind control. Nice! I thought.

Donagh tugged at Devon's shirt to get his attention, "Devon, I really didn't try to hurt them. I just wanted to have fun."

"I know, Donagh," Devon said.

Tom continued, "But, Donagh, humans don't get you like we do. We know you wouldn't do anything. Why don't you come by the apartment sometime? T would love to see you."

At that last statement, we heard T through our headsets, giggling, "Tell him I'll make some fish crackers and honey porridge for him if he does."

Tom conveyed the message and, with that, Donagh's face lit up into a huge grin. He agreed and spun off toward the playground swings.

We walked back to the cars and Devon said, "Thanks for coming down, Garik."

"No problem," Garik replied, "I've got a couple more runs to do tonight. Do you mind doing the paperwork on this one?"

"Tom?" Devon said.

"Sure. I've got ya covered, Garik," Tom responded. After a few more pleasantries, Garik got back into the police car and drove off.

I asked, "How old is that guy, anyway? He looks like he's thirteen!"

"Well, you're close," Tom said, "I think he said he was 15 when he was turned in 1940. He's the oldest vamp in the department, besides Acair. Just don't tell him he has a baby-face. He gets pretty pissed off about that."

"No problem," I said and then remembered why we had been there in the first place. "By the way, what the hell was that thing that was chasing those kids?"

Tom snickered at my response to the little creature, but Devon said, "Donagh is an Urisk from Scotland."

"Did you bring him here with you?" I wondered.

"No, he was here long before me."

We got into the car and Tom said, "They are some seriously misunderstood creatures."

"Care to elaborate?" I asked.

"Well, all they want to do is play, but with a face that not even a mother could love, they usually get the reaction you just saw," Tom noted.

After that, conversation was quiet in the big, deep blue beast of a car. Only the sounds of rain pounding the windows and the repeated squeak of the windshield wipers trying to battle it off were heard. I was sucked into my own thoughts; the kids in the playground had reminded me of some fun times when my high school friends and I had actually hung out in that same place. But I was also conflicted with thoughts of T and the teasing that we had done back in the apartment. Tom peeked from the backseat to lean his head onto my shoulder, "What'cha thinkin'?"

"Nothing," I replied. I didn't really want to share any of my confusing thoughts about Maddie and T, no matter how irrelevant the flirting seemed to be. *Especially with an over-protective brother.*

"Oh, you never want to talk anymore," He pouted and squeezed my shoulders playfully, but still feeling like a vise grip.

Devon reached over and smacked Tom upside the head, "Stop acting like such a girl, Tom."

"How would you know what a girl acts like," Tom said, "You've never had one."

I smirked at that comment.

"Like you've picked up anyone since you turned, Mack Daddy Tom," Devon joked.

Tom held his heart and fell back against the back seat, defeated. *So dramatic.*

"Seriously," Devon turned to me, "What's going on in that little, tiny, pea brain of yours?"

"I don't know, Devon, I just have a weird feeling about this," since that was the other thing running in my brain besides the two women in my life. *Wow, two women? What a stud.*

Except they aren't really in my life or even close to my playing field, are they?

"Well, what is it now, boy?"

"I don't know," I repeated, "Something important is going to happen. I just don't know what. I mean, come on. What the hell was all that about back at the apartment with Mr. Carmichael? What the hell is that?"

"I don't know, Keen, but stranger things have happened."

"No, Devon, I mean, what the hell is THAT?" I pointed out the front window at a dark shadow hovering over the road that had caught my eye just a second before.

"Oh shit," Devon said all too calmly as he slammed on the breaks and tried to swerve around what looked to be a person forming from the shadow. As the car skidded, the man, now looking like he was wearing a long, black raincoat over regular clothes, put his hand out as if to brace himself against being hit. A loud smack sounded and the engine died. The car stopped after turning a

180, facing itself in the exact opposite direction it had come from. Devon and I looked at each other and then at the road.

Nobody was there.

Tom, who was lying upside down with one foot above the backseat and his head behind my seat, broke the silence, "That's it! Next time, I'm driving!" He righted himself, "What the hell are you two doing? Trying to get us all killed? Again?"

Catching each other's eyes and thinking the same thing, Devon and I jumped out of the car without a word to Tom. I stooped down at the place where I thought I had seen the human standing. Devon looked around the small, dark city block with his far-reaching eyesight, trying to sense any movement. All that was to be seen were broken windows, boarded up doors and a few stray cats.

At my feet was an old beat up pocket watch. It was bronze with gold edging. I picked it up and opened it. The watch was heavy; it was real bronze and gold as far as I could tell by the weight of it. And it was still ticking. I closed it and turned it over to its backside. Engraved in an intricate design were the letters "A.C."

Tom had gotten out of the car and approached us. Looking at my hands, he asked in his kid-like way, "What'cha got there, Special K?"

I handed the watch to Tom as two blurs of motion were happening – Devon's hand grabbing the watch out of Tom's hand and Tom only grabbing air. Tom could only protest.

Devon shot him a look, "Chill." He looked at the initials on it and then glared around again at the city, trying harder to catch a glimpse of whatever had dropped the watch. But even with his acute eyesight, sharp hearing and sense of smell, he couldn't pick up anything out of the ordinary.

Nothing.

Everything was silent within the city block.

I took the watch back, mumbling, "A.C."

"Hmm," Devon absentmindedly responded.

"Would anybody like to tell me what is going on?" Tom asked.

"How 'bout letting me in on it too," came T's voice over our earpieces.

I responded to both of them, "Devon almost ran somebody over, except that whoever it was decided they didn't want to get hit. So they just disappeared."

"Man, how many times do I have to tell you guys to stop taking crack before you leave?" T joked.

"Well, you know me. I've been trying to quit, but once you take crack, you never go back."

T laughed but then said, "Keen, were you able to get an aura reading on the guy? Are you sure he was human?"

I had to think about that for a second, "No, there seemed to be a smoky, black fog around him. He was hazy."

Devon asked T, "Did you catch any of that on video from the car?" referring to the button sized camera attached to the front of the rear view mirror.

"But of course, sir."

"Good, try to find out what it was."

"Aye, Captain. Will do," she said whimsically.

"Oh and T? Order us some Thai food, will ya?"

"Who's payin'?" she asked shortly.

"Whoever answers the door," Devon teased.

"Ha. Ha." T replied sarcastically.

"Dinner is on Mr. Carmichael, Sis," Tom said.

Devon turned back to us, "Well, let's start looking around."

"We're not going to find anything," I predicted as I turned the watch over in my hand, "Whoever it was meant for us to see this and only this."

"Yeah! A wild goose chase," Tom smiled, "I just love me a wild goose chase."

Devon replied, ignoring us both, "Humor me."

I had a horrible feeling that we were being watched as we looked around and then returned to the car. As Tom was getting into the back of the car on my side, I glanced high up onto the buildings. My neck prickled in warning and I could've sworn that eyes were staring back at me. But as I couldn't get a good reading on it, and it was only serving to freak me out further, I got back into the car and shut the door. We took off, all silent in our own thoughts of the weirdness of the night.

Chapter 8

Even Stranger Things

☆ ☆ ☆

Discussions over Thai Food

We headed to the apartment since we were all hungry and we wanted to take a better look at the watch. I only vaguely realized that I had been fidgeting with it the entire time.

When we got back, T was stretched out on the couch, surrounded by opened Thai food boxes from the all-night restaurant that catered mostly to us freaks. She had obviously tried everything at least once. Having been tracking us through the cameras, she didn't spook when we came in.

Looking at the mess of boxes, I said, "Save anything for the boys?" I wasn't ready to try human food yet as it still smelled rotten to me. Thankfully, it wasn't nearly as putrid and vomit-inducing as it had been when I had first moved in. It seemed that since someone was always eating human food in the apartment, the burning sensations in my nose had slowly diminished and I was able to stay in the same room with it. It was like Devon and Tom were teenage boys eating their way through house and home. And T? Well, let's just say that T had no problem keeping up with the boys at all. She could've won the Annual Lobster Roll Eating contest and still have had room for blueberry pie.

"Little person, big appetite," she smiled and then belched through a bite.

"Niiiccce. Real sexy there, sweetheart," I responded amused, impressed and slightly disgusted at the same time.

"What did you get on that video, little sis?" Tom said.

Devon moved to where the video screens and computer were as T replied, "Nada. Nothing more than a haze or mist or something."

"You're kidding, right?" Devon said more as a statement then a question, "We saw him."

"We saw something," I balked, second guessing myself.

"Well, whatever you saw did not want to be seen because none of the sensors picked up anything more than the rain with a little fog. But if you don't believe me, check it out for yourself." She slinked into the chair in front of Devon and pulled up the video. She ran it in slow motion several times, but as she said, there was nothing unusual except for a random mist in the street that could've easily been caused by the rain and humidity.

"I wonder," Devon took the helm and dragged the computer mouse to box in the mist. He magnified it and moved the view of it around. He enhanced it through some sort of software program that I had yet to figure out.

"Ah, see that?" Devon finally said.

"See what?" Tom said through with a mouthful of Thai food, now crowding around into us to get a look. My nose immediately wrinkled with the foulness of the food and his poisonous saliva mixed together. *Ech! Didn't anyone ever teach you to eat with your mouth closed.*

"Is that a hand?" T sounded almost appalled.

I pointed at the screen, "That looks kinda like the watch," and pulled the watch out of my pocket where I had absently put it earlier.

"I don't believe it," Devon said, "First a rogue gargoyle now this."

"Now what?" I questioned again, not sure I really wanted to know the answer, "What else have we gotten ourselves into?"

"That is an Aswang."

My right eyebrow arched up, *Hadn't I just heard that term before?*

"A Changeling."

I know I still looked clueless since that was how I was feeling.

"A shapeshifter," Devon tried to get my pea-brain to understand the names he was using – like I had heard them all before and I was being a complete imbecile to not get what he was saying now.

"Good luck catching that," T sounded excited at the thought.

Tom, however, did not, "And the hits just keep on comin'."

"A gargoyle and a changeling. Now all we need is a wicked stepmother and a good witch and we'll really have ourselves a good old-fashioned fairy tale." I said.

T smiled, "We already have a good witch. Veleda."

So I repeated my sentence with that minor adjustment, "Ok, fine. A gargoyle, a changling and the good witch, Veleda. All we need now is the wicked stepmother."

"This is serious, Keen," Tom replied.

"How serious?" I said flippantly.

"Serious enough to refund the Thai food Tom and T just ate and turn down the rest of the money," Devon responded.

"Let me see the watch," T requested. I handed it over. She depressed the button on top to open it and check the inside. There was nothing unusual within except, unlike the outside, its face looked as if it had never been viewed and it seemed very expensive. She closed it and opened it. Closed it. Opened it. Closed it. Opened it. She flipped it over and around and then closed it again. Once more, she opened it.

"Hey, what time is it?" She finally said.

"3:15 am," came the response from Tom.

"This clock is set to 8," She pulled on the area that acts as both the face reader and the timing mechanism and turned the knob. As the hands passed 1 on the face, a small, barely audible click occurred and the back of the watch, the side with the initials, A.C., swung open. A piece of folded parchment fell out. Black polished nails caught and opened it. T read it and handed it to Devon.

"2125 North Eastern Promenade," Devon read out loud. "Google it, T."

✲ ✲ ✲

A Destination Uncovered

It was just past mid-morning and we were getting off *Carmilla* to head toward the Eastern Promenade and the address that had slipped from the pocketwatch. I had requested to go back out to Sweet Haven's at sunrise and watch my parents eating breakfast on the island. I don't know what it was, but I just wanted to be part of their day, even if I couldn't really be part of it. I missed them and it was tearing me up inside. Devon understood when I asked if we could just keep that standing time with them for a little while until I got myself together. As long as it didn't interfere with PD obligations, he said he wouldn't mind taking me out there daily. I was grateful to him. One day I might not need to visit them, but that time had not come yet.

It didn't take long to drive from the docks up to the Eastern Promenade as it was only a mile away. The day was beautiful, the sky was bright blue with clouds moving in from the west and the bay was only a slight bit ruffled from the wind. As we got out of the car, I locked my attention back onto the investigation and put thoughts of my parents aside. The three of us, as T was back at the apartment doing homework for her afternoon classes, stood in front of 2125 North Eastern Promenade. *What's left of it.*

"It looks like a bomb exploded here," Tom said, "And not a well-planned bomb at that."

The stone house had been completely gutted out. What had once been a three story house was now a culmination of stone walls with grooves for where the wood floor had been carved into them. Only one chimney stood untouched, like a soldier still on duty for a war that had already ended. The inferno had been so hot that glass from the windows had melted into pools of dark bubbles mixed with ash.

We walked around the first floor. *Really the only floor now.* Bits of wood from what must have been chairs and tables, scarred like burned flesh, laid about on soot-embalmed pieces of rug. We could tell the fire had occurred several years before as Mother Nature had been greedily reaching at the ruins with long, green fingers of grass and plants. To our supersensitive noses, however, the sweet smell of smoldering wood was still in the air.

We moved toward the center of the floor-plan where there was more debris. As Devon stepped on a pile of crisscrossed pieces of wood and debris, we heard a grinding noise, not audible to the human ear. It sounded like metal scraping against wood. Devon bent down and moved the burnt pieces out of the area, exposing a trap door. Metal, heavy and dull to the touch.

"This isn't normal for houses in this area," Devon said, "On the Promenade, houses with basements were made with normal door entries, not floor doors."

"Look at the markings on the door," I took out the coin Mr. Carmichael had given us. "The drawings are the same, only on the door, it looks like a language of some sort."

Tom pointed his head down a little bit and spoke into his headset, "T, we're sending you some footage. Can you see what these markings mean?"

"On it," T's voice was short.

"Wait a minute," Devon turned to me, "Do you still have that dagger?"

I pulled it out from behind my back and handed it over. He took the coin as well. *That's where I've seen those markings before.*

"These are exactly the same," Devon said as I was finishing my internal thoughts. Devon moved both items to one hand and then used the other to pick up the heavy steel latch. He pulled.

Nothing.

There was a slit under where the latch had been. I saw it as Devon picked it up. I had an idea, "Devon, give me the dagger."

He returned it to me. I took the sheath off, revealing the sharp blade which, again, glowed briefly. I placed the tip into the slot and turned it. The lock moved to the right. I pulled on the latch and the door came up with my motions.

"Neat trick," Tom said.

We all looked through the doorway to see a narrow, circling staircase.

I bent over the space below and then looked at Devon, "I nominate you to go first. Who's with me?"

Tom added, "Yeah, not it."

Devon stood up, "Chicken shits."

"That's fair," I replied with a stupid grin on my face.

Tom smiled, "I'll agree to that."

Devon turned around and began walking down the winding stairway at just slightly faster than average speed. I followed and then Tom. What little light from the sun that had passed through the hole quickly trickled away as we made our way further down.

The passage, with its stone walls and wooden floors covered in the dankness of sea salt and moss, creaked under our weight. Our vampire eyes adjusted quickly to the dimming light, all ready to see even in the blackest of darkness. Unlit sconces were in place on the walls – not covered in dust or cobwebs like one might expect, but not used recently either. A draft was coming from below and the faintest sounds of water began to shift into a clear roar as we continued downward.

Since I was still getting used to my vampire senses, I felt claustrophobic and a slow knot of dread built in my stomach, "Anyone else getting a little bored with this? I mean, remember, what goes down has to come back up, and this qualifies as too many stairs my ass doesn't want to have to climb."

"By the sounds of it," Devon started, "We're heading toward the underground estuary system that flows back into the ocean. All these houses 'round here were built on top of the tide zone. My guess is this will turn into a passage with an opening into the bay."

"And the car?" I asked.

Devon said in his no-nonsense manner, "It's secured. We'll pick it up later."

We continued down the stairs and, just as Devon suspected, it turned into a path. Though the streams were not yet visible, the rush of water could be heard on either side of the walls and even the dirt path and wood ceiling seemed to ooze with sound. Stopping just past the threshold between the stairway and the path, I sniffed the air, "Ok, I get the pine and salt. But what is that burnt undertone?"

"You're smelling pitch," Devon answered, his voice sounding annoyed at the question, like he was trying to concentrate on the surroundings and my questions were pestering, "These walls and floors are waterproofed. At this level, we're probably surrounded by the ocean."

As we walked forward, further into the pathway, I noticed that our steps shifted from sounding like we were walking on gravel rocks to walking on something crunchy like cracking open a lobster shell. I bent over to pick up what was causing the out-of-sync noise.

Bones.

"Arrgh!" I jumped back in surprise and right into Tom, dropping the item I picked up. My eyes explored the floor, *Bones everywhere!* I called the other two vamp's attention, as Devon was walking ahead and Tom was rubbing his foot where I landed on it, "Guys? Please tell me these are all animal bones."

We scanned around our feet and the surrounding area. Some of the bones were still soft and fleshy. *Leathery.* Devon crouched down, picked up a bone, scrutinized it, and then tossed it a short distance away, "Well, they're mostly animal."

A chill crept up me, "I'm not sure I really want to know who decided to have their snack all the way down here."

"For someone who just got a bunch of kick-ass abilities, you sure are a twitchy fellah," Tom said to me.

"Yeah, well," I shrugged, unapologetically. *I still feel so human, though. At least, I think I do.*

"Ok, we've wasted enough time. Let's keep going," Devon said and then took off into the black distance. Tom and I shot a competitive glance at each other and then ran to catch up.

As fast as peregrines in flight, we reached a wall at the far end of the tunnel with a rusted metal ladder heading up about three stories. We had been running hard for almost ten minutes through the winding, bone-strewn path, but not a single bead of sweat dropped from our brows. Tom slapped me on the stomach with the honor of having beaten me to the end.

Mentally we did the rock, scissors, papers routine before Tom realized he was the only one that hadn't gone first in any situation. He started up the ladder. At the top, there was a trap door similar to the one we had descended through. He was able to unlock it from that side and pushed it open after pausing to listen for movement from the other side. He passed through and disappeared for a minute or two before showing his face and calling us up to ground level.

We climbed up into a small room constructed from granite, brick and wood, in which Tom was too tall to stand up straight. There was an open space where, presumably, there had been a window at one time. Looking around, there were three other trap doors that were identical to the one we had climbed through. Each door had similar markings similar to the one back at the Promenade. I opened each one only to find them filled to the top with salt water.

A small door opening on the opposite side of the room led us to an arched corridor. The right side had more of the same small rooms and to the left was a large courtyard with evenly spaced granite columns running around the sides.

Why does this place look so familiar?

As we stepped out into the courtyard, the gray, sunless sky greeted us with a swirling light above, hitting the clouds at regular intervals. *The clouds moved in quicker than I thought they were going to.* A ship's horn sounded – deep and hollow, breaking the silence of the day. The courtyard opened before us in a surreal vision. Rough, old stone walls with trees growing from their tops surrounded us. The structure had six sides, with five of the walls equal in length creating angles that formed a semi-circle. We had come from a corner where one of the small walls met up with the long wall that ran the diameter of the building. Four-foot-high alcoves led to heavy-barred window holes. Rusted cannons still sat guarding the coast of the mainland.

"I know this place," I said, dreamily walking further into the courtyard.

"You should. We pass it twice a day visiting your parents," Devon said.

"This is that old, island military base, the one you can only get to if you row to it," Tom concluded.

"Yeah, it's Fort Dune, 'the last strong hold,' right?" I asked.

Devon was thoughtful for a second, "I think that's what they called it back in the Civil War era."

Ocean water hit the walls with the rising tide. It clouded the atmosphere with echoes. Suddenly, a bad feeling crawled up my neck with its razor-sharp intensity and a split second later we heard a weird sound from above us. A whooshing sound beat against my ear drums, pushing and pulling at the internal pressure, and wind blew across my face as if a small homemade helicopter was hovering.

We all looked up at the same time.

"Oh!" I started.

"Shit!" Tom finished as he too began to back away.

But he wasn't quick enough.

Three silver arrows came raining down on us as Devon and I used our super-speed to back out of the courtyard. Tom was hit with one of the arrows in the shoulder and let out a snarl of pain that made all of our fangs jolt out in anger. With a screech, he yanked on the arrow, panting as the silver head came out dripping like it had started to dissolve in Tom's flesh. The arrow dropped to the ground and Tom fell to his knees in agony as his body began to dispel the silver and heal the wound.

Forgetting just how quick my vampire responses were, I misjudged the distance to get back to the corridor and knocked my head into one of the curved archways. I dropped to the ground and began to lose consciousness as hard stone dropped around me. I tried to shake my head back into awareness. *Probably not the best idea.*

Little green and blue starbursts flooded my eyes. *Stay awake, stay awake! The guys need you!*

I tried to get up but fumbled back down, smacking my chin and sending a whole new wave of sparks through my eyes.

Devon recovered quickly from the surprise attack and flashed his fangs. A yelling snarl escaped him, "Gargoyle!"

He jumped fifteen feet up and at an angle as he flung himself onto the wing and neck of the large, muscular creature.

I tried, the best I could, to follow the action and get myself back into it. I was failing miserable.

The gargoyle was nine feet tall with deep green, stone-like skin, weathered, old, and cracking like a Greek ruin. Its 7-foot wings expanded and contracted quickly to keep it afloat and beat hard wind around it after Devon jumped on. The beast stretched out its right arm to grab at Devon, who clung to its neck. It grabbed him easily with four chiseled claws and tossed him below. Devon's body folded into a neat pile, almost like he had fallen asleep in the dent he made in the ground upon impact.

Tom, having recovered from the arrow, ran at the beast, leaped up over it and side kicked him in the jaw. The gargoyle grabbed his foot and used Tom's momentum to throw him over to the third floor of the garrison, where he crashed through the concrete blocks and into a cannon room.

I tried shaking my head of the stars I was seeing, but I couldn't straighten myself out nor could I get to my feet. I was too dizzy. The pain was more than what I would've been able to stand when I had been human, but *I am just not strong enough yet.*

As the gargoyle landed, Devon got back up and attacked again punching him with lightening fast uppercuts and side jabs. The gargoyle easily slipped past some hits to get in some of his own and Devon started to look like he was taking a beating. White-ish splotches appeared on his dark face where the gargoyle had hit him. *Anti-blood equals anti-bruises?* I thought as I saw my own clear blood dripping to the ground.

The gargoyle turned its stone black eyes to Devon's and punched him hard in the face. Even with the strength of Devon's age behind him, he was no match for the granite fists of the gargoyle. Devon landed, bloodied, on the flat courtyard. Then I saw something odd. *I must be hallucinating. Is this what happens when vampires have concussions?*

It was as if the gargoyle began to change. *IS changing. But I'm not going mad, am I?* The shape of the body began to diminish; its wings began to fold in on themselves. The gargoyle half floated half walked past Devon. He looked like he was heading toward me.

This is not good. Get up! Get your lazy ass up, Keen!

As I pushed myself up with arms that felt like lead, my eyes caught on his and I fell back to the ground. All the while, the colors of his aura were going in and out, changing hues and denseness as his physical appearance turned. Twisting and struggling in itself. *Is he going to implode?*

And then, the gargoyle was no longer just that. He was a man in a black trench coat. I watched as little dust-ups swirled around the bottom of it as he flowed toward me – his feet not yet touching the ground. It reminded me of the vampire Acair briefly, but this creature was no vampire. *Nor is he human or a gargoyle.* His aura stayed blue and pulsed from the center of his body, not around his form as other peoples' auras did.

Realization hit me as my eyes closed into the darkness of unconsciousness, though I fought like hell to force them open. Two gnarled hands reached down to me and the trench coat, which now resembled more of a cloak, surrounded me. I heard the vampires scream, snarling in protest. I felt the air swirl around me and thought, *Oh crap, the Aswang has me.* And then, everything went black.

✵ ✵ ✵

Enter Reality, Stage Right

I was sitting on a bench in Lincoln Park, just watching the water flow from the fountain that was in the center of the big square commons. There weren't very many benches there, and even though it was a busy day, I was fortunate and was able to get one by myself. Of course, I had arrived early enough and watched as the park filled with morning runners, mothers walking in pairs with their children in strollers, and sun bathers. Young children were creating their own adventures on blankets laid out for picnics whereas the older children were looking for ways to be up to no-good.

The bench I was on faced away from the fountain, so in order to view the water, I had to force my body into an awkward angle. But it wasn't uncomfortable – quite the contrary. I just used the battered armrest to lean against and, occasionally, I shifted my focus from the fountain to do some people watching.

Three little boys walked by me, giggling and telling dirty jokes. They were probably headed down to the ice cream trolley that had just pulled up. They stopped just past me to dig through their pockets and pull out any change they had. A brown hand, a white hand and a tan hand all held out in the center of the group, they counted quickly and began to even up the change between them. Once they were happily settled on the division, they nodded seriously, closed their hands in tight fists around the money and ran like the wind to go get their prize. A couple walking in from the direction of the ice cream trolley had to quickly jump out of the way in order to avoid getting hit by the rambunctious boys. They were on a mission, and that was clear enough.

The chimes from the church down the way rang hollow and quick like it didn't really want to be bothered in telling the town what time it was. Another church further up wind mocked the other one by playing a bright and delightful song in its electronically tinny sound. Pigeons squawked at the battling noises and flapped away from the brunch of seeds that someone had thrown down for them.

It was eleven o'clock in the morning and the day was already warm. The sky was a bright blue with very few clouds floating around.

I thought about how I hadn't been there in a long time, and how, for being in the middle of a down-town area, it still felt secluded. It wasn't like being on the water or hiking in the forests, but it was peaceful enough for days I couldn't get away.

I smelled the sweetness of her perfume before I saw her. I heard her sigh and I turned toward the sound.

Maddie.

Beautiful, loving Maddie. *She found me. I knew she would.*

She approached and I stood; I could see her hesitance in it. She wrung her hands nervously in front of her, they were tan against the baby pink tank she was wearing. Her floral skirt danced around her and I followed the length of it down her amazingly toned legs to the strappy sandals that wrapped from mid-calf to her feet, a throw back to Greek styling. She put her hand up to my face to touch my cheek to see if I was real. "You're alive?" she whispered in a melodic voice.

I nodded, but I couldn't resist her closeness, *It's been too long.* I picked her up. She felt so light in my arms it was like I had picked up a butterfly. I spun around and took in her beautiful smell as her body pressed close to mine. She cupped both hands around my face and kissed me gently again and again, breathlessly saying my name in-between kisses. "It's really you," she said, sounding relieved, "But..." She drew her head back and held her hand up to my cheek. She searched my face quizzically, "Something looks different about you."

I held her hand to my face, reveling in the warmth of it and her body that I still embraced with my other arm, but I didn't answer her. My only thoughts were, *So many things are different – I wonder if she'll be able to accept it. Accept me.* I closed my eyes as my thoughts warred between the emotions of seeing her: sadness at what I had become and incredible elatedness because she was finally in front of me. Instead of speaking, I sighed and set her down.

God I missed her so much! The scent of her lingered on me and it was so much stronger with my new senses. *So entrancing.* Her skin danced in the light. Her blue eyes sparkled. *This is where I belong.*

With her, in my arms. "I've missed you, Maddie," I whispered as I hugged her again.

"I missed you too, Keen. You have no idea," she sighed as she stepped back from me. Maddie reached for my hand and entwined her long fingers around mine, "I know we should talk, but I just want to be with you right now."

We turned from the fountain and she guided me off the path to one of the giant maple trees in the park. She put her hands on my shoulders and pushed me down to the grass. It was still a little dewy and I could feel the moisture from the dirt through my jeans and boxers. But I didn't care as my love looked down at me, her sweet smile quirked. I took her hands in mine and pulled her towards me. She laid her head on my chest, tracing it with her fingers.

The park completely disappeared from us. Even the sounds of the people walking by, the cars honking their horns on the other side of the fence and the pigeons vanished from my awareness. All I could see was her.

I pulled my hand through her shiny, silky hair. It was stunning.

"You're so beautiful," I whispered.

She looked up at me, smiling. Her lips were bright and inviting. She slid her hand upon my chest, pushing my shirt up and surprising me, "Maddie," I said as I pushed her hands back, "There are people around." Although we had moved off the path, there was a chance that someone could walk by us.

"Shh," she said as she moved my shirt to show a little skin again, "They won't see us." She pouted – the expression she always used to get me to bend to her will.

How can I resist that look? But then her fingernails cut into me, drawing clear liquid on my chest. It hurt, and with my surprise, I caught her hand up in mine. Since I didn't want to hurt her, my grip was very light and she pulled free of me easily. She began unbuckling my belt and went to slide her hand down my pants.

"Maddie?" I looked at her, questioning. She'd never been this bold before. *What's going on here?*

She put her hand back on my chest and looked up at me again, but her eyes were no longer blue. They were black. Their shape had become less round and more narrow. She came at me with black eyes, bared fangs and night-dark, curly hair.

I woke up with a start.

✿ ✿ ✿

The Glow Stick

Fuzzy. Everything is so fuzzy.

Blinking my dazed eyes clear, I realized that I wasn't in my room back in the apartment on Exchange Street. A few seconds later, I remembered what had happened. I shot straight up and onto my feet. I had been lying on a bed. My hand went up to the back of my head, remembering the smack I took against the fort's wall. Thankfully, it didn't hurt. If I had been in my previous form, I would've woken up with a killer migraine and a huge egg on the back of my head. But, *Sometimes it's good to be a vamp!*

My hand went down my back and I lifted up my shirt. No dagger.

"Shit."

I reached into my ear.

Nothing. *Crap, the ear piece is gone.*

I threw off my left shoe. Devon had made me give it to him before we had left the day before. He'd cut a small hole in it. I assumed that it was for a tracer. Unfortunately, that was gone too.

"Damn it."

Time to search the room.

There were no lights on, but my cat-like eyes could see every shape of furniture, every painting on the wall. All the colors were dull though, washed out, almost gray. There was a dresser across the way and two nightstands on either side of the bed with a lamp on each. I reached over to the one on my right and turned the knob below the light bulb. I clicked it to the on position, but no light came on.

I quickly tried the left one.

Neither of them worked. *No light. That's mildly annoying.* I checked under the delicately frilled shade. "Don't these people believe in light bulbs? Electricity isn't that expensive," I said out-loud, annoyed.

There were two doors in the room, one to the left of the dresser and one on the right-side wall. Walking at a slow-for-me speed over to the door to the left of the dresser, I put my ear against it. It wasn't necessary since my vamp ears made it possible for me to hear at least two people breathing in the house. But, out of habit from watching too many bad horror movies, I felt it was a good idea. For good measure, I held my breath and listened for movement that I already knew wasn't there.

I turned the knob and opened it slowly. Sliding my hand up the smooth wall, I flipped the switch up. A harsh, yellow light flooded the room and I blinked to clear the momentary shock of green spots from my eyes. It was a bathroom.

The light spilled into the bedroom as I backed out of the doorway. The colors were muted reds, golds, and greens around the room. The massive four-post bed was antique, dark mahogany wood with rich comforters and pillows dressing it. There was barely an indentation where I had been laying.

The rest of the furniture was the same antique mahogany. The floor was wood with a rug that spanned the fullness of the bed and nightstands. It came out about three feet at the bed's end. I went over to the other door. It was very thick, but I wasn't sure what it was made of. I breathed in deeply. It smelled modern. *Like painted metal to look like wood?* The walls along it seemed very thick as well. I tried to open the door anyway, but after pulling hard on it, all I got was a shiny door knob for a prize.

Hearing footsteps getting louder from the other side of the door, I backed up against the wall, preparing to jump whoever walked through. The door flew open. I leapt at the form that came through and...

I fell straight onto the ground, completely missing my target.

A hard laugh came from the inside corner of the room, opposite the door entry, "You're going to need to be quicker than that, Vampire, if you wish to catch me."

Ass.

A slight clicking sound confirmed that the door had shut again. *Damn it, I missed my opportunity.* As I gathered myself up, my attention shifted to the corner where the voice had come from. *What the hell is this thing now? It looks like a human-shaped glow stick.*

His aura color shifted from blue to gray to green to brown and back to blue. Sparks of red and black were highlighted through it. The colors changed as his body continually contorted into different shapes – first a furry, wolf-like beast, then into the familiar stone gargoyle, then into something that looked like a scaly lobster, then a turtle, then a moss-covered boulder form.

The changes were so quick, though, that I imagined all a human would have seen was a head, two hands, two legs and a blur of constant motion around his body. Maybe *of cloth whipping around in the wind*? Either way, it was a nauseating motion and I turned away for a second to clear my head. After a few minutes, I did notice that his aura did not go away. It was constantly in flux around him, shifting like light from a prism on a wall as sun and wind hit it.

The glow stick thing was a few inches shorter than me and that light was also radiating from his center. His hands were two burned shells with blackened, withered fingers. *I remember him. This is the jerk that grabbed me back at the fort.*

I immediately went into a ready-to-strike stance, a snake-like hiss escaping my lips as I bared my teeth.

The figure rolled his eyes at me. As he did so, his core movements slowed down and the light around him began to dim as he changed into a completely human form. The light emanating from his chest did not lessen, though it settled to a blue.

"Welcome to the home of Mr. Carmichael, Sir." The figure was formal in tone, a husky, scraping voice that spoke like reeds shaking against each other.

"I would thank you, Sir," I returned formally, as I straightened my stance, "but I would have rather woken in my own bed, preferably with some hot, young chick keeping me warm."

Dropping the pretense, he said in a harsh mocking voice, "That hell hole? I've seen it. No woman would be in their right mind to join you there. Except for that pretty little girl.. What do you call her? Oh yes, 'T.'"

I really did my best to not flinch when he said T's name. I didn't like it at all that he knew any of us, "At least our place has working lights, unlike here where I have to use a human glow-stick, or whatever you are, to brighten the place up," *Ok, immature, but whatever.*

The figure flashed a hint of red before returning to a calm blue, "Mildly amusing, Mr. Panofsky, but you should already be used to the dark, why would you even need light?"

"Ok, fine. Whatever. How about we skip the crappy small talk and you tell me why I'm here," my patience was wearing thin.

"Oh no, I don't think I could do that," He pulled two gloves from his pockets and put them on over his hands.

"How about who you are, then?" *Give me a fricken break.*

He bowed deep and low, making a sweeping motion with his hands, came up and smiled.

This guy is a real asshole. I struck my best Scotty, from Star Trek, voice, "Will you be tellin' me anything, or am I just gonna play twenty questions all by me lonesome?"

The figure laughed, "All in due time, young vampire. All in due time. Your host will speak with you shortly and then he may or may not tell you anything."

He winked with a horrible, half human-, half-creature-looking eye, "In the meantime, stop trying to find a way to escape because there is none. All the doors in the house are vampire proof. But do try to get settled in because you may be here for a while," He paused and shrugged his thin shoulders, "Or maybe not."

Geez, he is just full of information, I thought, sarcastically.

The light began to slowly build from the creature again as he walked across the room to the door. He waved his crispy hand along the area where the door knob had been. It opened, no need of a knob. As the figure took his leave, I stood there, glaring at him. Hating him. With a lock of the door, I was alone with only the bathroom light shadowing the room. I decided to search the room more thoroughly and ram myself against the door to the outside a few times, but the guy had been right, there was no way to escape. Nor was there anything I could use either. There was nothing under the bed; the frame came all the way down to touch the floor like the beds you find in hotel rooms to keep you from losing articles of clothing. The dressers, too, were empty. No coats were hanging in the closet. No secret compartments – I know because I knocked. There wasn't even a speck of dust to keep me company.

I grew tired of searching, so I just paced back and forth between the antique bed and the tall dresser. Back and forth. Back and forth. Back and...

I slumped down on the bed, bored and annoyed.

✷ ✷ ✷

Meet Mr. Carmichael PT 2

I was starting to get hungry. *Real hungry.* It had to be near day break, or so my internal clock was telling me, but without windows in the room, I couldn't be sure. The good news was that I didn't have too much time to dwell on it, as the door to my room opened again. The human glow-stick waiting patiently outside said, "Mr. Carmichael is ready for you," and with the sweeping motion he seemed to love to do, he gestured toward the door as if he was a mere butler showing a guest around.

I walked out in front of him and waited outside the room, my eyes adjusting to the light, causing a slight headache that would pound for a second, heal, pound again, and then heal. *This is so weird.* I didn't like it at all – it was like a hammer hitting a metal pipe, pinging against it. *Ping... Ping... Ping. Ech, this blows.*

The door to the room I was in was at the end of a very long hallway. The walls were adorned with heavy, dark-textured paper and chandelier-esque sconces that made the hall take on an obscenely long-looking length – Gothic and disturbing. *I'm never going to get to the end of this thing.*

I followed the guy down the way to a gently curving stairwell. The first landing broke off in two directions: down another hallway that was very similar to the one we had just come from or down another set of stairs.

We took the stairs.

The next landing opened to a grand stairwell, with the same dark and heavily patterned walls and carpet as before. The grand effect of them gave me a shot of vertigo and I stumbled over myself as we started down the final set of stairs. It was so slight and barely out of step, but the glow-stick noticed anyway.

"Not too graceful for a vamp, are you," my guide said.

Not too graceful for a vamp, are you, my head mocked in a teenager's voice, but verbally, I didn't say a thing.

When I straightened up and looked around, I noticed more doors to my right, but, oddly, there were no wall hangings, pictures, mirrors or anything. Only a chair rail and the many doors seemed to break up the pattern.

Two sets of stairs came together, meeting to form a balcony that joined in the middle to create the final steps. These led to the next floor down. From the grand chandelier above the center stair, I ascertained, *This must be the main entry way to the mansion.*

My eyes darted around so fast that in an instant I was able to take in any potential exits. If there were windows in this place, they were few and far between and very hidden. There was no natural light to speak of, only the dull yellow of the wall sconces and the bright glittering from the chandelier. Small, colorful prisms danced on the floor and walls as the crystals hanging from above broke up the beams. In my mental mapping of the room, I found the front door. It was unguarded, but there was something odd about it.

No door knob.

There wasn't even a dead lock on it. Nothing but an empty thick wooden door. *Well, maybe it was wood.* There wasn't even a panel to the side of the door for a keypad or any kind of locking mechanism. *Bizarre.*

As if reading my mind the guy said, "I told you there was no way to escape. These doors are magically bound. Only those with permission from Mr. Carmichael can open them."

Ok, that's pretty damn cool, if I say so myself. Crazy. But cool. I tried to look unimpressed and not as worried as I was. *A place without exits was not a good place to be in.*

My guide, who looked more like a human the more steps he took, led me into a room left of the stairs. Like in all the old, creepy movies, the room was a library with floor to ceiling books, mostly in worn leather bindings. "Please wait here," he said, "and don't touch anything. Some of these books are worth more than the Devil's own soul and he's still pissed we have them."

Glaring into his half human-shaped eyes, I couldn't help but wonder, *Is he joking?*

Man, I hope he is joking.

I nodded and watched as the glow-stick backed out of the room, closing the French doors behind him and locking me in. Turning back around to the room, I quickly took in the lay of the land. There was a large, mahogany desk at the back side of the room. It matched the design of the furniture in the room I had woken up in. Two couches in front of the desk sat facing each other. They were deep, burgundy leather with gold studding around the edging. A glass table with mahogany legs was in the middle of the couches.

I walked around the walls of the library, every once in awhile dodging a sliding ladder that I was half tempted to try out to see how far it would roll with one push. But I reminded myself I was a guest in the house. Until something bad happened to me in his company, I wasn't going to be malicious or give in to childish whims. *No matter how much I want to.*

Reading the labels, I found some of the most obscure titles on the books. Some were old, some newer, but all were hiding behind leather bindings with gold, engraved titles. Some books were just so old that they were bound originally in leather.

"These are not your parents' Encyclopedia Britannica's," a familiar male voice startled me.

I've got to get better at using these vampire skills or I may get voted off the island.

Chapter 9

The Prophecy

✼ ✼ ✼

In the Library

"Ｈow is your head feeling, Mr. Panofsky?" Mr. Carmichael began, "Eammon tells me you knocked yourself around a bit in the old fort. We were afraid you may have given yourself a concussion, if that's possible. I had Eammon remove the lights in your room as to not bother you."

Well that explains the lack of light bulbs, and here I thought it was just to freak me the hell out. Which it didn't do, but... I glared at the glow-stick standing behind a tired looking Mr. Carmichael, "So you do have a name."

"Of course I do, silly boy. You never said the magic word," His voice was raspy and sharp, like I was a child being scolded.

"Oh excuse me. I'm sorry.... Was it supposed to be 'Who are you, Asshole'?"

Eammon's center light flared red.

"Temper, temper, Amy," I eased into a smarmy smile – my lips pursed in sarcasm. *I really do not like this guy.*

The aura around Mr. Carmichael had temporarily changed from just blue to blue with bright, lemon-yellow flashes as he stepped in, "Eammon, will you please bring our guest a couple of bottles of Bloody Captain? And I would like some tea,"

"I'll take the beers, but hold the poison, Amy," I grinned, liking this mispronunciation of Eammon's name.

Eammon smiled a sneer but nodded and walked out, closing the doors behind him.

Mr. Carmichael moved to stand next to a large and comfortable-looking leather chair behind the desk. "Mr. Panofsky, I know that you are wondering why I had Eammon bring you here, so I won't delay us any further."

He triggered a button under the desk. Several areas around the room, amongst the shelves of books, flipped up. The new spaces held laminated, glass boxes, each holding a single book. There were thirteen books in all and they were bound in silver, gold, copper, or black leather. They were all different sizes and one was even triangular in shape.

Mr. Carmichael walked out from behind the desk and over to where the first box appeared in the room. I used my vampire speed to move next to him. He didn't flinch but only shifted his eyes down to the glass box. I followed his glance. It contained a book made of six pages of gold. The pages were covered in a text that I could not understand and had an image of a horseman on it.

Mr. Carmichael stuck his thumb on an unlocking mechanism and, after it read the thumb print, the casing opened up. Mr. Carmichael put on a pair of white lint-free gloves that were lying behind the book. He gently picked it up.

"This book is over two-and-a-half thousand years old and written in Etruscan, a lost language of the people who once lived in what is now Italy and Corsica. Among antique dealers, it is thought the oldest book known to humankind, although I will show you otherwise. It was only discovered half a century ago in a tomb in Bulgaria by a worker building a road. The 'paper' is made from 24-carat gold and it's priceless."

Mr. Carmichael replaced the book, removed his gloves and closed the box, reengaging the lock on it. He then proceeded past two other cases and stopped at another one.

"This book is not really a book," he continued. I looked down. It was actually a black leather box with yellowed, thin, almost see-through paper attached to card stock. I recognized the script as Hebrew, but couldn't quite make out the words.

Mr. Carmichael continued, "This is writing on toilet paper by a prisoner who was held in Palestine after the British captured him in 1939. The man who wrote this fought, after his release, for Palestine against the Nazis in World War II, played a large role in the capture of Jerusalem during the Six Day War and later became Israel's Defense Minister. These letters were to his wife about life in the prison during the two years he was there. When I bought these, they were worth just under six million dollars."

His quirked up lip suggested that they were worth much more than that, but any million dollars was too high of a number for me to fathom.

We walked on, with Mr. Carmichael continuing his recollection of each book and their values as we passed it. It was as if he was seeing them for the first time, like he was surprised he owned all of these rarities. The best word for it was 'odd.' It just seemed odd to me. Well, to be quite honest, the whole situation seemed odd to me. But hey, what did I know? Up until a few weeks before, I would've thought anyone who mentioned anything about vampires, gargoyles, aswangs or anything of the sort was odd. *Or just out of their freaken' minds.*

But, seriously, the way Mr. Carmichael was moving around and looking at things in the room was more than odd. It was as if the tour we were on was the first for him as well. But I guess, maybe he was just admiring his handy work at procuring such precious gems. I couldn't afford spending more than ten dollars at a half-price book store for three books. And this man had spent millions for one.

I was shaken from my thoughts when Mr. Carmichael rushed gracefully, but purposely, to the end of the room. Luckily he didn't notice that, for a split second, I hadn't been paying attention. I'm sure he would've thought that very rude. But as quickly as my thoughts processed these days, I didn't think anyone would have noticed if I sat around trying to resolve the theory of time travel.

"This," Mr. Carmichael said excitedly as we reached the last holding case in the room, "is why I brought you here. I bought this at an auction 3 years ago. It took me fifteen years to track it down." He paused, "It's over forty-five hundred years old."

I peered down at the glass case. In it wasn't a book, but a six-sided, intricately designed, sterling-silver scroll holder that was about fifteen inches in length. The top of the case had a dome that ended in a bulbous crown shape. The bottom had the same dome as the other end, but with a crank on the bottom to help draw the scroll back in. The latch was wing-shaped, each feather showing soft detail, like they were flying in wind.

Did something just move on it?

Getting a little closer to the case, I saw that the cylindrical body of the scroll holder had red, black, green and white swirls moving and shifting in snakelike patterns around it. They appeared to be floating inside and out of the scroll case, around all edges, passing in and around each other. *Melting? No,* not quite melting as they touched, but rather brightening for a split second when they parted. At one point, the swirls shaped into what could have passed for lettering, but I thought I must be seeing things. Being this close, I realized, too, that the intricate silver designs on the faces of the holder were also moving – shifting at a much slower rate than the black and green swirls. *That has got to be the weirdest thing. Ever.*

"Can you see the movement on the surface, Mr. Panofsky?" Mr. Carmichael asked.

I stood back up to look at him. His eyes were wrinkled with hardness. I nodded.

"I can't," He said, bluntly. "I only notice that something seems different each time I look at it. My eyes only capture the movement of the colored streaks. A few months ago, Mr. Panofsky, this scroll cover had a bas-relief of the story of Passover. The domes were embroidered, for the lack of a better word, with red, green, black and white wings on the upper and lower domes that matched the scroll-release handle you see there."

"You're saying that the holder changed to look like this? Why? How is that even possible?"

Not answering my question, he went on with his own, "Your adopted parents raised you Jewish, correct?"

My ears perked up in sudden warning; my neck hair prickled. "A – How do you know that I'm adopted, and B – how do you know about how I was raised?" I was getting concerned. I don't like strangers to start talking about people I know and love. It's like an unspoken threat. I still didn't even know if this guy wanted to do me any harm. I would have definitely been able to put up a fight with my new abilities, but I'd already been overtaken once and that had been by my own hand… or really my own legs running me into that wall at Fort Dune. And I wasn't sure what the heck that thing, Eammon, could do since I had already seen him turn into a gargoyle. *Not cool.*

"I know a lot of things about you, Mr. Panofsky. A great deal more than you know about yourself."

"How 'bout you enlighten me then, Mr. Carmichael?" My concern was becoming anger at his nonchalance.

"Patience, young Mr. Panofsky," he patronized.

I hate it when adults say stuff like that. *I'm not young, and I'm not five years old.* In fact, all of the craziness was causing me to mentally feel like I was eighty years old.

He continued past my inner monologue, "I'm about to, but all in good time. You need to know the beginning before you can know the end, Son."

Yeah, there it was... The 'son' word. My brain wanted to shut off in spitefulness, but I reminded myself that this guy was old and probably called everyone 'Son,' including people older than him.

"This," he pointed at the scroll again, "Mr. Panofsky, is the original writing of the Exodus, what we would consider a Haggadah, or the story of Passover. Do you remember the story of Passover?"

"If my twelve years of Sunday school and all the matzo I've never wanted to eat in my life serves me right, it's the story of the Israelites' release from slavery under the Egyptian pharaoh."

"Do you remember what occurred that finally forced the Pharaoh's hand?"

"The ten plagues."

"More specifically, the reason why we call it Passover in the first place?" He continued to try to guide me to the answer he wanted but I was just not getting it.

"Would you like me to break into the singing of the 'Four Questions,' Mr. Carmichael, or would you like to get to the point?" 'The Four Questions,' is actually called the 'Ma Nishtana' in Hebrew, meaning "What has changed?" Traditionally, these are dreaded by every child sitting at the Passover Seder, or dinner ceremony, who is the youngest in their families. Or, as in my case, the only child. It was my job to ask: why, only during this time, do we eat matzo? (*a constipation inspiring "bread" made without yeast*); why do we eat maror? (*tear-inducing bitter herbs*); why do we double dip our greens? (*still confused on this one*); and why do we get to eat in a reclining position and not just a normal sitting position? (*bring on the pillows*).

Mostly, all kids understand is that if they get through this part of the ceremony than the search for the Afikomen, part of a matzo that's hidden in the house somewhere, was only a few minutes away and prizes were always given, even if you didn't find it. Well, at least that's how it worked in my family Seders.

At my reference, Mr. Carmichael's lips twitched involuntarily with a small laugh as he reached above the glass casing and pulled out another book – a Torah, part of the Jewish bible.

He opened it to Exodus 12:29.

וַיְהִי בַּחֲצִי הַלַּיְלָה וַיהוָה הִכָּה כָל־בְּכוֹר בְּאֶרֶץ
מִצְרַיִם מִבְּכֹר פַּרְעֹה הַיֹּשֵׁב עַל־כִּסְאוֹ עַד בְּכוֹר
הַשְּׁבִי אֲשֶׁר בְּבֵית הַבּוֹר וְכֹל בְּכוֹר בְּהֵמָה׃

I translated in English. Although a little rusty on my Hebrew, I said, "'It was midnight. God killed every first-born in Egypt, from the first-born of Pharaoh, sitting on his throne, to the first-born of the prisoner in the dungeon, as well as every first-born animal.'" I thought more of the Passover story and how the Israelites rubbed the bloody shank of a lamb over their doorposts so that they would be "passed over" – their first-born children protected from death.

"Very good, Mr. Panofsky," he put the Torah away and then he released the silver scroll from its glass prison, put his white gloves on and went to reach for it. I was startled by his movement toward it. No normal scroll would ever have a binding that had color that writhed and snaked around it. *This thing is dangerous. Other-worldly.* I grabbed his hands back in a sudden reflex and then dropped them just as swiftly when I realized I may have done so too strongly and hurt him.

"How touching, but it is quite safe, for now," Mr. Carmichael said after rubbing his sore hands and again reaching for the scroll. I was mildly embarrassed, but, *Oh well, better safe, than... whatever.* The colors continued to swirl around the scroll case menacingly, except for the areas where Mr. Carmichael touched it. There the thin traces would go around, encircling his fingers before moving on like thick oil paint that spread away from his hands as if it was hit with paint thinner. He placed it on the flat surface that was next to the glass box – a study area.

He unlatched the wing catch and pulled it gently away from the scroll case. As he rolled the first few inches out, the weathered parchment, about nine inches in height, was ripped and the jagged edge had been stitched down to a newer piece in order to connect to the catch better. The colored streaks that had been on the cover ribboned out onto the parchment, twining around the Hebrew words. The snake-like lines didn't touch the newer paper, though, just everywhere else.

"It's not whole, the parchment looks like it was torn away," I said.

"You are correct on one count, Mr. Panofsky. The scroll is not complete, but the parchment is actually papyrus – made many millennia ago. I will only be able to tell you what we know is in this section. We can only speculate and discuss the legends of the second half."

He unrolled the scroll to the middle, letting the rest of it flow down the length of the table. He picked up a sterling silver yad, a pointer that is used to track where you are reading without allowing your fingers to touch the delicate paper, and read in ancient Hebrew the same passage. This time, however, the phrase included 'Shalach at hamelan shel mout,' meaning, 'Sent the Angel of Death.'

Mr. Carmichael explained, "This version is the original story of Moses and the Israelites flight from Egypt. As you can see, it's quite a bit bigger than your family's Haggadah."

"Yes, that looks like it would be a lot longer than the usual four hours the Passover Ceremony takes," I joked.

He took the handle of the case and began wrapping it around to bring the scroll paper in, the colored lines retracted from the paper at the same time, and he latched it shut. He returned the scroll to its glass showcase, locking it, and moved to sit behind his desk. "Please join me for a few minutes. I would like to tell you about the story of Passover that is recalled in that scroll." His ears perked up slightly and he quickly pushed the button under his desk. All of the glassed treasures returned to their hiding spots within the walls of the library. A second after they were all closed up, Eammon walked in with a tray of blood brews, tea and biscuits.

That's interesting timing.

"Thank you, Eammon. That will be all for now," Mr. Carmichael was more than dismissive.

Eammon nodded curtly, glowered at me with annoyance and left, closing the doors.

I sat on one of the couches and Mr. Carmichael came around the desk to sit across from me. He handed me a blood drink and put two sugars in his tea cup along with a little milk. Looking at the bottle in my hands, I was nervous to drink it in front of a human other than T. *And I'm still not positive that Eammon didn't manage to poison it some how.*

"Please drink, I know you must be hungry and I do apologize for that."

I twisted the bottle around. The label looked different from the other blood beers I had drunk, though it was made by the same brew masters. The label was remarkable, like that of a fine wine, 'Veal blood, a smooth texture where the canvas of umami lives on.' *Whatever that means.*

Mr. Carmichael sipped his tea through tight lips as I popped open the bottle. When I had entered this room, tension in my body had kept me from remembering how hungry I was before I got here. I downed the first bottle, a little barbarically, and opened the next one, waiting for him to begin to speak.

I didn't have to wait long.

"The most important part of the story actually occurs after the ten plagues. God sent the Angel of Death down to slay the first born Egyptian sons. This included anyone who had Egyptian blood, as you so delightfully translated, from the Pharaoh to the prisoner and included the first born animals owned by Egyptians."

I nodded, somewhat not paying attention as I knew this story very well.

"He was to take their souls directly to the deity Ra," Mr. Carmichael continued.

"Huh? Ra? Who's Ra?" I suddenly became interested. The story had deviated a lot sooner than what I was expecting.

"Ra is the Egyptian deity of the sun," he rested, thinking, "Ra had also been unhappy with the Pharaoh for treating other humans so poorly. At that time, humans were still fairly new creations and all the gods loved them."

All the gods?

He sipped his tea, "However, that is really neither here nor there. The angel that was picked from the fourteen Angels of Death to follow God's will, according to Rabbinical lore, was Abaddon. After the first-borns were killed and delivered to the foot of Ra, Abaddon went to see Moses. Moses thanked the Angel of Death and, as was courteous in that time period, offered his youngest daughter, Rebekah, to him as gratitude for helping the Israelites."

Wait a minute, I thought. I knew the story of Moses back and forth – even without the Charlton Heston version, "Whoa, whoa, whoa. Moses only had two sons with Zipporah, there's never been any mention of a daughter."

"That's very true, there is no mention of her. Many stories were left out of the Bible," Mr. Carmichael sipped on some tea, and then continued again, "Also, there are many things that relate to the Angel, or Angels, of Death that do not show up in our testament, but do show up later on in the New one."

Mr. Carmichael continued, "During the exodus through the dessert, Rebekah gave birth to twin daughters. Ra, after hearing the mournful prayers of the Pharaoh over the loss of his son, decided to steal one of Rebekah's daughters to console the Pharaoh. The stolen girl was named Bast, the Eye of Ra. The other child was raised under Rebekah's care and called Basya, Daughter of God."

"No, that's not right," *I know my Hebrew lessons,* "After Moses parted the Red Sea and the Jews passed through, the Pharaoh and the Egyptians drowned when the water closed up."

"Bibles were written by man, Mr. Panofsky. First told and retold then written and rewritten. Think of the possibility. Over the centuries, don't you think the stories could have changed? Parts were either forgotten or lost once they were written out."

It's like the old joke about the monks transcribing books when one decided to look up the original version of the document. He cried out to the others in his revelation, 'I knew it! It's celebrate, not celibate!'

Before I could laugh at the thought, Mr. Carmichael continued, "Abaddon grew angry with the treachery and begged God to intervene. But God would not make any more war upon the Egyptians. This, of course, did not sit well with the angel. He waited and bided his time until he heard whispers of unrest amongst the other angels on the different levels of choirs that followed under God or Ra."

Mr. Carmichael gave himself a moment to gather his thoughts before continuing, "It has always been thought amongst the higher energies that the gods favored humans. Even more so than their own half-breed humans. And so, the Angel of Death began feeding a flame of doubt. Anger flew within the ranks, played on other's emotions, and Abaddon began to get his own following. In the end, Abaddon led a war against God and Ra. But the deities prevailed, and the Angel of Death and those who fought with him were sent into exile."

"To where?" I interrupted.

"I do not know. That is where we have lost the line of the story. We had to decipher what some of the words on the last page of the scroll actually meant and even that is a guess to us."

Dead end. Fantastic. I asked, "So what happened to the children?"

"Time passed and the girls grew. But differences became quickly apparent due to their parentage. When they hit the age of adulthood, thirteen back then, they began to age more slowly. They grew stronger than the strongest men in their villages. Quicker than any human or animal. Their teeth grew sharp and deadly. And they began needing sustenance other than the typical harvested food. Their tribes feared them. They were called 'Motzetzi Dam.'"

I didn't recognize the word. I raised my eyebrow in a questioning manner.

"Bloodsuckers," he said matter-of-factly.

Ah. That I understand.

"However, God and Ra found them very useful. They each charged the girls with protecting the pure humans from danger – from their own father and his minions."

"What does all of this have to do with me, Mr. Carmichael?" I asked. *Do I really want to know the answer to that question?*

He poured himself another cup of tea, dropping in two more cubes of sugar and milk. For a small cup, he really did like his tea sweet. Up until now, I had forgotten the second bottle of frothy blood brew in my hands, but with his pause I took another sip, preparing myself for his next words.

"The line of Bast and Basya has always been female. In centuries, there have never been males born to them. The females marry and turn their husbands. They procreate and the children are turned after they come of age. Anyone not born of the line are not truly vampires, but half breeds, though just as deadly," he drank some more and added as an after thought, "Rogue vampires, you might say."

I hate to have things spelled out for me, but I seriously was not getting this old man. And he was sounding crazy, "You lost me."

"You only become a vampire if you are bitten by one of the descendants of Rebekah and Abaddon. But, also to survive it, you become a vampire if you are, by birth-right, part of the vampire family. Your genetic disposition protects you from the poison. Otherwise, a vampire's bite would be the last thing you ever feel."

"That doesn't make sense. If that were the case, then why are Devon and Tom both vampires? They've never mentioned anything like this and they both were bitten by vampires that aimed to kill them, not turn them," *his theory is incredulous.*

"I don't know why, but some humans not related to the family either have enough of an immunity or the poison was too slow to course through their veins that they were able to become rogue vampires."

"What do you mean 'rogue.' There are differences in vampires?"

"Only one. A direct descendant will have four sharp teeth. Like yours, there are two very long top ones, and two sharpened, shorter ones on the bottom. Those who have been bitten and are rogue, only have the top two canines. However, knowledge of how vampires were created is kept only to the descendents. The story of their line, et cetera."

"But what about the rogues? Are there the same laws for them or something?"

"They are ruled differently. Ruled by modern times and modern laws. Sometimes they keep intact the laws from the time in which they were bitten, sometimes they stick to the laws of the time period they are in. For example, your friends Devon and Tom, they remind those coming into the harbor that they are to abide by the laws of the town. 'No hunting within city limits,' am I right?"

I nodded. I guess that makes some sense. *Wonder if Tom's and Devon's makers were of the family and just went rogue, or were actually these half-breed rogues he's talking about. It's not like I really noticed how many sharp teeth they had – that seems kinda personal to ask 'Excuse me, can I see your fangs, please? Nope, not one of us.'* As for me, what Mr. Carmichael was saying began to make sense. *It feels right for my circumstances.* The back of my neck began to prickle again, tensing up with caution. "So, you're saying that the process that got me these," I pointed to my teeth, "was not an accident." That was more of a statement than a question.

"No, Mr. Panofsky, it was not. The vampire who bit you knew who you were."

"And who am I?"

"If I am not mistaken, you were adopted minutes after you were born," He leaned back against the seat he was on, a very relaxed-looking position.

I, however, began to get even more on edge, "Well, I can't remember that for sure, but, yes, I'm told I was adopted as soon as my biological mother had me, as she had died in childbirth."

"And your bite? Were you not just bitten about two months ago?"

I nodded again. He already guessed this before, *What game is he playing at?*

The alert in the back of my head began to start drumming a low, warning song. My muscles tensed further. For the first time, I started thinking I really was in some kind of danger there. *And he looks like such a nice old man.*

"You were brought back into the circle. But, you weren't the only one born minutes before your adoption. You have a brother. A fraternal twin born minutes after you," he paused, "Rebekah's blood flows through you, as does the Angel of Death's. I knew when you were bitten because the scroll changed to the form it is now."

This was what I was waiting for. *The punch-line where my life becomes forfeit.* I jumped up in a blocking position, hissing a deep growl, waiting for some unknown attack. *Eammon, maybe? Had he been listening to all of this and was just waiting for a sign from Mr. Carmichael?* I scanned the entire room again, looking for anything that was now out of line with where it had been before.

✤ ✤ ✤

The Missing One

"Please. Please sit down. I do not mean to hurt you in any way," Mr. Carmichael leaned back from his position on the couch and reached over to his desk, pulling a small photo frame back with him. He handed it to me, "The man I sent you to find is my son. He is also your twin brother."

I glanced over the picture, loosening my defense position as I did, "Are.. Are you telling me that you're my father?" Flashes of Lord Vader saying 'Luke, I am your father' popped into my head and I had to stifle a laugh.

"Regrettably, my dear boy, I am not. I adopted Adam after your mother's passing. Please sit. I can tell you some things but what occurred that day needs to be told by another. It's not my story to tell. But for now, I will tell you at least all that I know."

As I moved back to the couch, I asked, "Why didn't you tell me this while you were holding a gun to my head at the apartment? Why all the smoke and mirrors, not to mention, the possible concussion from my little run in with your butler?"

"I'm sorry for all the drama. Really, I am, but I needed to separate you from your 'clan' and make sure you were who I thought you were. I've been looking for you ever since the scroll turned and was advised of your missing status."

Mr. Carmichael looked sincere, but I still didn't trust him, so I asked, "Who told you I was missing, and how do you know I'm this twin?"

He leaned towards me and pointed at my face with a manicured finger, "You have a shadow of a birthmark on your cheek. When did you get it removed?"

Why does this man insist on answering all of my questions with a cryptic one of his own? "I didn't remove it. The mark all but disappeared after I was bitten."

"Fascinating," he mumbled so quietly that I doubted a human standing next to him would've been able to hear it.

But I could and I was not at all fascinated by it, "So?"

"Look at the picture, at your brother again. Tell me what you see."

I focused more intently on the photograph again. And then I saw it. Instinctively, I reached up to my right cheek when I saw the same mark I used to have on a person who looked nothing like me. The birthmark on Adam was on the exact opposite side mine used to be on. It ran from his left eye down to swirl around his left cheek.

Mr. Carmichael spoke, breaking me from the sadness I suddenly felt about my missing birthmark and the brother that I shared it with, "It's the mark of the Dragon."

Huh. I knew I was right.

As he breathed deeply in a hesitant pause, it made me think that I wasn't going to like what he said next. And I didn't.

"Keen, the dragon represents the mark of Abaddon," he waited for my response.

And because I didn't know how to react, I changed the subject. *An excellent self-preservation method.* Eammon gave me the perfect opportunity as he walked in and began clearing the tea tray from the room. *Ignore the bad subject and maybe it will go away.*

"Didn't you say your son was taken by a gargoyle?" I asked, remembering our first conversation that had been back in the apartment. I handed the picture back.

"Yes, that is correct," he said flatly.

"Well, your pal here, Amy," I glanced quickly at Eammon to see his reaction of my nickname for him. He flashed red as I continued, "knocked my friends around in order to get to me. Why don't you ask him where your son is?" Being s*mug is fun.*

Mr. Carmichael smiled, "Eammon was standing next to me when it happened. He's also, as you may have noticed, a Changeling. No. The animal that took Adam was indeed a gargoyle. Have your friends made any headway with finding him?"

"No, we were led astray by Mr. Thing here," I impassively waved my hand at Eammon.

"Again, I do apologize for that," Mr. Carmichael responded, "I was hoping they would've found something out about the coin that was left when Adam was taken."

"I'm pretty sure that right now they are searching for me and not looking to find your son." *At least I hope they are.*

"You hope," Eammon mimicked my thoughts.

He's in my head almost like Alexandra. And I do not like it.

"That'll do, Eammon," Mr. Carmichael said and Eammon left with the tray.

I waited until the door was closed before I asked, "What about the scroll you showed me earlier. The Haggadah. Where is the missing piece?"

"Unfortunately, I do not know. Like this piece, I imagine it had been misplaced over the years. Sold, stolen or just lost. It was more luck or fate than anything that I came across it. I was the only one at the auction who knew what it was. I've been hoping for the same luck for the second half. We need to know how it ends."

"Again, Mr. Carmichael, what does this have to do with me?" *Seriously, can I get a straight answer?*

"Mr. Panofsky, you were bitten for a reason. The vampire knew you were a descendant even though you are male. As I said before, the line has only been female up until you and Adam were born. That, alone, means something and apparently something worth trying to kill over. Adam has been taken for a reason. The scroll changed when you were bitten. I'm sure that he was bitten too as the same night he was taken, the first color, red, disappeared from the domes and began winding around the entire scroll and the engravings slowly changed."

I ignored what I thought was an implication, "And this happened again?"

"Yes. Over the past six months, a total of four times. The last time was with you."

Not being able to hold in my emotions anymore, I looked at him in disbelief. *No way. No fricken way. That's not even possible.*

"I'm sorry Keen, I know this is a bit of a shock to you. But you really were bitten for a reason. This was no mistake. The vampire that bit you knew your line. Your parents have been trying to protect you since your biological mother gave you to them. I don't know the complete reason why all of this is happening, but there is a reason and we need to find it."

He made the next part very clear, his eyes darkening, his posture leaning in towards me, his voice steady and strong, "We need to find Adam and the other half of this scroll as soon as possible."

He sat back, breaking eye contact with me.

"I have been protecting my son, your twin, since I first laid eyes on him. I have failed. I can only hope that he is," He paused, tears welling in his eyes, the first real emotion I had seen of Mr. Carmichael.

Mr. Carmichael pulled out the kerchief from his suit pocket. He dabbed at his eyes, "I'm sorry," he whispered, "I know he is not of my blood, but you have to understand, I raised him. He is my son," he broke off again, "And I could not protect him."

Without knowing what kind of reaction I should feel, the shock, the anger, the fear, I became a stone instead, separating myself from the reality of it, "Mr. Carmichael, we will find your son. I promise. We'll figure this thing out," *Man, I hope I'm not lying.*

He looked up at me, his gray eyes piercing, "Since my son has been taken, I have been doubling my efforts to find the second half of the scroll, to find out what is supposed to happen, what is to come. We need to know how to protect you and him from the changes that are coming."

Mr. Carmichael went back to his desk and pulled out an object, "This is yours, I believe."

I put out my hand and he dropped my dagger in it with its sheath.

"Very interesting dagger. Do you know what it is?"

"No," I responded, "Devon told me he had gotten it in Egypt after beating an adversary. Do you know what it is?"

He shrugged.

I guess that's an answer I'll get at a different time. "So what now? What else can you tell me?" *Patience is not my strong suit.*

"The real story behind your adoption should be told by the woman who was with your biological mother as she gave birth to you and Adam," he paused. I could tell he was contemplating his next words. "It's time to see your mother." We were both silent for a few moments, letting everything sink in. He got up and pressed a button on his desk phone, "I'm going to have Eammon take you back to your clan. They should know so they can help protect you."

I nodded.

"Mr. Panofsky," then he said more gently, "Keen. You need to see your mother. She needs to tell you about the day you were born. She knew your biological mother and the workings of her family. And she misses you."

My mother. *I miss her too.*

✿ ✿ ✿

Back to the Apartment

This figure came flying at me, almost as immediate as my reflexes, but, thankfully, I was faster and able to catch T before she careened into me, causing,

I'm sure, what would be a lot of pain to her tiny body. She gave me a hug and then let go, a slight blush on her face, "Uhm, we've been, ah, worried about you, Keen. Where have you been? Are you all right?"

"I'm fine," though I wasn't sure if I was at all. She gave me a look, so I responded, "I'm fine. I promise."

The apartment looked exactly like the last time I had seen it – crap everywhere. "Where are the guys, T?"

"They went looking for you. Devon thought it might help to retrace your steps to the fort to see if they missed anything. I'll call them back."

"Cool." There was an awkward pause before she turned around and went to the computer where the radio was to contact the guys. Today, her hair was in dreads with a red bandana tied around it. She was in an off-the-shoulder, cotton shirt and a brown, floor-length-skirt. Very hippie-ish.

Geez, she's just cute in everything she wears.

I really needed to stop thinking like that.

✵ ✵ ✵

Outside the Panofsky's

I was standing on the back line of my parent's yard. Again. Waiting. *Again.* I was watching from the dirt road just outside the property line. It was barely past six in the evening. The sky was a bright blue, the sun was starting to think about descending for the day. I focused on the reggae music echoing up the spaces between houses from Gordon's Landing.

"Go on," Devon said from behind me, "It's time."

This morning, when Tom and Devon had returned to the apartment, I had told them all that had transpired between Mr. Carmichael and me. They had apparently been working with T's connections at the FBI to find out about Mr. Carmichael... who apparently wasn't Mr. Carmichael at all, but a man named Joel Kachman. He also happened to be wanted by the FBI for tax evasion. I stored that information in my brain to think about at another time. *Was he lying about all of this? If so, why? And what's it got to do about me anyway?*

Talking to my mom seemed to be the best way to go, even if it pained me to do so, mentally as well as physically. I made sure I had drunk several bottles of Bloody Captain's but I was still concerned. Guilt washed over me when I remembered seeing, scratch that, attacking my mother the last time I was home.

I should've taken a nap this afternoon before coming here. Unfortunately, my brain had been too full of drama to take the two-hour shut-down my body needed to recuperate its strength. My mind was tangled in thoughts about what Mr. Carmichael had said and thinking about what to say to my parents. *When they find out what I've become, will they still accept me as their son still?* I was afraid to find out, and even with Devon here, I wasn't sure I could do it. I didn't move.

He reassured, "Do you want me to wait here or go with you?"

When did I become such a chicken? "No, I'll go alone. I'll probably stay until the last ferry. I owe them that much. I'll see you back at the apartment later on tonight."

Devon turned to go. I knew he would be out of there in a flash, so I quickly said, "Thanks, Devon."

He clapped my shoulder and then he was gone. Just a little dust kicked up from his motions.

It took less than a second to cross the yard and get up the steps. My movements were becoming so natural, so much a part of me, and that helped take away any kind of hesitance I was feeling. It didn't give me time, really, to waver.

I knocked on the back door. It didn't feel right just to walk in after I had been gone for so long. In an instant, I was pulled into a gigantic bear hug by my adoptive mother and father. Their blue auras enveloped me in warmth.

Mom. Dad.

They smelled so good. They smelled like home. *Nothing edible about that...*

But I am glad that I had that last bottle of blood beer.

Chapter 10

Finally Home

✿ ✿ ✿

My Only Family

Still holding me in a tight hug, my mom asked, "Are you all right? We were so worried about you! We thought we lost you."

"Let him breath," my dad said. It was so good to see them. I didn't really want to let go of them, but I knew, as my dad released his grip and gently pulled my mother's arms away from me, that it was time.

My mom grabbed my face with both hands, like she always did no matter how old I'd gotten, and began kissing my face. She kissed my forehead, my lips and my cheeks. She had this way of suctioning her kisses that always tickled me, so I did what I always did when she kissed me like this – I pinched her side to tickle her. It was a game we always played. I was definitely mommy's little boy... *Still.*

She laughed and let me go.

We moved into the kitchen and sat at the breakfast bar. My mother and I grabbed seats facing the kitchen and dad stood across from us. They looked so happy. *Finally,* I was relieved, *but there's still so much more gray in their hair now, though,* I frowned inward. *They're too young to be old. And it sucks that I'm the cause of their sudden, rapid aging. Hopefully, they'll slow back down now that they know I'm alive.*

Hearing a small meow, I bent down to pet Bree who had been twining around the legs of our chairs. She sniffed at my out-stretched hand, then bent down to the ground, butt in the air, eyes wide and ears stiff against her head like they had been sewn there. A horrendous yowl pierced through her throat right before she went to bite me. I pulled my hand away well before she had time to clamp around it and I could hear her jaw snap shut. She hissed and spat, then ran off out of the room. *I guess someone's not happy I'm home. Hope it's not like that with mom and dad.*

My dad laughed at the exchange, "Don't worry, I'm sure she'll come around. You just haven't been here to give her treats."

Yeah, right. I'm sure that's all it is. It couldn't possibly be because I'm not human anymore. Even the cat thinks I'm evil... But I smiled at him in agreement, no matter what my thoughts were.

My mother turned to me. She put her hands on mine and brought them to the counter. I looked down at them. My mom's hands were always smooth compared to my dad's callused ones. She was a hard worker, just like my dad, so I never knew how she kept her hands so soft, so mom-like and loving.

"You've been bitten," She didn't ask a question. She said it as a statement, in her moms-always-know voice.

I didn't say anything. Saying it out loud would be admitting to people I know that there is something seriously wrong with me. And besides, like a little kid who fell off his bike and scraped his knees, I knew as soon as I started talking, I wouldn't be able to stop the aggravated tears that would fall. *My thick, bitter, inhuman tears.*

"This is all my fault," she said, her shoulders slumping, "I promised I wouldn't let you out of my sight and someone got you anyway."

She started crying. *Crap.* I had to look away and blinked back my own tears. I could feel the thick, mucousy gel of them become heavy under my eye lids.

"This is not your fault, mom. How could I even blame you for something as screwed up as this?" I was not really doing a great job in reassuring her, but I was trying to do my best. I gripped her arm lightly to get her attention. She turned to me with tear-streaked cheeks, "This is not your fault." I repeated as I looked at her, willing her to believe me.

"Come on dear, boys will be boys," my dad said, trying to break the tension. We looked at him with matching thin smiles. He got the message – now's not the time to joke. He remained quiet.

"I guess that if I would've known something like this could ever happen, than I would've been more careful. Maybe." *At least, I hope I would've been.*

"I thought if we could protect you, we would never have to talk about it. This would all just pass." She took in a deep, calming breath, blew it out very slowly and then said thoughtfully, "I guess that just made it easier for you to walk into it."

She hugged me again, "I'm so sorry, baby. I am so, so very sorry. Can you ever forgive me?"

"Mom, there is absolutely nothing that needs to be forgiven."

My mother sniffled. Dad got her a tissue and she wiped her face. I could tell she wasn't convinced, but maybe in time…

"So what have you been doing with yourself these past few months, Keen," My dad asked.

"Oh you know, a little of this, a little of that," I smiled my mischievous smile.

He grinned at me, "That's my boy!" and hit me on the arm, and promptly realized that it was a bad move. He shook out his hand and laughed, "So I see quite a bit has changed about you."

I shrugged my own laugh, "What can I say? Perks."

Taking a few minutes, I told them what had happened to me since I left that night for the bar with the guys, leaving out the gory details that included Alexandra. *Let's just keep this version PG.*

I decided that it was time for the necessary conversation. Now was just as good a time as any. "Mom, who is Mr. Carmichael?"

"Why, did you see him? Is he all right?" *There was more concern in her voice than I expected.*

"Yes, mom, he's fine. But his son was kidnapped."

"Adam? He's still missing? I had hoped that the letter Joel sent was a mistake, that maybe he came back and that Joel had just forgotten to tell me," the worry in her voice was thick.

The letter I saw when I first came back here must've been because of us. "Yes, my twin brother is missing," *No sense in beating around the bush as to what information I do and do not know.*

There was definitely a strong silence that overtook my parents. Then my mom spoke, "So you know about Adam."

"Only a little. I was hoping you could fill me in on things. Like what happened the day I was born and who is Mr. Carmichael, to start," I smiled gently, to encourage her. Although, my fangs stuck out a bit, so I wasn't sure if that was more unnerving or what. But my mom continued without flinching. *I guess that's a good sign.*

"Mr. Carmichael is actually my older brother. His real name is Joel. Joel . Kachman," My mother admitted.

"Is our real name Panofsky?"

"Yes. I took on your father's name when we got married, but my maiden name is Kachman, not Weitz, as you've always known it."

"Why did you both change your names?"

"Well, I guess I should just start at the beginning. It might be easier."

My mom got out of her chair, and went into the other room. I could hear her rummaging around and breathed a sigh of relief when she finally found what she was looking for.

She came back with a small box of photographs.

✳ ✳ ✳

About Bio Mom

There she was, smiling up at me, a picture of my very pregnant, biological mother. She was beautiful, with dark reddish hair, light eyes and high cheek bones. Her face and arms were thin and strong. Sculpted. But she resembled a human who had swallowed a beach ball whole. I looked nothing like her, so it was hard to be convinced from the picture that she was the woman who birthed me. Adam, however, was a spitting image of her, just in male form.

Both of my mothers were hugging each other, cheek to cheek. My poor biological mother's stomach was turned at an angle so they could be as close as they could get.

"She was my best friend," the mother that raised me said, "Her name was Lisabette. I called her Liz, she called me Em." My mother's name is Miriam, but most of her friends, and what I knew of as her family, called her Miri.

"We met in kindergarten at the Hebrew School and were inseparable," She stopped. Memories washed over her and my mom smiled. Right before she broke into tears again.

"She had the kindest heart," she choked out, "she was always there for me. When my parents divorced, when my younger brother died on tour in the Gulf.

She was always there. We were there for each other. I was there when she… when she was turned. The least I could do was care for her children."

I patted her shoulder gently, trying to be less impatient and more sympathetic, letting her regain her composure first. I owed her that much. After a couple of minutes, I asked, "What happened on the day I was born, Ma?"

My mother stood up and paced around the room a minute. She crossed her arms and brought one hand up to her mouth, biting her nails.

Nervous.

I waited.

"Your mom went into labor while we were eating dinner at their house. Her face was so comical. She was half trying to be calm, but she was definitely saying 'uh oh!' in her mind when her water broke. As we were grabbing her overnight bag to take her to the hospital, we were attacked. Your parents were well protected. Just not protected enough. We ran for it. Your father, your biological father," she stressed the word 'biological,' "stayed behind to fight. Your dad, he was my boyfriend at the time, and I got your mother into the car and we drove to my brother's house. Joel. I thought it was the safest place for us. No one would know where to find us."

She sat back down next to me. My dad had made some tea for her and him and handed me a bottle of Bloody Captain. Moose. *Just what I wanted.* He smiled at me and winked. "How did you know to be stocked for me?"

"I knew I hadn't dreamed seeing you that night," my mother said.

Oh shit. My face must've hit complete mortification because she said, "It's all right, Keen. I wasn't hurt. I was just surprised and worried about you. But I knew what had happened right away. I knew someone had gotten to you. I just wished that I would've been able to explain before you headed out again and we could've gone through this together. As a family."

I swallowed hard. My mom could really make me feel guilty without even trying, so I diverted back to our original subject of my biological parents, "So what happened at Joel's house?"

My mom continued her story, "Your mom begged us to take you both and hide you. Keep you safe. We tried to move her, but she was too weak. No matter how much blood we gave her to drink, she just couldn't get enough strength. We told her we wouldn't leave her behind. But she refused to move. She knew they were coming for us," her next words were breathless, "She always knew when something bad was about to happen."

My ears perked and my neck prickled slightly, *Just like me.*

"What happened?"

"We heard them coming."

"Who?"

"There were some vampires and other creatures who found us. The ones who had attacked before. Joel, your father and I took you boys from the house. There was a trap door in the floor of the kitchen. Joel shut the door behind us. I had you; your father was carrying Adam."

She shook her head down, "We didn't make it down the steps before we were knocked to the ground by the explosion. I knew in my heart that there was nothing left of the house and that your mother was gone." She began to cry again. I took her hand and rested her head against my shoulder and let her cry it out. When her human tears stopped, she continued the story. "We ran to.."

"Fort Dune," I finished her sentence.

"Yes," she paused again, thoughtful. "Joel called Eammon. He took all of us to Canada, to a safe place. We talked it out and decided that Joel would take Adam and we would take you. We thought it was best to separate you two. We all went underground for a while. Popped up with new names, new everything."

My dad spoke up, "Joel got us a marriage license and birth certificates for you and your mother. She and I had a quick ceremony a few months later to make it more official to us."

"Wait, you married after I was given to you?" *They had always told me they had been married two years before that day.*

"I loved your mother and knew we would one day get married. We just got some things thrown at us that moved the date up a bit," he caught my mother's eye and smiled in a loving, but mischievous way, causing her to blush like a teenager.

Bewilderment hit me as I realized that even the smallest details of my life had been a lie, "'Some things thrown at you?'"

He shifted his stance from side to side, "Well, yeah. What can I say? I always wanted a son." He grinned boyishly.

Oh-kaaaay. "Why did you come back here? Didn't you think someone would recognize us?" I asked.

My mother answered this one, "Sun Tzu once said 'The opportunity to secure ourselves against defeat lies in our own hands, but the opportunity of defeating the enemy is provided by the enemy himself.' We needed to find out who did this and why."

"Did Lisabette," I couldn't call her my mother, "did she know anything? Give you any information at all?"

"Unfortunately, we haven't found out anything about the attack. Your mom knew who she was. She told me the story a long time ago. Before she was turned. The ceremony was beautiful and much bigger than any Bat or Bar Mitzvah I had ever seen," she said very matter-of-factly.

My Bar Mitzvah, or coming of age ceremony in the Jewish tradition, was a two-day event starting with leading a Succoth service on Friday and then leading the temple again for three hours on Saturday morning. Reading from the Torah signifies becoming a true part of the Jewish community as an adult. And then, once you get done with the nerve wracking part where your voice cracks from singing, in Hebrew, at high and low ranges that no human should really try to sing, the real party comes. Usually complete with DJ, drunk uncle, hundreds of dollars in decorations and thousands more for the food that friends you know, and family members you will never meet in your life again, will eat. We had two hundred and fifty people attend. It was like trying to put together plans as large as a wedding for a thirteen-year-old.

She continued on, "Very few that are not of the family get to see it. But I was her best friend and she wanted me there."

Well, this sounds nothing like my own ceremony. I wonder what else I missed!

"Liz told me when we were 13, and I had just celebrated my Bat-Mitzvah, that she was part of a family that could track their lineage through the maternal side all the way back to Moses and that they had special gifts. I didn't believe her at first, but then I started to pay attention to her family when I was over. They always had special drinks in hand and, well, you clearly see the differences you have now," she waved her hand at me as if I was one of the prize items in the Show Case Showdown on the Price is Right show.

Through the open window in the living room, I heard a kid walk past the house. Nothing unusual there, as kids walked through our yard all the time to get to the playground across the street. My parents never had the heart to put up a fence, so there were always people. I put my hand up to my mother to warn her that someone was near and she tightened her lips.

When the crunch of grass died down, I nodded to give her the go-ahead. As she continued, a brief scent invoked a memory as a breeze blew through the house. I couldn't place it, so I just let it slip back into my collective memory of all things island.

"She told me about how, in a few years, she would be changed to become more like her parents. I guess I should back up a little. First of all, all children born to vampires have been female and are born with the vampire chromosome. Once the woman is bitten, the gene from the adult vampire initiates the process and the human becomes a vampire."

I remember this part, "Joel said I had some sort of predisposition to counter the poison and not die."

Her face scrunched up in sudden anger, "Don't think of it as a poison. How can you say that?" her voice was distraught, "This is their life force. Your life force, Keen."

"But it kills others," *If I had been born before the blood beers were created, than I would've had to kill others just to survive.* But I didn't want to point out the obvious.

My dad broke in, "So do nuts and bee stings. Most people will have a reaction to a vampire chromosome, but this is who you are now. Don't think of it as a curse."

"Well, it sure as hell isn't a blessing," I was getting mad, a slow-boiling heat was rising in me. *Breathe, Keen. Relax. Don't get yourself upset at your parents.* I didn't know how dangerous I would be to them if I got angry and I didn't want to find out anytime soon.

Mom regained her calm quickly and with a soothing voice said, "You can't choose whose family you are born into. Just as you can't choose allergies or immunities you'll have. You just have to take it as it comes. Deal with the changes and live your life."

"For now, Ma, let's just agree to disagree," dropping the subject was the best way to calm myself.

She shrugged in agreement, "Ok. For now. But we'll talk about it later."

Typical parenting. I rolled my eyes, "Fine. So you were telling me about this 'coming of age' process with vampires."

She grudgingly began on the topic again, "Fine. This task is usually done in a ceremony that includes a Rabbi as the over-seer, the vampire-to-be's parents, if they're still alive, and local vampire witnesses in the community.

"Centuries ago, this used to occur around age thirteen, but as people began living longer, the age jumped up to twenty-five. Although, sometimes it can be done as early as twenty or as late as thirty. It just really depends on the circumstances," she smiled slyly, "Besides, who wants to raise a teenager for longer than you have to."

I smirked back at her. I knew I hadn't been the best teenager, but I was most certainly not the worst. I mean, what she didn't know couldn't kill me. *Right?*

"How many people are usually there for the ceremony?"

"Since it's a highly religious and rare ceremony that lasts for days, an upwards of five thousand vampires might be in attendance."

"Geez, I thought my Bar-Mitzvah was rough with all the hundreds of people you invited," I laughed.

"Yeah, I can only imagine how nervous Liz was when it was her turn to change. But she took it all in stride. She was ready for it. She was also in love and wanted to have the change completed before she was married."

"Was my biological father a vampire too?"

"Yes," then she mended her statement, "Well, not at first. Elijah and she met when they were finishing up college. Both were twenty-one. They were instantly in love with each other. He didn't even flinch when she said what it would take to marry her."

"And what precisely is that?" *I don't think I have ever asked this many questions about anything. Even when my parents wanted to talk about 'the birds and the bees.'*

"In order for them to be in a valid marriage according to tradition, she would need to bite him to make him into a vampire. They would become eternally bonded. Well, until 'death do they part,'" her last sentence held a sarcastic and sad tone.

"Your father and I were there for that ceremony too. In fact, that's how your dad and I met. He was your father's best friend. As humans, we stood as witnesses and protectors of their secret, helping when we could."

"And keeping out of the way when we couldn't," my father jumped in. He had just finished woking up some meat and vegetables for dinner, "Do you want any?"

My nose cringed at the smell of it, "I wish, but I think I'll stick with my beers. Do you have any more?"

"Absolutely," he went back into the fridge and brought out three different kinds, putting them on the breakfast bar in front of me. "Take your pick."

Moose, Shark Bait and Black Bear. I'd had them all before.

Hmm, something light. I took the 'Shark Bait' pale blood ale. *For a blood that bites back.*

He laughed, "You're so predictable."

He put the other two back in the fridge before coming back to the table and sitting down with a glass of wine.

I fidgeted with the Shark Bait bottle while I asked, "Do you have anymore photos of them? Any of my dad at all?"

My mom shook her head side to side, "No, these are all I have of your mother and we never had any of your father. It just happened that way. They didn't really like to have their pictures taken."

I totally get that. I hate being in photos. But, for the first time, I was sad that I would never see my biological father's face. Now that I had heard their story, it was much easier to feel their realness – feel the relationship that I would never have.

Moving as slowly as my parents, we went over to the dinner table. I didn't want to look any less normal than I already did. We sat down in our usual spots with dad at the head of the table and mom and I sitting across from each other. We said the Jewish blessings over the meal. Since they were eating rice, they said, "Barukh ata Adonai Eloheinu Melekh ha-olam, bo're minei m'zonot."

'Blessed are You, Lord our God, King of the universe, Who creates varieties of nourishment.'

Even though I hadn't said any prayers since my change, having said them several times a day till then, I hadn't forgotten them. Drinking the blood beers satiated my hunger, but I didn't know who I needed to raise my voice in prayer to for having them. *Seriously, what kind of prayer does one do over the consumption of someone else's life force?*

I was happy to be home and with my family. If it had been before, Maddie would've been here eating dinner with us. My parents loved her; they had already accepted her as part of the family and were just waiting for me to make it official. She'd been on my mind since I got here, as my parents would be my only link to her now. I thought about asking how she was doing, but I was too much of a coward and didn't want to hear if she had already moved on. *I don't think I could take that kind of hurt.*

I shoved those random thoughts to the farthest, deepest, blocked-off area in my mind and looked at my beer. "Any ideas what I should say over this," I joked slightly, tilting my beer back and forth.

My father answered with: "Barukh ata Adonai Eloheinu Melekh ha-olam, bo're p'ri ha-gafen."

I laughed "Of course." *The prayer over wine.*

I repeated the prayer, raising my glass and said, "L'Chaim."

"Cheers," Dad clinked my glass with his.

"L'Chaim," Mom repeated back the Jewish saying meaning 'To Life.' We all took sips of our drinks like it was any regular family meal and I wasn't sitting there drinking blood.

My dad smiled and then looked at his wife, "The thing about Liz is that she had heard all of the stories throughout her life about the prophecy of the twins. But who in their right mind would ever think that she would become part of a prophecy. Certainly not a twenty-something-year-old who was just starting a new job and a new life with her new husband. The only thing she was thinking about was her school bills. She didn't want her parents to pay for it, so she decided to work to pay for it all. She was like that. Very independent. Like you."

I smiled. *That's nice to hear.*

"What exactly is the prophecy of the twins? Uncle Joel said Adam and I carried the mark of the Dragon. That it was the Angel of Death's mark," *An exiled angel. An evil angel.*

"Liz once told me long ago, well before she had ever become pregnant about a saying that had been passed down through generations to her," Mom stared straight ahead into her own little world as she remembered the words, "'And the line that was once broken will bare two by two, completing the pact and restoring what was once taken. Two by two different, but the same, whence both by both are brought back to the fold, rightful power will reign once more.'"

What in the hell does that mean? But what I said was, "What does that mean?"

"No one in her family knew for sure. But does that seem good to you?" My mother replied.

"Well, no. Not really."

She was suddenly light and joking, "Yeah, well, no one else thought so either."

Dad smiled along with her, a quirky grin.

"People were frantic once your mom found out she was having boys," she grew serious again, "Practically all of the community joined in the research to find out what the end of the prophecy was supposed to be. Even families that Liz knew from Europe and the Middle East went through all of their historical papers."

"But," dad started, "no one had been able to find anything out by the time Liz and Eli were murdered."

"My brother's been working on it ever since to try to keep you and Adam safe," mom paused, smiling in memory, "It's scary how things can change so quickly. When she found out she was pregnant, she and Elijah were ecstatic. They wanted to have a big family, and although she knew she could only have girls…"

"Or so they thought," my dad said sheepishly.

She gave him a funny look that was half amused and half death-glare, "they wanted to adopt boys after having a couple of girls first."

"Would they have been able to bring adopted children into the family?" Both of them understood my double meaning. *Would they survive being turned?*

Dad took this one, "Well, just as Elijah originally wasn't a vampire, there are others out there who are not just of the family. If the vampire," he paused, unsure of the right word, "gene mixes slowly into the human body, then the chances of them surviving are greater. So my guess is that they would've asked the boys if they wanted to take the risk."

I noticed my mother was just pushing the rice and meat around her plate, "When she found out she was having twin boys, though, she became very, very concerned. The entire community felt it too. It was like something in the planets began to shift. Something in the undercurrent of life was changing, but no one knew what or how or why. We all began to prepare for the worst."

She stopped eating and took my hand, "And now we know that the worst has started. We just don't fully know what that 'worst' is."

"What happened to everyone else in the community?" I asked.

My dad answered, "We don't know. After we went underground, we didn't try to reconnect with any of them. We didn't know who we could trust and, as I mentioned before, we never did find out who attacked us."

"Could they still be out there? I mean, how long does a vampire live, or would they all be gone by now?"

My mother replied, "Our friends were killed along with your father at your parent's house. Other vampires may just have died over the past few years, but vampires live a long time. Hundreds of centuries even."

Long life. Wow. Even longer than Devon and Tom thought. There was nothing much else left to say and I didn't have any more questions for them at the time. We all finished our dinners in silence.

Helping my dad with the dishes afterward, for a few moments it was like I was still a human son trying to splash him before he could get me. I did show off a couple of my new abilities, but only slightly and just to be funny with it – acting like I had dropped a plate and then catching it at the last minute – letting him time how fast I could put the dishes away. *Less than fifteen seconds.*

"Impressive," he told me, "why don't you come home every night. I'll pay you to be our maid."

"Yeah? I don't think so," I said while wiping off the dining room table. Once we were done cleaning up, we all sat down and watched a couple of stupid reality shows. I missed being with them, but when I saw them yawning around 11 p.m., way past their bedtime, I knew I needed to get back to the apartment. I got up to leave.

"Do you want to stay the night? Your room is exactly how you left it," My mom was hopeful.

I kissed her on the forehead, "It's ok mom. I'll be home again soon. I promise. I need to make the last ferry though, so I should probably get going."

My dad stuck out his hand to shake mine. I grabbed it and he pulled me into a hug, "Stay safe, son. Let us know what's going on and how we can help."

Yeah right, like I would bring them further into this!

"Mom, I do have another question about all of this."

"I'll try to answer it as best as I can."

"That's all I'm really asking. The guys that I'm staying with, Devon and Tom, they were bitten too, but it seems like it was very random. Why would vampires change people outside the family line?"

"Hmm. Well, along the centuries there have been rogue vampires, and I'm not just talking about the ones that were not part of the family. I mean there have been some evil vampires in the past that would create other vampires to use as weapons. Hell, even something like spouses 'stepping out' on one another and creating a vampire out of lust is possible."

Dad added, "Don't forget that every vampire experiences humanity at first. That doesn't mean that they experience humanity at its best either, and those traits still carry over once they are changed. You are still you, Keen. You are just an enhancement of what you were. That's all. And you will always be our son, no matter what."

Before I stepped out the back door my mom turned me to her, "Keen, I don't know for sure what's been set in motion, but I do know that you need to find your brother and keep him safe. I also know that if he hasn't been bitten already, he needs to stay that way. He cannot be brought back into the family. It's not safe for either of you two."

Inwardly I cringed, remembering Mr. Carmichael's theory that Adam had already been bitten.

I promised I would do my best and walked down the steps of the patio. I turned around and waved at them when I got near the edge of the line where the light from the house faded into nothingness. I knew both of them would be standing there, waiting for me to disappear. They waved back and I walked into the shrouding darkness.

✶ ✶ ✶

To Do List

Even with my fast speed, I almost missed the ferry back to the mainland. I didn't go back to the apartment right away, though. I walked around town for a while, just taking in the sights and sounds of the night – the occasional squawk of a seagull settling down for sleep, the water lapping against the boats, the random pedestrian heading home from the pub.

There was so much to think about. *So much to do.* I didn't even know where to begin to find my brother. *No, not my brother. My twin.* Walking down the old train tracks, the ones that are used as a tourist train ride around the port, my head felt like it was swimming:

Do I start with tracking him down? Figuring out what the weirdness is behind the dagger I'm using or the coin that Mr. Carmichael gave us? And what about Alexandra? What does she have to do with this? Are there any more vampires out there trying to track me down or kill me like she wanted to do? I mean, even with Devon and Tom at my back, am I really all that protected? And what about T? Is it really safe that I'm around her? I don't think I could live with myself if her beautiful body were hurt.

Oh, hello! Bring it back in from left field, you still have a girlfriend.

Maddie, Maddie, Maddie, I repeated in my mind.

Yes, that's the one. You know, the girl you're still in love with. The one you want to marry. No thinking of other women, the guilty, little angel-side of me said.

Of course, the little devil on my shoulder whispered in my ear, *Maddie thinks I'm dead. I might as well be dead to her. Why can't I look at other women?*

The angel answered, *Because you and Maddie are not done yet. Your death doesn't officially end things with her.*

Oh, I don't know. Death seems pretty final, my devil-side argued.

You are walking, talking, breathing.. ok, not breathing, but you're doing the other things. You are alive and you still have a girlfriend... whom you love.

Even the devil-side of me couldn't argue with that. I really did still love Maddie. With everything that I had left in me. Not with my non-beating heart or the air that I couldn't take into my lungs, but with my soul and my mind. *Do I really have feelings for T? I don't know. Maybe she's just a distraction from all this so that I don't have to think of Maddie.*

That's gotta be all that T is, I convinced myself, *Find a way to get back to Maddie.*

OK, I'll add that to my To-Do list, I laughed at the thought, but at least it brought me full-circle back to the task at hand, which was to figure out what to do next. *Adam's the most important piece. Everything else can wait. The dagger, the coin, Alexandra, Maddie, and T. All of those are just gonna have to wait.*

Finally, I headed back to the place I had called home for the past while and decided to sleep for a couple of hours since the last time had been at Mr. Carmichael's, *I mean, Uncle Joel's house.* I smiled a little at that. Even if his methods were a little skewed, he was my mother's brother and I had even more family to find. For now, though, I needed to reboot my system before I could do so. *A short nap and then off to save my own brother.*

Chapter 11

The Last Hold on My Humanity

✧ ✧ ✧

An Unexpected Visitor

It had been a week and we were still no closer to finding out where Adam had been taken or where Alexandra had been lurking. The significance of the coin and the blade had kept us busy too, with trails that led to other trails, but nothing of significance – yet. We couldn't find a story, a mention or even a person that could tell us more about the mysterious prophecy I was supposedly a part of. While I reviewed online forums and websites about Jewish mythology, Devon and Tom had tried looking through the city and college libraries. T even went to the local Jewish temples and spoke with Rabbis under the guise that she was doing a college term paper on early Biblical stories. *Vampires, apparently, don't write anything down.*

I had begun to really like the fact that vampires only needed two hours of sleep a day. Besides looking into my little conundrum, we still had to do night patrols of the harbor. There had been an influx of vampires during the past week, but Devon said that was to be expected this time of year. *I guess vampires are tourists, too!*

There was a knock on the door, but none of us moved. T was at the computer reviewing DVDs of footage from the cameras that were installed all around the city in order to find where Alexandra had run off to. She had been at it for the past few days as there were several tens of disks to review. The only good news was that Alexandra had one of those looks that stood out in this area. So we kept our fingers crossed and our asses out of T's way.

In an effort to do that, Tom was reading a magazine on the couch. Devon and I were playing a game of Slap Jack – which can be a bit painful when you're playing against a vampire. Fortunately, we heal quickly. On that last jack he had turned up, however, I was just not quick enough and *Wham!* Broken finger... and then we watched it mend. *So cool!*

The knock happened again.

We all looked at Tom.

"Oh all right," Tom exasperated, "I'll get it."

He got up and trounced down the steps to the front door.

I was just about to whack Devon's hand as a jack fell on the stack of cards when my ears perked up at the sound of a voice and a scent that lingered up through the stairwell and into the apartment.

I knew it so well.

My attention moved away from the game and Devon's hand rapped so quickly against my knuckles that skin drew off to the bone and that oozy, clear blood dripped. Not even the stinging sensation pulled my eyes away from the direction of the apartment entrance. *It would heal before she saw me.*

Maddie.

"We have a visitor," Tom shouted up the steps, as any normal college student would do to get their dorm-mates attention. It was also code for 'Pack up all the shit as to not freak out the human.' Devon and I flew around the room hiding the weapons and maps. *We really need to try to put things away after we use them. Crap, I'm beginning to think like my mother.* T pushed a button at her desk and all but the normal computer peripherals went bye-bye.

Tom stomped up the stairs dramatically and slowly to give us more time, not that we needed it. I could hear her tiny footsteps behind him, hesitant and nervous. By the time they reached the top of the steps, we were all back to our places acting like we had always been there.

Maddie saw T first and a flicker of jealousy pained her face for a second. I smiled to myself, *That's my girl!*

Her eyes continued around the room and then landed on me. A look of regret from her dropped my internal smile immediately. But I showed her the dashing, happy face that was saved just for her. I tried to put all my heart and love into that one smile to reassure her. I got up and moved toward her. We stood there, taking each other in, noticing any subtle changes in the other from the months apart. She had on a tight, green T-shirt and blue jeans that showed her belly button piercing. *So sexy.*

Tom said, "Well we should probably just…"

I glared at him.

"Yup, yeah, we're going… now," he stuttered.

I nodded my thanks.

Devon said, "Let's give them some privacy," as T began to protest that she was about to beat her high score for Bejeweled 3 on the computer. Devon picked her up and swung her over his shoulder like she was a sack of potatoes.

Once T was out of Maddie's ear shot, I heard her say, "You never let me watch the good parts."

Good? I thought, watching Maddie's face, *This is anything but good.*

☆ ☆ ☆

Reunion

"Hi." We both said in unison. Her voice was bell-like, a subtle high nervousness to it. Her voice was higher pitched than most women I knew, but not in the way that would make you want to pierce your inner eardrum just to deafen yourself. Hers was the kind of voice that made you think of bees gathering pollen from wildflowers that were waving, carefree, in the wind. Not too high, not to low, just right on the ears. It made me want to instantly relax into old habits with her even though I knew that wasn't possible, so I dropped my gaze. She had done the same shy motion as well.

She was the first to speak again, "Hi."

I lifted my eyes and smiled. She looked at me and then looked around, clearly uncomfortable with my new living quarters since she was so used to the museum that was my parents' house.

"How've you been?" I asked.

"Ok," she answered, "You?"

"It's been a little crazy," *How much can I tell her? How much should I tell her?*

She walked around for a few minutes, picking up things here and there, I think more out of nerves than curiosity.

My memory didn't capture her voice nearly as well as I thought it had. Wanting to hear more of her beautiful voice, I asked a very stupid question, "How's your summer been?"

She put down the magazine she had been mindlessly flipping through and gazed at me with sad eyes, "It's been difficult."

"Yeah, I know what you mean." I mentally smacked myself in the forehead, *That was probably not the best way to start this conversation off.* I put my hands deep in my pockets, pushing down on the material a little bit in frustration. The chayyim medallion was tucked away in my right pocket and I could feel its cool metal against my fingertips, but I found no comfort or calm of having it there.

Suddenly, Maddie came over to me, more confident than she had been when she had arrived. Her eyes darted all over my face, not looking at my eyes. Her eyebrows pinched slightly in her expression of confusion. "Something looks different about you," she said as she brought her hand up to my cheek.

I jerked back in surprise and caught her hand reflexively as I flashed back to the dream I had at Mr. Carmichael's. I dropped her hand just as quickly, *This can't be happening again, can it? She has to be real this time, right?*

My impulsive and unearthly movements stunned her and she backed away from me, stopping only when she hit a chair that had been a few feet behind her. I caught her before she fell over it, righted her, and then moved back to the spot where I had been before she approached me. Her face went from disbelief to fear-struck before she was able to gain her composure.

"Maddie, I am so sorry," *I hope I didn't just wreck this. I must've scared the crap out of her.*

She walked over to the window and stared out of it. I kept my distance, allowing her some time to overcome how freaked out she must have been. *This is going to be awkward.* I couldn't help watching her though, even if she was turned away from me. I couldn't believe she was there. *Am I dreaming again? If so, I don't want to wake up to have her gone or changed or something.* I don't think I could take that again.

"How did you find me?" I blurted that one out unintentionally. *Ah well.*

"Every few days, I visit with your family to see if they have any news on you. I went there the other night. As I walked past the window, I heard your voice.

I wasn't sure at first. I thought I was just willing it to be there, but then you spoke again and I knew."

Oh! I thought as realization struck me hard, *The 'kid' that had walked past the window, the memory I couldn't place. It was her. I was just too focused on my parents at the time to realize it!*

She looked down, embarrassed, "I'm not proud of this, Keen, but I heard some of your conversation. I was just so, I don't know, lost after I heard," she paused, fumbling for a way to say what she needed to say, "after I heard what you are going through, I ran off over to the back of the island. You know, to our spot."

Of course, I knew. The cliffs. On the back shore there was a place where dropping just a few feet in the water could literally kill you, either by crushing you against the rocks or pulling you out to sea in a quick second. *Even with death being that close, or maybe because of it, it was one of the most beautiful places on the coast.*

She continued, "I didn't know what to do, so I sat out there for a while. You were so close to me and I couldn't will myself to move and go to you. I was shocked. I'm not going to lie about that."

Her eyes moved back to mine again, "When it got close to 11, though, I headed back to the docks to make the boat."

"I didn't see you on it," *Or smell you, I should've been able to do that at least!*

"I know. I was up on the top level while you were standing where you always go."

The bow. I smiled, thinking about the wind in my face. *That would've put her down wind from me and my mind had been too far gone in thought about the prophecy to sense her.*

"Besides, you looked very thoughtful yourself," She joked and then turned serious again, "I followed you around when you left the ferry. I wanted to know where you lived."

"Why did you wait so long to come find me again? It's been a while since I spoke to my parents." Although, just that morning I had been on the island, watching them from afar. *Still not used to the fact that they are ok with me the way I am.*

"I needed to think about this. About us. About all of the changes going on in your life. I wasn't ready to see you suddenly, knowing that you've been alive all this time and haven't even come to see me," Her voice sounded hurt although she was trying to put on a good front.

"I'm sorry, Maddie. I've never stopped thinking about you through all of this. Seeing you in my mind… It's what kept me going. Keeps me going now. But I didn't know how to approach you after all of what happened. I thought you would run. Far."

I paused, "Really far."

She grinned a little at me, "You know, in my heart I knew that you were still alive somewhere. Hiding for some reason."

"How?"

"There was a picture of us that I put on the shriney-kind of thing that everyone put together on the spot where you, uhm, where they thought you disappeared from. I visit there often," she became shy, "I like looking at all of the crap our friends left and I'd sit there thinking that maybe you'd come back one day unharmed. I don't know, I guess it was stupid for me to think like that."

She didn't give me time to try to console her, whisper words to tell her that everything was ok, before she continued on, "Some of the stuff there had been knocked around one night so I tried to put things back up in place. I noticed our picture wasn't there. It could've easily fallen into the water," she looked directly in my eyes, "but I knew it was you. It had to be."

Oh my God, she never gave up hope. She knew. This could turn out ok.

"You're right," I pulled the picture out of my back pocket. It was folded, bent and slightly misshapen from keeping it there, but it was always with me. *Always.*

She took the photo from me, glancing at it deep in thought, and then put it down on the table. I didn't reach for it. With her there, I didn't need it anymore. *Not with the real thing in front of me. The live and breath-taking version right here. Right now.* "Do you want to take a walk?" I asked, "I know we need to talk and I want to explain everything to you. Answer what I can."

"That sounds nice," she replied.

I walked toward her, trying to figure out if I should reach for her hand, slide my arm around her waist or something else that would take us back to the way we had been. *I'm not opposed to playing dirty.* But I didn't. Instead, I swept my arm out in a 'After you' gesture and followed her back down the steps. I locked the door behind us and we turned left to walk up the street.

We made it to Lincoln Park in complete silence, walking next to each other, trying hard to not bump the other. For me, it was for fear of her flinching if she touched me and finding out that our chemistry had changed since the last time we were together. *That my skin was different. Cold. Unmoving. Dead.*

Of course it's changed, Dipshit. You're a vampire now. Get it through your thick head! Shutting down the mental argument, I said, "Seriously, though, how are you really?" We headed toward the center of the park where the fountain was and sat down on the bench closest to it. *It's like déjà vu.* It was exactly how it had been in the dream I'd had when I was at Mr. Carmichael's. *Hopefully, she won't turn into Alexandra this time.* I shuddered at the thought.

She shrugged, "I'm ok. You?"

"I'm all right. Better now that you're here." I smiled and she returned it. It made me hopeful, thinking again that *Maybe this really could be ok.* "Maddie," I started.

She broke into my words, angry, "What happened to you, Keen? Where have you been?"

I didn't answer at first. *What can I answer? Or should?* I looked around instead, trying to choose the right words, ones that would keep her with me even if for a little while. *Since asking for forever might be a little much right now.* It was beautiful out. The sky was blue. The grass was dark green. People were laying out on blankets and towels having a picnic or just reading a book. More than a few people were out rollerblading through and around the park, too. I quickly took in everyone around us, checking their auras and making sure they were all blue. They were. "Maddie, I've changed."

"I can see that," she teased, less mad at me, and lightly punched me in the arm, "Ow." She shook her hand out.

"Yeah, sorry about that. That's part of the change, too."

She looked confused.

"Ok, where to start?" It was more of a question to myself than to her, but she still answered.

"How about you start on the day you disappeared."

"No." I responded tersely.

"No?" She was taken aback at my short response.

"No. That's too confusing," *And would get me into a shit-load of trouble. Need to play my cards right. And right now, my cards are calling for the sympathy play.*

I thought for a minute, "Maddie, I found out who my biological family is."

"That's great!" She sounded excited and then she saw my face and asked in a more unsure voice, "right?"

"Well, yes and no."

Over the next few minutes, I filled her in about my new-found family, my reactions to it and how the thoughts of just seeing her had gotten me through all the craziness of the journey.

We sat in silence as she absorbed what I had told her. If I had a beating heart, it would've been thumping like I had kayaked a long-distance race or run the Boston marathon – it would've been trying to jump out of my chest. I was so scared to tell her about everything and I wasn't really ready for it either. In our conversation, I didn't tell her that before the incident, I had been thinking of asking her to marry me.

After about ten minutes I asked her if she was all right.

She played with her hands in her lap, picking at something invisible in them, and then got up after a moment. She took my hand, pulling at me. We walked, slowly hand-in-hand around the fountain. Maddie stopped suddenly, turning to face me and I knew it was coming. "I can't be part of your world, Keen. I'm afraid for you," She said calmly.

For me? "Don't you mean 'of me'?" I gritted my teeth trying and failing to not show her that my heart was breaking. I had loved her since the day I met her. I couldn't believe things were going to end between us.

"I'm not afraid of you. You're the nicest guy I've ever met," She smiled and put her hand on my arm, reassuring me.

"Wow, and I thought I'd delivered the kiss of death," I mocked in short anger.

"Please don't be mad. You know I love you, but I just don't think I can do this. Please don't ask me to."

"I'm not mad, Mad," I used her nickname to shelf the blow.

Sad, hurt. Loneliness was beginning to brew. And fear. *If she couldn't love me – no, would not love me – then who would ever love me now that I was no longer human?*

"You know, if only you were an elf.." She trailed off, smiling mischievously.

I smiled, too, *If you only knew.* Devon had told me terrible things about elves, none of which I was going to mention to her.

It's time to be a man about this, though. "Maddie, I am always here for you. I love you, but I won't ask you to be with me if you can't be. I understand. I didn't want this either. It's been so crazy these past few months. I never thought it would be this way," I pulled away from her and dodged her sorrowful eyes, "I was still hoping you could see me as a human. No that's not right, because I will never be that again."

Sighing, torn and no longer able to hold my feelings in, I caught her eyes with mine and turned her body gently to me. Laying my hands on her shoulders, dropping the protective wall around me, I made one last plea, begging, "You know, before all this began, I was actually hoping to ask you to marry me. I'm still hoping that you can see me as your husband and you as my wife. But I don't want to put you in danger either. And I'm not sure how to do both. Is it possible? Can we try?" My words were so soft it was like I was trying to convince myself as well as her.

I bent down to kiss her on the lips, her eyes closing as I approached. Gently, trying to convey all the years we'd spent together and all the ones that I wanted to spend with her… *All the years that would come. We could live for centuries together. How's that for a fairytale ending?*

Pulling back to look at her face, I noticed that her eyes were still closed.

"Your wife," she whispered, her lips curling up at the edges into a tiny smile.

I took in a sharp breath, trying not to get my hopes up, but wanting her to tell me how crazy I was for thinking that she could be in danger while she was around me. *Could she actually be considering it?*

Her eyes opened with love and desire in them. But her smile dimmed. "I can't, Keen," she broke away from me, her eyes to the ground as she continued, "And it's not because of whatever this danger is. I don't care about that."

I took her chin, softly, in my hand, guiding her head up. I wanted to see those beautiful eyes, see if she really believed in what she was saying, "If it's not the danger, what is it? Besides the obvious, is there something else about me that I can change?"

My thoughts took on an irrational pleading tone. *I mean, was this coming before I changed? Had I been a horrible person to her? Had she been growing apart from me? I can't think of anything other than being so happy with her. Was I missing something? Was she in love with someone else?*

She took my hand in hers, "I guess I should say that I never fantasized about how big of a wedding I was going to have or if I was ever going to get married. That has never been important to me. The only thing I ever dreamed about was growing old together with someone. With you."

What in the hell does that mean? I tried not to show confusion.

"I've thought about this. I want to grow old, Keen. I don't want to outlive generations of my family. I want to grow old and then I want to move on from this life."

An emptiness filled the pit of my stomach and I felt sick as I realized the meaning of what she had said to me. *She wants a life I could never give her – one with a chance at a natural death.* "Is there anything I can do to change your mind? This does have its perks, you know?" I tried to smile and make a joke, but it came out more like begging.

She smiled sweetly, knowingly. But she shook her head, "I can't." She stood up on her toes, closing her eyes again, and kissed me on the cheek.

A goodbye.

But that wasn't enough for me. *If this is 'goodbye' then I'm going to do it right.* Wrapping my arms around her tiny frame, I pulled her into my chest one last time, feeling her take in a swift breath of surprise. Touching my lips to hers, I pressed into her. I slipped my tongue past her parted mouth and searched for hers. They joined together, mingling in her mouth. She leaned into me and I could feel her tears, wet against my face.

It really is over. I broke the kiss, as my un-beating heart shattered, and moved toward her ear. "I love you," I whispered, letting go of her warm body. *Letting go of her. Letting go of us.*

I left before she could open her eyes. Running my now normal pace, putting distance between her scent, the park, the wind and salt and the sea, I did not care if anyone noticed a human-looking blur brushing by.

It was either my wishful thinking or my inhuman hearing, but I swear I heard the words carry in the air around me, "I love you too, Keen."

☆ ☆ ☆

Reaction

The woods passed in streaks by me – bright and dark greens infiltrated by brown, vertical blurs of the tree trunks. It was mile after mile of the same. Each passed like they had never been there in the first place, but I couldn't stop running.

I didn't want to.

Stopping would mean thinking.

Thinking would mean defeat.

If I stopped running then my life would catch up to me and what was my life without Maddie? I mean really without her. I guess I knew she could never be part of my life *and now... She's gone.* She had left on her own decision. But my heart didn't want to accept it. The pain of it rumbled through me as I thought of her choice. The choice to leave me because of what I had become. Something so hideous. So dangerous.

So dangerous, to her.

So much for wanting the 'Til death do us part.' A sarcastic laugh bubbled up from my stomach, catching in my throat. What was I talking about? *I did die.*

Murdered.

My life with Maddie, my friends, even my family had been completely taken away from me by an evil, murderous vampire. The thought of it all turned my sadness into heated aggression.

A laugh burst through my throat, followed by a sound that came from so deep in the pit of what was left of my body that I thought I was going to be torn apart by it.

The scream echoed in the forest.

I stopped and bent over. I wasn't winded. My vampire muscles were far from exhausted. I just needed to stop, to dig down where that scream came from and do it again. All the frustration, the anger, the sadness bottled up from the past few weeks was finally catching up to me and exploding.

I screamed again. It came out in a horrible, painful shriek. A steam boiler exploding. An earthquake shattering glass. Of similar power were the sounds coming from me, my vampire lungs. *My inhumanness.*

It felt awful.

It felt releasing.

A flock of Canadian geese flew up from their resting place just to get away from the sound.

To get away from me. My sensitive hearing picked up movements of other creatures running to leave the area around me, *The big bad vampire. I don't blame them. I want to get away from me, too.*

I am a bomb waiting to explode. I want to get into a fight where I could lose. I want to do some damage to myself. I don't know, maybe run into a black bear and get mauled? Could I even lose against it? Would it even hurt? Physical pain is much easier to deal with than this shitty mental anguish.

"I am so tired of this!" The scream and pain in my voice scared even my own ears. I was tired of feeling inhuman no matter how cool the unintended effects were. I wanted to be a real person again – one with moving internal organs. I wanted Maddie to want me. *I want to be human for her.*

This needs to be a dream. I wanted to wake up the next day and go play a pick up game of street hockey with the guys. I wanted to laugh with my friends, the ones I'd known since grade school.

Hell, I even want to do some homework.

Something normal.

"Anything but this!" I yelled at the forest.

I breathed in deeply, trying to calm myself. I took my iPod from my pocket and hoped the music would help silence the small rips in my otherwise quiet heart. Or at least hoping the music would melt away the emotions that I wished were gone from me – wishing they would've left when I died. *Because this is a bitch.*

Gold flickered to the ground when I pulled the iPod from its resting place. I bent over to pick up the disfigured medallion. *'Life,'* the symbol meant. I held it in my open palm, staring at it, trying to find some reason, some meaning behind the word, but only seeing the bite mark that Alexandra had left in it, forever marring it. *Like me – bitten, dented and almost broken.* Fighting the instinct to throw the chayyim as far from me as my strength would allow, I let it retreat back to the pocket it had fallen from. I wasn't ready to let go of it yet.

Turning the iPod on and locking it in place so the tracks wouldn't jump around, I ran. *I need to get away from these thoughts.*

I ran out of the trees and towards the rocky coast. Climbing the cliff shores unseen was easy now that I had made it so far north and I was far enough away from civilization. I was too fast anyway. *A blur.* Tom Petty sang the last few bars of *Wildflowers* before it changed to the Gnarls Barkley song, 'Just a Thought.'

I listened to the lyrics about love, lack of understanding and a brief thought of suicide. It fit my mood perfectly. The song ended with the singer saying that although he's thought so many crazy things, he's actually fine.

Am I fine? I mused, *Am I really?*

Yeah, I'm fine. At least I will be.

I think.

Coming out of my blind running stupor, I stopped to gage my environment. Patronizing myself, I thought, *Yes, yes, I'll be fine, but where the hell am I?*

The cliffs were still rocky where I was standing, but up on the hills were several one story houses and lobster shacks. All of them had a white flag with a red maple leaf on it.

Canada. Swell.

I'll have to go back the way I came since I don't have my passport on me.

But my mind turned to a wicked thought, *Not that breaking out of a border-crossing jail would be that hard with my strength, but I'm not in the mood to deal with anyone just yet.*

I breathed the deep scent of pine and maple – the maple was stronger there than it had been a few miles back in the US. I realized I liked the maple smell better than the pine, but both calmed me down. It was getting dark; the skies were beginning to turn from deep blue to black, the clouds were shot with streaks of bright neon pinks, yellows and oranges. Looking at my watch, it had taken me only four hours to run a trip that would've taken me the same doing slightly faster than the speed limit in a car. Still surprising to me, nothing on my body was sore.

Physically, I didn't feel tired. Emotionally, well, that was a different story. I sat down on the rocks and watched the black waters roll in and out, foaming hard bubbles as they did.

"What am I going to do?" *I am all out of answers.*

"Do I keep going on like this? Living a life without Maddie, without anyone to love or share it with? Am I destined to be alone like Tom and Devon?"

Am I even that independent that I could do it?

I'd like to think that I am, but really, when was the last time I was without a girlfriend?

I'd had other girlfriends, but Maddie was my first for everything real. And I mean everything. We grew together and became the personalities we were by learning things together. *Can I give that up? Can I just walk away from the love of my life?*

"Should I fight for her?"

Would she want me to?

I shook my head 'no' at the thought.

"Would I want to?"

Think about her safety and what it means to have her in my life. The danger with all this bat-shit crazy stuff going on? With Alexandra still being out there, somewhere. Any human would be unsafe until this thing got settled.

"Then there's that whole prophecy crap. Real or not?" I said to myself.

Does it matter? People believe in it. That makes it real enough and dangerous for anyone around me, including Tom, Devon, T and my parents.

So again, would I want to fight for her?

"It's just not safe for her. Maybe one day I can go back to her."

Maybe. But today is not that day.

For now, leave her to live her life. Figure out this prophecy thing. Find my brother.

In my misery, I had forgotten all about that. Forgotten about him. *My brother.* I stood up in an instant.

Purpose. Focus. These are good things. I'll throw myself into them.

"I'll concentrate on finding Adam," That would leave no time to think of Maddie.

I smiled to myself.

Problem solved.

Chapter 12

All Things Come to a Head

✧ ✧ ✧

Run in with Evil

Only it wasn't. Over the next few days I threw myself into trying to find my brother. And during that time, I went through the different stages of getting over someone. Usually, this took weeks for me, but maybe the hours that I spent awake allowed me to go through them all the more quickly.

First there was sadness that Maddie and I had broken up – the continual ache in my empty body, the goopy tears that would shoot out of my eyes spontaneously. It was embarrassing; I felt like such an idiot. T tried to console me, Tom tried to joke with me and Devon just became uncomfortable and annoyed at me.

Then there was anger at being rejected and thoughts of *How can she do this to me, to us?* A flame would heat the bare cavity of my heart and I'd break things accidentally, *Or purposely,* not paying attention to my strength like when I was doing the dishes or taking out the empty bottles of Bloody Captain's. *Or when I shredded the crap out of the photo of me and Maddie.*

Denial was the next phase, *There is no way she meant it. I need to go find her right now and just tell her that she can't break up with me.* The guys had fun with this stage – Tom would hold me back while Devon would tell him to let me go. At least Tom tried to talk some sense into me.

The sadness stage would come back – the depression of not having her in my life and the tears that couldn't come to me except in thick gel-like seepage.

Reality was the last stage. I recognized that I needed to give her up and find out where life was going to take me. Then I would go through all the phases again. But after the third round of craziness and pain and inhuman tears, strength came back to me as I hardened my heart against loving anyone again. And I was ok with that. It may have not been a true reality, but it was the reality I was going to buy into. *For now.*

"Anybody thirsty?" I asked. It was day four after the 'Big Breakup' and I owed the guys big-time for putting up with my ridiculous Dr. Jekyll and Mr. Hyde personality disorder. Getting them a drink was the first start in trying to make up for being the ass I had been.

The answers I got were "Yes," "Yes," and "Gross!"

Ok, so that's two blood beers for the vamps plus one for me and nothing for the human.

It was around 2 a.m. Saturday morning. T was still on DVD duty, tracking the movements around the city for Alexandra, but she hadn't found anything yet and we were still keeping out of her way. She could be such a machine sometimes. Her being a human, I don't know how she was even doing it! She was taking a three-credit, summer art course that was the equivalent of taking a four-month course and slamming it into 3 weeks. She went to class for five hours a day and went back for the lab portion well into the evening and sometimes early in the morning. It was sheer madness! She spent almost as much time awake as we did and it seemed like she never really tired.

In the meantime, Devon was sharpening his knives and Tom was playing a mafia game on the Wii. I moved in a flash over to the fridge and opened it. *Well crap!* Two beers left. *Ah well.* It was my turn to go stock up from the liquor and market store downstairs. It was convenient that it was right next door to us, I must admit, especially on those extremely lazy days where none of us really wanted to move to go get essential items.

I threw the guys their brews with full vampire speed. Tom didn't even look up from the game when he caught it.

Show off. "I'll be back. Need anything else from the packie?"

All three began firing off lists at me for junk food, milk, blood brews, garbage bags and Moxie, a drink that was like an anise spiced Dr. Pepper on crack. Anyone who was truly from here, not 'from away,' had drank Moxie by the liters since 1884. It was an acquired taste, something only Northerners actually got into. And I was not one of those people that liked it. Now, I couldn't even stand to be in the same room with it since I went through the change. Horehound spice was just so over-powering that it felt like someone was putting fire up my nose and laughing.

Glad I have super strength to carry all this crap. Now if only I had more hands!

I wrote down the list with a speed I wished I'd had while taking my first semester college exams and then headed below to the store. *Too bad my memory didn't improve with all these changes, but I guess I can't have everything!*

It was nice being able to walk into a place that I used to go to all the time as a human. It made me think how disillusioned I had been in my 'previous' life, as I had no idea that it had this otherness about it – that it actually provided supplies for 'alternative' lifestyles, and not just Vegans and organic food lovers. In fact, after 11 PM, if T tried to walk into the store by herself, she would get as far as the curb in front and think the place was closed. Tons of wards were set up to keep the regular population out of it late at night.

I went outside our door, turned to the right and went in the door not 10 feet away from ours. Walking up the three old, wooden steps was like walking through a time warp of a century with each one. I could hear the voices of the ghosts of sailors within each creak of the boards. They were calling me to add my own sound.

Smells of fish and beer and oil leaked into them, wafting up at me with every movement. Each intake of my senses was its own history lesson – a story of all those who stepped there before me. I even caught a whiff or two of my human self.

The design of the shop was small and cramped, yet every inch of it called its customers to become part of its rich mish-mash. To the right, at the top of the stairs, was an old table-top coffee machine against the wall with two chintzy, ripped up, high-back chairs underneath it. The only thing they had in common was that they each were made from some semblance of leather and were probably constructed in the 1960s. In front of me was a table that had a checkers board stained into it. The table was surrounded by two metal chairs that seemed to have given up as places for people to sit on. Foam and fluff were oozing out of their cushions and their twisted, metal arms were streaked with rusted scratches. *Can a vampire get tetanus?* I didn't think so, but I stayed away from them anyway.

The store floor was made from the same dark, ancient wood as the steps. I imagined they were made from planks of old pirate ships, but that was just the kid in me daydreaming. The wood was raked with cuts and dents; dirt from forever ago was trapped in the cracks, chunks were knocked out of them. *There is character in that wood, that's for sure.*

The wares in the store, themselves, seemed random at first glance. There were two racks of crappy junk food sitting behind the checkered table. Devil Dogs, Funny Bones, Utz BBQ chips, Humpty-Dumpty Salt & Vinegar chips, Cheeze Whiz and Funions were choices of mine during my human years, depending on the mood of the day.

Prior to Alexandra, my fall-back plan of what-should-I-snack-on-today had always been to grab a bag of Ruffles and head over to the right wall where the refrigerated cases started to get a tub of Helluva Onion Dip. The sweet, caramelized onion flavor mixed with smooth sour cream always made my mouth water. *Well, until recently.* With my discriminating sense of smell, it just made my nose tango with its sharpness – and not in a good way. *If only I had the taste for those!*

Next to the chip dips and salsas were the bottled water, teas, sodas and beer. The back of the wall continued the beer choices and then the very cheap, but very drunk-inducing, wine and the even cheaper wine-in-a-box. *Fun at tailgating, no matter what sport.* All of the blood beers were hidden, with the rest of the alternative dietary needs, in refrigeration units in a back room. *Don't want to scare the humans!*

I turned to my left to ask Dennis, the store owner and a vampire wizard who was surrounded by stale cigarette products and non-winning lottery tickets, *Well at least I never won anything,* for my order of blood beers. My goal was that while he got the beers, I would make my rounds to get the rest of my shopping done.

That goal did not happen. *Best laid plans never do.*

When I turned, I saw the back of *Her!* With her black, magnificent hair and body wrapped in Gothic leather, even with her curls straightened, I would have known her anywhere.

Alexandra.

Shit.

She smelled completely different to me from when I was a human and if I hadn't seen her, I would've never noticed her until it was too late. I must not have smelled the same either, because she remained focused on Dennis ringing her items up. She was more sensual than I remembered her being, with the aroma of new rain in a flower garden. It was freaky how entrancing she was and *I need to shake my head from those thoughts and think about how I can get the hell out of here without her noticing!*

As long as she didn't look up into the security mirror, I would be able to back up and call for the guys since I knew the windows were open to our apartment and I hadn't left without my ear piece this time. Just as I was thinking about my next move, she looked up into the mirror and smiled. Her red-painted lips bared very long and very sharp fangs. Even her lower ones jutted out and *She is still sexy.*

Shit again. I have no manner of luck whatsoever with this woman! The sight of her made my body turn involuntarily toward her, wanting the pain and pleasure of our last meeting. My feet stuck to the floor in agony of choice. *Stay or go?*

"You," her voice said in my head, in a pointed but not surprised manner. At the sound of her I finally gained control – her voice was so much of a threat that even my lust couldn't shake off my flight instincts.

I dropped my grocery list and reached for the dagger hidden on my back. I pulled to release it and threw it with lightening speed at her. She grabbed it out of the air like I had gently tossed it to her, then she repelled it back at me with the same quickness, only less shaky, as my aim.

My thoughts were slower than my body, but, thankfully, my body moved on its own and ducked out of the way. The dagger slammed into the coffee pot, shattering it and spraying day-old coffee everywhere. The smell of burnt earth shot through my nostrils as if the coffee beans had been roasting for eons instead of a couple of hours.

I looked at it and then at her and sprang. But when I landed, she was no longer there. She had grabbed her stuff, left the balance in money and was gone. *How in the hell did she do that?*

Dennis didn't even flinch at our actions; this must've been a regular occurrence in his store. He just said, "You're gonna have to pay for that," and gestured at the coffee machine.

"Put it on Devon's tab," I said and dashed back to the dagger. I pulled it from the back wall and then took off out the door opposite the one I had entered, the one Alexandra had left through.

I ran up Exchange Street, following her scent. My pace was being matched, which freaked me out until I realized it was Devon and Tom in pursuit with me. "How?" I asked as we made it to where the street split left and right.

"T," was all Devon needed to say.

My guardian angel.

Alexandra had gone left. We had sight of her ahead of us by several dozen yards, but it was so odd that I didn't think I was seeing her correctly. She was flashing in and out of sight. She would disappear and then, like a strobe of lights hitting someone, she would appear again a couple of yards away. It was disconcerting to watch, but we were beginning to gain on her – especially Tom. *He is just wicked fast!*

She ran down another left, making her direction go toward the water.

She's trapped herself now.

With that last turn, Alexandra had dodged herself down a dead end. We halted ourselves at the entrance and looked down the street, waiting for a possible attack as we glanced around the corner.

Nothing.

No crazy hot, evil vampire.

There wasn't even a garbage container in sight. She had completely disappeared. We ran to the end of the block. There were no doors for her to escape through. It was just three sides of solid brick windowless walls.

Devon spoke into his microphone, "Where did she go, T?"

"I don't know, Devon. I lost her when she left the store. I only picked up Keen's and your movements on the cameras," T sounded as if she were at a loss as to what the heck was going on.

"Whoa," Tom said, "No vampire can move that fast, can they?"

I turned to Devon for his answer. He didn't. I was frustrated, "Fantastic! Just freakin' great. Not only is Alexandra hot and dangerous, but she can go invisible, too? No freakin' way!"

We all studied the environment around us. Devon fixed his eyes downward, "T, anything in the sewers?"

There was a pause and a couple of clicking noises over our earpieces and then, "Not even a rat is out."

Good, I hate rats.

Devon cussed in that strange language of his, "All right. She couldn't've just disappeared. She's around here somewhere."

Tom meowed, "Here Kitty, Kitty."

Devon ignored him, "Tom, you go up and check out the roofs. The kid and I will take the sewers."

Oh great. Don't I really just have all the luck tonight?

Tom grabbed the wall, his fingertips and boots gripping like a cat up a tree and he climbed straight up five stories in just under four seconds. He was by far the fastest of all of us. I marveled at it briefly, almost jealous.

Meanwhile, Devon had thrown back the manhole cover. It clanged against a wall, sparking before it landed in a thud on the ground. It was a good thing there were no windows because I was sure someone would have been curious about that sound.

He jumped down and I gave him a second to move out of my way before I followed. I splashed into ankle deep water and almost hurled from the overwhelming stench of shit and piss, some human and some animal. There was rotten food, decomposing flesh and bodily waste. The smells were so compounded that I heaved again. Although it's fortunate that vampires can't puke, dry heaves weren't much better.

"You forget you're not human," Devon said, a small smile on his face.

I gawked at him, still trying to get used to the smell, which was impossible.

"Stop breathing, idiot. You won't smell anything."

"Oh right. Force of habit."

"Newbies," he said under his breath while rolling his eyes.

Yup, I'm an idiot. I am totally aware of this. Relief came immediately when I stopped the intake of air through my nose and mouth and I was able to quickly glance around the sewer. We were in a tunnel that was barely taller than me. It was circular with a center river of nasty, which we were standing in, and two walkways on either side of the walls.

We'd have to stand hunched over if we wanted to use them and since we were already standing in 6 inches of feces, *Yuck*, we just stood there for a second.

"You go that way," he pointed off to the right tunnel direction, "I'll take this way," he thumbed his hand over the back of his shoulder.

I nodded.

"Don't approach her on your own, Keen. IF you see her, stay unnoticed."

"I can take her," *I would just love to run into her again.*

"No you can't," he said bluntly, "Just remember what happened the last time."

"I am," I answered, and I really was. *Revenge for taking my real life would be nice.*

"Keen, don't make a move without me. I'm dead serious," his eyes were dark with just exactly how humorless he was.

"We're wasting time," I gritted my teeth, insulted, but more annoyed that he was probably right. I doubted I could take her, even in my new form, *But, damn it, if I see her I'm sure as hell gonna try!*

He glared eyes of stone at me, the pupils blackening across the whites of his eyes. He knew what was in my head, but he turned around and took off. He vanished behind a bend in the tunnel and I ran the other way.

☆ ☆ ☆

The Sewers

It was hard for me to not breathe no matter how unnecessary it was. I was just too young of a vampire to have stopped thinking like a human. I was in awe of all my new abilities, but my brain hadn't changed, my conscience hadn't changed and I still looked mostly like I had before the change, now that I was back to full health. But while I was down in the sewer and I opened my mouth or flared my nostrils to 'breathe,' I was quickly reminded of how useful it was to not be a human.

When I did accidentally take in air, the century old muck and grime would fill every pore of my body and I'd choke, tripping myself in the meantime. A couple of times I was just barely able to hold onto my balance and keep from falling, face-first, into the watery stenches. But there were just so many things to think of at once.

Don't breathe.

What am I running in? Nope, don't wanna know.

Why did Alexandra show up now?

Was it random? It had to be, right? She was buying groceries, right? It just happened to be right next to the place I live, right?

Thinking of which, as I rounded another bend and a light from a manhole or grate flashed on a few bottles of Bloody Captain's.

Another few feet ahead of there was an unopened can of lobster meat, though why a person wouldn't want to just buy it fresh in this town, I didn't know.

I dared a whiff of the sewer again to figure out where I needed to go as I was at a branch that split three ways. *Ach!*

But underneath the gross was her smell. She was in the forward tunnel and very close. I briefly thought about whispering into my mic to let the guys and T know I was on her path, but *I want to take care of her myself.*

I slowed up when I saw the paper bags containing all the rest of Alexandra's wares. They were in a heap against one wall with some of the items scattered randomly. Or, actually, maybe it was not so randomly. I wasn't sure. My brain yelled at me then. My bad-stuff-is-about-to-happen warning alarm went off and I had a distinct feeling that I was heading into a trap. *Not cool.*

The problem was that beyond the sweet smell of her, I could smell others, but I didn't know the number that was lurking in wait for me. It seemed to be several small hints of earthy and sensual scents folding around the other nasty stinks. There was another turn going to the right. I stopped several feet before it and took in my surroundings. I shut my eyes, listening to my warnings, *Where was I going to be attacked from? Which direction?*

I decided it was definitely going to be from around the corner ahead. *Would they just expect me to run right through to them? Should I crouch down or go up to the ceiling?* It was higher than in the first tunnel I had been in, so I thought maybe that would be a good vantage point.

Ok, I have my decision. Sliding to the corner, I got close to where the wall turned right and yanked the ceiling's gritty surface. I brought my legs up so quickly that even the water was not disturbed. It was so easy to hold onto the ceiling by my shear muscle strength that, for a second, I thought I was floating. *This is totally amazing!* I briefly thought before coming back down into complete reality of the situation. *Get back to business. Vampires are trying to kill you, remember?*

Hmm. Good point, but my inner monologue can be such a downer.

I peaked my head ever so slightly around the corner, just enough for my eyes to take everything into view. An absurdly short glance told me that there were six gray auras hiding in shadows behind Alexandra's. She was standing in the middle of the water like I had been. I counted five men and one woman as my eyes took in as much as possible before backing my head up.

I heard one of them speak in Hebrew, "Hol Chaan"… *He's here,* I translated mentally.

Well, crap! I backed up all the way, pulled my dagger out of its sheath and jumped down silently onto the side walkway.

"Hello there," a smirky, masculine voice said. Standing in front of me was another vampire who was not part of the group I saw around the way. He had a Middle Eastern accent. I twisted my neck slightly, keeping him in view, but checking behind me as well.

Yup, now I am surrounded. Shit. This is a fine mess I'm going to have to get out of now. There were a total of seven vampires behind me and one in front. Sarcastically, I thought, *Huh, I wonder which way I'm going to go?*

Alexandra spoke in her soothing, purring way, "Well, it looks like I have a second chance at killing you."

Oh, does she smell sweet! I shook my head inwardly to clear it. Not taking my eyes off the guy in front of me, I said, "You missed me the first time, Alexandra. What makes you think you'll get me this time?"

Several deep and throaty laughs lingered in the air behind me.

Ok, enough of this. I need to get out of here and they are distracted. Everything slowed in my mind. I could hear the dripping of the condensation from the ceiling to the floor, the rustling of other vampires' clothes, the gleam of their fangs as their lips curled with smiles of blood lust and the swirling of the sewer water around their ankles as they got ready to attack.

A couple of vampires sprang up behind Alexandra and at me. Even though I was turned away from them, I could hear their movements and was ready for it. I jumped up the side of the wall I was closest to, like there was no gravity in that space, and I ran up the curvature of the ceiling. I was upside down and my hand automatically slashed at the vampire in front of me with my dagger glowing blackly. The vampire's head slid quickly off his shoulders, a cauterized spine kept him up briefly, the body not knowing the mind was gone yet. I pushed at him and his body fell backward, leaving me enough room to get by him.

And I ran.

Angry, awful hissing followed. It sounded like feral cats stealing a prize mouse from each other and my shoulders cringed toward my neck from it.

Continuing to run, first on the ceiling and, as that was making me a little dizzy and confused from the angle, then on the ground again. The other vampires flew at me from all directions and angles behind me. Some had gone up to the ceiling as I had; others were on the side walls, while still others were on the water path behind me. I willed myself faster, my body taking queues from my non-human side. I was so fast I barely touched the surface of the water. *Fascinating.*

But no time to think of that. I spoke determinately into my mic, "T, a little help here."

She replied, "The guys are on their way. I'm going to get you to them. Just keep running, Keen. I can't track the raven head, but the others are on your tail and gaining."

"Where do I go?" I asked, coming up to a split in the pipes.

I heard a vampire vault toward me and I turned my body an instant before he hit. Instead, he landed head first into the wall of the pipe. The metal took the shape of his head. I grabbed his shirt and rocketed him back down the way he had come. I heard the thud as he hit the back wall. More hissing and screeches came at me as vampires caught up to where the vampire lay.

I had lost my sense of direction. I asked agitatedly, "T?"

"Your right," she paused and then yelled, "No, your other right, Jerky! You went down the wrong tunnel!"

"Ok, yelling at me is not going to help! Now what?" I asked as I hit a dead end with not even a manhole above me, only a 12 inch pipe with water running out of it was in the wall.

"Turn around and head back," she said, "And haul ass, Keen!" Then she mumbled, "Stupid, direction-senseless vampire."

I moved and got back to the tunnel crossroads in a hurry, but not fast enough. Six vampires blocked my path, all smiling eerily. They were grouped together in such a tight space that I knew I wasn't going to be able to get around them.

They were all wearing fairly dark clothes. Jeans and flannels adorned the three vampires that were obviously lobstermen by their muscular and rough builds. Two of them were white, the other was Latino. Behind them were two Middle Eastern men dressed in complete black and an Asian woman dressed in black jeans and a low, v-cut, blue knit shirt. The vampire I had thrown was one of the lobstermen and he stood with them, all head wounds healing as he glared at me.

I swung my dagger in a threatening motion. It glowed black, the hilt feeling hot in my cold hands. It still dripped with the clear goo of the nameless vampire I had beheaded.

The vampires smiled, mocking my somewhat defenseless and definitely awkward posture. I had hoped they'd take me a bit more seriously after cutting the head off of their friend and knocking down the other one. *Really, even I admit, I'm not that much of a threat.*

The vampires began parting like the Red Sea at Moses' command. Alexandra stepped through them. She didn't need to touch them, they seemed to move by her will. Her advances were graceful and scary. My mind raced to find an answer to 'how do I get the hell out of here,' but I couldn't think of a single one.

Alexandra glanced down at the knife I was holding and her smile slipped ever so slightly. But in an instant, her red lips were evil again, "I see you have found the Pharaoh's Dagger."

The vampires behind her hissed and murmured to each other in fascination.

"The what?" I said, *Idiot!* "I mean, of course I have. It belongs to me."

She was not fooled, "No matter. My clan will dispatch of you anyway. You're no match for us."

She's right on that point. It wasn't like I was going to be able to go all karate-punching, bullet-dodging Neo from *The Matrix* style on her. I'd be able to take down two, maybe three, with me. *Oh who am I kidding? If I'm lucky, I'll get two, but there's no way I'm getting out of this alive. I wonder if it'll hurt this time when I die. Stop thinking like that and concentrate! Jesus! Get a grip, Panofsky!*

I smiled inwardly and changed my position to a more stable and confident attack stance. *At least I'm not going to show them fear. Let's see how many of these bastards I can drop.* That would be a good end game.

Just as I was about to jump at them, a form appeared in-between Alexandra and I. It was so sudden, I jumped back. One moment, nothing was there, the next there was a full form of a man in a duster. It flowed slightly around him in the water and he looked familiar even though he was facing my would-be assassin. His aura glowed gray, *Oh great, another one.*

"That's enough, Vampire. You will not be taking him," the new vampire said.

"And who's going to stop me? He's certainly not, and you may get some of us, but you won't get all of us," She smirked.

"No, but we will get whoever he doesn't," a deep and threatening voice said. *Devon! Ha! The cavalry has arrived!*

Alexandra turned toward the voice. The way the seven of them were standing didn't leave much room to maneuver. They were sitting ducks even with just four of us, assuming Tom was with Devon.

"I suggest you depart, Alexandra. You and your clan," Devon said.

She hissed at him but stayed in place. A full minute passed in silence as she and Devon stared at each other. The tension was as thick as the smell. The other vampires were still. Even the water was hesitant to move. I tried to remain as motionless as possible, hoping to sense any movement that would help me pre-empt an attack.

Finally, she faced me, looking around the vampire between us to get a better view, "Don't worry, my child, I will come back for you." Her voice, her posture, even the air around us told me that someday she would find a way to get at me and kill me. She walked back through her clan and made her way down the tunnel we had come from. They ran off in a blink of hisses, flashing fangs and wet clothing.

In my head, I let out a sigh of relief. My savior turned to look at me and I said, "Thank you. You're Acair, right?" I thought I recognized him as the vampire that Devon had nodded to on my first night out on the town.

He nodded 'yes' and replied, "You can put that away now."

The dagger had stopped glowing, but it was shaking slightly in my hands as I realized I still had it in an attack mode. I relaxed and brought the dagger to my waist. I wiped the vampire blood off on my shirt and sheathed it. Devon and Tom were next to us in a second.

"Let's get back to the surface," Devon said.

"Yeah, the stench is awful," Tom whined.

"I'll meet you up top," Acair said and then disappeared as quickly as he had come.

"That is a really neat trick," I mused.

The tunnel Devon and Tom had been through, the one I was supposed to go into originally, had an access point to the surface. We climbed up the ladder, one at a time, allowing the vamp ahead of us to get totally up and out of the way, lest we have shit-water fall on our face. But even with that kind of pause, it didn't take but a few seconds to ascend.

Acair was waiting for us.

"Thanks for saving my butt back there, guys," *That was probably the best thanks I was going to be able to give.*

"You have a knack for finding trouble, Newbie," Tom said.

I shrugged, "It's part of my charm."

"You should try listening more," Devon was steely in his anger with me.

"All kidding aside, I will try not to let that happen again. I promise," I felt ashamed and stupid for getting caught in such a dangerous situation. *Geez, and I thought only my parents could make me feel guilty.*

"What the hell happened down there, Keen? I told you not to go near Alexandra if you found her," Devon said in his cold voice. He didn't yell at me which actually made me feel worse, like I had really let him down. *Or myself.*

T's voice came to my defense over the ear speakers "Go easy, D. They surrounded him. It was a trap that any one of you could've gotten yourselves into."

Aw, that was nice of her. I am going to have to give her a hug when I get back.

She continued, "But had he not been such a direction-senseless dumbass, you all would've been in a better position to get some answers from them."

Scratch that hug. Not helpful.

"He did manage to take one of them down though, before they trapped him at the dead-end tunnel," T said.

Hug's back on!

Tom admired, punching me in the shoulder, "Really? Way to go, Newbie."

I smiled at him, but it wasn't a happy smile. I had killed another being. Granted, he wasn't human and I'm pretty sure he was going to try to kill me, but still… I took a life. I felt something between being ecstatic about my strength and remorseful for my actions. I slumped at the sudden weight of it.

"It gets easier," Devon said, reading my face.

"Yeah, you keep saying that, but what if I don't want it to?"

"I'm not sure you're going to have much choice," Acair said, "From what little Devon and Tom have told me, these vampires are after you for a reason, and you may have many more times where it's either you or them."

We were quiet for a few moments, then he asked, "Why does the leader of that clan want you dead?"

"I have no idea. She turned me a few months ago. Apparently not on purpose either. She meant to kill me. If it hadn't been for Devon and Tom interrupting her, she would've been successful."

"That's twice we've saved your ass, Newbie," Tom joked.

"Three times, actually. Don't forget the Water Spirit."

"Kaellan? Nah, he could never've got the drop on you… he's all washed out," Tom chuckled.

"I'm not even going to dignify that sucky pun with a laugh." *Tool.* But I laughed anyway.

"Actually," Devon explained, "He is only dangerous when he's in the water. He mostly goes after ships and sailors. He just comes ashore when he's really bored and wants to know what's going on with the world."

"Yeah, huge fan of YouTube."

Uhm, Ok. Odd.

"Getting back to the subject," Acair said, "what is going on? What did you do to piss her off? Vampires don't go for the kill unless it's for a gain."

I looked at Devon to see if I should let Acair in. Devon shrugged his normal I'll-let-you-decide shrug. Since it was my show, I gave him the '*This is Keen's life for Dummies*'version. When I got to the here and now of the story, I remembered something Alexandra said.

"Devon. That knife you gave me, Alexandra called it 'the Pharaoh's Dagger' or something like that. Since you found it, do you know what she was talking about?" I was hopeful.

"I have no idea," He responded.

Hope deflated. Damn it.

He continued, "Like I said, I found it in Egypt on a guy who owed me more than the life I took from him."

Acair said, "Well, this is the first I've heard of this dagger or the prophecy you speak of. But then again, I don't know who my maker was or why I was brought over so long ago."

Ooh, curious, "Why not? What happened?"

"Hmm. I'm not sure, actually. One minute I was a Roman warrior battling against the Franks who invaded our territory around, what, I guess the third century, if I remember correctly. I was hit by the back end of a battle axe. My next memory, I was alongside wolves and birds of prey, feeding on the dead and decaying warriors. No live human was in sight. I wandered for many years, eating when I needed to, sometimes regretting it, sometimes enjoying it as I enjoyed battle. I didn't run into another being like me for over a decade. She told me what we were. I remember hearing a word similar to 'vampire' as a child, but it had always been in a story my father had told us to get us to behave."

He looked thoughtful and then continued, "My love and I stayed together for many, many years. Centuries."

"What happened to her?" I wondered aloud, not really meaning to get an answer as I didn't know if it was a touchy subject for him.

"We were ambushed in 1490 during the beginning few years of a massive witch hunt in England. She was caught and I couldn't protect her. There were other vampires among the hunters who were hiding their true identities, so it was easy for them to hold her down for capture. Like the witches, they burned her to death. I left a couple of years later, sailing to the unknown... at that time, I guess. Eventually, I made my way up north and settled here."

I couldn't even fathom his age and what he had seen. My mind just couldn't bend around the concept of a vampire's longevity yet. Hearing about living centuries and actually living centuries were two different concepts to me. But there was one more thing I had to ask, "How do you do that disappearing trick? Is that something I'll be able to pick up, too, after centuries of being a vampire?"

He laughed, "Actually, before I was turned, I was able to, I don't know what the word is in English, but think myself somewhere within a few feet of where I was standing. Sometimes, even a couple of yards. My entire family had the gift.

When I changed, the ability increased and I've been able to improve upon the art of it ever since."

"Wicked cool."

"Yeah. I know," He smiled.

"Well," Tom said, "I don't know about you, but I'm tired of standing around in these nasty clothes. Besides that, the town is going to wake soon."

We all nodded in agreement.

I had forgotten, at least briefly, that my pants were beginning to become dry crustiness covered in nasty and my shoes were sloshing. *Ech!*

"Acair," Devon got his attention, "Since you helped save my clan member's stupid ass, can I buy you some new clothes?"

"No thank you, Devon. That is very kind of you. However, this thing," he shrugged at the duster, "has seen worse days. I went to California very briefly during the gold rush, and, well, the Romans were a far cleaner-living people. I'll just put it that way. Nothing a brisk dunk against a wash board won't fix."

"What about the boots?"

"My feet smell worse. Besides, they don't call them 'shit kickers' for nothing," He laughed again.

"Thanks again for your help tonight, Acair." I put out my hand.

He shook it, "Try to keep yourself out of trouble, young man. But if you need me again, just let me know. Devon knows how to reach me."

"Will do."

"Gentlemen," He nodded at Devon and Tom. And with that, he disappeared.

We walked back to the apartment through the back alley. We tossed our thoroughly soiled clothes, including socks and shoes, into the dumpster next to Devon's car – we decided the clothes just weren't worth the hassle since we could easily pay for more. *It's so nice to not have to worry about those things.* Not that my parents were poor or anything, but we kept clothes as long as possible just because of our nature to be thrifty and not wasteful. But even I didn't want to think about having to touch those nasty, sewer-smelling clothes again.

We climbed the fire escape to get into the apartment. I was so deep in thought that I forgot that we might have an audience. But then I heard T's sarcastic and lovely voice, "Niiiiiiiccccce!"

Her eyes moved up and down my body in a female predator kind of way. If vamps could blush, I would've been the color of a tomato. At least Devon and Tom had undershirts and boxers on. Earlier that day, I had made the unfortunate pick of tighty-whities. *Not remotely what I want to show a girl – especially not T.*

She whistled and catcalled while the other two laughed. I threw a couple of couch pillows gently, but hard enough to hit her with a satisfying thump, and managed to get behind the door to my room before she could retaliate. Even after I came out of the shower fully dressed they all still laughed. *Apparently, I am here for their amusement.*

The guys had been quicker than me in getting cleaned up, but I am a bit of a control freak when it comes to being clean, so I made sure to run the hot water all the way out before I got out of the shower.

I coughed, "Shall we get down to business?"

T still smirked, "Already begun, Special K. Since the symbols on the hilt have brought up nothing, I tried searching on the name 'Pharaoh's Dagger,' but nothing's come up yet. Do you think that Mr. Carmichael might know anything?"

"I'm not sure. He didn't say anything about it when he handed it back to me. He didn't even seem interested in it. And I didn't think to question it."

"Hmmm," She became quiet and thoughtful, "Well, it's worth a shot."

"True," I admitted, "I'll go this afternoon."

"We'll come with you, seeing as how you always seem to need a bodyguard these days," Tom said.

T suppressed a laugh.

Yeah, everyone's a comedian.

"In the meantime," T stated as she got up from the computer and notched the button to hide all but the normal peripherals, "I still have some lab work to do. I'll be back in the evening." She grabbed her things, a jacket and an art portfolio, and left down the stairs.

✳ ✳ ✳

Meet Mr. Carmichael PT 3

The time was just past five in the evening and I was waiting for the guys to come back from a trip to Mike's Lobster Bake. When I was human, that would've been the bomb. Thick, delicious, mouth-watering, creamy clam chowder and the best crab cakes in the city, but now... *Well, now, not so much.* I still couldn't stomach food smells. Everything seemed rotten and, as of right now, I was content to drink the blood beers. *Mmm, fresh animal blood with spice. From all organic meats.*

My stomach growled. We were out of Bloody Captain's and the boys were supposed to pick some up for all of us on their way back up since I hadn't finished my shopping spree after last night's run-in with Alexandra. I know I could've gone downstairs after I had taken my own nap, but I didn't want to risk my instinctual reactions taking over on the mostly human occupants of the store at this hour, nor did I want to risk running into the sweet and lethal Alexandra either.

I called Devon's cell to see how much longer they would be. I was sure they were still tearing into the hard shells of their lobster meals, all barbaric in manner, but I was getting hungry and wanted to make sure he had the full shopping list.

Just great. Voice mail.

In my quickened vampire speech, I listed off all the things I was supposed to get the night before and then some. My stomach ached in a fiery pain. *Grrr.*

To keep my mind off things, I took out my dagger. The blade glowed in its blackness briefly, like an empty space into nothingness. It was bizarre and it only happened when I first touched it or when it was attacking something. I'd seen

T, Devon and Tom all handle it, but, in their hands, it never was anything more than a knife. No glow, no cauterizing slices through flesh – or so Devon told me. He had used it on the guy he took it from and it had only cut through Devon's prey like a normal knife would have. It only 'worked' for me.

Very strange.

The vamps came back in, bringing me from my thoughts and I darted over to them, knocking over a chair in my haste to grab the beers. I didn't even wait to chill them. *Dinner! Finally!*

"Mmm, good," I belched and went back over to the chair to right it and sit down.

"Don't let my sister hear you do that." Tom said, threatening.

I looked at him quizzically.

"She's liable to get into a burping contest with you... and win."

Devon said, "She's beaten the best of us, I'm sorry to say."

"Sad. That is just sad," I said, shaking my head in disbelief.

After two pints of Shark's Pale Ale, *Even with a spicy bite, it definitely is as smooth as the label claims,* I was more mentally aware. More focused. More able to remember important things like where dear old Uncle Mr. Carmichael lived. His house was in Lewiston-Auburn, or L.A. as everyone around called it. Though, I'd been to the real L.A. on a family vacation and this one was nothing close to the craziness that is Los Angeles. *More like the laid back-of-the-woods, no cares in the world, alternate universe version of Los Angeles.*

We took Devon's car out. The sound of the motor humming was like listening to your best friend telling old stories on a Saturday night around a bonfire – risqué stories that should never be retold. The car had such presence that it seemed other cars rushed to move out of its way. It purred like it was just daring the other cars to race. If it was in a parking lot and you were leaning against it, you knew no one would mess with you. *Sweet ride.*

We pulled up the long, wooded drive and through the curved main way that led to the front door. I had only seen the house briefly before Eammon had driven me home, but getting out of the car and really getting the time to check it out allowed me the admiration it deserved. It was a three story, Tudor-style home with a five-car garage. The turrets at the corners, with cone-shaped tops, made the place look more like a castle than a house where two people lived.

It's amazing.

We walked up limestone steps. I briefly thought that it was funny he didn't have more security, but remembered that Eammon said the place had wards and magic around it to keep it impenetrable. Keeping that in mind, I was wondering where the hell the doorbell was since we wouldn't be able to just walk right in.

Or would we?

As we got closer, I saw that the door was very slightly ajar. It had just missed the latch. If I hadn't been in the condition I was, my eyes would've been too poor-sighted to tell that it was amiss without actually touching the door and feeling its give. But, with my better vision, it was so blatant to me.

I put a hand up to halt the other two vamps.

"What's up," Devon asked.

"Door's open," I replied, "I'm not getting a bad sign like we're in danger or anything, but I don't feel good about this. It doesn't seem right."

Devon approached around me and knocked on the door. It promptly relented. He caught it before it could swing further than a couple of inches, then he called in, "Hello? Hello? Mr. Carmichael?"

He glanced back at me, "What was the name of that butler of his? Oh yeah," He turned back to the door, having answered his own question, "Eammon? Hello?"

Devon peered around the door and then opened it completely. We were dumbstruck. Not even Tom could say anything. The place had been completely ransacked. Broken glass was everywhere – on the floor, on the stairwells. Light glittered off of them in a million reflections. I glanced up. The chandelier was in pieces too. Wires and metal held onto shards as if they were mountain climbers hanging onto each other for dear life – one stuck firmly in the ice with all the rest dangling precariously, hoping not to disappear in the crevice below.

The ceiling looked as if it had partially caved in. Crown molding and chunks of the wall were pealed back like they had melted in the sun. Even the wall sconces had been knocked askew or shattered.

Tables and chairs from other parts of the house were thrown about and lay crumpled. Three large claw marks, each two inches thick and at least an inch deep, tore through the walls and across closed doors. Papers were strewn around like confetti.

"What the hell happened here?" Tom asked.

My mental heart began to race; I was suddenly very worried about my uncle. And then another frightening thought came to me. *Mom. Dad.*

Ok, one thing at a time.

I listened, but couldn't hear any human sounds, no shallow breathing or anything. "We need to check the house," I barked orders then, my crisis mode overtaking me, "Tom, take the top floor. Devon, take the second. I'll look around here for Mr. Carmichael and Eammon."

"We know at least one gargoyle was here," Devon advised, "we need to find out if more creatures were involved."

Tom and I both nodded and then the other two ran in a blur up the stairs to begin their search.

I began opening doors in a counter-clockwise move, starting with the door on the right that was closest to me. Only mere seconds passed between opening each door and calling for Mr. Carmichael. I yelled his name mostly, calling for Eammon as an after thought. *I have much less stock in him.* I listened for signs of life in each room, but it seemed to take forever to me, with nothing coming up.

I made it to familiar French doors and the back of my neck hair prickled up. *I should've started here first,* I realized too late for rational thought.

It was the library. When I pushed the door, it only opened a few inches. Something was blocking it.

"Mr. Carmichael? Eammon?" I was frantic now, "Uncle Joel?"

Why hadn't I come here first?

I paused my calls and heard a gurgling breath coming from across the room. It was weak and came in quick pants followed by long stretches of pauses. But I could tell from the scent that it was my uncle in there and that there was very little time left for him. The blood smell was heavy and savory, and my eyes began to narrow with the longing for it. I pleaded with myself to shut that instinct off, and, as best as I could, tried to make it smell less appealing. *The intensity of it...* I craved whatever was leaking life. It made me hungry and it made me hard to control. *Chill out, Keen. This is no time to freak out.*

My eyes came back to my human-type of senses and I searched the floor on the other side of the door, as much of it as I could see. My uncle's desk was what was blocking me. I couldn't see my uncle at all in the two inches of view I had. I just had to hope I wouldn't hurt him. *More than he is.*

I backed up a couple of feet and ran straight through the door, splintering it and the desk with a large smashing sound.

I searched the room, looking for any kind of glow of aura, "Uncle Joel? Eammon?" I listened again and heard the strained breaths.

At the back of the room, there was a pile of couches and desk chairs, topped by the coffee table which was broken in half. Blood was splattered around the room, focusing on the pile. Several rungs of the book ladder and book shelves were also piled on. I ran over to it and began throwing off all the furniture and pillows. I needed to know who was under there.

"Oh shit," I whispered when I found Mr. Carmichael. I turned my head, partly to clear it from the mess I was seeing. The other part was trying to fight off the vampire instinct that had clicked in and decided it was dinner time. I filled my head with quick thoughts of my parents, my family and that this buffet in front of me was my uncle. I called quietly to the others, "Guys. He's in the room below the stairs on the left."

I knew it wouldn't take more than a whisper-tone for them to hear me and I didn't want to frighten the broken man I was stooped next to.

My uncle was half twisted on his back and rolled on his side, partially balled up in a broken wrongness. *Whole bodies are not meant to be in this kind of position.* I took a couch pillow and placed it under his head. Blood was coming from his mouth and he had three claw marks that dug deep into his neck. Three more in his chest. His aura was blue, but fading quickly into a whitish-pale color. I didn't know how much time he had left. But I did know that what time there was, he was going to be in pain. I said a quick prayer that it would end soon for him.

His shocked, wide eyes turned to me, but didn't really see me, "Adam? You're here."

"No Uncle," I took his hand as he reached for my face, "It's me. Keen."

His eyes focused and he knew who I was, "Have you found my son yet?"

I shook my head, my voice quiet, shameful and full of guilt, "I'm sorry."

He blinked his eyes closed and I spoke his name to keep him awake. As heartless as it was, I still needed to get information from him, "Uncle, who did this to you?"

"Eammon," he breathed, barely audible, keeping his eyes closed. And I suddenly knew what would be missing from the house. "He took the scroll. I couldn't stop him." Now he sounded shameful. Weak. *Human.*

"It's not your fault," I steadied my voice, but my mind flared in anger. *Traitor! Murderer! I'll kill him when I get my hands on him.*

I felt Devon's and Tom's presence, but they stayed back, just inside the threshold of the room.

Devon said, "We've called the captain. He's sending an ambulance and the crime scene unit."

"It'll be too late for an ambulance," I said under my breath, only audible for the vampires. *I'll never get to know him.*

Devon was next to me in an instant and bending close to my uncle with his mouth an inch to his ear. Devon said, "Mr. Carmichael, I can heal you. Turn you. The ambulance won't be here in time to save you."

"No!" His voice was forceful and his eyes fierce as he opened them in anger, "I'm not meant for that kind of life."

His voice was once again calm and quiet as he squeezed my hand as hard as he could, which was nothing more than a limp grasp, "Find Adam. You must find him."

"I promise," I said, though I didn't know if I would be able to keep it. I needed just a little more time with him. I pulled out the dagger, "Uncle, do you know what this is? Can you tell me? The vampire who attacked me, Alexandra, called it 'the Pharaoh's Dagger.' It's very strange."

He tried to focus on it, his gaze going in and out. He shook his head side to side, "I don't know what it is. The symbols are the same as the coin."

His eyes blanked out past me as if trying to remember something, "Eammon… Eammon… He burned those markings around this house and the one on the Promenade."

His words became rushed. Urgent. "He said they were for protection. They were religious symbols. I had never seen them before I met him, though."

Blood suddenly choked up out of his mouth. He moved to speak again, though, "Protect the dagger from the one who turned you. And the coin. I'm not sure what it is either, but they will be of interest to Eammon and you need to keep them safe."

He paused for a second, gasping for breath before he continued, but in a different, unearthly voice. A voice of a person who knows that death is near, "Protect your mother."

That caught me off guard, and I could feel sludgy gel flow from one of my eyes. I brushed the milky, thick tear away.

"Tell Miriam," he paused and started again, "tell my sister that I love her and that I'm sorry I couldn't protect you and Adam better."

His eyes closed as if resting. Without warning, they charged back open and he sighed. The rest of the air in him drifted out. His aura turned from the pale blue to white and then began to vanish as his heart stopped beating and his eyes lost the confident fire in them.

Chapter 13

Under Attack

✪ ✪ ✪

Save My Parents

Idon't know how fast I was driving and I don't think I want to know, but I got over to the dock where Devon kept his boat within fifteen minutes of leaving my uncle's home. Normally it was a one-hour trip. *Thank God for back roads, no traffic and no cops.*

Tom and Devon were going to help the captain and special homicide team search the remainder of the house for any clues. I wasn't exactly on the payroll yet, well, not officially, so I dodged out as soon as I could. My only concern was getting to my parents before something happened to them – *If it hasn't already.*

Don't think like that. It'll be ok. Reassuring myself was not really helping, though. I needed to see them in person. See their faces, hear their voices. And I wanted to see them intact and unharmed.

I untied the front and back of the boat, making the short jump onto it without any problems as the tide started pushing it away from the bumpers. I started it up and breathed easier as the boat passed the 'No Wake' signs on the docks, allowing me to push the boat to full throttle. The sun hadn't set yet, though it was heading that way, so I had to remind myself to keep to a human pace once I landed on the island. Technically I was still a missing person and I didn't want to cause suspicion among nosy neighbors.

Fortune was with me, though. When I docked and ran up the slight hill to cross Island Avenue, I didn't see anyone. *Such a rarity.* I took the back path to the house, just pushing what would have been my human limits. No one was around – human or otherwise.

Once I got under the protection of the trees in our property, I hauled ass onto the patio and into the house... which was, again, unlocked. *What the hell!! They are killing me! When are they going to learn to secure their doors? Not that locks or bars would stop anyone from breaking in anyway, but my parents might get a fighting chance or at least a warning to call 911 if they heard a noise. But, good shit, that alone could make the difference between life and death.*

Moving through the sliding door was like entering through the door at Uncle Carmichael's house all over again. The cupboards and drawers had been turned out. Dishes had been tossed and broken; like my uncle's place, furniture had been upended and piled up. The television was broken, bedding and clothing were in slices and strewn like streamers around the room – like a party had gone incredibly wrong.

"Mom? Dad?" I yelled. I was standing in the kitchen and nothing was upright. Not even the fridge. My Adam's apple jumped to my mouth and my stomach dropped in anxiety as I realized that there were deep claw marks along the walls and door frames – the same shape as the ones at Mr. Carmichael's house. I tore around the house yelling for them and throwing items out of my way, in case they were buried underneath something.

Please, please, please. Not my parents! I'm not ready for that. Those thoughts kept repeating in mantra as I checked their bedroom, the basement, the mudroom under the patio, the closets and even my bedroom upstairs.

There was no smell or sight of blood or anything else – only their lingering presence. I relaxed momentarily, *They're not here.* But I didn't know if that was a good thing.

Suddenly, I heard footsteps coming up the front porch. The door opened and closed on the first entrance into the house, which faced the street. Originally, it had been an open porch, but we had built walls around it a few years back and made it into a small exercise room.

I hid in the bedroom next to the door, ready to jump whoever had come back to attack my parents. The outside door would swing open right next to my hiding spot. It wouldn't matter who they were either. *They are going to tell me everything.*

I took the dagger out as I distinguished between the two sets of feet crossing the few steps of the front porch and over to the main door. The weight of their steps made them sound a little shorter than me and I thought, *I can take whoever it is and I'll promise not to kill them until they tell me where my parents are.*

The two people stopped. They were silent and steady for a moment.

The door began to open and I heard…

Laughter?

Mom! Dad!

Thank God!

I put the knife away and I heard my mom intake a breath in fear as she crossed the threshold and her eyes took in the sight of things.

"What the hell?" My dad said, dropping the grocery bags he was carrying, "Miriam, call the police."

"Wait!" I said a little too loudly, scaring the bejeezuz out of them. They both jumped and turned in my direction.

"Son, did you do this?" He asked in reflex.

Suddenly I was no longer just a man relieved to see my parents alive, but I was their teenager sneaking in past curfew. I felt oddly embarrassed that he would jump to that conclusion. I had changed, but I hadn't changed so much that I would want to destroy anything of theirs while simultaneously scaring the crap out of them. "No dad. It was like this when I came in," I said recovering.

They stared at me. I thought they were trying to believe me, but I wasn't sure. They were definitely not coming any closer, but I couldn't blame them for that.

The silence between us was awkward and lonely. It made me think that even though they knew when I was born what I might become someday, that *Maybe, just maybe it scares them now. I wonder if we'll ever truly be a family again. It was so different the last time I was here. They welcomed me without fear and with love. Maybe after seeing the damage that has happened here, they realize it isn't safe around me. Maybe they don't truly trust that I'm still their son.*

My mom was the one who finally broke the intense quiet. She set her bags down and approached me. I stood completely still, not really sure what she was going to do nor what my reaction was going to be. Their blood still drew my stomach into pains, like all other humans I had been around. I had been able to control myself… But I had never been this full of emotion, this wound up, not even when I was surrounded by seven very unhappy vampires.

So I waited.

She was close and I tensed, trying to regain composure. Then she put her arms around me and hugged. She started to cry as I bent down to hug her back, finally relieved and feeling like everything had been forgiven – that I was still a normal kid. My dad eventually came up to us, too, and surrounded us in his big arms. *My family.*

I didn't want to break up our group hug, but matters were pressing and their lives were clearly in danger, so I pulled gently away from them, "Mom, Dad, I think you both need to sit down."

They looked around, wondering where the best place would be for them, so I turned over the couch and put the stuffing-torn cushions back into place within a blink of their human eyes. I probably shouldn't have done that, but time was wasting and I needed to get them out of there. My mom sat, but I think dad was a little pissed off about the shape his house was in, and so he paced.

Angry. Violated. I could read that from his blue aura that darted with mustard and brown colors through it. "Uhm, Mom?" *Where to begin?* I sat down next to her, squeezing her shoulders gently.

"What's wrong?" She asked quietly, always able to get straight to the point.

"I went to Joel's house. I had some questions," My voice trailed off.

How do I tell her that her brother is dead. Murdered violently. And all because of me.

She immediately stiffened, "He's gone, isn't he." It wasn't a question. She always knew things. She may not have been my biological mother, but she always knew everything going on in my head. *Mothers just know.*

I couldn't answer her and I bent my head, not able to meet her gaze. Inside, I felt this deep sense of cowardice that I couldn't even break the news about my mother's brother to her properly. She started to cry again.

"I'm so sorry mom. When we got out there, it was too late. He'd been attacked. The house had been destroyed on the inside."

"And the scroll?" She whispered. *Damn mother's intuition thing.*

"Stolen."

My mom shook with emotion and tears.

Dad came over to sit next to her, taking her into his arms and turning her head onto his shoulder like he had done with me when I was a kid and had been hurt or upset by something.

I got up and grabbed the tissue box, handing it to him for her. As her tears slowed, my dad said, "Do you know who did it?"

I nodded a 'yes,' "Eammon."

My mom looked up at me with fierce, unbelieving eyes, "No. That's impossible. Eammon protected Joel. He wouldn't do anything to him. Joel was like a father to him."

"I don't know, Mom," I tried to explain with carefully chosen words, "When I first met Joel, we had asked him if Eammon was capable of hurting Adam and he essentially told us no. But the last time I saw him, Joel didn't seem to trust Eammon. I don't know what changed, but…"

Pausing, not wanting to give her more bad news, "Mom. Joel told me it was Eammon. I was the one that found him." I didn't mention Devon's suggestion of turning Joel to save him; *Somehow, I don't think she would react too well to that.*

I took her small hands in mine, "He wanted you to know that he loved you very much and that he was sorry… sorry for everything."

My mom turned away again towards my dad and cried harder. Dad handed her more tissues while cradling her and rubbing her back.

"It's not safe for you anymore," I said, getting up and motioning to my dad to come into the kitchen. He gave my mother one more hug and then followed me. Not that it was far enough away that mom couldn't hear us, but I wanted to give her at least some semblance of privacy in her grieving. "We need to get you out of here."

"Yes," he agreed, "But where?"

"Another vampire that I'm staying with, Devon, gave me keys to a place he owns further north. It's not owned under his real name, so there should be no problems," *Hopefully.*

"All right. I'll make some calls to my work and your mother's."

"I'll pack some stuff up for you two. It'll be quicker if I do it," even using normal speed, I would be faster. When I was younger, I had watched my parents go through the pain of packing for trips and they always took forever, no matter if they were in a hurry or not.

"If I miss anything, you can just buy it up there," I took out my wallet from my back pocket, "Here's some money. Don't use any credit cards up there or your cell phones. Don't even use your laptop to get on-line."

My dad smiled at me in a quirk of his lips, "Geez, when did you become the dad and I become the son?" He smiled bigger and patted me on the shoulder, but he looked proud. And, of course, he pushed my handful of money gently away; he wasn't taking any of it.

"Dad, you're the only parents I've got and it's time for me to take care of you."

He pulled me into a humongous hug and sniffled as manly as possible. I wish I could've returned the pressure of his hold without breaking him. Instead, I just patted him as sympathetically as possible.

We looked over at Mom; she had stopped crying and was staring out the dining room window with a hard and determined guise on her face. The cat had jumped into her lap and Mom was petting her without noticing.

We both sighed and then I said, "Actually, I'll have Mom start packing."

"What are you going to do?"

"Straighten things up around here. I'll just take a few seconds and then I'll help her."

"Ok," he agreed.

"Mom, we need to get you packed up. Can you take Bree and get her things ready? I'm not sure she'll let me get near her enough to put her in the carrier," the cat hissed at me in agreement as I came near.

Backing off, I said, "Once you're finished with Bree, let me know and I'll come help you."

As I started clearing the mess in the living room, I heard my dad talk to the temple and funeral home about arrangements for my uncle. As per Jewish custom, as soon as the police released his body, he would need to be put into the ground.

Unfortunately, I wouldn't be able to help my mother and father sit Shivah, the customary seven day period where my parents would mourn by sitting close to the ground on low stools, covering all mirrors, praying and honoring his memory, for my uncle. It's the Jewish way of coming to terms with loss. There were many things my parents were not going to be able to do during this time, such as cooking, cleaning or caring for themselves, so I called Devon to have him send someone he trusted to help them through. He called back a few minutes later to tell me that the body guards he had up in his northern place would do what was needed and to not worry.

A huge weight lifted off my shoulders when that was in place. I didn't want anyone my parents normally socialized with to know where they were located and I knew anyone Devon could count on would be individuals that could be trusted. *I really owe him. My life and theirs.*

✡ ✡ ✡

Dagger Discussion

We were out of the house within an hour. *Humans move so slowly,* I thought as I tried not to roll my eyes with impatience. I had the house picked up and fixed before my mother had finished getting the cat's things together and my dad was still on the phone. So I helped complete packing their luggage and hurried them out to the boat. We were under the cover of darkness when we headed up north.

Once we were in international waters, I slowed the boat in order to talk to my parents so they could hear me at a normal voice. I didn't feel much like yelling and I don't think they realized how they could just whisper and I'd be able to hear them. I wanted things to be as ordinary as possible between us, so I tried to act like a regular teenager around them as much as I could. However,

I needed more answers about my vampire history that, oddly enough, only my human mother could tell me. *How weird is my life?* I handed my mom my knife with its sheath on, "Mom, do you know what this is?"

She took it in her hands and carefully loosened it from its casing. As was typical, it didn't glow in her hands like it did in mine. I was hoping it would do something when she held it, but I was realistic that it only did it for me for whatever reason.

"This looks like a ceremonial dagger to me. Where did you get it?"

"Devon," *lie,* "uhm, found it in Egypt and gave it to me," *Good, that response keeps the dead guy out of it – don't want to freak out the parentals more than they already are,* "I've run into other vampires who recognize it. They called it the 'Pharaoh's Dagger.' I had gone over to Uncle Joel's to ask him about it before," I didn't continue.

She understood, glancing down and away at first and then back up at me, "I'm sorry, Keen, I don't know what it is."

"Well, say this is a ceremonial dagger, do you know what it was used for?"

Her face thinned in thought, searching for a memory, "As far as my understanding of them from some of the history classes I took in college, they were used for several things. Sometimes Pharaohs were buried with them to show their stature in the afterlife. Sometimes they were used in marriage and other religious ceremonies. And sometimes, they were used to remove the head of prisoners or enemies."

"This is going to be a crazy question, but were any of them thought to be magical?"

"All of them were thought to be so, as any superstitious people believed. And almost every culture back then was superstitious. Why?"

"It's best if I just show you," I held my hand out and she put the hilt of it in my palm. The instant it touched my skin, it glowed a deep black."

She gasped slightly, "I thought that was just legend."

"What, Mom? What legend? What haven't you told me?" *Good lord. What the hell else could possibly...*

My mother's voice broke into my thoughts, "There was once a dagger that had been carried by the line of Ramses that was supposed to be a dagger of such power that it could kill evil and good."

"What does that mean?" I didn't really like riddles.

"Demons, angels" she said. And then more quietly, "And gods."

Well, that would be a good reason why Alexandra was so intrigued by it.

The blade dulled as I re-sheathed it.

"Are you sure Devon just found it? That dagger, if it was even real, was said to have been lost centuries ago," my mother asked.

I shrugged. It was in my possession now and Devon didn't seem to care about that, so I couldn't imagine an ulterior motive for him giving it to me, "Mom, I don't know what the circumstances were, but I'm pretty sure he thought it was only a decorated knife. I chose it as a weapon when I first saw it. The dagger doesn't react to anyone like it does to me and I don't know why."

"Don't let anyone get that," she said, sternly, "I don't know the significance, but it could have something to do with the prophecy."

Well, I guess I'm not the only one who thinks that, but I'm not sure that's good either.

Mom had no more information for me on the matter. We continued our travel on the water in silence – only *Carmilla's* engine rumbling quietly through the waves.

When we reached our destination, I was sad and worried about leaving them where I couldn't protect them. But after I said my goodbyes and felt their warm, comfortable hugs and kisses, I turned the boat away from them and back south along the coastline.

I regretted not saying 'I love you' to them one last time. But I hoped I would get another chance soon.

☆ ☆ ☆

Attack on the Homestead

I really did not want to go back to the reality that was waiting for me: my uncle dead, my parents in hiding, my twin brother kidnapped and myself in who knew what kind of danger. So I did what any person does who has things to do but doesn't want to. I procrastinated.

Steering Devon's boat along the coast, I checked out all the inlets on the way back home, wasting as much time as possible. Eventually, I found myself not only having lost a ridiculous amount of time, but also having exhausted all of the gas in the tanks. *Carmilla* choked to a halt, like an angry woman crossing her arms and planting her feet until she was apologized to. Except for drifting with the tide, we didn't go anywhere. *Oops.*

Part of me wondered if my new special skills would allow me to paddle myself back to shore. It was dark; there were no other boats in the area and no moon to give any weirdness away if anyone did travel too close to me. But with a boat this size, I couldn't figure out the logistics of it without putting myself completely in the water or turning myself completely in circles, neither of which sounded very promising.

As luck would have it, the radio worked, so I called Devon. And, of course, he laughed...

And laughed...

And laughed...

I hope that means he's coming. So I waited...

And waited...

And waited...

Feeling nostalgic, I listened on my iPod to some songs my parents used to sing to me when I was younger. Beatles, The Byrds, other bands like them, and then I felt a bump against the boat. My eyebrows furrowed. *Crap! What was that?*

A strong arm wrapped around me and lopped me quickly upside down in front of a very sharp face. I could feel the suction cups of her tentacles begin to squeeze me. *Oh man, I hope Scylla remembers me.*

"Hi Scylla-girl!"

Her eyes narrowed at me, but I concentrated on her very large, pointed beak – that was where most of the damage could be done. "Devon's friend?" *Come on, remember me.*

After a few tense moments, she shook me up and down and then put me back on my feet in the boat. *Phew!* "Good girl," I said and leaned over the railing to pat her cheek, *I guess that's her cheek,* when she moved her face closer to the boat.

She wrapped a couple of tentacles around the boat railings and bobbed it up and down, clicking her beak and making water flood over the railings like I was on a small bath toy and she was an ornery toddler trying to dunk it. *Ah, the little girl wants to play.* There were still a few tires roped off in the holding part of the boat. I untied one and held it over my head to catch her eyes. "Ready?"

She clicked her beak once.

I feigned right. Her eyes followed, but she wasn't fooled. She didn't move. I instead threw it over her head and, as it was just about to get out of her reach, she shot an arm out and grabbed it like a gigantic yo-yo, wrapping a tentacle through and around it. *Impressive reflexes.*

"Ok, girl, give it back and I'll throw it further this time. I know that was a pretty bad one." I wasn't sure if she could really understand me, so I motioned for the tire and patted the railing in front of me. She brought it closer to me and I grabbed on to it. I tugged, but she didn't let go, "Now, Scylla, I can't throw it if you hold on."

Giving me a look that I can only describe as mischievous, she tugged me off balance. She squealed happily, almost like a laugh, as I fell into the rail and then to the floor. Bringing the tire over to where I stood, she dropped it so that it encircled me. Apparently she thought that was hilarious because she started splashing her other tentacles, continuing to squeak and click her beak.

If this wasn't a fifty-ton creature I'm playing catch with, I'd say she'd be cute as a pet. I picked up the tire and huffed even though I was completely amused at her. I put it over my head again so she could see it and I tossed it over the other side of the boat. It went about a mile, maybe two, out. She bobbed her head and then ducked under the boat, taking off after it. *Man, she can haul ass.*

A couple of minutes later, she dropped it back on the boat. "Again?" I asked, trying not to talk to her in baby-talk, but it was really difficult.

She bobbed her whole body up and down in excitement.

I threw it out again and she gave chase. While she was away, I scanned the dark horizon, hoping to see a boat heading my way. After about the fourth time of me playing catch with Scylla, I finally saw one. By the time she brought the tire back, Tom and Devon had arrived with Acair in his boat. *About time.*

Scylla came back very quietly, barely breaking the surface of the water. She was hesitant with the new boat, but not as if she was afraid. No, she had the hesitance of a stalker – a cat about to pounce on a bird. *Or in her case, a lion attacking a giraffe.* Her tentacles slowly drew out of the water and wrapped themselves around Acair's boat. She was about to tear the boat in half when Devon hopped over from Acair's boat to stand next to me, placing himself in her line of sight. She slowly backed off, to the relief of Acair, who had only just noticed the movement from her.

Acair anchored his boat several feet away and then he and Tom jumped over. Devon and Acair worked on adding fuel to *Carmilla* and began bailing out the water that had gotten into the engine from Scylla dipping the boat up and down. Tom and I took turns keeping Scylla occupied by tossing multiple tires across the bay.

After a few minutes of quick work by the two vamps, the boat engine turned on. Tom and I cut some of the extra tires to leave behind. Devon petted and talked to Scylla for a while in what I can only say would be baby talk. I don't know about the others, but I was highly amused.

As we were preparing to leave, a red light on the radio began flashing and a series of beeps started. It sounded like a pager going off. "What's that?" I asked as Devon and Tom looked at each other, their faces intensely strained.

Tom grabbed the radio mic and whispered into it, "Tom to T, what's wrong? Over."

No answer.

Stealth be damned, Tom's voice turned loud and panicky, "Sis? Answer me or at least give me a sign that you're ok."

Devon turned to Acair and in his calm, cool, deep voice said, "T set off the house alarm, or there's a breach. Can you help?"

"Of course," Acair inclined his head and he jumped the distance back onto his boat like a deer over a fence. It was quick and graceful, his duster flapping in the wind like bat wings. He took up the anchor and started the engine. Both boats turned south towards the main land.

Scylla immediately understood our body language and backed away from the boats, flowing seamlessly under the murky water and dragging her toys down with her. As Devon thrust the boat into full throttle, the boat radio cracked back on with T's voice. She was calm, but on the edge of hysteria, "Who the hell are you?"

Tom visibly tensed.

A familiar woman's voice answered, "Where's your little friend?"

"What are you talking about?"

"Don't play with me little girl, you know who we're looking for. Where is Keen?" Alexandra was menacing, *Psychopath.*

"Keen who?" T mocked ignorance.

Don't goad them, T.

"Oh goodie, she's into playing games," a male voice intimidated and teased, "let's play the 'how many pieces can we split the human into before she screams' game."

"I have a better idea," T stood her ground, "Let's play the 'dead vampire' game instead." A sound like a taser going off came over the radio, with a teapot-pitched scream following it.

"I win," T said.

"Good girl," Tom muttered under his breath with a smile.

"Enough!" Alexandra said, "Where is the one that is called Keen?"

"Suck on this, Bitch," the taser went off again and must've hit another vampire from the sound of the scream. *I hope it was Alexandra.*

We could hear a struggle, then T forced out a choke, "Let go of me, you crazy psycho ho!" A hiss was followed by a scream – T's scream. *Oh my God! T!* Tom looked like he was about to crawl out of his skin and through the radio. Devon moved the boat faster, Acair on our wake.

"Keen," Alexandra's voice was clear over the radio, although there were sounds of a struggling T behind her, "We'll be waiting for you. If you want to see your feisty tart in one piece, you'll show up alone at the monastery on Sweet Haven Island with that pretty dagger of yours, as I see it is not here."

I grabbed the radio mic from Tom's angry, trembling hands and tried to sound commanding, "I'll be there. But not until you let her go, Alexandra."

"Ah, you are listening. Good boy. But I think I will take her with me just in case I need a little snack."

"Don't you touch her," I gritted through my teeth.

"Right. Because you are so frightening, young one," her sarcasm was unbearable, "Oh yes, and bring the Seal of the Gods with you as well. Oh wait. Never mind. Here it is. You know, you really shouldn't keep precious and powerful artifacts just lying around. You never know who might take them."

"I'll come to the monastery," I sounded defeated even to me.

"That's my good pet. Be there by midnight tonight."

The radio connection broke, only white noise crackled from it. The only other sound was of the boat engines. It was a couple of minutes before any of us could speak, we were all so pissed and worried. I could feel the heat of anger waft off of Tom. His aura was so gray, but I could've sworn I saw brief flashes of muddy red sparks. I shook my head. *Maybe it's just my own red anger flashing through me.*

"Don't even think you're going there alone," Tom said angrily when he saw me watching him. "She's my sister and I'm not just going to let you fall into that crazy vampire's hands as well."

"I know better than to go alone. I don't have a death wish for T or for myself. I know a trap when I see one. We need a plan. I need all the help I can get!" *I'm not so delusional that I can't see or feel the danger that is coming.* All of the warning bells ringing in my head told me that going to the monastery would be the last thing I ever did. But I needed to get T back. *If anything, T has to be saved and nothing is going to stop me from getting to her.*

✧ ✧ ✧

Call in the Troops

We couldn't get back to the docks fast enough. As soon as we were within jumping distance, about sixty feet, Tom flew off the boat and headed toward the apartment. We were a few seconds behind, as we had to tie off the two boats first.

The apartment was more of a wreck than it had been before we left. But T had gotten all of the weapons and computer equipment hidden back into their holes before our uninvited guests had shown up. Two bodies of male vampires were on the floor, partially disintegrated, dissolving into dust. Each one had two metal clips and wires coming from them. I recognized their faces as the lobster-men that had been in the sewers.

"What did she do to them?" I asked.

"She carries a specialized taser on her. Let's just say you can't get them from any normal weapon stores," Devon said.

"Devon came up with it," Tom explained, "The things have enough juice in them that it's like attaching your enemy to a power station, instantly frying them."

Tom picked up the taser that had been dropped next to T's desk and he said more to himself then for us to hear, "Way to go, baby sis."

"So is this what happens when we die?" I asked, not happy with what I was seeing.

"Ashes to ashes. Dust to dust," Devon said, "We always return to the ground. Some just faster than others. For example, her taser just sped things up for these two unlucky bastards."

"What do we do now?" I couldn't look at the dissipating corpses anymore, *Please make this quick! I don't want my two hours of sleep to be filled with nightmares.*

"First things first. We call in to the department and get as many non-humans for backup as we can. It's ten o'clock, so we have two hours to get prepped and over to the monastery. Do you know which one she's talking about?"

"Yes," I had been there often while playing around as a kid, "it's on the back part of the island."

"Good, then you'll be able to guide us in."

Devon went over to the police radio, "Sarge to radio?"

"Sarge, go ahead," Mo's heavily accented voice responded.

"Mo, it's Sarge. I need the captain and we're going to need backup... a lot of back up."

Chapter 14

Battle at the Monastery

☆ ☆ ☆

Counterattack

It was thirty minutes to midnight and Acair's and Devon's boats were tearing across Casco Bay, around Fort Dune, heading north around Chandler and Deckard Islands. We were going to come back down and park ourselves near Deckard Island so that one team could enter the monastery by water through an outflow below it and the other team could go over the old chapel wall.

Devon's boat carried me, Tom, two very tall leprechauns and a witch. The leprechauns, Cayden and Quinney, were a married couple that had started on the force about three years earlier to help curb money laundering and insurance scams; they could smell money and who was lying about it. Both men were over six feet tall and skinny, but muscular. Cayden had short, curly blond hair that clung tightly around his head like a cherub. The other, Quinney, had bright red, shoulder-length hair.

Veleda, the witch, was petite even for a female in her late 20s. She looked familiar. I could've sworn I had seen or met her *Before I was bitten?* But I just couldn't place where. T and she had been best friends since grade school. She was the one who had given T the book about my ability to read auras. She was cute, with pink, chipmunk cheeks and waist-length, blond-streaked, brown hair that came to a widow's peak in the middle of her forehead. She had some really cool abilities which I was about to see.

Acair's boat carried him, Captain Jameson, Mo and four vampires split evenly between males and females. The captain was a burly man with a red beard and mustache, which was not quite trimmed, but only a little unruly. He had a full laugh and a comedic streak when he wasn't on duty, but he was incredibly focused when he was. The other human, Mo, normally played dispatch for us, but tonight he was there to help watch the boats while our attack on the monastery was underway.

Garik, the vampire that had helped us at the playground, was on Acair's boat. He looked so different from the first time I met him. If possible, he looked younger without the standard police officer uniform on. And since he wasn't wearing a hat, he showed off short, spiked hair that was blond to the point of being white. He was so thin, it seemed like the muscles on his body hadn't caught up to the length of his bones.

The other male, Harbuu, was originally from the United Republic of Tanzania. All Devon told me about him was that his family had come here seeking refuge after they had been attacked by aggressive vampires, soldiers of a warlord whose idea was to use vampires for taking over other tribes. Harbuu was also thin and his face was etched with the traumas his family had gone through and endured – every line and every crease deep with hardship. His hair was buzzed short and around his neck he wore two strands of tribal beads that were colored yellow and white.

The sight of Garik and Harbuu standing next to each other was like seeing a full moon greet the night sky. Garik was so incredibly white, he was porcelain. And Harbuu was as dark as coffee beans. Garik had that baby face and Harbuu looked well into his fifties. But they were both deadly and disconcertingly so.

The women were beautiful *I'm not going to lie*. It was hard not to drool over them. I had slowly been figuring out that it was good to be a vampire – especially for the women. No skin issues, no hair out of place, perfect white teeth, well, other than fangs. Lachina had auburn hair cropped in a pixie cut. She was 5'8" and had a lanky build. Her black outfit was so tight that it hid nothing of her body. It seemed to be like silk against skin and it was hard for me to turn away from her knowing that my brain was about to take a nose dive into the gutter of fantasy.

Unfortunately, aiming my attention at Ermelinde was not much better. Actually, with two visions of beauty in front of me, my body wasn't able to keep itself in check. Ermelinde had gorgeous wavy blond hair and was shorter than Lachina by a few inches. She was, what my friends would call, ten miles of bad roads – curvy in all the right places. *Hot!*

All four vampires worked in the Special Operations department. From what I'd heard, they were all good at their jobs. They had worked together many times before in undercover stings and they were able to do whatever it took to diffuse the situation and get everyone out alive – well, 'alive' as much as vampires could be. That helped me back off my worries a little at least. Especially when I noticed that they were covered head to toe in heavy artillery, all water proof since they were the ones taking a dive for us.

Ok, time to concentrate. I turned my attention to Veleda. She was studying me with her precise hazel eyes behind square-rimmed glasses. Where everyone else was wearing black, she was wearing my clothes. They were comically baggy on her since I was a good eight inches taller than she.

As we got closer to Deckard Island, Veleda took off her glasses, placing them in a bag near her feet, and began mumbling to herself. I could tell the words were a chant, but I couldn't understand what language they were in. It sounded close to the way Devon cussed in his non-English way. She moved her arms around slowly in circles and up and down. The air around her tightened and expanded at the same time, like a small tornado was sucking the air out of our little area. She stared at me intensely, almost hypnotizing me. As she did so, she began to grow in body size. Her legs and arms elongated and became more muscular. Her hair shrank into her skull, turning all blond. Her features became sharper, the concaves of her curves began to broaden. Her eyes lightened in color.

A thin mist appeared around her and her aura suddenly changed from yellow-green, the color witches have, to the gray of vampires before disappearing back into her. Within another few seconds, I was staring at an exact image of myself. I moved and she mirrored the actions. In my awe, I reached out to touch her shoulder. Her hand moved exactly in the same way and then…

She hit me. Hard. It felt like Devon had hit me; she had taken on all of the characteristics of a vampire. When she bubbled into laughter, it was my voice, but not my laugh. It was me in a girlish laugh. *I know this is all part of the plan, but come on, this is just weird.* But as she changed her girly giggle to a manlier snicker, I could see why she worked in the undercover unit on special occasions.

Out of curiosity I asked, "So are you all vampire now? Or are you still human?"

"At this moment," she said with my voice, "I am mostly vampire. I can take on some attributes like you have, like your strength and speed, but there are no other gifts."

"Like you can't read auras like I can?"

"Nope," she responded with a hard 'p' on the end of it.

Morbidly, I questioned her with, "What about how vampires die?"

Veleda looked down with my eyes. *So that's what I look like with puppy-dog eyes. Crazy.* She whispered, "No, that part of me is still human."

My neck pringled at that, *Why are we letting her go in there? Shouldn't it just be me?*

As if Devon read my mind, he said, "Just as we discussed before, had you been paying attention back at the apartment, Veleda has the capability to quickly find out where T is and communicate that back to the teams immediately. She's trained to save people's asses. You are not. You would get yourself killed."

"Well, still…" I said defiantly.

"What? I'm a chick – is that it?" Veleda took on my manly stance with her feet spread apart and her arms crossed.

"No, of course not," I sputtered. It wasn't a total lie, "It's not that you're a girl," she glared at me, "I mean, a woman," I amended, "But you're human. These are, at the minimum, a bunch of vampires. Who knows what the hell is over there?"

"Keen," she assured me by putting her hand on my arm in a completely feminine maneuver, which again seemed bizarre coming from someone who looked exactly like me, "I can take care of myself."

Well Ok then, I thought and remained quiet, but I didn't really believe it. But we had gone over the plan. She was going to put an invisibility spell on Devon and Tom so that she appeared to be alone. If all worked well, Veleda would draw attention to herself and pull any bad guys inside the monastery toward her. With her spells she should be able to get information out of someone there as to where T was located. If she got into trouble, she would go invisible. If she got into really deep trouble, then Devon and Tom would be there to protect her.

The leprechauns, Acair and I were to wait until Veleda gave us T's where-abouts, then we would jump over the ocean wall of the monastery, hopefully landing somewhere in the small courtyard to the side of the church sanctuary. By using Veleda's instructions, we would go get T and get the hell back out as quickly as possible.

The group waiting underground was there for support in case things went drastically wrong. Hopefully, they would not be needed and could sneak out as silently as they had gone in. Although we discussed the plan once more on the boats, *Why do I feel like this is a suicide mission?*, it seemed relatively easy – we probably even out-numbered Alexandra's vamps, but *I can feel it. Who isn't going to make it back from this?*

We were going in blind – we didn't know how many vamps were with Alexandra since we didn't have time do to reconnaissance on the place. *How many others does she have on her side besides the ones in the sewer? What if they're not all vampires, but something worse? What is Eammon was there? Could we handle another attack by him?* Also, we had no idea about any weapons or what kind of security they had set up around the small, walled church.

I hated the fact that we had such little information on the place, but Alexandra had left us with no choice. It wasn't safe for T to stay around such volatile creatures. *I know. I'm one of them and I don't even trust it when she's around me alone. Alexandra can take her life without a single thought or care. T's only human. Is she ok?* I really didn't want to think of the possibilities or outcomes anymore; it made me ache to know what danger she was in. *It is what it is for right now, just turn yourself to the task at hand and worry about what shape T is going to be in later. Just find her and get the hell out.*

We anchored just off the east shore of Sweet Haven Island. The captain and Mo roped the boats together as four of the vampires on Acair's boat dove quietly into the water and were away in an instant. They were going to enter the monastery through the underground water pipe.

My boat of people, the rest of the vamps, the witch and the leprechauns, got into a motorized, elongated raft that had been trailing behind Devon's boat. Veleda spelled it to move us towards the island without having to use the motor. The boat quickly and quietly landed on the shore. My team got to the wall without incident and Devon, Tom and Veleda, still bewitched to look like me, headed to the front of the monastery by way of a stone path around the outside of the church that led to the front of the building.

As we waited, I took out the chayyim medallion, *My lucky charm,* and then randomly thought, *Veleda should be carrying this. Not me.* Once the words swam in my head, open like that, I knew we were in trouble. My body percolated with hyperawareness *And fear.* A deep paranoia had sunk into me and I was ready to jump at everything.

I quickly placed the wounded talisman back into my pocket and set my attention to Devon, Tom and Veleda's direction. I listened to their footsteps, memorizing whose was whose and waiting to hear my voice, which was not mine, speak. As soon as they stepped through the door to the church and it shut, I closed my eyes and sent senses out to listen for other beings inside, like Tom had taught me weeks ago. But I was still too young of a vampire to be able to differentiate between the good guys and the bad guys just by their breathing. I sighed, *Maybe one day.*

My attention to the building as well as the ear piece I had on caused a delayed stereo sound effect and I quickly withdrew my focus from the first, concentrating only on my headset. The hair on the back of my neck began to stretch toward the sky as I heard the faint sound of Alexandra's voice come across the airwaves. *She must be standing far away from Veleda. I hope that's a good sign.*

"So, you came alone, young Keen," Alexandra said in a mocking voice, "Came to save your little human friend?"

From the corner of my eye, I could see the leprechauns. They were itching for a fight. Their muscles were tense, their eyes were lusting for it. On my other side, Acair was listening, but relaxed. We waited for Veleda to give the sign that we should start our attack.

"Where is she?" Veleda asked, using my voice without any trace of fear, but with sure authority of her own.

Acair hit me on the shoulder and said, "I think she makes a better you than you do."

"Gee, thanks, Acair. It's your sense of loyalty as you drive that knife into my back that I've always liked about you," I responded.

Acair chuckled quietly.

We listened to Alexandra, "Oh, she's safe. Though why the real Keen didn't come himself, we'll just have to find that out ourselves won't we my friends?" Guttural laughter suddenly filled in our ears and I counted seventeen other voices in the room with Veleda, Devon and Tom.

Oh shit, suddenly focusing completely now, *We're busted and out-numbered.*

Acair's face darkened in realization as well and he whispered, "I'm going in." And before I could protest, he was gone.

The response of, "What?" was only halfway through Veleda's lips when we heard the swirling sound of a sword cutting through her. Snarls and hisses of excitement from several vampires came over. *Oh my God! Veleda!*

✧ ✧ ✧

The Start of the End

A voice I didn't recognize yelled, "There are three more in here! Two are somewhere near the dead witch and the other one is hiding. I can smell him."

Alexandra responded angrily, "Quickly! Go after them! Bring the heir of Basya back to me. I want to kill him myself."

My senses flinched, but I tried to remain calm and separate from her words, as if it wasn't me she was talking about.

To my surprise, Devon sounded on the mic next, in a tranquil and composed voice, as we heard a couple of his tasers go off, "We could use some back up. Any day now, guys."

But then we heard a scream. It was a blood-curdling, pain-filled one that reached through the headsets freezing me in terror. Tom yelled through the headset, "We're in some serious shit here guys. Veleda is gone and Acair is down."

Suddenly, our ear pieces crackled, as if someone was moving a headset from one place to another. Then, the voice that came over it was not Devon's or Tom's. It purred in a sing-song manner, "Will the real Keen Panofsky please stand up?"

Alexandra. Every part of my being shook violently in anger. *What did that mean for the others? Are they still alive?* I couldn't think straight. I didn't know what to do. I looked wildly at the leprechauns. They were beginning to climb the wall as explosions rocked the ground underneath us. *Plan's gone to hell. Time to improvise.* I jumped up and over the fence in one quick leap with the leprechauns following.

The three of us landed on the other side of the wall and right behind three massively huge vampires. Their attention was toward the church building and we caught them completely off guard. With one sweeping motion, I reached behind me to unsheathe my dagger and ripped it diagonally through the vampire closest to me. The slash cauterized him from neck to mid-back, slicing his spinal cord. He screamed as he dropped face-first to the ground. I thrust the dagger one more time into his back. A final scream slipped from his lips as his movement stopped completely. The dagger burned with a black fire. Clear liquid from the dying vampire dripped from it, sizzling where it touched the blade, smoking as it dropped onto the ground.

I glanced around to see how I could help Quinney and Cayden. One of them had tased the bigger of the two standing vampires. That poor unlucky soul was quickly turning to ash on the ground. And the leprechauns were both now battling with the last one.

The last standing vamp was incredibly strong and in an instant had swiped at Cayden, knocking him over my head and into the wall behind me. Just then, a door burst open next to where the limp form of Cayden landed. Lachina and Harbuu, having made their way through the basement, charged the vamp who was still trying to fight Quinney. He had lost concentration briefly when Cayden had gotten bashed, but looked like he was beginning to gain the upper hand. The enemy vamp took one look at the incoming threat, punched Quinney so hard he flew over the wall we had come from and took off running.

Lachina and Harbuu grinned evilly at each other and doubled their speed to catch up. They whirled by me, a flash of wind breezing my face. A third vampire came through a different door into the courtyard. Ermelinde yelled at me, "Keen! Help me! I found the prisoners!"

Prisoners? That is not good. "Hold on," I charged back to her and ran over to the lifeless leprechaun. I bent down and put two fingers on his neck. *No pulse.*

"Eh Boyle!" A voice called to me, "You'll nev-ar find a pulse thar!"

I looked over to the wall where Quinney was climbing back over, "Where can I check then? It doesn't look like he's breathing."

He laughed, clearly not worried, "It's a lot low-ar than his neck. And if you touch me husband there, I'll kick yar ass."

I immediately brought my hands away from Cayden in a 'whoa-not-going-there' gesture, "Ok, I'll let you check then."

Quinney was next to me and feeling for Cayden's pulse – and he was right, I was not going there! Pleased at what he felt, as I turned away for a second, he asked me, "Got any money on ya?"

The question threw me off, "Huh?" And I looked at him.

"We're leprechauns. Nothing heals better than someone else's money," His grin was huge, and the light from the church hit off a diamond stud in one of his teeth.

My face was frozen in probably a very dumb and confused look, I wasn't getting it.

"Give me a five dollar bill," He put a hand to Cayden's arm, shaking him gently, "No, better yet, a twenty. Ya got a twenty on ya?"

I reached for my wallet in my back pocket, thinking this was not really the appropriate time for loaning out money. I pulled out a twenty and handed it to Quinney. He put it in Cayden's hands. The money glowed bright green and then gold. His aura began to match the brightness of the crumpled bill and the unconscious leprechaun began to stir.

Somehow, I don't think I'm going to get that back.

I was mesmerized. Quinney slapped me on the shoulder as he stood up, "Don't worr-ay, I'll take Cay ta the boats and make shawr he's all right before comin' back. Get T."

Hearing T's name shook me out of my stupor. I jumped up and, with a swift motion, went to follow Ermelinde.

✳ ✳ ✳

Finding Prisoners

Ermelinde was fast. It was wicked hard to keep up with her. She practically flew down the steps. I think I moved even faster than when we were in the underwater tunnel to Fort Dune. *Geez, that seems so long ago. Was that just days ago? Weeks?*

The walls rushed by us in a meld of golds, earth browns and deadened whites. We may have been three or four stories under ground. The monastery was beginning to look more like a happy version of a dungeon, if that was possible. It wasn't dark or dank or even scary. But at the bottom of the steps, the corridor opened to a hall of barred cages. Oddly, they were well kept, clean and without rust; the structure's appearance was deceptive for its age. For a structure that was over one hundred years old, everything looked new. From what I saw of the rooms as we raced by, they were large; a few had cots and a dresser in them and the ceilings were fairly high. *God, I hope they use this place as a touring museum!*

We heard threatening screaming in front of us, "Stand back!" and "Look out!" An explosion rocked the basement-dungeon, hurling rocks, cement and dust at us and knocking us off our feet. "What the hell was that, Erm?" I asked hurriedly, trying not to panic.

She was just as surprised as I was. We got up and ran slower toward the explosion, but when we came to the end of the hallway, where it split left and right, we saw that the right corridor was completely blocked with debris. And in the left corridor was... *Oh man, poor Garik.* The hall held what was left of Garik's white-blond head and, *An arm? A leg? Maybe?*

In horror of seeing what was also now beginning to turn to ash, I moved my eyes away from the body to stare further down the corridor. Even in the dust cloud, it was still easy to see two vampires, their auras gray and dead. They were gleeful. One had some sort of explosive that, upon seeing us, he lit and threw an easy fifty feet.

Ermelinde stepped in front of me, putting her hands up and yelling a long, "Nooooooo!!"

I turned away from the explosion, covering my head and ducking down behind Ermelinde. *Ok, I can't believe I was just that big of a coward. What the hell is wrong with me?*

Self-preservation.

Like that is going to help?

I need to stop talking to myself.

The explosion hit.

But not us.

I peaked around from my crouched position. Ermelinde was slowly bringing her hands down. The explosion had happened at the other end of the hall. The other two vampires were now in smaller pieces than Garik had been.

Oh my God!

T and another person were in the cells behind the exploded vampires. The bars to the cages were a twisted mess. I could see T lying crumpled up on the floor. *At least she's in one piece.*

Yelling her name as I ran for the cell, my throat became tense and hoarse. I think I must've been screeching her name, but I was half out of my mind – scared at what I might find. I couldn't see her aura. *Where the hell is her aura?!?*

In what was probably an instant, but seemed like eternity, I crashed through what was left of the twisted metal cell doors. Ermelinde was on my heels, dry sobbing. *Don't blame her if anything happened to T, she was just protecting us. She may not have even seen T and the other prisoner. Right?*

I stole a short, uncaring glance at the other body in the small cell. It was a male vampire. His aura was a strong gray. He seemed to just be knocked out. Ermelinde headed to him as I got up to T.

T's body was so small against the cold floor. She was on her side, curled in a little ball and still, like a little porcelain doll that had fallen from her stand. Her wig was flung about her face in a spray of auburn. It had shifted off her head and I was surprised to see her cream-colored scalp. There wasn't even a hint of buzzed or shaved hair. *She must be completely bald.*

My hand went to hers and as soon as we touched, her aura began showing a faint blue. I bent down, moving my face level to hers. T's eyes fluttered open, her lips curled up. I breathed a sign of relief, not realizing I had been holding my breath until then. *Thank God,* I thought, *I'm not ready to lose her.* But suddenly, T's eyes rolled back into her head, closing. Her aura blinked out and her body went limp.

No, no, no, no, NO!

I shook her gently with both hands, "T! T! Come on! Don't do this to me, come on T!"

Ermelinde said, "I got this guy. Get her out of here."

I shouted a little more angrily at Ermelinde than I anticipated, "Get him back to the boat. I'll take care of T."

Turning my attention back to the lifeless form on the ground, I straightened her body and began pressing on her chest to get her heart started again. I controlled the pressure, hoping not to bruise or break her ribs, but my motions were rapid and clean. Maybe a little too rapid, but her heart began to beat on its own again after a few seconds and her aura returned. Dull at first and then stronger.

I straightened her wig back on, covering her up delicately. *If she doesn't want people to know why she wears wigs, than I'm not going to give her secret away.* I gingerly picked her up in my arms, cradling her limp body, vowing to protect her from any other dangers.

Ermelinde was already ahead of us and out of the cell. She had flung the knocked out vamp over her shoulder as if she was tossing a jacket there while taking a stroll on the beach. The sleeping vamp's head bobbed up and down with her motions of running. Every once in a while I caught sight of his face and realized I recognized him from a few weeks earlier, but *Now is not the time to care.*

I moved faster to keep up with Ermelinde. We ran up the steps, taking five at a time with our long, graceful strides. As we got to the doorway to the courtyard, we almost bumped directly into Devon and Tom bursting in from the other side. Tom was limping slightly and Devon had bite marks on him that were already beginning to heal. Devon called out to us, "Let's get the hell out of here."

Tom almost pounded into me to grab T. But, even to her brother, I didn't want to give her up. Seeing her on the ground before, her faint aura dancing in and out around her, the smile she gave me when she saw me – something protective and fierce had clicked in me and I couldn't let her go. *Not yet. Not until I know she's safe.*

Tom was screaming for me to give him his sister.

"Tom," I said gently, but predatorily, "She's ok. I've got her. Let's just get her out of here."

He shook his head in surrender and took point with Devon, Harbuu and Lachina to fight off any creatures that came out at us – Ermelinde was as encumbered as I was. It didn't take long for several vamps to attack us.

A small, mouse-like, teen-looking vamp came from a side door and knocked into Harbuu's knees, rounding on him like a bowling ball, making the larger vampire fall over backward. The 'kid' was on Harbuu in a second. Tom wrapped his arm around the attacking vampire's chest, thrusting him back and off of Harbuu. Immediately, Harbuu jumped up and went to help Lachina, who had been assaulted by two female vampires.

One of the vampires was from the sewer. Although she had changed her clothes to all black, her high cheek bones and almond-shaped eyes were clearly recognizable. The other female also looked familiar, though she wasn't in the sewer. She was tall and had blond hair. *I know her, but how?* The two vampires had long swords that curved at the tips and Lachina was having a heck of a time trying to get at her taser as she scrambled to dodge the wielding weapons. She was backed into a storage room off the main courtyard and the women were on the move to go in for a final strike.

Harbuu yelled at Lachina to turn away as he threw a flash bomb into the center of the three women. Lachina shut her eyes just in time, but judging by the screams of the other ladies, they were momentarily blinded. Lachina finally managed to un-trap her taser and zapped both of the distressed vampires. They dropped to the ground immediately, though only stunned. They would heal from their wounds as would the 'kid' that Tom had finally wrangled up and tossed over the monastery – out toward the front of the buildings and away from where we were heading.

The vampire male that Devon was fighting wasn't so lucky in his outcome, however. He was also one of the vampires I met in the crap-infested waters under the city. I didn't get to see much of that fight, but it ended with Devon ripping the other vampire's head off. *Remind me to always stay on his good side!* With T in my arms, I kept my head tucked and my body hunched over to protect her. *Time to get the hell out of here.*

I angled my head to the side to see where I was going and was suddenly hit from my unprotected right side. My knees crashed into the concrete-tiled courtyard floor, cracking it. T's head began to gravitate toward the ground and if I didn't catch her, she'd hit it so hard there would be no chance to save her. Sliding my arm up as quickly as possible, my hand got under her head just in time – the tiles shattered underneath me, kicking up shards and dust onto her face, making small pinkish slices, *No blood, thank God,* but she was safe, *For the moment.*

A short, squat vampire, about fifty when he was turned, came at me, "Ah, the heir of Basya. You're coming with me." He reached for me and I had just enough balance on my left leg to stay on that and sweep my right leg out to trip him. The motions happened in a blur of blender-like movement and he almost fell. But my luck ran out and he regained his own balance before I could get myself and T out of the way. *Crap!*

He grabbed T's leg and pulled. I went along with the motion, hoping she wouldn't be torn in half from his strength. Using our momentum, I rammed him with my head straight to the chest – which, by the way, I won't be doing ever again. But the stars that burst in my sight went away as quickly as they had come and at least that motion did knock him down. For a split second, the vamp stayed where he was and I yelled for Tom to help. Up the gray-haired vampire came like a bursting jack-in-the-box and he nailed me in the jaw with a right hook. My hands were full with T, so I couldn't do anything to block him and I hadn't turned back in time from calling for Tom to dodge the blow. I could taste the nasty, gel-like blood in my mouth as my fangs bit down into my tongue. I ran backward when the vampire tried to hit me again and, finally, Tom was able to break away from the brown-skinned vampire he was fighting to get in-between me and my adversary.

Great! I'm outta here! I turned tail and ran to get to the back wall, to the area we had come in from earlier. Lachina and Harbuu joined me as Devon went to help Tom fight off the remaining vampire. We hopped onto the wall and switched our view to the fight. But I guess the old vampire didn't want to continue after he saw Devon approach, because he bolted through one of the monastery side doors. *Don't blame him at all!*

Staring at the mess we were leaving, I realized we had been attacked by wave after wave of vampires. Some of them were regenerating as I watched, but it seemed they were too weak or too smart to try to come after us again. There were enough truly dead vamps and other beings from both sides that none of our team did anything to completely kill anyone else. And I was absolutely fine with that.

Tom and Devon practically flew over to Ermelinde and the unconscious vampire we had rescued from the prison cell to help them both up. They had been beat up pretty hard and both had cuts on their faces and arms that bled clear, thick blood even as they healed. Tom helped Ermelinde to the wall and Devon picked up no-name vamp and hefted him over his shoulders. All three of the walking vampires jumped onto the wall to land in-between us. Tom and Devon reached the raft-boats first. Tom hopped on and reached his arms out, picking T out of my own arms so quickly I couldn't react. Judging from his face, and the faint warning growl he gave me, that would've been a bad idea anyway, so it was good that I just let it happen. I didn't want to get pulled limb from limb trying to keep her. *This could get complicated.*

Well, that was an odd thought.

Landing in the waiting boats was effortless, noiseless. Everyone moved so incredibly silently. It was eerie, quite honestly, after the rush of noise we had made not two minutes earlier.

Lachina and Harbuu were helping Ermelinde with the rescued vampire. He was just beginning to stir and we all knew how fast he would be able to go from unconscious to freaked-out vamp when he woke, so they were taking precautions. I had freaked out too when I woke up 'captured' by other vampires and not knowing if they were friendlies or not. Of course I was tied down at the time, so I couldn't do much about it.

The three vampires held the semi-conscious vamp's legs and arms in place on the bottom of the raft they were in. One of them stuck him with a needle which I can only assume contained the same sleep-drug stuff Tom gave me when they found me fighting Kaellan, the water spirit. The vampire didn't stir any longer. The small engines to our two boats were started and we moved quickly away from the island.

I stopped thinking about anything and went on staring at T as she was being taken care of by Tom. He was looking down at her with such a look of worry and helplessness that I didn't think he was going to be able to keep it together much longer.

Devon stole sideways glances at them, worry on his face. He tried to look ahead to where the main boats were, but he couldn't hold the mask of apathy that was his norm for these kinds of situations. We were all silent on our way back to the bigger boats and as we boarded them. The Captain and Mo were waiting for us.

I glanced back at the monastery wall as we got further away. Surprise and fear hit me when I saw Alexandra and several other beings staring at us with abhorrence. I thought they were going to attack us – they could've easily, as we weren't that far from their shores yet. But they stood their ground. Alexandra's dark hair curled around her face, masking the snarl that was formed on her lips – turning the ugly expression of contempt into something beautiful. My body felt the pull towards her like it did the first night I met her at the bar. Thankfully, the memory of her deadly bite was enough to shake off my desire for her.

She motioned for the men beside her to hold their positions and let us go. One of them was a bald-headed witch, his aura burning yellow-green with flecks of red. The other three beings standing with her, two males and a female, were vampires – the gray of their auras wrapping brightly around them before disappearing. The female vampire was one of the women that Lachina had been fighting. She had apparently recovered from the stunning taser a lot quicker than I had assumed she would. Seeing her made me wonder where the Asian woman from the sewer had gone to and I half-expected to be attacked at any moment.

One of the males was a tall guy with short blond hair. He had light eyes and looked like he had been turned around the same age as I had been. The other guy was shorter than Alexandra and had shoulder-length blond hair. *Why do these vampires look so recognizable? Why do I feel like I've met them before? Did I know them before my life as a vampire? Did I meet them afterward? Why can't I place them?*

Alexandra and her group glared at us for a few seconds more before jumping backward to land on the inside of the monastery where they were blocked from our view.

I shifted my attention back to my beaten and battered team. I counted the occupants of both boats. I counted again. And again. Missing were Garik, Veleda, and…

Acair.

I said his name to Devon. He glared at me and I looked at Tom for an answer even though I guess I already knew it.

So Acair wasn't just 'down' as Tom said. He had fallen.
Damn it. Damn it all to Hell.

Mo and the captain drove both boats back to the mainland. I took the opportunity to really look at the team during the trip. The leprechauns were battled and bruised, but Cayden had recovered, still waving my glowing twenty dollar bill around. It had shrunk into the size of play money, almost as small as Monopoly money, but was still viewable. His husband was cradling him against his chest, singing softly in a lilt and gently stroking Cayden's hair. Quinney had a black eye and a bruised cheek, but he was fine. *Nothing a five dollar bill won't fix.*

Devon had a big gash down his chest and another one on his right arm. The index finger on his left hand was missing. However, the cuts were healing slowly, the bite marks were all but healed and his finger was regenerating. *A couple of blood brews will heal that.* Tom seemed ok other than the limp, but I couldn't fully tell since he was curled around T, talking to her to coax her to wake up. The other surviving vamps were bloodied with their own and other vampires' clear jelly blood. Their clothes were ripped, but the cuts underneath seemed to be healing. *Quickly.*

I checked out my own arms and body. I had been hit with metal shrapnel from the cage explosions. My skin was starting to push the foreign pieces out; clear ooze flowed from each of the tiny holes as they healed. *So cool and yet so very unsettling.*

"What happened in there?" I asked Devon.

"They had seers," he was sullen, defeated, like he should've known that ahead of time.

"Seers?"

"A witch was there. He could see past Veleda's magic. One of the vampires could feel that we were in the room. He could sense the number of 'presences,' or something like that. I could tell he didn't know exactly where we were until Veleda's last heart beat, then her spells disappeared completely," for once, Devon's hard unemotional shell cracked and sadness seeped out of him.

Or regret, I thought in understanding. *I knew we shouldn't have let her go in.*

He gathered himself before he continued, "She stayed alive long enough that we were able to get out of the room before they could see us. Once she died, though, Tom and I became visible. We set ourselves up around the corner and took out a couple of them as they came to attack. Acair appeared in order to help surround a few more, but the vampire that killed Veleda came up behind Acair as he was fighting two guys. He wasn't quick enough to disappear again."

Devon was silent for a moment and then added, "He was a good guy."

I could only nod my head in agreement, *I liked him too.*

His fricken duster.

His ability to save my ass from Alexandra. Saving Devon and Tom, too. I didn't know him very well, but I knew I would miss him. *All of them,* I amended in my head, *Acair, Veleda and Garik. Our fallen friends.*

Chapter 15

Cleaning up the Mess

✡ ✡ ✡

Lost Friend

We docked the boats and headed quickly across Commercial Street, up the darkened alley ways to Front and Exchange Streets. It was easy to dodge any regular people that were out at that time. We stuck to the shadows, or, when we had to, we acted like we were walking with drunken friends. Since T was the worst off and still hadn't woken up, Tom took a longer way back home in order to completely dodge the humans.

I was the first to enter the apartment. My bad feeling hit as I opened the door. *Someone's here.* I took my dagger out and ran full force up the steps expecting Alexandra or one of her minions to jump out at me, wondering how they could've beaten us back there. *But come hell or high water, I'm taking out whoever it is!*

The lights were off in the apartment, but the glow from his gray aura lit his pained face.

"Acair!" I sheathed my dagger, almost missing the holder in my surprise.

He stumbled and fell toward me. Taking two large and quick steps, I caught him before he could land on the hard wood floor. The clear fluid, marking him a vampire, flowed out of his mouth and he sputtered wordlessly.

"Devon," I called out, "I need you up here now!"

In a blink, he and the rest of the entourage were up the landing. Harbuu carried the still-unconscious vampire from the monastery to one of the couches. Newspapers and crumpled clothing were thrown quickly to the floor as space was made for the hurt and battered team. Tom made it back and rushed T over to the available couch. The captain was on the phone immediately, calling a doctor that specialized in all creatures other than humans. She would be arriving shortly.

We put Acair on the dining room table, Devon clearing the mess off with one sweep of his large muscular arm. Acair did not look good. One arm was almost completely cut off right above the elbow. His leg had a deep gash and it was not healing like it should.

We got out packets of real blood from the fridge. It was an emergency stash of O negative, just for such occasions. Devon had gotten it from a connection at the medical center up the hill. We cleared Acair's mouth of the thick fluid and began dripping the blood down his throat.

A knock at the door alerted us that the doctor had arrived and Mo let her in. In glancing at her aura, I narrowed her down to not human, not vampire, not witch and not leprechaun. But other than that, I had no idea what she was.

Her aura gleamed bright red with black twisting around. She sparked blue, though. So whatever she was, she was at least a calm being. I could work with that.

She moved with vampire speed to Acair, brought her tools out and began examining him. "These cuts are from a spelled weapon. We need to take the arm off completely and close up the leg wound or else the magic will pass through his system and kill him."

"Will his arm come back?" The captain asked the question that was on everyone's mind.

"Not in this century, if it ever does. It's a miracle he's still alive. You see these marks on the cuts?" She pointed at black, scaly skin, "The poison is spreading incredibly fast."

"What do we need to do?" Devon asked in a cold, detached voice.

"We need a sharp, sterilized knife and hot water in a bowl. We'll take the arm off first and then heal the rest of his wounds," the doctor commanded.

Devon turned to me, "Keen, give her your knife."

I didn't hesitate. I flipped the dagger out and went to hand it to her.

She shook her head, hurriedly speaking, "You'll need to do it. I'll show you where to cut, but I need to prepare the poultice." A bowl of hot water had been placed in front of her by someone and she was already pouring sweet smelling powders into it.

I was horrified. I looked at the knife as it glowed its crazy, black glow. *What would this knife do to Acair if I cut him?* I had only used it to kill with. *Does it know the difference between friend or foe? Would it kill him too?*

My face twisted in agony and Devon put a hand on my shoulder. "I'll do it," he said and I let the knife slide from my hand as he took it.

Immediately, the glow went away and it looked more or less like a normal dagger. He approached Acair, and I knew I couldn't watch. I didn't want to watch as a weapon of mine possibly killed someone who had saved my life. *Maybe in Devon's hands it wouldn't. I can't believe how lame I am that I can't do this myself.*

I went over to Tom and T instead, turning my back on a friend and allowing someone stronger in heart than me to do the job Acair needed done. Tom was stroking T's face with a hot washcloth, wiping away dried blood and dirt from her. Sitting on the coffee table across from them, I picked up her hand and held it, feeling her cold fingers out-cold my own. Her aura brightened briefly and then dissolved back into her.

Tom dropped the washcloth onto the floor and I scrutinized the damage she had received. Her face was criss-crossed with reddened cuts and a bruise had formed on her cheek bone. I reached out, forgetting whose company I was in, and touched the darkening contusion. I streaked my fingertips against it, not wanting to cause her any pain, but fascinated with the mark just the same.

Tom cleared his throat at me expectantly. *Oops.* I leaned back and took T's hand again. But I noticed something odd, "Tom?" I said, questioning. He looked down at T. The area where I had touched T had begun to lighten.

The discoloration had changed from the deep purple of a new bruise to the yellow, ugly-brown shade of a healing one and a scrape near the bruise had disappeared slowly.

Oh my God. Did I do that? Did I just heal T? No way! How awesome would that be?

Careful Keen, the reasonable side of my brain started, *you might get a god-complex and nobody likes a showoff.*

Nothing else changed about her, though. "Tom?" I said again, but with more concern in my voice.

"She's fine," he said curtly, "You can hold her hand, just don't touch her face again."

He had spoken to me as if I was a toddler and it made me wonder what he wasn't telling me about her. But I ignored my intuition. I was too concerned about her. *A bruise and cut may have healed, but her aura hasn't gained any strength.* My anxiety got worse. A marathon of memories popped into my thoughts in a stream of episodes, like I was watching only the best parts of my favorite television series.

Like the night we met. Man, I thought she was going to die from boredom and her brother thought she was going to die because of me. A small smile crept to my face as I remembered that tiny misunderstanding that almost landed me dead before I got started.

Oh, and that time when she was harassing me in the bathroom the first night I was let out of the apartment. Recollections of her continual mocking of me surfaced – *Sure, goad the untrained death machine.*

Her ridiculous wigs, *The green one that really brings out her eyes.*

My smile turned into a sigh, *Her eyes... The odd jade color the ocean turns after a storm at sunset. So warm... So alluring, even while her wit cuts you down. But all in good fun, eh?*

But her eyes always lit up when she twirled her way into the room. And she was striking – a complete knockout. I found myself frowning for a second, *I don't know what I would do without her.*

What? Wait! Back up. What was that last thought?

I think I just thought that... No, never mind. I'm being an idiot. I just got over Maddie, there is no way that I could be in love with T so soon. But then, the empty cavity in my chest ached again, and I looked down at it, hoping the feeling was only my stomach growling in hunger. I had no such luck. *Oh shit.*

Realization hit like a whale running aground, *I am in love with her.*

When did that happen? I questioned myself, my thoughts cycling through the past few weeks in detail to look for an answer, a sign, anything.

Was it just now? When I was remembering all of those times hanging out with her? Or was it when she kept joking with me while I was trying to let go of Maddie? I mean, I had thought about how hot she was the other day when we flirted, but that was just flirting, right? Had I been feeling this as an undercurrent ever since we met and I shook her hand – when her aura first showed to me?

My mind immediately thought 'Yes' and the feeling that I was right clicked like it was absolutely true. *I have been in love with her since we first met. Everything else has just been distractions – even Maddie. To be honest with myself, I knew from the time I ended up in the estuary and saw my reflection, there was no way I was going to be able to keep Maddie.*

Oh, crap. This is not good. Not good at all. I know how I am when I'm falling for a girl. I trip over myself, am completely tongue-tied and I do really stupid things that I don't even want to remind myself that I do. How did I not see this coming? Oh man. What am I going to do? I can't fall for T? That's just fricken crazy!

But you already did. Weeks ago.

And then I remembered something else…

Tom will kill you if he finds out you like his sister. Just get the thought straight out of your head right now. You didn't realize how you felt about her and you can un-realize it just as quickly. And for the love of God, don't look at Tom.

Shit. Too late.

My eyes went directly to Tom. And by the way he was glaring at me, I knew my face had given away everything I was thinking. *How long has he been staring at me? Before the smile? After the sigh?*

His normal comical smile was screwed up in anger. *Oh, man. Must've been before the smile.*

I relaxed my features, trying to put a poker face on to hide anything else my traitor self would give away. But Tom's lips pressed together, a crease formed in his forehead and the realization reflected in his eyes made me understand my thoughts even more clearly. *We both must've come to the same conclusion at the same time.*

I hastily dropped T's hand. It hung awkwardly, but I could've sworn her fingers angled as if to reach for me before falling limply down again. *Maybe, wishful thinking?*

Tom's body posture began to change. He pulled T in, protectively, and at the same time began getting up aggressively like a giant silverback gorilla shielding his family. His eyes narrowed and he bared his fangs at me in the look of 'touch-her-and-die.'

I put my hands up in a 'hey-I'm-not-going-to-hurt-her-I-mean-touch-her' gesture and quickly backed my ass off the coffee table. I kept my eyes directly on Tom, though, preparing for the attack.

A scream of pain, rage and despair knocked us out of our silent conversation and we both turned our sights to the kitchen.

We saw Acair's severed arm being moved away from the table. He was writhing around, knocking people about in his strength. The doctor was yelling, "Hold him! Hold him! I need to get the poultice tied on."

The surrounding beings jumped on his legs and chest to keep him immobile, but he was still struggling and I heard Devon cuss in pain. He had been trying to hold Acair's shoulders down. Apparently, though, Acair's strength had not diminished so much that he couldn't untangle himself from the others and bite the closest person to him – Devon. Devon reeled his hand back into a fist and punched Acair between the eyes. The table splintered from the force and all quieted as Acair was knocked out.

"Not really what I had in mind, but effective none the less," the doctor said wryly. She wrapped a gooey, green-blue dyed towel around the point his arm was cut at. She secured it and began placing sweet smelling cloths into the deep wounds on his legs.

She looked up at Devon, "you want anything for that bite?"

"No thanks," he replied as he was already healing from it.

With that crisis averted and me clearly not welcome to be near T at this time, I went over to check on how the mysterious vampire we found at the monastery was doing.

✵ ✵ ✵

Can This Possibly Get Any Worse?

The leprechauns, who were fully healed, Mo and the captain had been watching the dark-haired vampire as the rest of our team had been tending to Acair or T. The vampire was beginning to stir and I could tell that he was taking in his surroundings while he kept his eyes closed. My memory flashed back to when I had first arrived at the apartment and had done a very similar thing.

He breathed the air deep into his body, and I could tell that he tasted it, trying to get a sense of how many beings were holding him captive. *I wonder if he is thinking about how many of us he could kill before we took him down. Or maybe he's just wondering where the hell he is.* His aura turned a strong gray as he flared his nostrils and flexed his hands.

The others were talking and not noticing the changes. I cleared my throat, "Looks like this guy's coming around. Someone grab a blood beer for him. He's probably going to need it."

As soon as I finished my sentence, I had one in my hand. I smiled, noticing that my actions were becoming just as fast as the other vampires. I had thought that if I sounded calm and helpful, the vamp might not freak out as badly and less harm would come to everyone in the area. *Boy, am I wrong.*

The damn vampire came up swinging. The beer smashed to the ground as I fell backward over the coffee table. *Jesus! That was hard.*

He lashed out at anyone close to him, but the other vampires were on him in a second, coming across the room in a blur of motion. They had maneuvered around the leprechauns and humans, pushing them to safety as they subdued the just-wakened vampire. Our new friend was held down in a sitting position on the reclining chair by Harbuu and Devon. He didn't look happy, and the affect of two vampires with a hand each firmly on his shoulders made him look like he had body guards.

Though not for his protection.

I turned the coffee table upright and moved it over to sit down directly in front of the new vampire. I asked for another beer. Although, this time, I drank it in long gulps like I was auditioning for a commercial, reinforcing how delicious it was. I could tell he was fighting the urge to reach for it as his hunger took over, magnified by the fact that he had been healing over the past hour.

I took a long look at him. He wasn't in bad shape, any major cuts or bruises having healed while he was sleeping. His short, black hair was a little askew like having bed head. His features were young, like he was turned around the same age as I had been. He glared hateful eyes at me and I finally recognized him.

Devon came around to my side as Harbuu kept his hands pressed firmly on the vampire's shoulders. "Karl, right?" Devon asked.

That's right! Now I remember! He was one of the vampires I had met on my first night out on the town after my training with Devon and Tom – *One of the New Zealand vamps. Wait a minute! Were the other vampires at the monastery?* I played the scenes over in my head – who we had fought and whether or not the others had been there. *Well, crap. I think I remember that short one, what was his name? Sherman. Yeah, that had to have been Sherman standing up there with Alexandra. And wasn't that blond wife of his there too? Fighting against Lachina? Hmm, this could get very bad, very quickly.* I dampened the warning bell that went off in my head, *I guess we'll just have to see how this plays out.*

Other than a sheepish smile, he ignored Devon and just continued to glare eyes at me so dark they looked black.

"Is that your real name?" Devon questioned.

He shifted his eyes down and to the left so quickly that only I was able to catch the movements before he looked back up into my eyes. Karl was clearly not his real name. He finally glanced over to Devon, "Not you." He nodded to me, "You."

Devon growled deep in the back of his throat, like the rumble of a truck passing by. He moved back to stand behind Deegan, taking his previous spot next to Harbuu.

Ok, fine. Not sure why he wants me to do all the talking, but I can do this. Right?

"Who are you and why did Alexandra have you in that cell?" Even to me, I sounded cop-like. I felt like I had a spotlight trained on the vampire, saying 'Where were you on the night of…?' It reminded me of a bad movie.

His ears perked up at the name and then he paused, interpreting the situation, trying to decide whether the truth would be good or bad.

Hoping to help make up his mind, I scolded, "Hey, we just saved your ass from those crazy vamps. The least you can do is tell us who the hell you are and why your ass needed saving."

He laughed at that. It was a deep snicker, though. Sarcastic and ugly.

"I am Deegan Botand," his New Zealand accent dropped before he fell into copying my New England accent, as if he had always been from there, "And you're Keen, eh?"

I was disturbed that he remembered me so easily, but, then again, I was confused that the New Zealand vamps had been fighting along-side Alexandra, yet this guy had been locked up in a cell. I tried not to show my surprise, "Yup."

There was a pause before he asked, "What are you going to do to me?" His eyes shifted back and forth to each of the vampires around the room, moving directly over the humans and leprechauns as if they weren't a threat.

"Well," I said thoughtfully, but with a little hint of menace, "That depends on why you were in that cell, Deegan."

He seemed terribly amused at something.

Annoyed, I said, "Start talking vamp, or we'll just lock you up ourselves."

"Or worse," Devon said from behind him.

Deegan shifted in his chair to really look at Devon and consider his offer. He shrugged indifferently.

His voice was calm when he brought his attention back to me, "Alexandra is my mother. Your friend," He pointed at T, "was supposed to be my snack if you didn't show up as requested. Or maybe even if you had."

Hisses went around the room and the grip from Devon got tight enough that I saw clear fluid begin to wet Deegan's shirt. He didn't flinch at the pain. If Tom hadn't been concentrating on T's sudden movements of waking, I'm pretty sure he would've pounced and there would have been no more Mr. Deegan Botand. *Alexandra a mother? No fricken way. Not that crazy, sexy, manipulative vampire!*

All the rest of the beings in the room slowly moved toward the insulting vampire. *Very menacing.* As if I had any say in it, I put my hand up to halt them. Oddly enough, they stopped. "Let's try something else. Why did Alexandra want me there? Why does she want me dead?"

I could hear T's movements behind us. Tom asked her again and again how she felt and if she was all right. I crooked my head towards their direction. He rearranged his body to give her a hug, cuddling her as only an older, protective sibling can do. To my amazement, her aura was a bright blue. *How did she do that? She was practically on death's door!*

I heard him lean in and whisper that her best friend, Veleda, was killed in the battle. Her light tears fell, hitting the cloth with little wisp sounds as he recounted how the brave witch, her best friend, had died. I tried to block the conversation out and concentrate on the enemy before me. It was hard for me to ignore T's pain as my thoughts jumped to the talisman, *I should've given Veleda the damn chayyim. It's kept me safe all this time. It would've kept her alive.* In my head, I knew that thought was total crap, that a good luck charm wasn't real and couldn't save people. But my guilt couldn't stop thinking about the 'what if.'

Devon cleared his throat to pull me back in. I listened for a few seconds more, until T got up and closed us off behind her bedroom door. Then, my full attention went back to the mysterious vampire.

Deegan's shadowy brown eyes stared at me in consideration. His voice was even, slightly cold, kind of uncaring, "Just like you, my twin brother has been abducted. We tried fighting the gargoyles off, but my brother and I were still human at the time and not much help."

"Gargoyles attacked you?" I looked up at Devon. He just shrugged back, not giving a guess as to what gargoyles wanted out of this. I nodded at Deegan to continue.

"Well, gargoyles, vampires and humans. The vampires weren't of the, ah," he paused looking for the right words, "family."

I nodded again, catching his drift.

He continued with a little more animation, "My father was killed in the battle. My brother was taken. And in all the confusion, I had been bitten. My mother stole me away to hide me while I was changing. The vampires you saw with me months ago have been my protectors as I hid out in Ireland and New Zealand.

"Whoever is looking for us is hell-bent on getting all four of us," he laughed at the end, more to himself, a secret joke.

I knew he was leaving some details out, but I tried to be patient. *Hopefully, he'll get to it soon.*

"To protect me," he said, sounding dark and chilly.

Ah, here it comes.

"To protect me," he repeated, "So I could come home, she decided it would just be easier to kill you or your brother instead. If the gargoyles can't get to all of us, then there's no fulfillment of the prophecy. No prophecy means I can go back to living my life as I had before, only now with a few extra, fun abilities," he cracked his knuckles in musing and I rolled my eyes at him. *Tool.*

But I had to take note of what he said, *What part could he and his brother possibly have to do with the prophecy? Adam and I were the twins. It's us. IT has to be just us.*

"I'm not going to lie. She went after your brother, what was his name? Oh right, Adam. She went after Adam first, but the gargoyles got to him before she could. She was finally able to find you. Imagine her surprise when she discovered that both of you lived so close together. It was smart to have you hiding in the town you had already been attacked in as babies. No one would think to look here."

My curiosity piqued, "How did Alexandra find me?"

"It was your picture in the paper when your high school won the state hockey championship," He pointed at my cheek, "We all had birthmarks shaped like dragons before we turned."

Both of us brought our hand to our own faces, gently touching where the mark of the dragon had been. We moved as if we were twin brothers. If the subject hadn't been so important, we might have laughed.

"Anyway," he went on, "She thought she killed you. It was nothing personal."

Yeah right!

"What, mother bear just protecting her cub, is that it?" I dripped sarcasm like water coming out of a broken faucet.

"Something like that," he sneered, but then continued in a calm, methodical voice, "So after a few weeks, when you hadn't resurfaced, she called me back. Of course, you changed the game when you showed up alive... Well, mostly alive, and changed. My mother had inadvertently moved us closer to the prophecy. I was in the cell for my protection in case any of those murderous bastards came looking for me."

"That didn't work out too well, now did it?" A familiar pixie voice said.

Shifting, I saw T coming over to us.

She had removed her wig. Instead, she wore a deep maroon and purple variegated scarf that wrapped around her head and was tied in a large knot at the base of her neck, somewhat below her right ear. The rest of the scarf hung like a thick ponytail surrounding her shoulder and caressing her arm down to the elbow. She had changed clothes too. Wearing holey jeans and a Count Chocula t-shirt, I thought this was probably the first time I had ever seen her wear normal clothes. Her face was tear-streaked and red, but her eyes were stone cold with strength. *She is so beautiful. Why did it take me so long to realize that?*

She shoved me over, not like she really could move me, to get a front row view of Deegan. *Oh yeah, she is so much just one of the guys, not taking crap from any of us.* In watching her in great detail, I realized something was amiss with her. *No cuts or bruises and her aura is wicked strong.* She had healed almost as fast as we had. *That can't be right. She's not a vampire. Then what the hell is she?* Then my thoughts went to the possibility that I had some magic that healed her. *But then why would Tom not be amazed with my new skills and thrilled that I had saved T? Something's up with her.*

"For all you know, we could be just as murderous," T threatened.

Seeming unimpressed with her, he said, "Yeah, my little human? Not likely."

I wasn't too sure about having her being so close to Deegan, so I glanced behind me at Tom and he nodded the 'OK.' *At least he trusts me enough to keep his sister safe.*

She was so close, her arm touching mine, that her skin felt on fire against me. A wave of feelings came over me seeing that she was alive and not terribly hurt. I couldn't help but smile. *Yup, I'm in love.*

Crap.

I felt a hand on my left shoulder and glimpsed up to see Tom suddenly hovering over me. His face was not happy – *More like a black bear being teased into a fight.* I smiled in embarrassment, moved slightly away from T and got my head back in the game. "What is the rest of this prophecy your mother is so concerned about?" *I can't wrap my head around this. Alexandra a mother? It just doesn't fit. It doesn't sound right.*

"What do you know?" He countered.

Everyone, except the unconscious Acair and the good doctor tending him, had joined in a small circle around us. This was the first time some of them were hearing about the prophecy and that I had something to do with one. They were all intrigued.

Ok, I'll allow a quick recap, "Mr. Carmichael, my twin brother's adopted father, told us that we were basically the relatives of the Angel of Death, Abaddon, and Moses' daughter, Rebekah. He mentioned that Abaddon had a falling out with God and Ra over the treatment of angels and vampires compared to humans. What else does this have to do with us?"

Really, I just cared about finding my brother and keeping my parents safe. I wasn't interested in this crazed version of a second cousin twice removed or whatever the hell he was to me. I felt T's closeness, but she was as motionless as any of the non-humans in the room and waited for him to answer.

"Have you heard of the Book of Revelation?" He asked all mysterious and hypnotizing. The room seemed to be vacant other than me and him, everyone was so quiet. Except for the humans and the leprechauns breathing, no one was making a sound.

"Yes, I've heard of it, but I don't know a lot about it. Hebrew school never taught us anything to do with the Christian faith."

"The Book of Revelation is supposed to be the prophecy handed to John while he was on the island of Patmos, from God. It concerns the battle between God and the Prince of Darkness," He laughed a low laugh at the nickname of the Angel of Death, "It's the story about how the people of the earth will be judged and how the world, as we know it, will cease to exist."

"Yeah, yeah," I waved my hand around and rolled my eyes at his over-dramatized statement.

"Keen," Deegan's tone turned sharp and sarcastic, mocking my lack of enthusiasm, "now pay attention to this." He leaned down on his knees, putting his arms down on them and getting very close to me and T. I scooted her over to put myself closer to him.

He ignored my motion, clearly not interested in her, which was good. His focus was completely on me and I mirrored his posture. Our faces were within inches as he said, "The real story is that the book wasn't handed down by God. Abaddon had been exiled and imprisoned on Patmos where he had heard about one of God's messengers, John. Abaddon sent for John to visit and manipulated John into thinking he was sent by God to pass a message to the people. He used the 'book,' the scroll that John wrote in, to curse the children of God and the people of Ra. The pure humans. And he was going to use his own children to condemn them."

"Explain," it was the only word I could think of – my mind had gone numb and my neck prickled with the biggest, strongest and worst feeling I've ever had. Even worse than at the monastery. *I do not like where he's going with this.*

"Well, to sum up the story in the scroll, the curse was that when four of his line were born male, they would unlock the seals, releasing the Angel of Death from his prison. As the dragon, he and his four sons would bring the apocalypse down upon the people of earth."

I think the humans just stopped breathing.

"My twin and I are the direct descendants of Bast, the daughter of Rebekah who was taken to live with the Egyptians. You and your brother are from the line of Basya, the daughter who stayed with the Israelites."

What? "Ok, exactly, how is that supposed to work? I mean, I would prefer not to actually bring reigning death upon my friends and family, so can't I just say 'No?'"

He sat back laughing, "Yeah, that would be the easy way out. Do you really think you can turn your back on your forefather? An angel at that?"

I gave him the look of 'Sure, why not?' with a shrug.

"Oh, dear, sweet, naive Keen. How adorable your world must be."

I got angry with him, my voice rising slightly, "There is no need to make fun of me, cousin. I want to know the options here."

"Why do you think my mother was trying to kill you or you brother. If there aren't four sons, then there isn't a prophecy."

"Aren't there any other options?"

"Other than one of us dying? No. We all needed to be brought over to the family. To become vampire. You and Adam were split up; we were hoping that that would keep one of you from being found and turned – and keeping at least one descendant human. But my guess is that all four of us have been turned."

I nodded, "Well at least we agree on that. Mr. Carmichael had part of the prophecy and the scroll's cover became, I guess, more alive as each of us were turned. Do you know what that means?"

"He had a scroll? Which part?"

"He only had the beginning, the Haggadah portion where Grandpa Death and Grandma Rebekah got busy."

"Where is it now?" He finally looked interested, his posture tensing.

"We think his butler, Eammon, got it. Eammon murdered my uncle," I maddened at the thought of it, digging my hands into the coffee table and leaving claw marks under where I was sitting.

"Where is this human?" Deegan was also fuming now, his eyes turning blacker.

"He's not a human. He's a changeling. He may be with the gargoyles since that seems like his form of choice," Devon said in a very military manor, his deep voice startling us both.

Deegan craned around to see the bigger vampire, "What do you know of them?"

"Not much, except they're really beginning to piss me off," Devon replied threateningly.

I wanted to get back on track, *Who cares about Eammon right now,* "So, ok, fine, now that we're turned, what's supposed to happen?"

"Well, the Cliff Notes version is this: if the two parts of the scroll are brought back together and the story read, the seals will be broken and we will become the four horsemen."

"I'm sorry. The seals and the four what?"

"The Book of Revelation talks about the four horsemen. Wait, do you have a Bible?" He glanced around the room to the walls and bookshelves that were in view from his angle.

I had never noticed if there was one in the apartment, but T jumped up and ran to her room. She was back in a couple of seconds with a larger and thinner than normal book. It was a giant children's book that had cartoon drawings of Noah and the Ark, Moses, Jesus, Mary and Joseph and other persons and animals on the cover.

I raised an eyebrow at the children's Bible "Bedtime stories? I thought you were a Wiccan."

She smiled, "I am, but I was raised by Christians. My parents gave this to me when I was younger. I think I read it once and decided the stories weren't for me."

Huh. To each her own, "Must be all the color."

Deegan gently took the book from her, not making any startling moves. He was slow and human-like. It was actually comical to see him, a dark and irritable vampire, holding a 'Jesus for children' kind of book. He flipped through it until he found the location of the specific passages. He looked up at T, "Huh, not really watered down, is it?"

She shrugged, "Our parents were Bible thumpers. Nothing was half-assed when it came to the good Lord, Jesus Christ their Savior." She said it with a smile and a wink to her brother – a personal moment of memory between the two.

He began reading, "This starts at Revelation chapter 6 verse 1. 'And I saw when the Lamb opened one of the seals, and I heard, as it were the noise of thunder, one of the four beasts saying, Come and see. And I saw, and behold a white horse: and he that sat on him had a bow; and a crown was given unto him: and he went forth conquering, and to conquer.'"

He closed the book, keeping a finger where his place was, "I'm not going to read all of this, as this is not the exact version we have that was passed down directly from the Abaddon's mouth. But here's the gist of it. The Angel of Death will loose four horsemen. One horseman rides a white horse. He is the carrier of pestilence and conquers with a bow. The second man's horse is red. He carries a sword, and with him will be a great war. The third horseman rides a black horse, he carries balances in his hand and brings famine to the lands. The final horse is pale green with sickness as he carries Death on his back."

He opened the book again and read, "'And I looked, and behold a pale horse: and his name that sat on him was Death, and Hell followed with him. And power was given unto them over the fourth part of the earth to kill with sword, and with hunger, and with death, and with the beasts of the earth.'"

T spoke up, almost in a trance, "'And lo, there was a great earthquake; and the sun became black as sackcloth of hair, and the moon became as blood; And the stars of heaven fell unto the earth.'"

"Very good," Deegan said as he held up the page that T had said verbatim. On it was a not-too-kid-friendly scene of the world coming to an end with four horses standing over the ashes and destruction, but with smiles on their faces as they watched men in white drifting towards heaven. He shut the book and handed it back to T, "You know your scripture. I'm glad we didn't kill you after all."

Not a wise statement by the vampire. Several low rumbles of growls went off around the room, making the room shake in surround-sound. T flipped through the book trying not to show any care about his flippant comment.

Deegan ignored them and said, "I have been aware of my fate for many years. My family has had the second half of the book since it was written. Your family had the first half. It was for the safety of everyone to keep them separate. Our book was taken at the same time my brother was. And it seems whoever stole it now has the other half. Our saving grace is that my mother now has one of the seals which she stole from you."

"Ah, the coin," I realized.

"You're quick."

Smartass. "What's up with the seals anyway?"

"There are four seals that introduce, for lack of a better term, the four horsemen to the world," he answered without hesitance.

"Introduce?" *Oh how I love one-worded questions.* I could tell it was annoying the crap out of Deegan.

"Transform us. But a theory, one that I would like to stick to, is that the books and the seals need to be in the same room."

"And?" *There has to be more to it than that.*

He replied in a bored voice, "And what, Keen?"

"And what about us? Do we need to be in the same room? And what about the lamb that you said opens the seals?"

Deegan shrugged, "No idea on either question. I'm not even sure if the lamb is important. What is important is that there are four seals out there and we have one of them. We can only hope that the others, the ones who have taken Adam and Gavin, don't have the other three," and then he said, mostly to himself, "Or else we're screwed."

"Why doesn't Alexandra just destroy the coin?"

"She's working on that now, but as far as we know, nothing of this human world can destroy that or the Pharaoh's Dagger," his patience was wearing thin with me.

Oh good, this was easy, "But we're not human, why can't she just destroy it by crushing it? Or using the dagger on it?"

He shook his head in exasperation, like I was the dumbest vampire he had ever run into, "We are still part human and we cannot destroy what was made by the gods or angels."

I asked, "Why didn't my uncle know about all of this?"

"My guess is that, unlike my family, who has been protecting our part of history since the beginning, the family that raised your brother and you were not told all of the details. More plausible is that they ran out of time."

Makes sense, I guess. I didn't like the answer, though.

Sitting in silence was awkward, but I didn't have any more questions at the moment. When Deegan was satisfied that I couldn't think of anything else ignorant to say, he continued talking.

"Keen, I know who I am to become. Our parents sealed our fates with the names they chose – whether it was on purpose or by some other guidance. My name means 'The black-haired one.' I am the carrier of the balances, the bringer of famine."

Resentment and anger flared in me like fire engulfing a house, *He is so nonchalant about it, so accepting. He's been told since birth, preparing all his life for this – like it's natural to be put on a quest to conquer all.*

"We have to find my brother, Gavin. He is the white horseman. Your brother, Adam is the red horseman."

My eyes met his in my understanding of what he was about to say. This was why Alexandra vowed to kill me after my brother was taken. *The prophecy.* It was why Mr. Carmichael and my biological parents had been killed. It all came down to who I was. *I'm not ready to hear this out loud.* I braced myself, feeling my stomach drop. Nausea boiled through my head and my body. I felt like my bones wanted to come up through my throat and run away. *Oh my God.*

"You need to come to terms with this. I know it's been fast. I had years to comprehend it and you only have a few days," he sounded sincere, "Keen," Deegan paused cautiously.

"I know," I was determined to get through the moment without gagging, "I am the fourth horseman. The pale one."

T gasped next to me, a sweet intake of air as she realized what I was saying. *I am death.*

Epilogue

The Sunrise

The gold of my chayyim glinted hypnotically as I stared at it in my outstretched hand. I paced back and forth, like a crazed animal, on the granite edge of the cliff at the back of my island. One step is all it would have taken to have sent me down the jagged teeth like a rag doll. *One step and I could end this – maybe damage myself enough on the way down for the dark waters to pull me to my final death.*

Who the hell am I kidding? Death won't come easily to an evil creature like me. And especially not to the one I'm to become.

Shit!! I threw my hands up in the air in dismay, *What the fuck am I going to do? Killing myself isn't an option – I like me too much.*

Run away? Maybe. Maybe that's the solution: stay away from the coins and the damn prophecy scroll. Get the hell away from here and let the danger follow me.

What else can I do? It was hard enough to struggle against the innate desire to kill humans that came with being a vampire. The nature of my prophesized self seemed like it would be impossible to out-will. *I mean, I really don't want to hurt anybody. But if I turn into one of the fucking horsemen... Will I be so far gone that I'll attack people I care for? My parents... Devon, Tom or...* I choked back T's name.

Aggressively, I sat down. Sharp rocks cut into me. The quicksilver way my flesh healed was an inflaming reminder of what I had turned into so many months ago. I looked out at the ocean and the haze of the rising sun cracking open on the horizon

And what about Adam? Is there a way to save him?

Oh, God! I pleaded at the purple-blue sky as if someone might answer me. *How is there even a way out of this without one of the four of us dying? My twin or one of the other two. Or me.* It didn't matter that I hadn't met Adam or Gavin. We were all brothers in this. Our destinies tied before we were born.

Faces from the apartment popped into my mind. *The horror on their faces had been directed at me.* Only Devon showed no fear or anger or *hatred? Could they possibly hate me? Could they be arranging my demise? Deegan's as well? Or did they kill him already?*

If the situation was reversed, what would I do?

The guttural laugh that escaped my lips was dark, sarcastic, angry and on the bridge of hysteria. *It doesn't really matter what I would do if I were them. They're not the ones caught up in this fate.*

"Well," I said with determination, "that settles it." *Getting the farthest away is the best option. I'll run and hide if I have to – stay away from the coins, give the dagger back to Devon, go nowhere near the prophecy scroll.*

Yes, this is the path... exile. Let the danger follow me, I thought again.

At least I've got my iPod, I could survive, I mused.

Yeah, until the power ran out.

My body shrugged in defeat. *I am truly alone. There is no other option.*

Leave tonight, my mind settled on that reality and my back straightened in the surety of it. *For now, just enjoy the last island sunrise you'll ever see.*

Just as my decision was made and I fully turned my attention to the wakening view, movement on the uneven rocks behind me broke the murmur of seabirds bobbing on the waves. But I didn't stir. I knew the scent that had flown on the wind; I knew who had come for me.

The air shifted as she sat down beside me. I could sense the lingering aroma of dye and hear the soft shifting of cloth of that same beautiful head scarf she wore a few hours before. No bouquet of make-up or perfume, she wore the same jeans and probably the same t-shirt, but with a fleece pull-over covering it. Though it was a summer morning, the wind blew in cold off the ocean waves. *She must've taken Devon's boat to find me.*

Her voice was quiet, "Thank you for saving my life."

I didn't expect that. Keeping my eyes fixed on the horizon, I kept my tone neutral for fear of giving away my feelings, "You saved mine weeks ago. I never got the chance to thank you for that. I guess we're even, right?"

She nodded quietly.

Another human I love that I can't be near. "I'm sorry about Veleda. I didn't mean for any of that to happen," I sighed, "For any of this." I folded my hand over the chayyim, hiding it in my palm.

T scooted closer to me, the gentle brush of her leg against mine made me disgusted in myself. *I want to be human. I want to tell her so many things, to show her exactly how much I appreciate what she did for me.*

The only way to show her now is to leave. Get some distance in before the light comes through enough to look in her eyes and doubt my decision.

Maybe knowing my thoughts, or maybe because the unhappiness was rolling off of me like waves rolling in the ocean, she leaned her head against my shoulder as a friend would. *As a sister would to a brother.*

We sat there listening to the ocean, trapped in our own contemplations – her with her head lying on my shoulder and me wanting, and yet not wanting, to touch her. *All I have to do is move my hand and it could be on hers.*

Her touch, her presence, was melting the resolve I so fiercely believed in a few minutes before. *This is not good. The decision to stay will not be a good one.*

It's only going to cause pain. Trying to reason with myself, I thought, *It may mean her death.*

I didn't want that, but my strength was wearing out. *How long can I run before Alexandra or Eammon, or whoever, catches up and finishes me off? Wouldn't it be better to stay and fight with those who would come together to help me? T's here – that's got to be a sign, right?*

Endanger your friends' lives just so you can live longer?

The selfishness of it made me ache. I felt like the dilemma would kill me, if no one else did. I cried out silently in my head, *Goddamn it! What do I do?!?*

T's hand covered mine, and I tensed at her touch. She said, "Whatever you decide, Keen, don't leave."

What was she, a fricken mind reader? "How did you know I was thinking that?"

"What else is there to think about?" I could feel her smile with her kidding.

"You," *Oh geez. Didn't mean to say that out loud.*

T brought her head up with a jolt, but she didn't try to pull her hand away, nor did I let it go. I peeked a sideways glance at her to make sure she wasn't angry at my Freudian slip. Her face was blank – no smile, no anger. I couldn't read anything from her. After a few moments, she put her head back on my shoulder.

Together, we watched as the sky turned blue with the day, the clouds lightened to a dark gray and the other bright colors began to fade away, *The sun's auras.* The world was waking up around us, slowly drawing the night to a close as the water began to flow home.

T jumped up to a stand with a slight smile on her face, melancholy in her eyes and her hand reaching out to me, "Let's go home, Keen."

I smiled at the thought of that, *Home,* and I realized, with that one word, that I had lost all of my ambition to leave. I accepted her assistance and stood up beside her. She moved closer, wrapped her arms around me, placed her head on my chest and gave me a deep hug. Her scent was so warming to me and I breathed it in, holding her, loving the feel of her delicate strength.

She leaned back from me, our arms still wrapped around each other, and smiled a brighter smile, like she was trying to fight off the last remnants of sadness. Her aura of resolve and optimism was infectious and I grinned back at her. Turning mischievously, she ducked under my arms and started heading back down the path away from the ridge we were on. My eyes followed her for a few steps, still grinning at her, but then I felt the little medallion still in the palm of my closed hand.

Looking at it, I frowned. The sun glinted off of the bite mark and I was suddenly incensed. The emotions swelled in me like a volcanic eruption, heated by that gold charm, *My life.* I knew what I wanted to do with it – this representation of my human life, the life I no longer had. I didn't want the damn thing anymore. I couldn't stand looking at it. Alexandra's mark on it repulsed me and I couldn't take the hate of it any longer. I whipped my hand back like a baseball pitcher, meaning to throw it as far away from me as possible. *Out of my sight!*

As I swung my arm forward, it caught on something and I was tossed back onto the ground with the momentum of it. T was on top me, straddling me, with one hand pinning my throwing arm above my head.

What the hell?

She was yelling at me and visibly shaking. Her aura sparked out around the edges with the murky-red color of anger, but with the pink of love, "No, Keen! Don't let it go. Not yet."

My surprise left me speechless as she heaved torrential breaths of air like she had exerted herself to the extreme. I relaxed my body underneath her, hoping that would help calm her. My thoughts scrambled to understand what the hell had happened. *T just knocked me over. T! The little, pint-sized HUMAN, just knocked... me... OVER!*

She slowed herself down, her aura snapping back into her, and showed her own face of shock, "I'm," she panted, "I'm so sorry. Keen. I didn't mean to, uhm." T looked around her and then scrambled off of me, "Sorry," She repeated.

"What the hell was that, T?" I asked, from the ground. She didn't respond. Flashes of scenes played out in my head of all the things that had seemed out of place to me since I had met her. But I couldn't grab onto the thoughts long enough to understand them. I remembered how graceful and quick she moved – her actions riding the edge of being normal. I finally realized that she kept the same hours as Devon, Tom and I. These were not regular human practices, no matter how much homework she had, lab work to do, or work for the police department – a human would eventually crash after being awake for so long. *But T? I've never seen her drag ass. She's always wide awake. It's not like I've seen her sneaking anti-drowsy pills or energy drinks every hour.*

I checked her aura, glaring at every particle and every spark that danced through it. It was blue, not gray. *She can't be one of us.*

But she isn't fully a human either. I was close to dumbstruck and I sputtered out the only words I could think of, "You're not like other girls, are you T?"

"No, I'm not," she looked away from me, embarrassed, and then whispered, pleading, "Please. Please don't tell Tom. He only knows that I've become a fast healer."

What is she? I tried to mask my shock, as I got up rapidly to stand in front of her.

She peered at me with sad, but defiant, eyes. "Please," she repeated.

I took her hand from her side, turned it palm-up and placed the gold, dented chayyim in it. It wasn't mine anymore. She had saved it, *Saved me,* so long ago. I wouldn't betray her. I closed her hand around the talisman and brought her in my arms again. I kissed the top of her head, on the scarf that covered yet another secret, wondering if she had hid that from her brother too.

No, I won't betray her. Feeling her breath against my chest and hearing her soft tears fall, I knew that I couldn't leave her or the prophecy – both of which had a tight grip on me. I knew then that I would have to see this new life of mine through to the end, no matter how or why it ended. My resolve to leave was completely abolished. *I need to protect her. I need to protect my family and whatever else was in the path of Abaddon's destruction.*

T gave me one small squeeze of a hug and then looked up at me with tear-streaked eyes, "Let's go home, Keen."

I nodded and I took her hand. *Yes, let's go home,* I thought, *There's a lot to do.*

The Pale

About the Author

A.D. Wittman was born in Indiana, graduated from Purdue University with a Liberal Arts degree and went on to achieve an M.B.A. from Franklin University. A.D. currently resides with a wonderful life-partner and their three cats.

An avid music lover, A.D. created play-lists for all of the characters in the books. A.D. thanks the following artists (and many more artists like them) who helped to keep the Muse dancing and creating while listening to a well-worn iPod:

For Keen: *Gnarls Barkley, Tom Petty, Mr. Reality, Paul Gross, Tech N9NE*

For Devon: *Gaelic Storm, Tartan Terrors, Billie Holiday, Michael Jackson, The October Project*

For Tom: *Eminem, Spiral Beach, Coldplay, Weezer, Live, Alabama 3, Goose*

For T: *Paramore, My Morning Jacket, Dixie Chicks, Evanescence, Aiden, Gosling, Imogen Heap, Tegan and Sara*

7373812R0

Made in the USA
Lexington, KY
19 November 2010